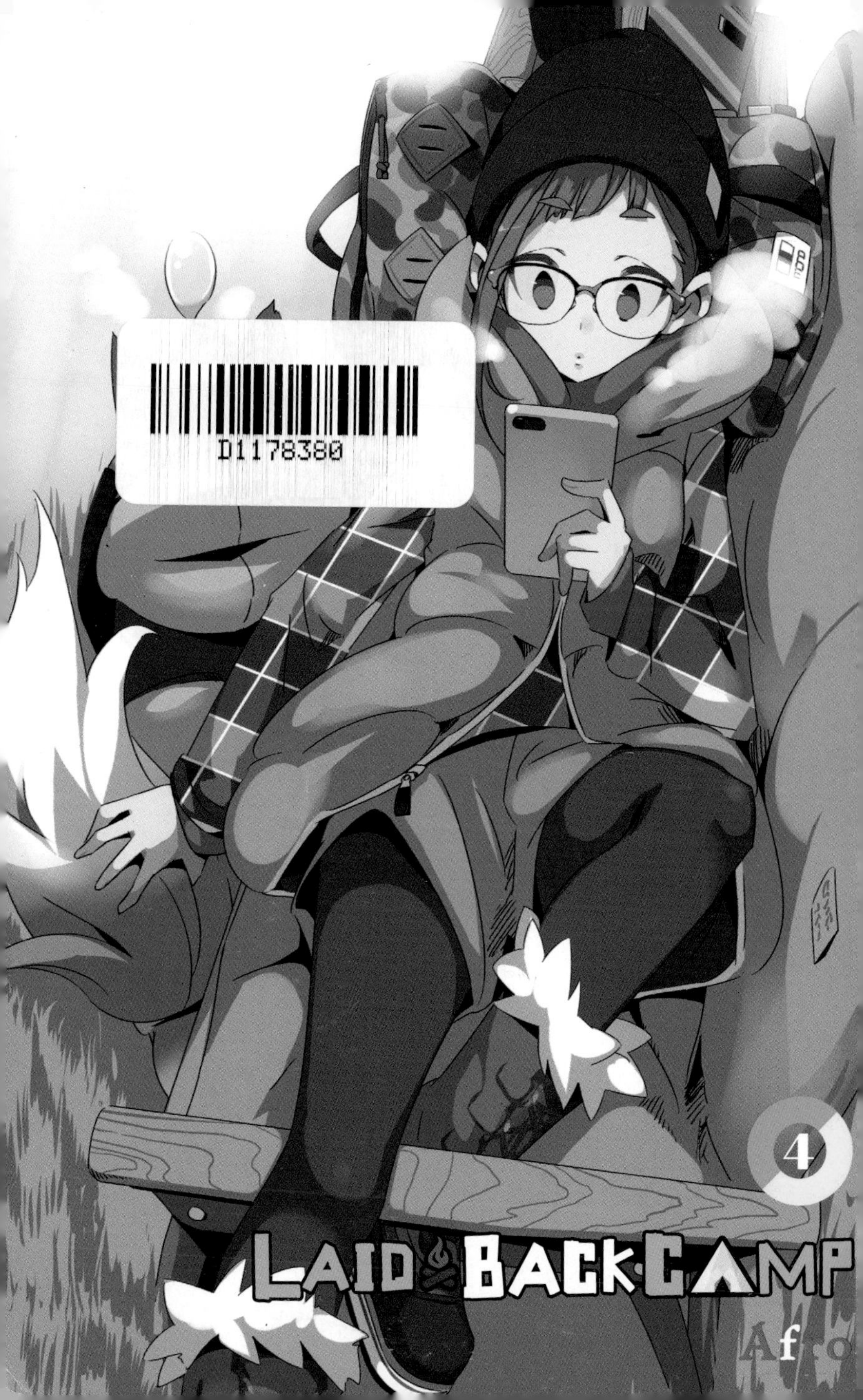
4
LAID BACK CAMP

4

LAID-BACK CAMP
contents

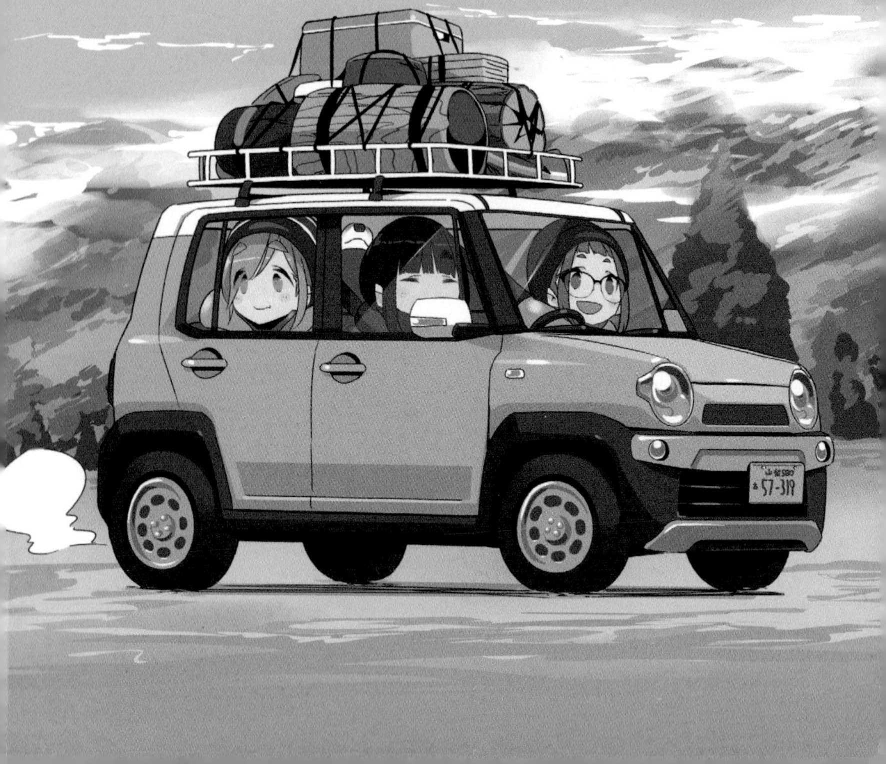

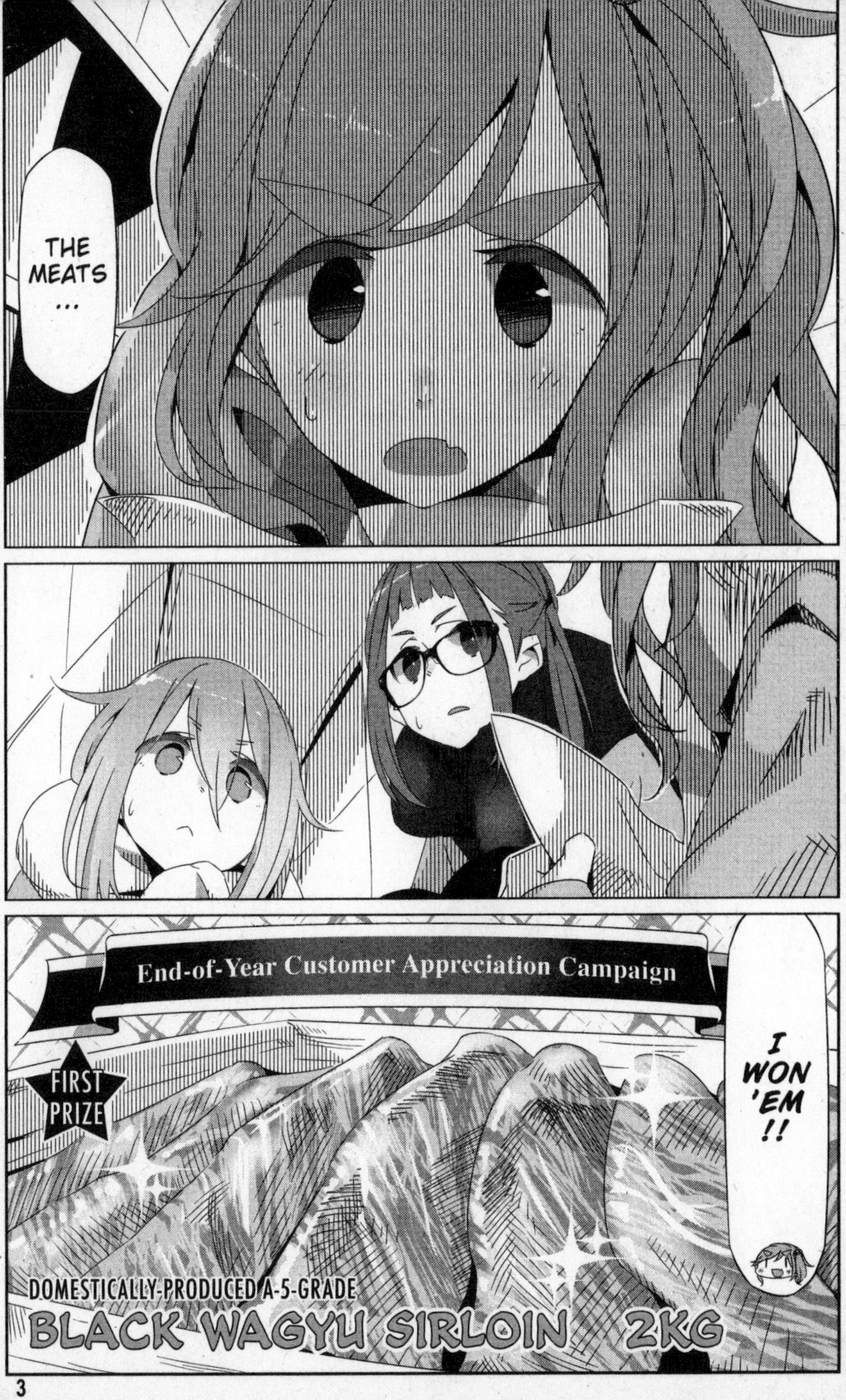
THE MEATS ...
End-of-Year Customer Appreciation Campaign
I WON 'EM !!
FIRST PRIZE
DOMESTICALLY-PRODUCED A-5-GRADE
BLACK WAGYU SIRLOIN 2KG

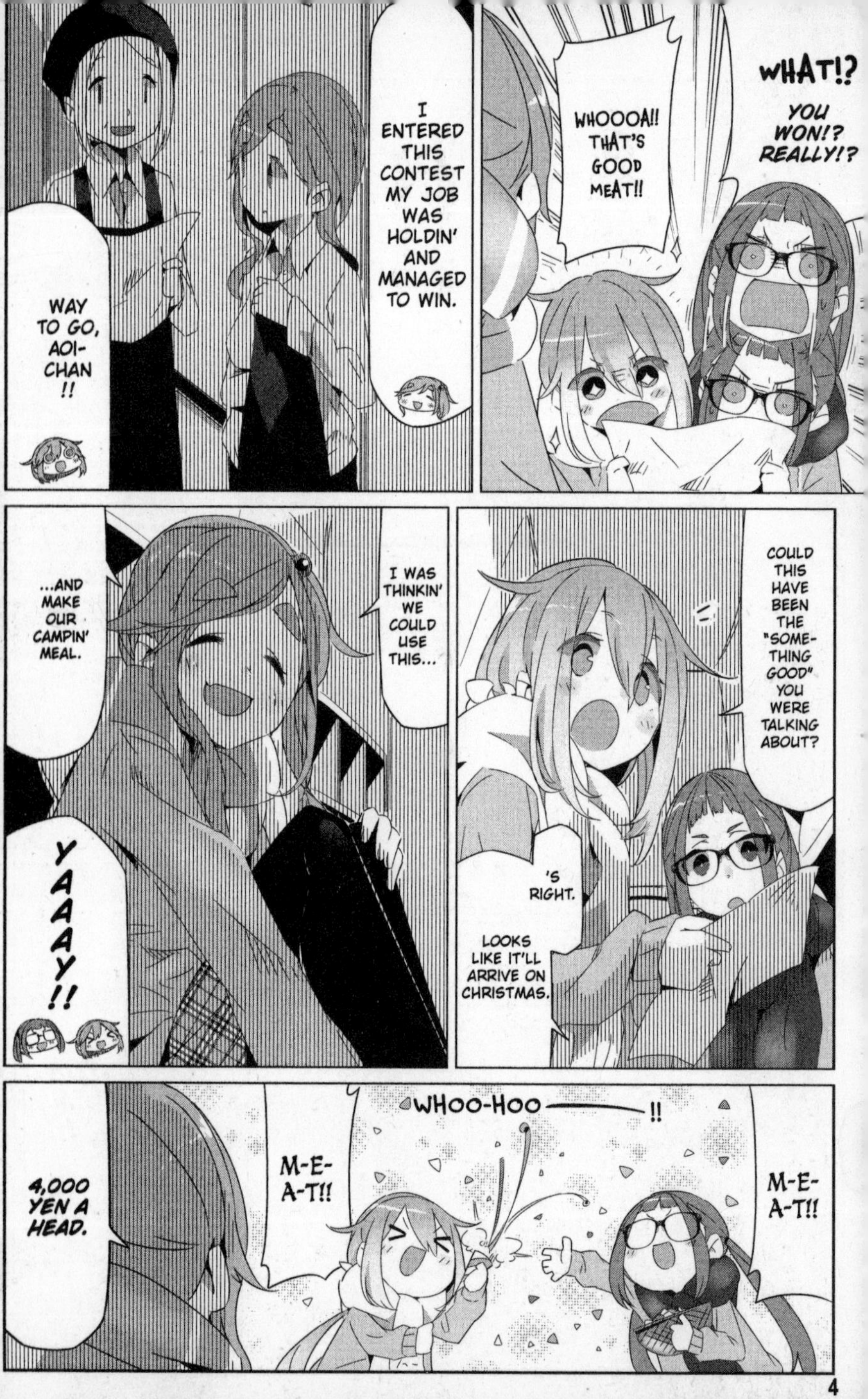
WHAT!?
YOU WON!? REALLY!?
WHOOOA!! THAT'S GOOD MEAT!!
I ENTERED THIS CONTEST MY JOB WAS HOLDIN' AND MANAGED TO WIN.
WAY TO GO, AOI-CHAN!!
COULD THIS HAVE BEEN THE "SOMETHING GOOD" YOU WERE TALKING ABOUT?
'S RIGHT.
LOOKS LIKE IT'LL ARRIVE ON CHRISTMAS.
I WAS THINKIN' WE COULD USE THIS...
...AND MAKE OUR CAMPIN' MEAL.
YAAAAY!!
WHOO-HOO——!!
M-E-A-T!!
M-E-A-T!!
4,000 YEN A HEAD.

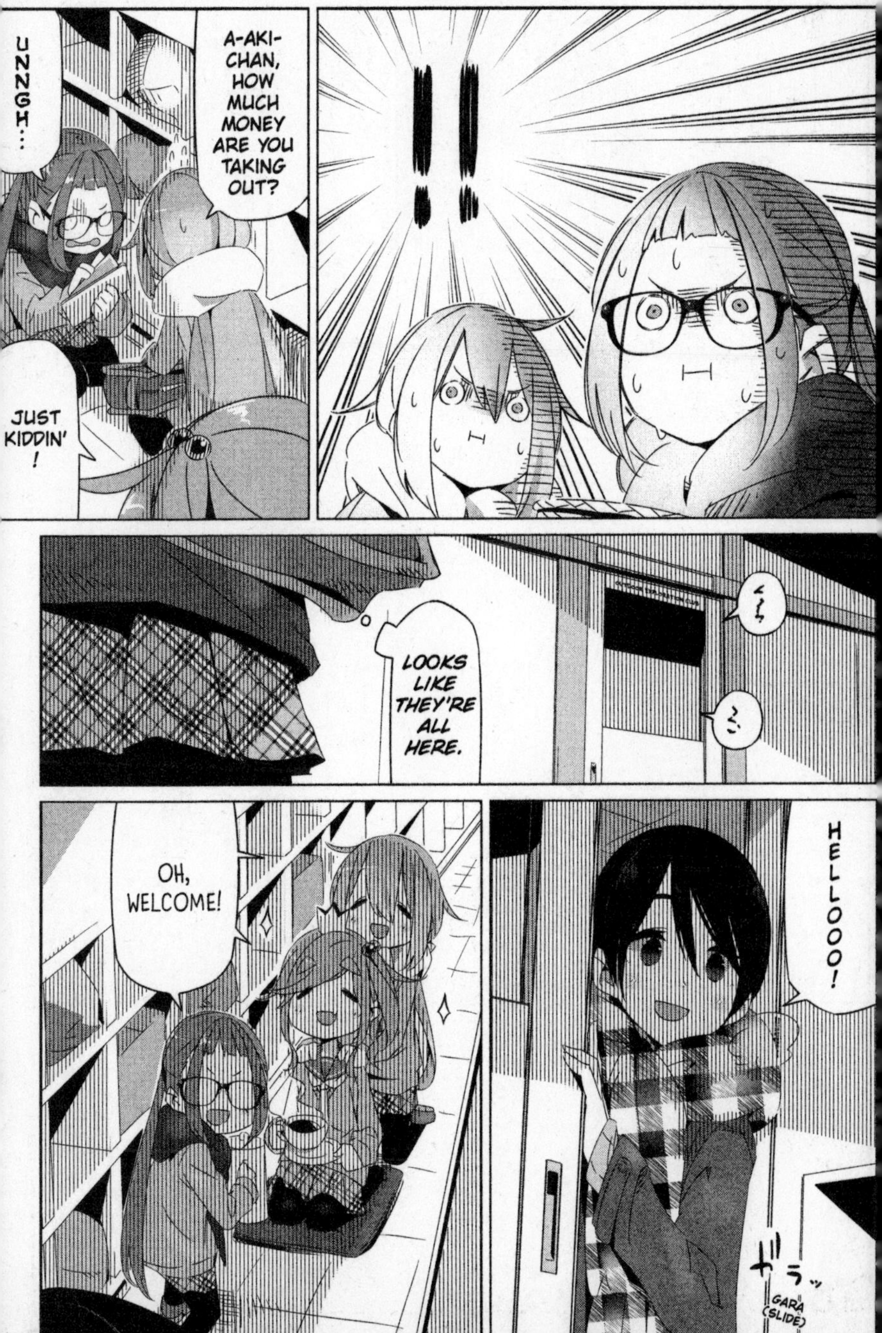
!!
A-AKI-CHAN, HOW MUCH MONEY ARE YOU TAKING OUT?
UNNGH...
JUST KIDDIN'!
LOOKS LIKE THEY'RE ALL HERE.
HELLOOO!
GARA (SLIDE)
OH, WELCOME!

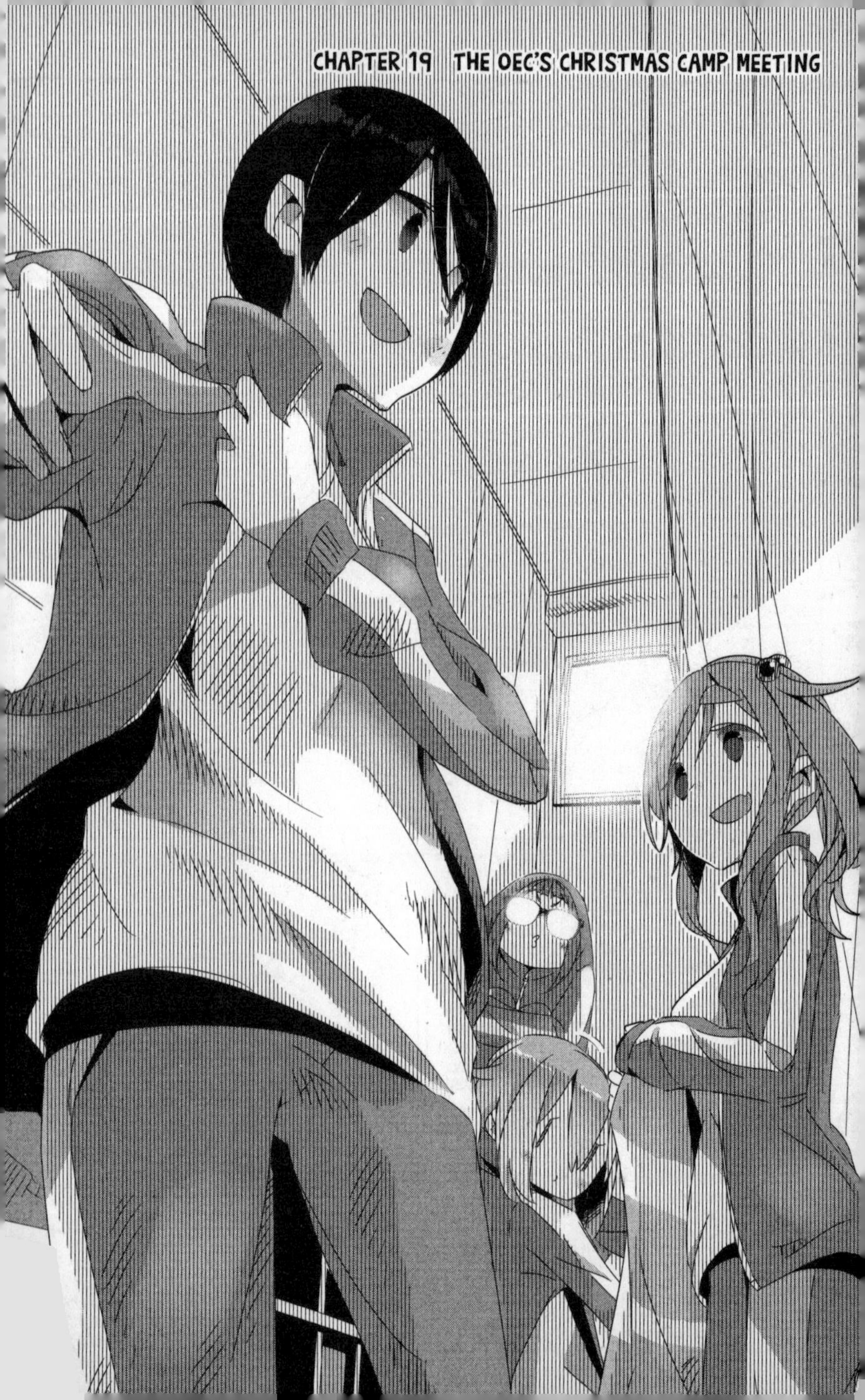
CHAPTER 19 THE OEC'S CHRISTMAS CAMP MEETING

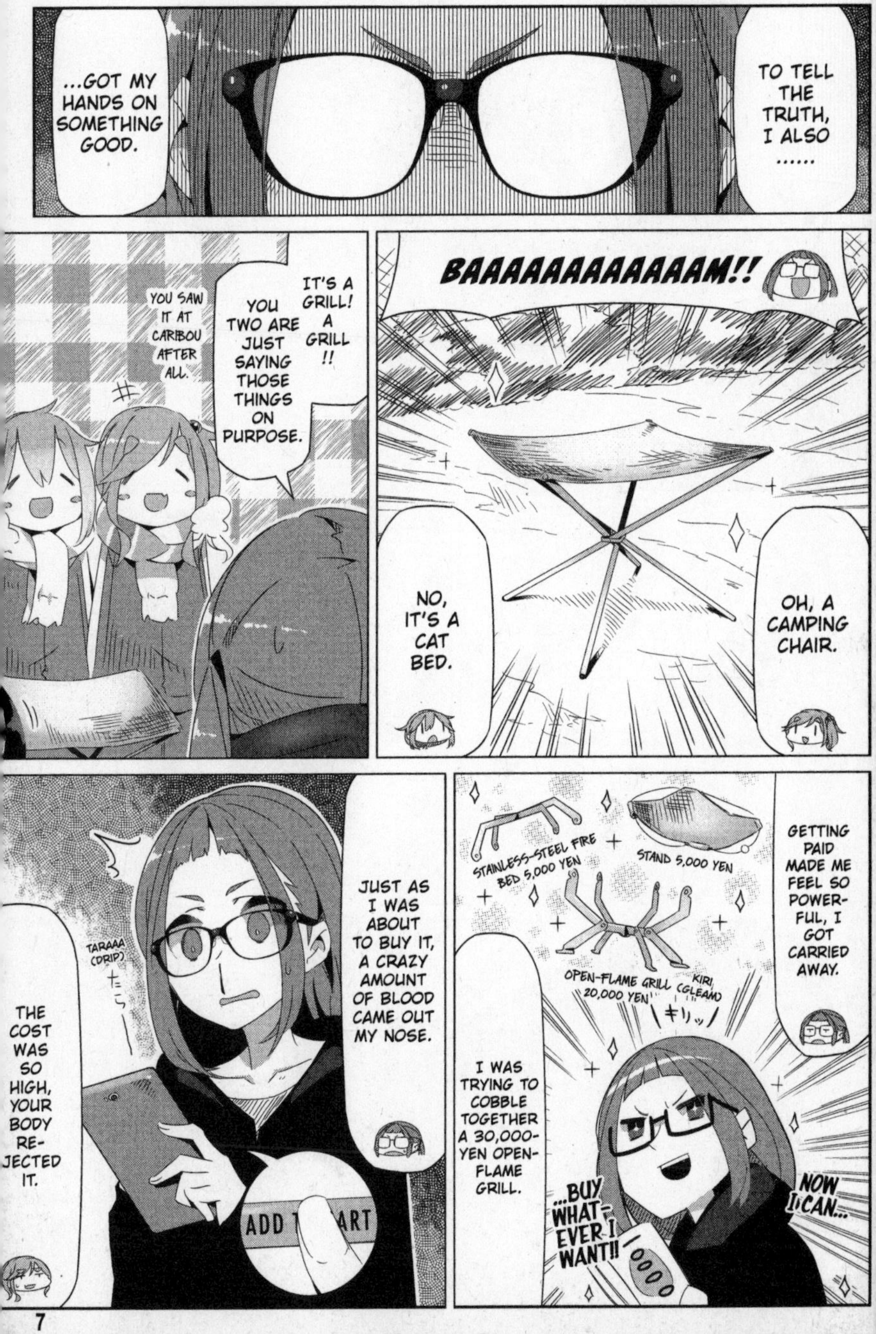

TO TELL THE TRUTH, I ALSO ......
...GOT MY HANDS ON SOMETHING GOOD.
BAAAAAAAAAAAAM!!
OH, A CAMPING CHAIR.
NO, IT'S A CAT BED.
IT'S A GRILL! A GRILL!!
YOU TWO ARE JUST SAYING THOSE THINGS ON PURPOSE.
YOU SAW IT AT CARIBOU AFTER ALL.
GETTING PAID MADE ME FEEL SO POWER-FUL, I GOT CARRIED AWAY.
STAND 5,000 YEN
STAINLESS-STEEL FIRE BED 5,000 YEN
OPEN-FLAME GRILL 20,000 YEN
KIRI (GLEAM)
キリッ
I WAS TRYING TO COBBLE TOGETHER A 30,000-YEN OPEN-FLAME GRILL.
NOW I CAN...
...BUY WHAT-EVER I WANT!!
JUST AS I WAS ABOUT TO BUY IT, A CRAZY AMOUNT OF BLOOD CAME OUT MY NOSE.
TARAAA (DRIP)
たら～
THE COST WAS SO HIGH, YOUR BODY RE-JECTED IT.
ADD T ART

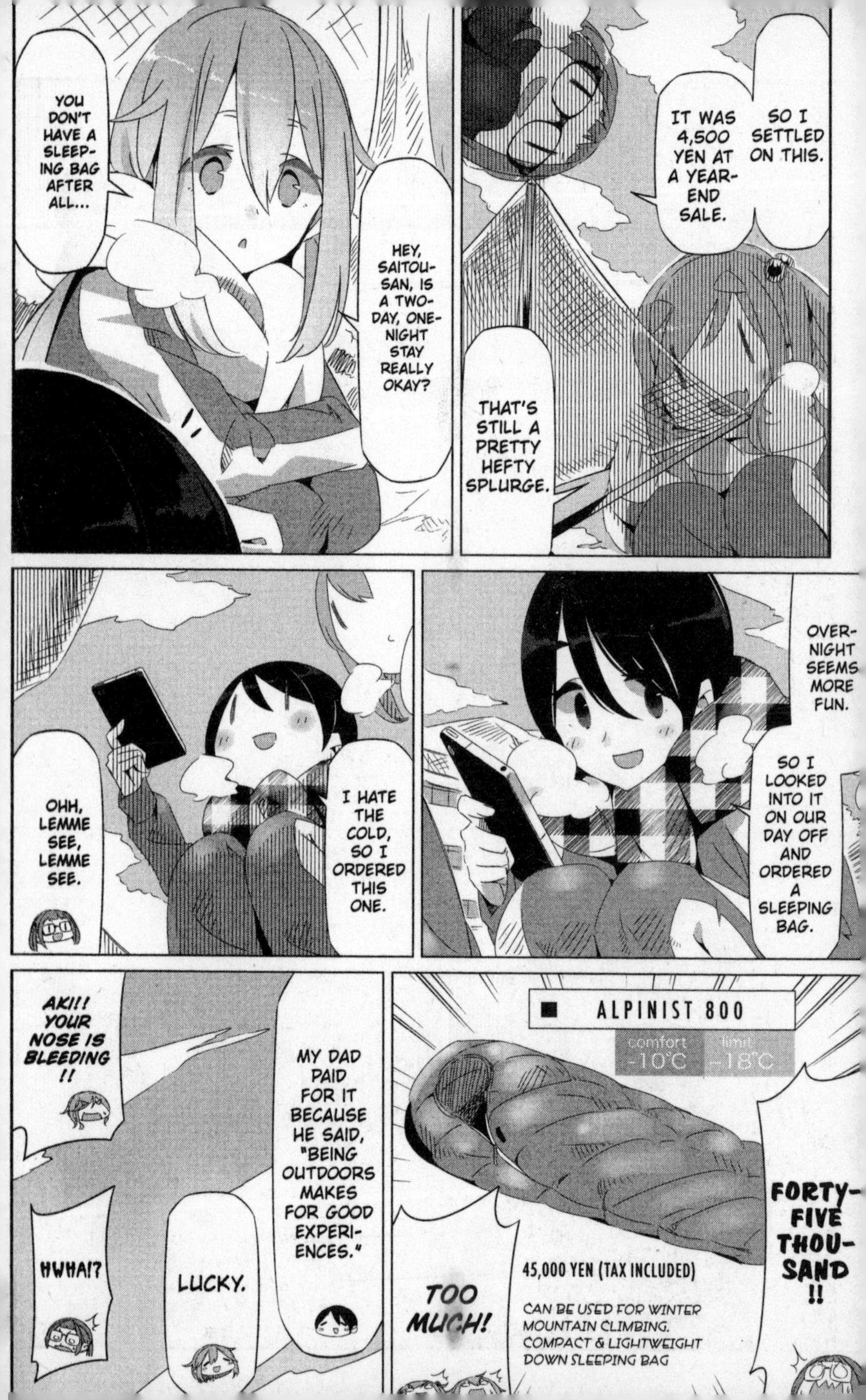

IT WAS 4,500 YEN AT A YEAR-END SALE.
SO I SETTLED ON THIS.
THAT'S STILL A PRETTY HEFTY SPLURGE.
HEY, SAITOU-SAN, IS A TWO-DAY, ONE-NIGHT STAY REALLY OKAY?
YOU DON'T HAVE A SLEEPING BAG AFTER ALL...
OVERNIGHT SEEMS MORE FUN.
SO I LOOKED INTO IT ON OUR DAY OFF AND ORDERED A SLEEPING BAG.
I HATE THE COLD, SO I ORDERED THIS ONE.
OHH, LEMME SEE, LEMME SEE.
ALPINIST 800
comfort -10°C
limit -18°C
FORTY-FIVE THOUSAND!!
45,000 YEN (TAX INCLUDED)
CAN BE USED FOR WINTER MOUNTAIN CLIMBING. COMPACT & LIGHTWEIGHT DOWN SLEEPING BAG
TOO MUCH!
MY DAD PAID FOR IT BECAUSE HE SAID, "BEING OUTDOORS MAKES FOR GOOD EXPERIENCES."
LUCKY.
AKI!! YOUR NOSE IS BLEEDING!!
HWHA!?

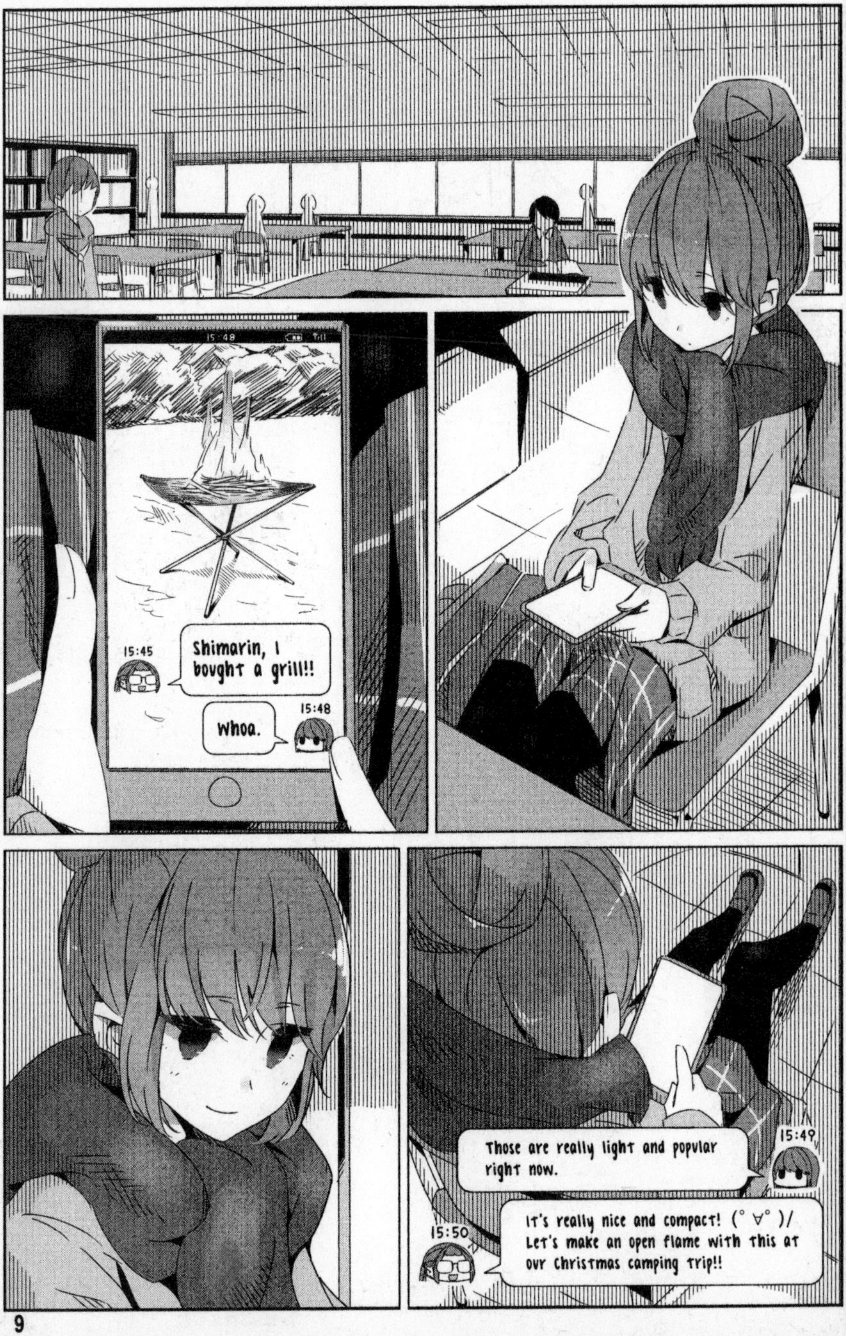
15:48
15:45
Shimarin, I bought a grill!!
15:48
Whoa.
15:49
Those are really light and popular right now.
15:50
It's really nice and compact! (° ∀°)/ Let's make an open flame with this at our Christmas camping trip!!

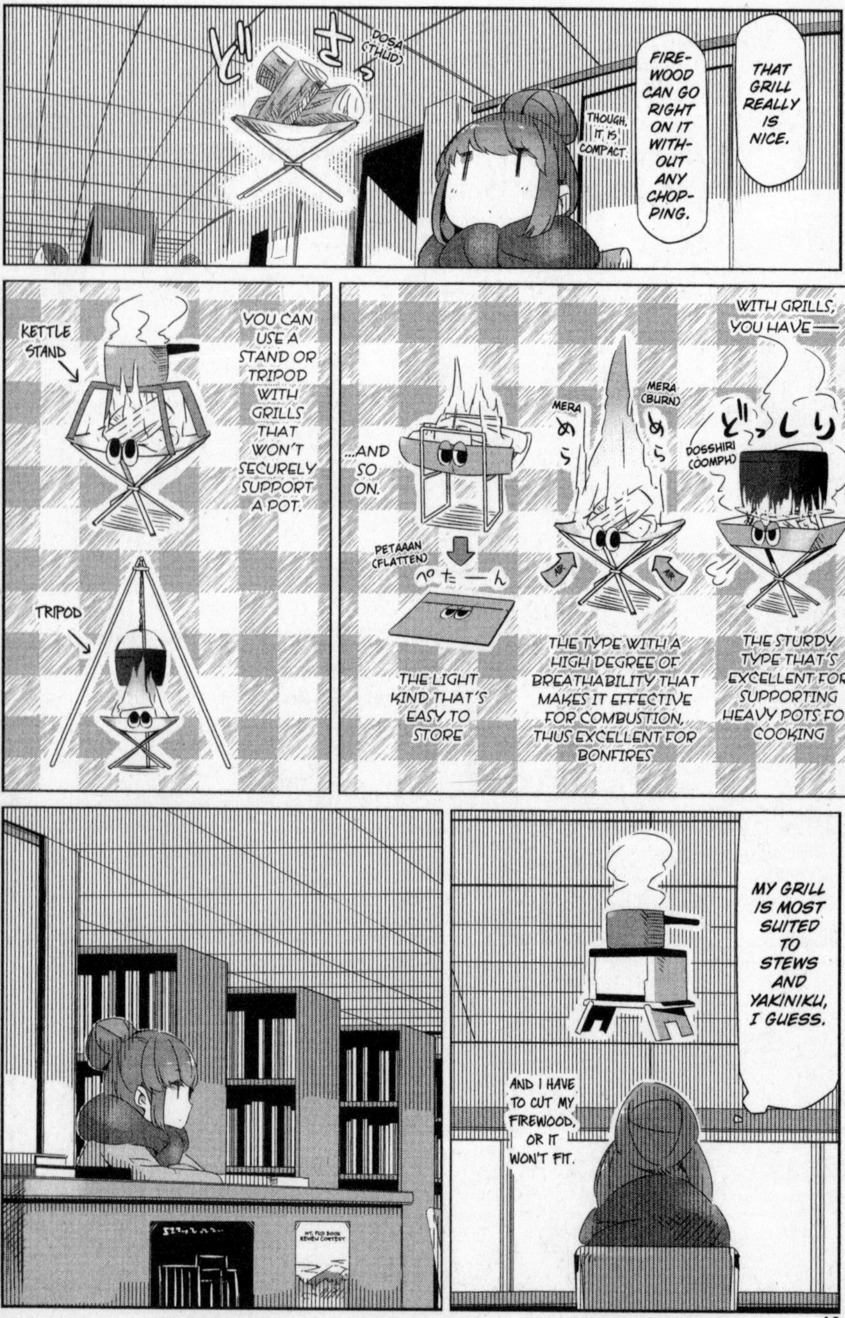
THAT GRILL REALLY IS NICE.
FIRE-WOOD CAN GO RIGHT ON IT WITH-OUT ANY CHOP-PING.
THOUGH, IT IS COMPACT.
どさっ
DOSA (THUD)
WITH GRILLS, YOU HAVE—
どっしり
DOSSHIRI (COOMPH)
THE STURDY TYPE THAT'S EXCELLENT FOR SUPPORTING HEAVY POTS FOR COOKING
めら
MERA (BURN)
めら
MERA
AIR
AIR
THE TYPE WITH A HIGH DEGREE OF BREATHABILITY THAT MAKES IT EFFECTIVE FOR COMBUSTION, THUS EXCELLENT FOR BONFIRES
ぺたーん
PETAAAN (FLATTEN)
THE LIGHT KIND THAT'S EASY TO STORE
...AND SO ON.
YOU CAN USE A STAND OR TRIPOD WITH GRILLS THAT WON'T SECURELY SUPPORT A POT.
KETTLE STAND
TRIPOD
MY GRILL IS MOST SUITED TO STEWS AND YAKINIKU, I GUESS.
AND I HAVE TO CUT MY FIREWOOD, OR IT WON'T FIT.
MT. FUJI BOOK REVIEW CONTEST

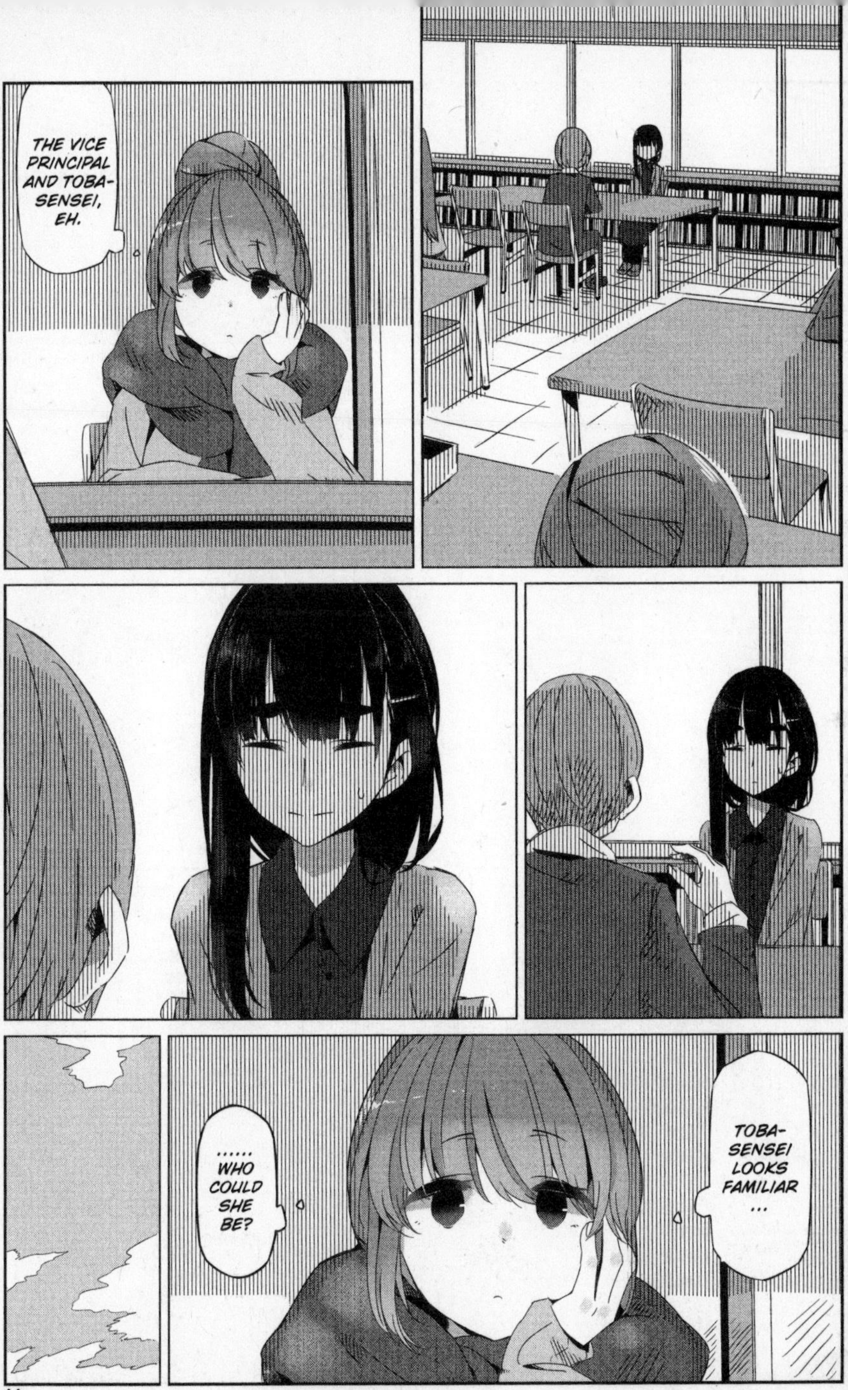
THE VICE PRINCIPAL AND TOBA-SENSEI, EH.
TOBA-SENSEI LOOKS FAMILIAR ...
...... WHO COULD SHE BE?

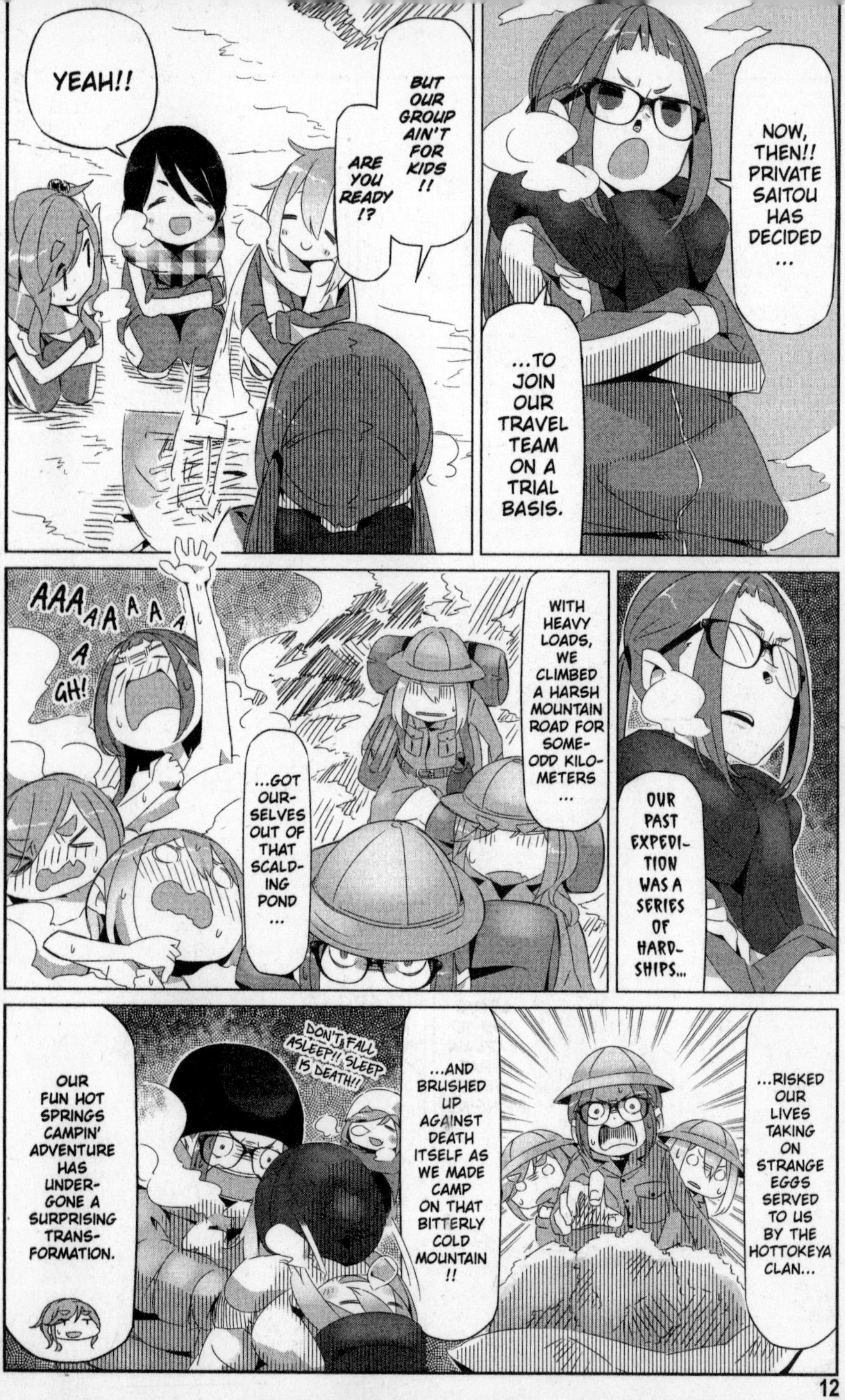
NOW, THEN!! PRIVATE SAITOU HAS DECIDED...
...TO JOIN OUR TRAVEL TEAM ON A TRIAL BASIS.
BUT OUR GROUP AIN'T FOR KIDS!!
ARE YOU READY!?
YEAH!!
OUR PAST EXPEDITION WAS A SERIES OF HARDSHIPS...
WITH HEAVY LOADS, WE CLIMBED A HARSH MOUNTAIN ROAD FOR SOME-ODD KILOMETERS...
...GOT OURSELVES OUT OF THAT SCALDING POND...
AAAAAAAAAGH!
...RISKED OUR LIVES TAKING ON STRANGE EGGS SERVED TO US BY THE HOTTOKEYA CLAN...
...AND BRUSHED UP AGAINST DEATH ITSELF AS WE MADE CAMP ON THAT BITTERLY COLD MOUNTAIN!!
DON'T FALL ASLEEP!! SLEEP IS DEATH!!
OUR FUN HOT SPRINGS CAMPIN' ADVENTURE HAS UNDERGONE A SURPRISING TRANSFORMATION.

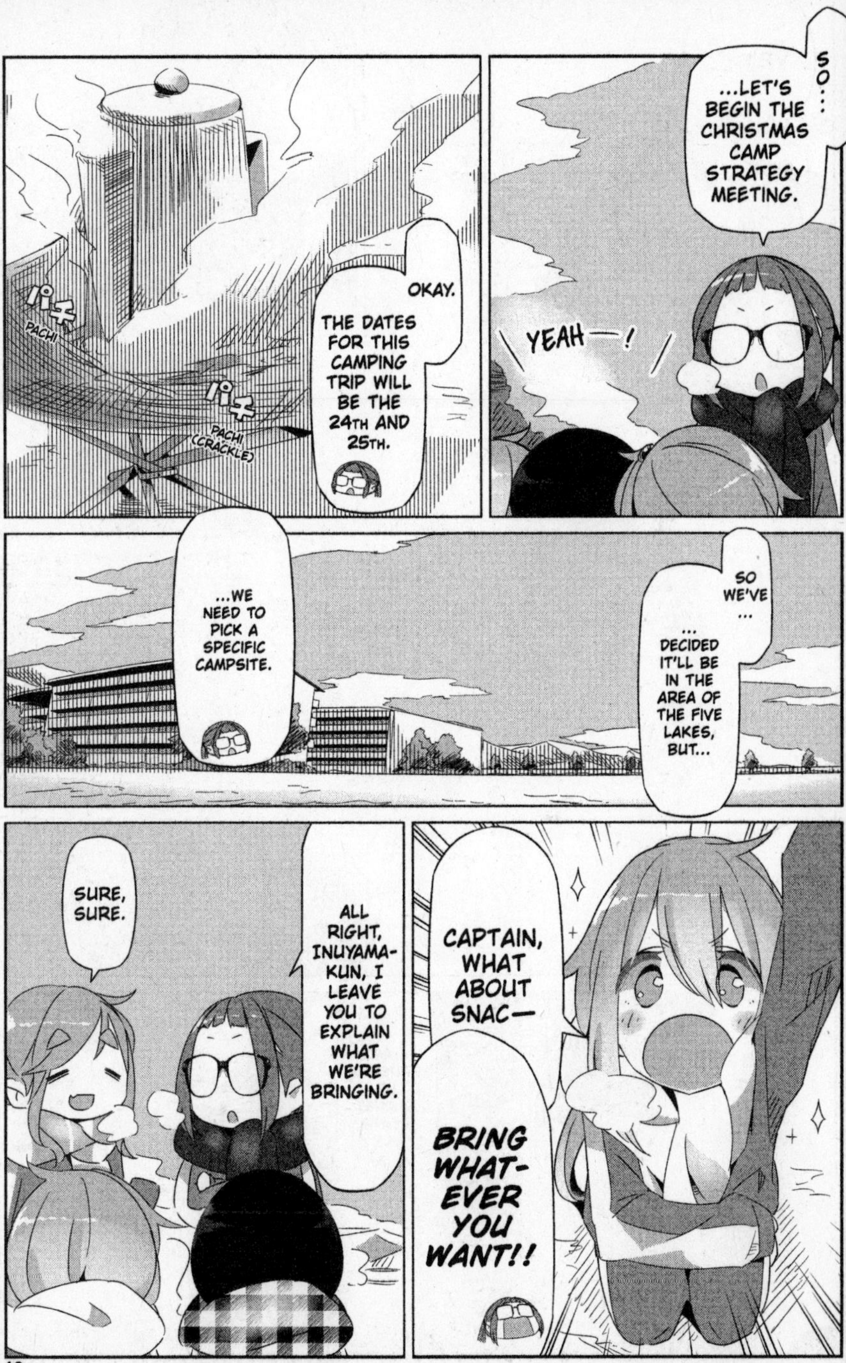
SO... ...LET'S BEGIN THE CHRISTMAS CAMP STRATEGY MEETING.
YEAH—!
パチ
PACHI
パチ
PACHI (CRACKLE)
OKAY.
THE DATES FOR THIS CAMPING TRIP WILL BE THE 24TH AND 25TH.
SO WE'VE... ...DECIDED IT'LL BE IN THE AREA OF THE FIVE LAKES, BUT...
...WE NEED TO PICK A SPECIFIC CAMPSITE.
CAPTAIN, WHAT ABOUT SNAC—
BRING WHATEVER YOU WANT!!
ALL RIGHT, INUYAMA-KUN, I LEAVE YOU TO EXPLAIN WHAT WE'RE BRINGING.
SURE, SURE.

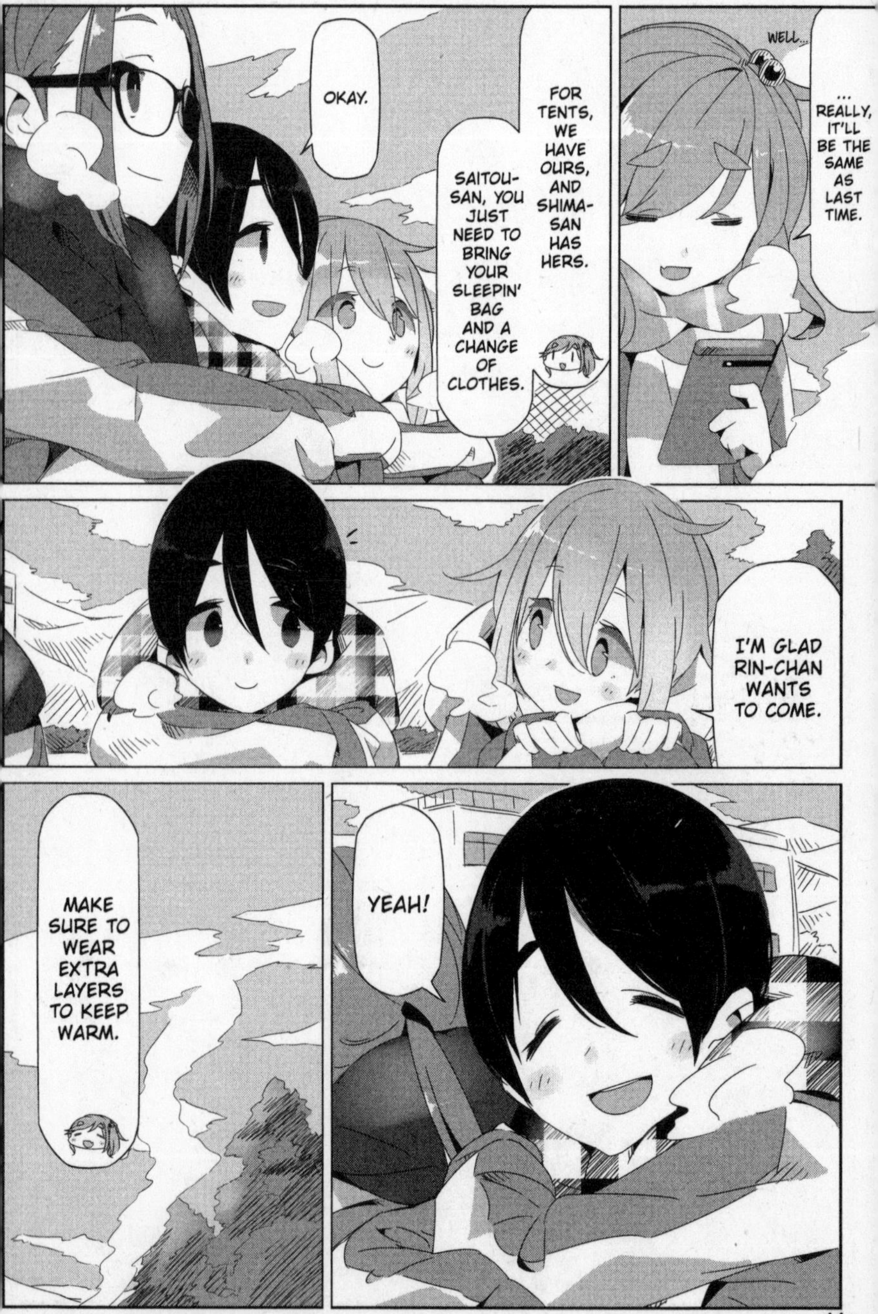
WELL...
...REALLY, IT'LL BE THE SAME AS LAST TIME.
FOR TENTS, WE HAVE OURS, AND SHIMA-SAN HAS HERS.
SAITOU-SAN, YOU JUST NEED TO BRING YOUR SLEEPIN' BAG AND A CHANGE OF CLOTHES.
OKAY.
I'M GLAD RIN-CHAN WANTS TO COME.
YEAH!
MAKE SURE TO WEAR EXTRA LAYERS TO KEEP WARM.

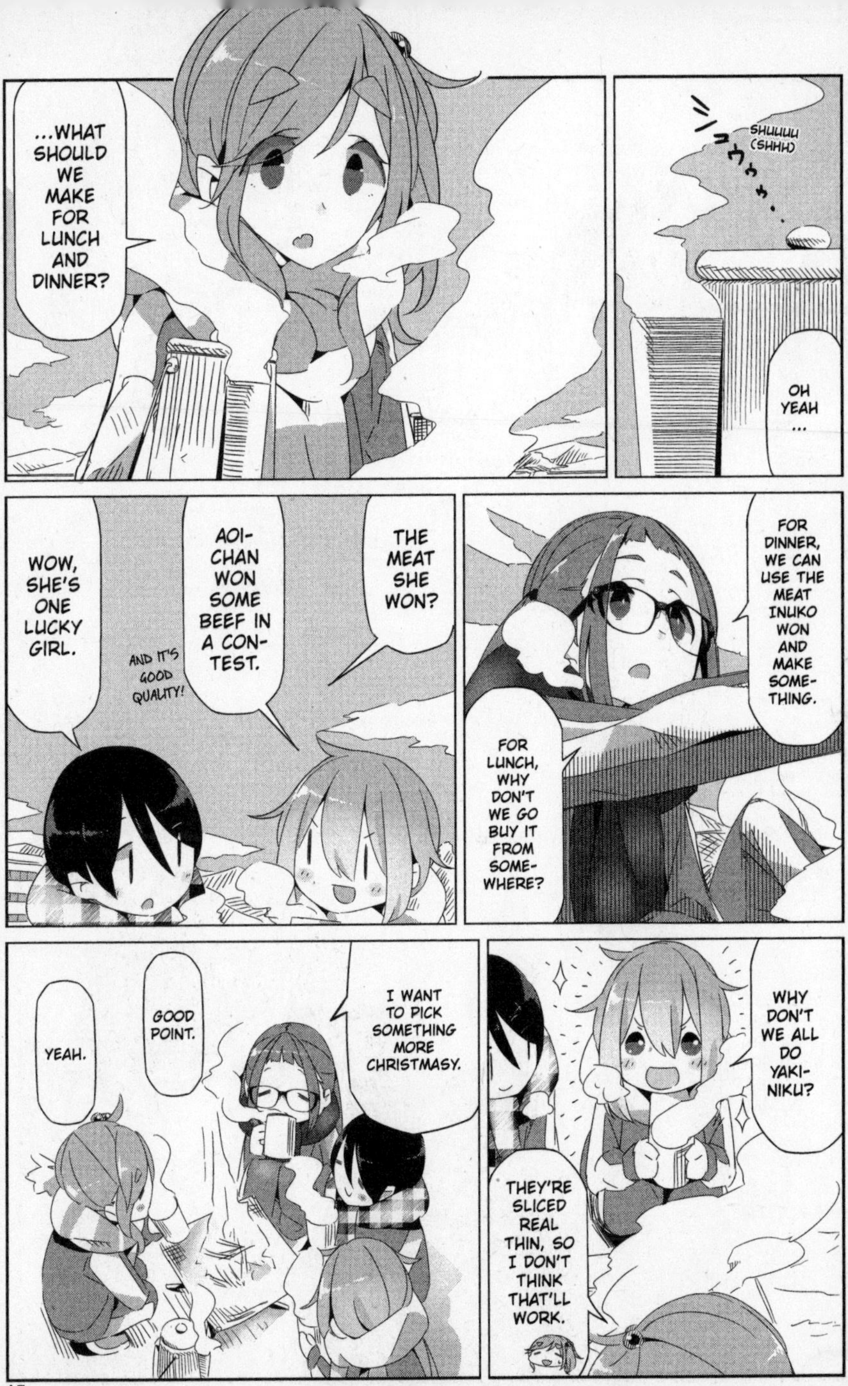
SHUUUU (SHHH)
OH YEAH ...
...WHAT SHOULD WE MAKE FOR LUNCH AND DINNER?
FOR DINNER, WE CAN USE THE MEAT INUKO WON AND MAKE SOME-THING.
FOR LUNCH, WHY DON'T WE GO BUY IT FROM SOME-WHERE?
THE MEAT SHE WON?
AOI-CHAN WON SOME BEEF IN A CON-TEST.
AND IT'S GOOD QUALITY!
WOW, SHE'S ONE LUCKY GIRL.
WHY DON'T WE ALL DO YAKI-NIKU?
THEY'RE SLICED REAL THIN, SO I DON'T THINK THAT'LL WORK.
I WANT TO PICK SOMETHING MORE CHRISTMASY.
GOOD POINT.
YEAH.

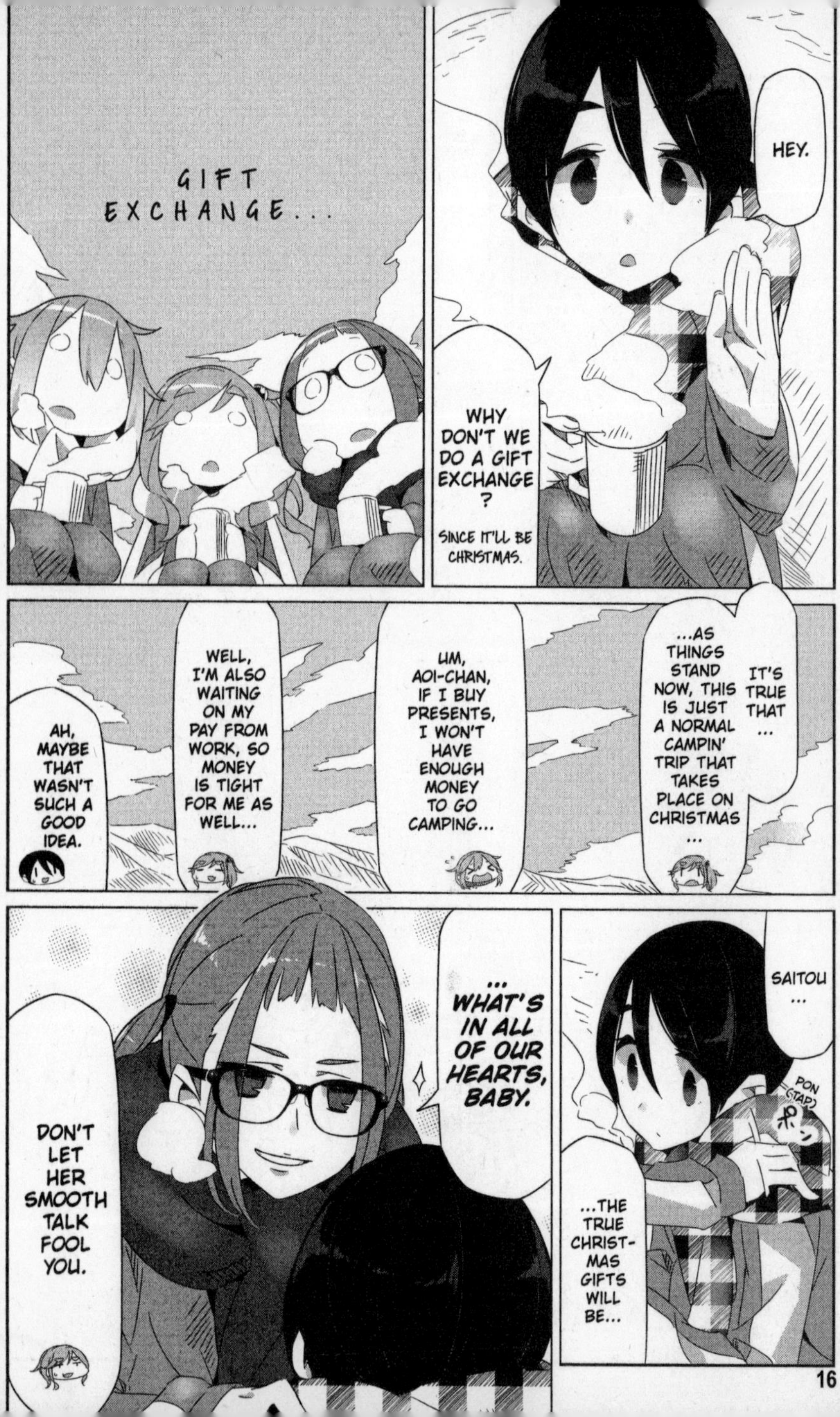

HEY.
WHY DON'T WE DO A GIFT EXCHANGE?
SINCE IT'LL BE CHRISTMAS.
GIFT EXCHANGE...
IT'S TRUE THAT...
...AS THINGS STAND NOW, THIS IS JUST A NORMAL CAMPIN' TRIP THAT TAKES PLACE ON CHRISTMAS...
UM, AOI-CHAN, IF I BUY PRESENTS, I WON'T HAVE ENOUGH MONEY TO GO CAMPING...
WELL, I'M ALSO WAITING ON MY PAY FROM WORK, SO MONEY IS TIGHT FOR ME AS WELL...
AH, MAYBE THAT WASN'T SUCH A GOOD IDEA.
SAITOU...
PON (TAP)
...THE TRUE CHRISTMAS GIFTS WILL BE...
...WHAT'S IN ALL OF OUR HEARTS, BABY.
DON'T LET HER SMOOTH TALK FOOL YOU.

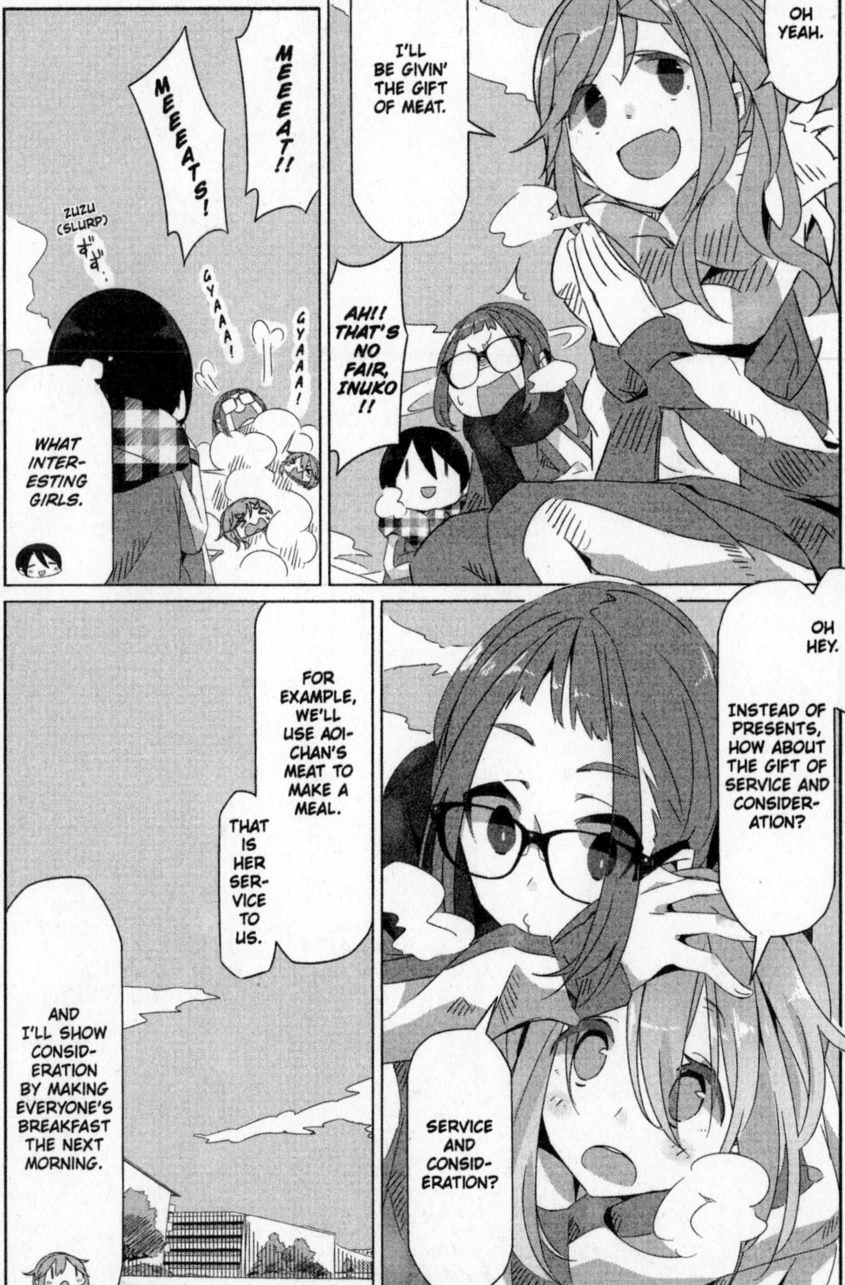
OH YEAH.
I'LL BE GIVIN' THE GIFT OF MEAT.
AH!! THAT'S NO FAIR, INUKO!!
MEEEAT!!
MEEEATS!
ZUZU (SLURP)
ずず…
GYAAAA!
GYAAAA!
WHAT INTER-ESTING GIRLS.
OH HEY.
INSTEAD OF PRESENTS, HOW ABOUT THE GIFT OF SERVICE AND CONSIDER-ATION?
SERVICE AND CONSID-ERATION?
FOR EXAMPLE, WE'LL USE AOI-CHAN'S MEAT TO MAKE A MEAL.
THAT IS HER SER-VICE TO US.
AND I'LL SHOW CONSID-ERATION BY MAKING EVERYONE'S BREAKFAST THE NEXT MORNING.

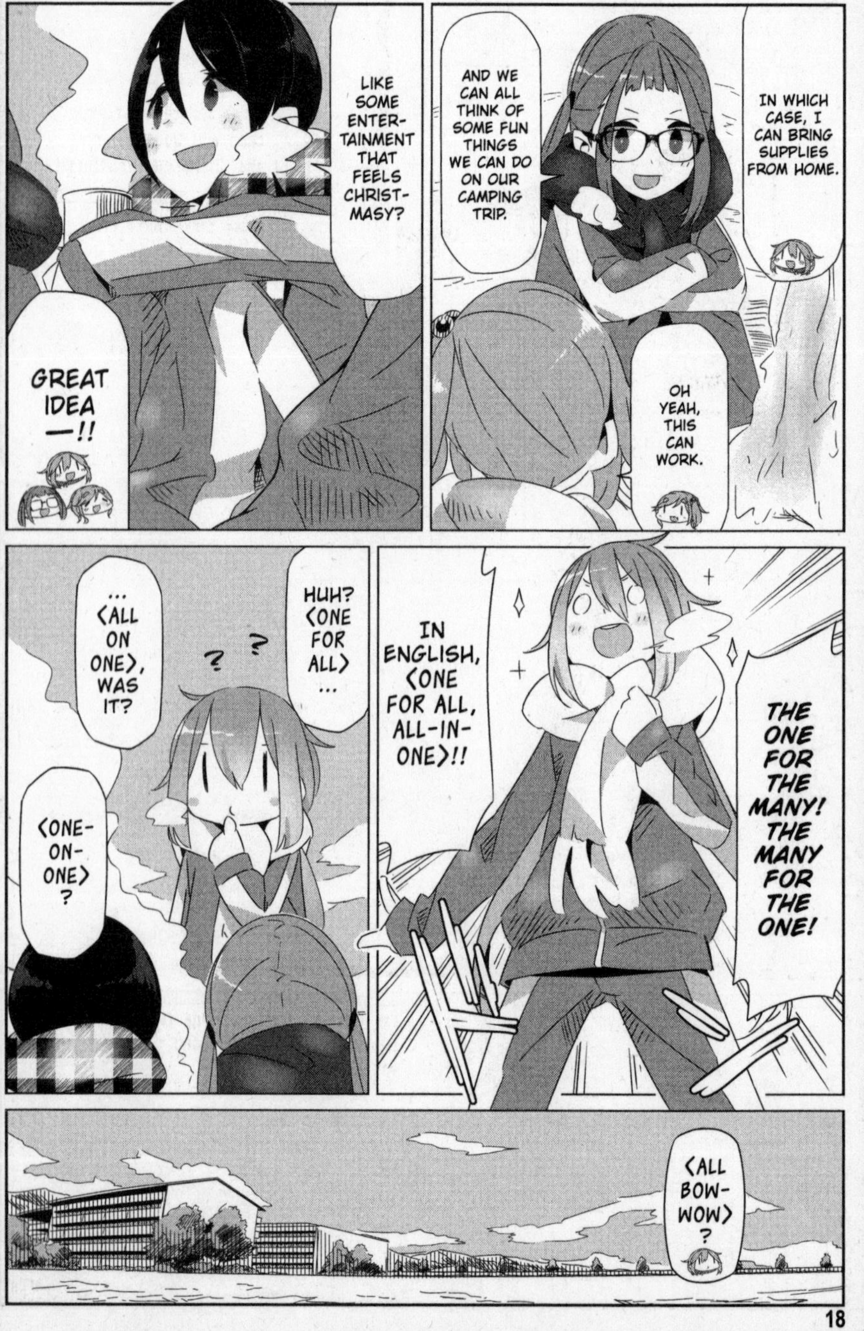
IN WHICH CASE, I CAN BRING SUPPLIES FROM HOME.
AND WE CAN ALL THINK OF SOME FUN THINGS WE CAN DO ON OUR CAMPING TRIP.
OH YEAH, THIS CAN WORK.
LIKE SOME ENTERTAINMENT THAT FEELS CHRISTMASY?
GREAT IDEA—!!
THE ONE FOR THE MANY! THE MANY FOR THE ONE!
IN ENGLISH, 〈ONE FOR ALL, ALL-IN-ONE〉!!
HUH? 〈ONE FOR ALL〉...
... 〈ALL ON ONE〉, WAS IT?
〈ONE-ON-ONE〉?
〈ALL BOW-WOW〉?

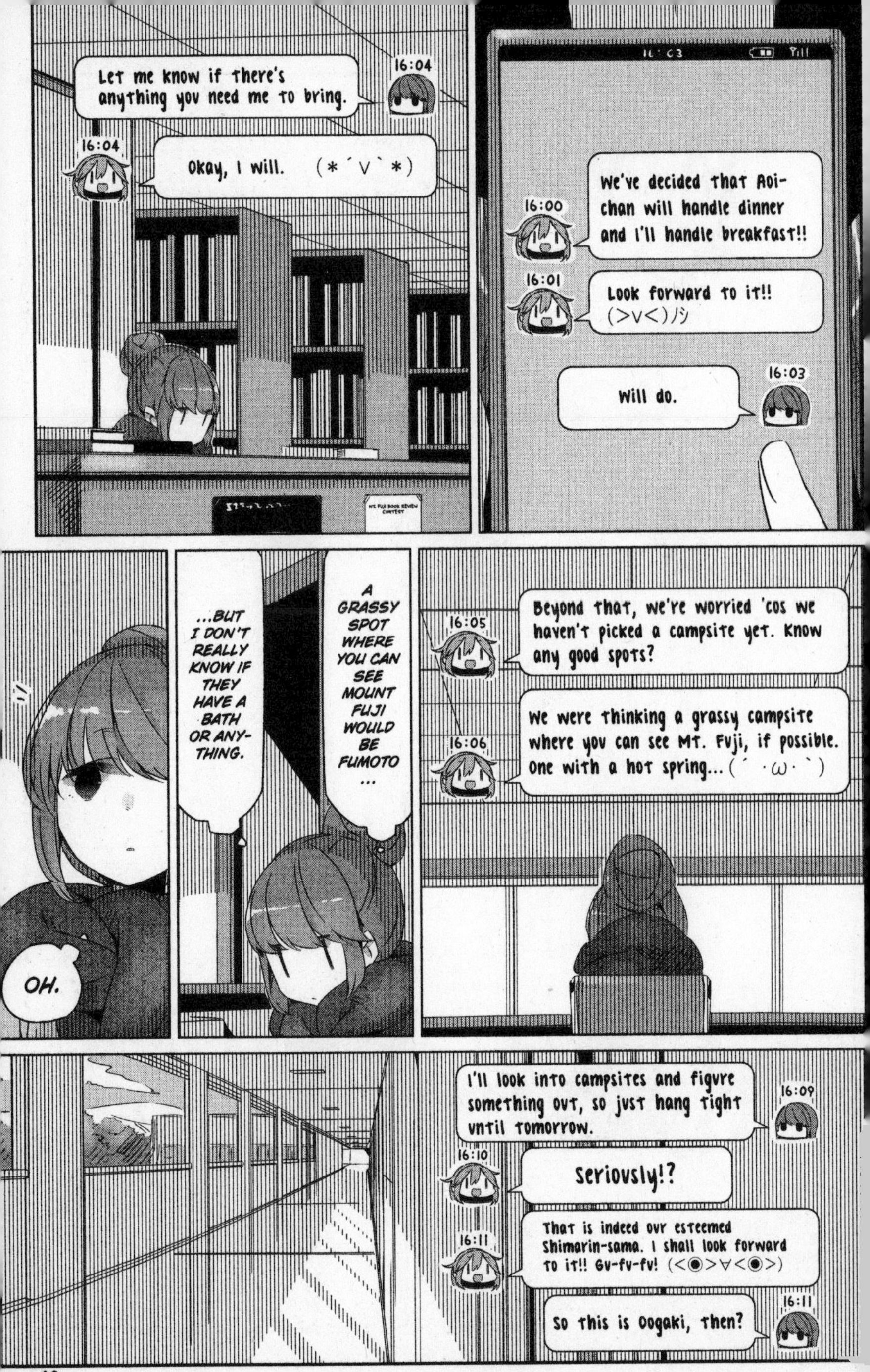
16:00
We've decided that Aoi-chan will handle dinner and I'll handle breakfast!!
16:01
Look forward to it!! (>v<)ノシ
16:03
Will do.
Let me know if there's anything you need me to bring.
16:04
16:04
Okay, I will. (*´v`*)
MT. FUJI BOOK REVIEW CONTEST
16:05
Beyond that, we're worried 'cos we haven't picked a campsite yet. Know any good spots?
16:06
We were thinking a grassy campsite where you can see Mt. Fuji, if possible. One with a hot spring... (´・ω・`)
A GRASSY SPOT WHERE YOU CAN SEE MOUNT FUJI WOULD BE FUMOTO...
...BUT I DON'T REALLY KNOW IF THEY HAVE A BATH OR ANYTHING.
OH.
I'll look into campsites and figure something out, so just hang tight until tomorrow.
16:09
16:10
Seriously!?
16:11
That is indeed our esteemed Shimarin-sama. I shall look forward to it!! Gu-fu-fu! (<◉>∀<◉>)
16:11
So this is Oogaki, then?

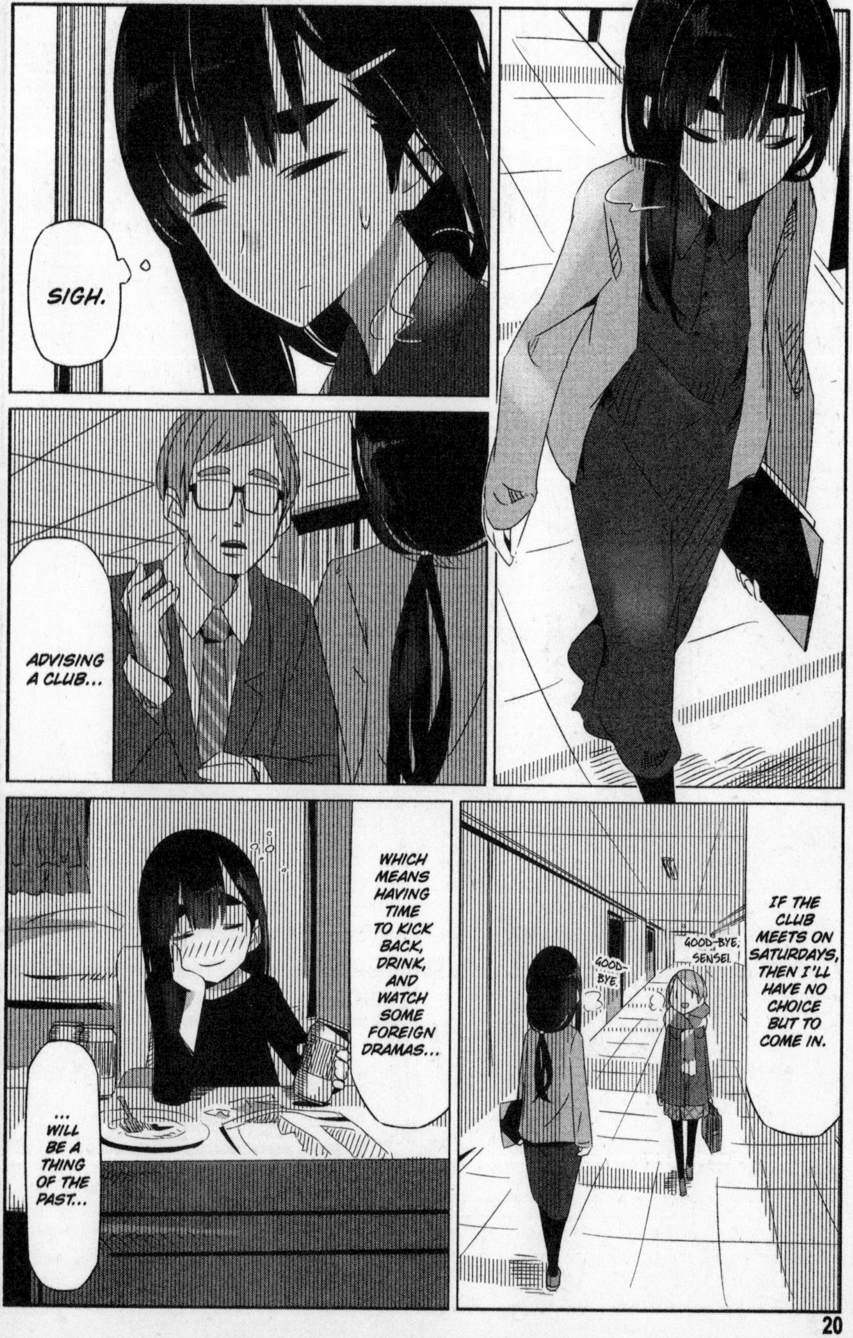
SIGH.
ADVISING A CLUB...
IF THE CLUB MEETS ON SATURDAYS, THEN I'LL HAVE NO CHOICE BUT TO COME IN.
GOOD-BYE, SENSEI.
GOOD-BYE.
WHICH MEANS HAVING TIME TO KICK BACK, DRINK, AND WATCH SOME FOREIGN DRAMAS...
...WILL BE A THING OF THE PAST...

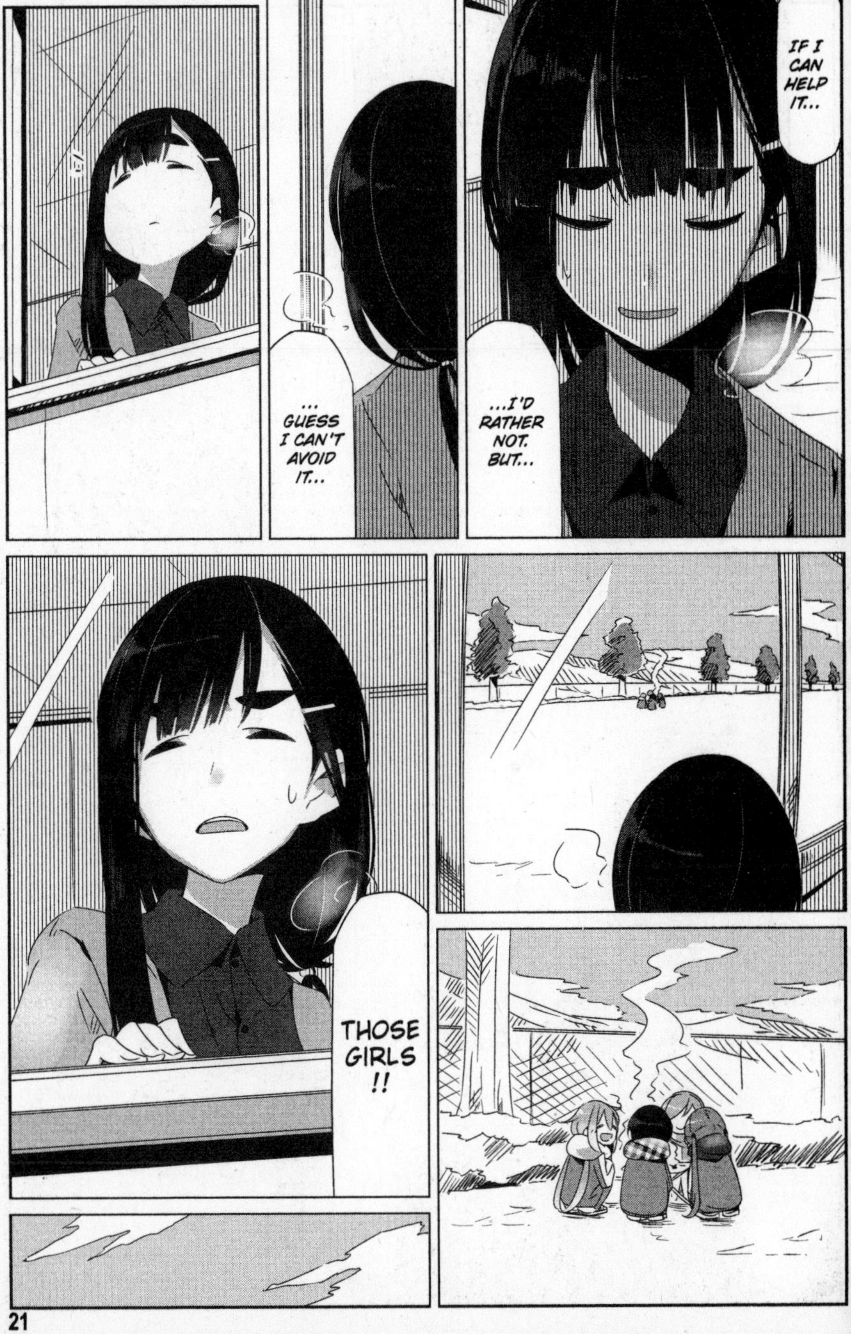
IF I CAN HELP IT...
...I'D RATHER NOT. BUT...
...GUESS I CAN'T AVOID IT...
THOSE GIRLS!!

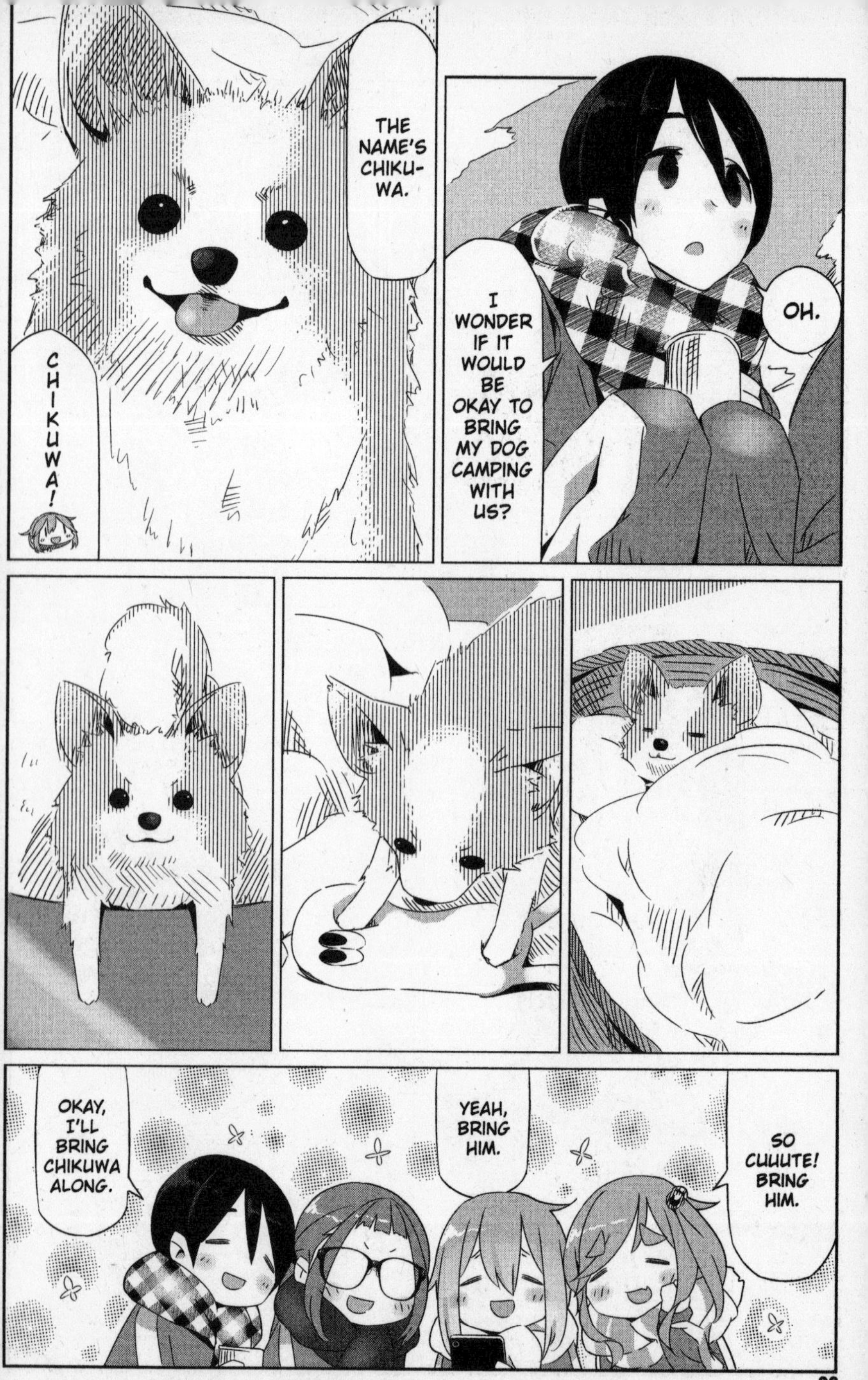
OH.
I WONDER IF IT WOULD BE OKAY TO BRING MY DOG CAMPING WITH US?
THE NAME'S CHIKU-WA.
CHIKUWA!
SO CUUUTE! BRING HIM.
YEAH, BRING HIM.
OKAY, I'LL BRING CHIKUWA ALONG.

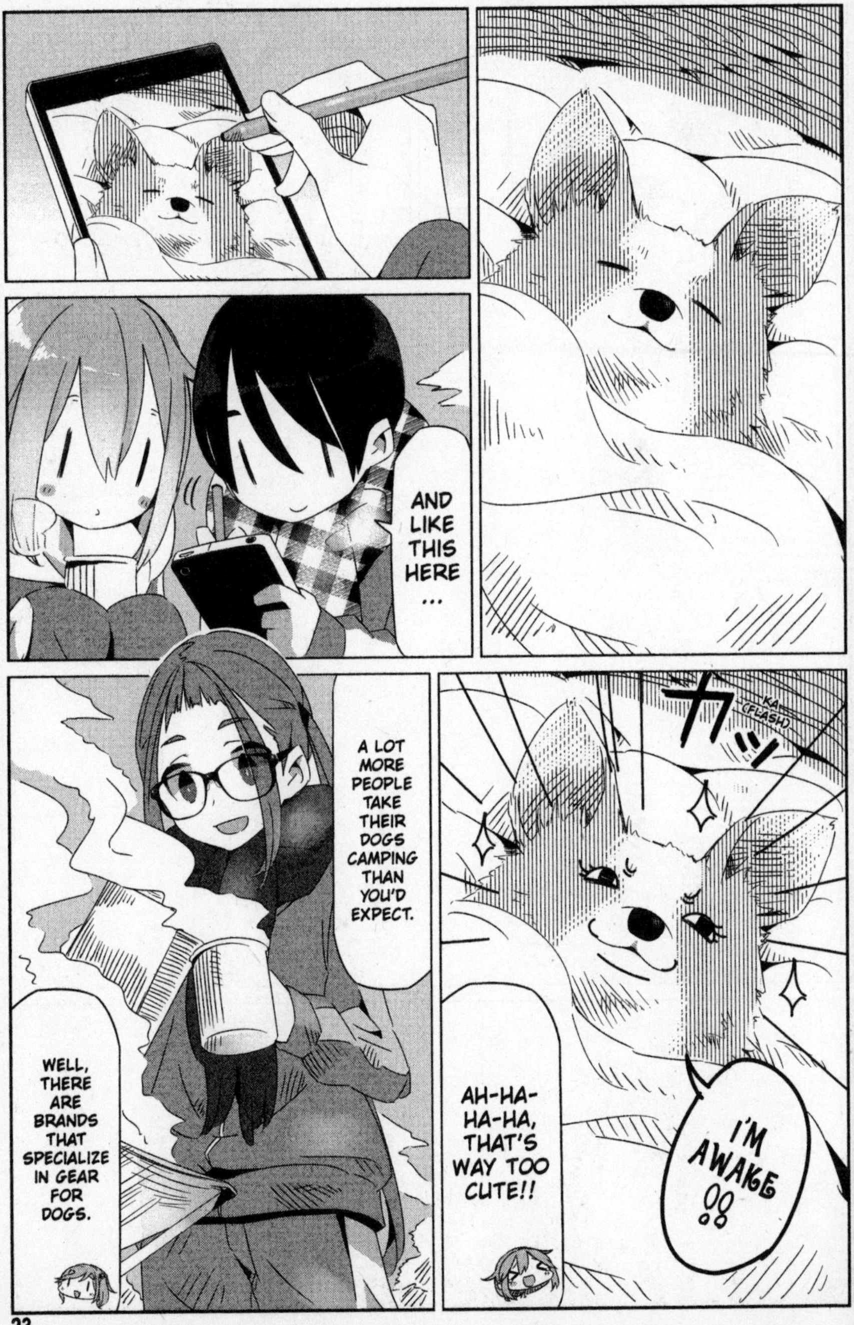
AND LIKE THIS HERE...
KA (FLASH)
I'M AWAKE!!
AH-HA-HA-HA, THAT'S WAY TOO CUTE!!
A LOT MORE PEOPLE TAKE THEIR DOGS CAMPING THAN YOU'D EXPECT.
WELL, THERE ARE BRANDS THAT SPECIALIZE IN GEAR FOR DOGS.

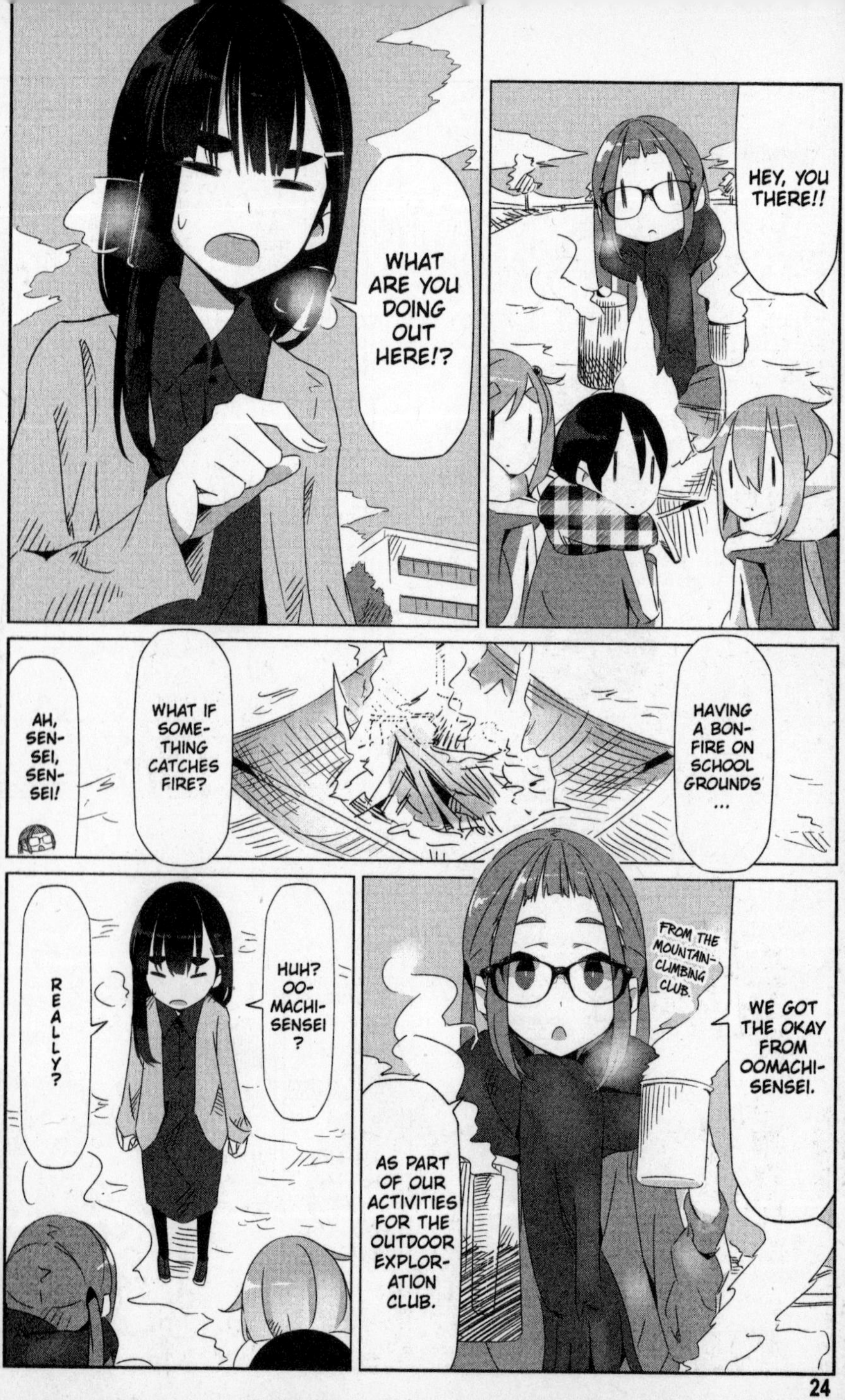
HEY, YOU THERE!!
WHAT ARE YOU DOING OUT HERE!?
HAVING A BONFIRE ON SCHOOL GROUNDS ...
WHAT IF SOMETHING CATCHES FIRE?
AH, SENSEI, SENSEI!
WE GOT THE OKAY FROM OOMACHI-SENSEI.
FROM THE MOUNTAIN-CLIMBING CLUB.
AS PART OF OUR ACTIVITIES FOR THE OUTDOOR EXPLORATION CLUB.
HUH? OOMACHI-SENSEI?
REALLY?

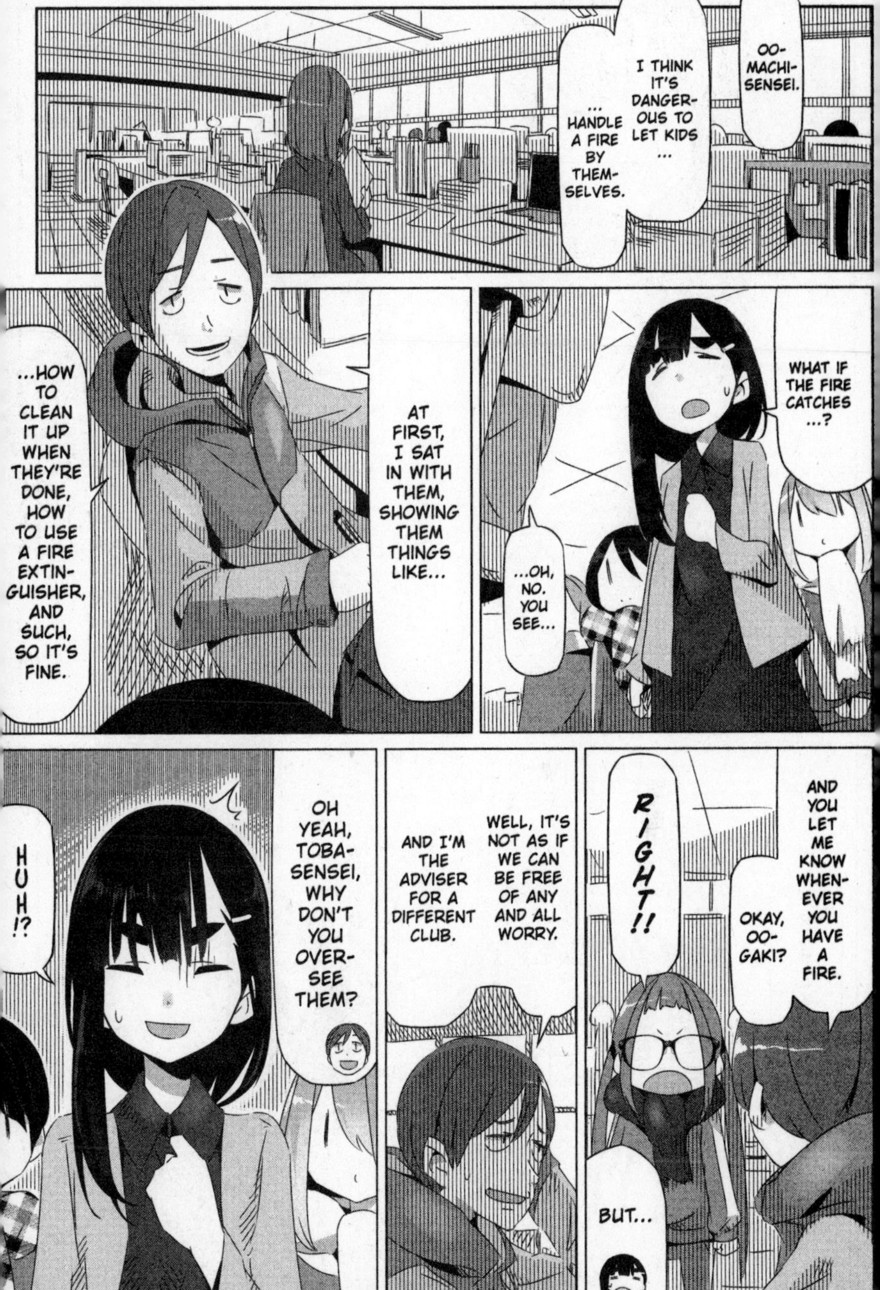
OOMACHI-SENSEI.
I THINK IT'S DANGEROUS TO LET KIDS ...
... HANDLE A FIRE BY THEMSELVES.
WHAT IF THE FIRE CATCHES ...?
...OH, NO. YOU SEE...
AT FIRST, I SAT IN WITH THEM, SHOWING THEM THINGS LIKE...
...HOW TO CLEAN IT UP WHEN THEY'RE DONE, HOW TO USE A FIRE EXTINGUISHER, AND SUCH, SO IT'S FINE.
AND YOU LET ME KNOW WHENEVER YOU HAVE A FIRE.
OKAY, OOGAKI?
RIGHT!!
BUT...
WELL, IT'S NOT AS IF WE CAN BE FREE OF ANY AND ALL WORRY.
AND I'M THE ADVISER FOR A DIFFERENT CLUB.
OH YEAH, TOBA-SENSEI, WHY DON'T YOU OVERSEE THEM?
HUH!?

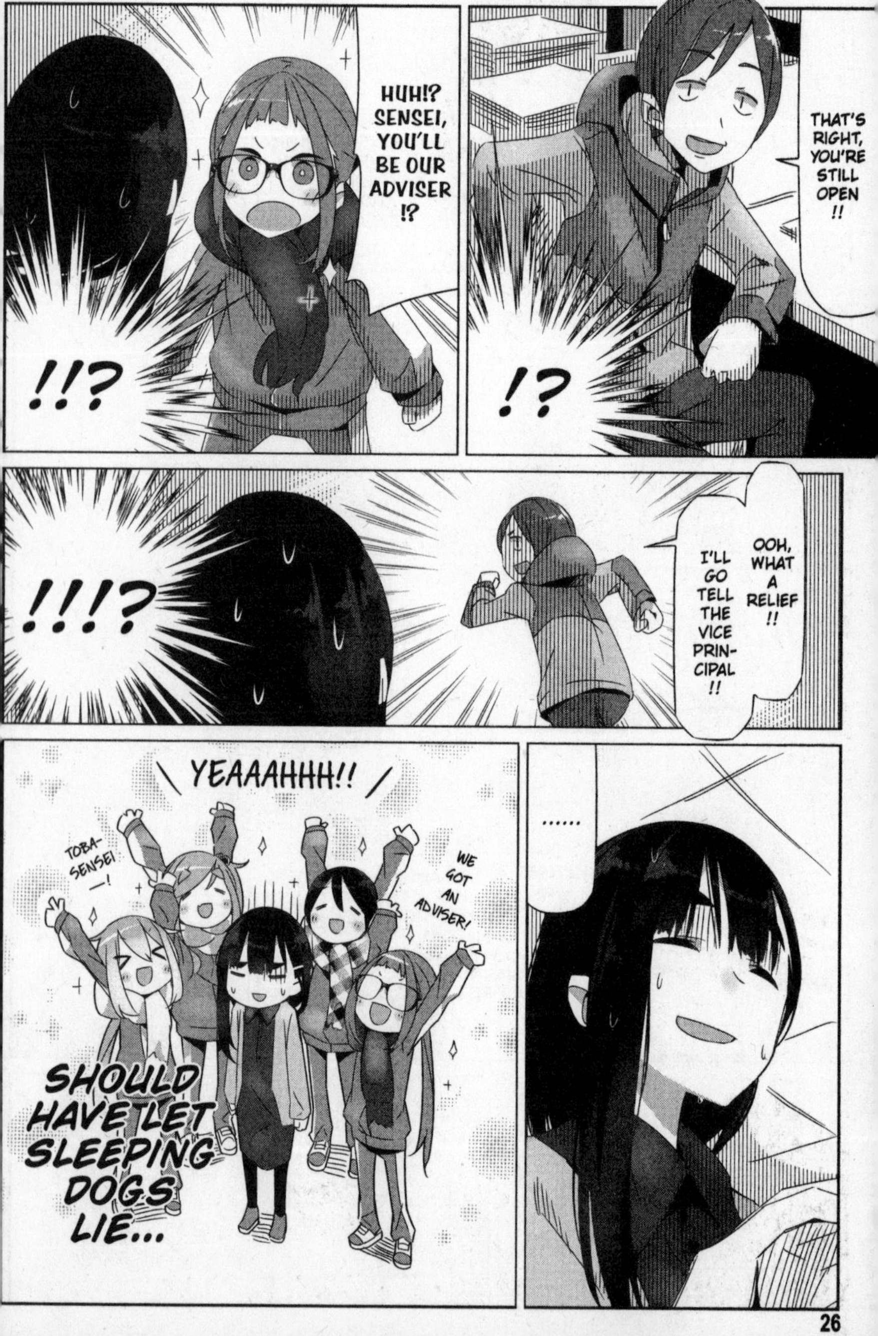
THAT'S RIGHT, YOU'RE STILL OPEN!!
!?
HUH!? SENSEI, YOU'LL BE OUR ADVISER!?
!!?
OOH, WHAT A RELIEF!!
I'LL GO TELL THE VICE PRIN-CIPAL!!
!!!?
......
YEAAAHHH!!
WE GOT AN ADVISER!
TOBA-SENSEI—!
SHOULD HAVE LET SLEEPING DOGS LIE...

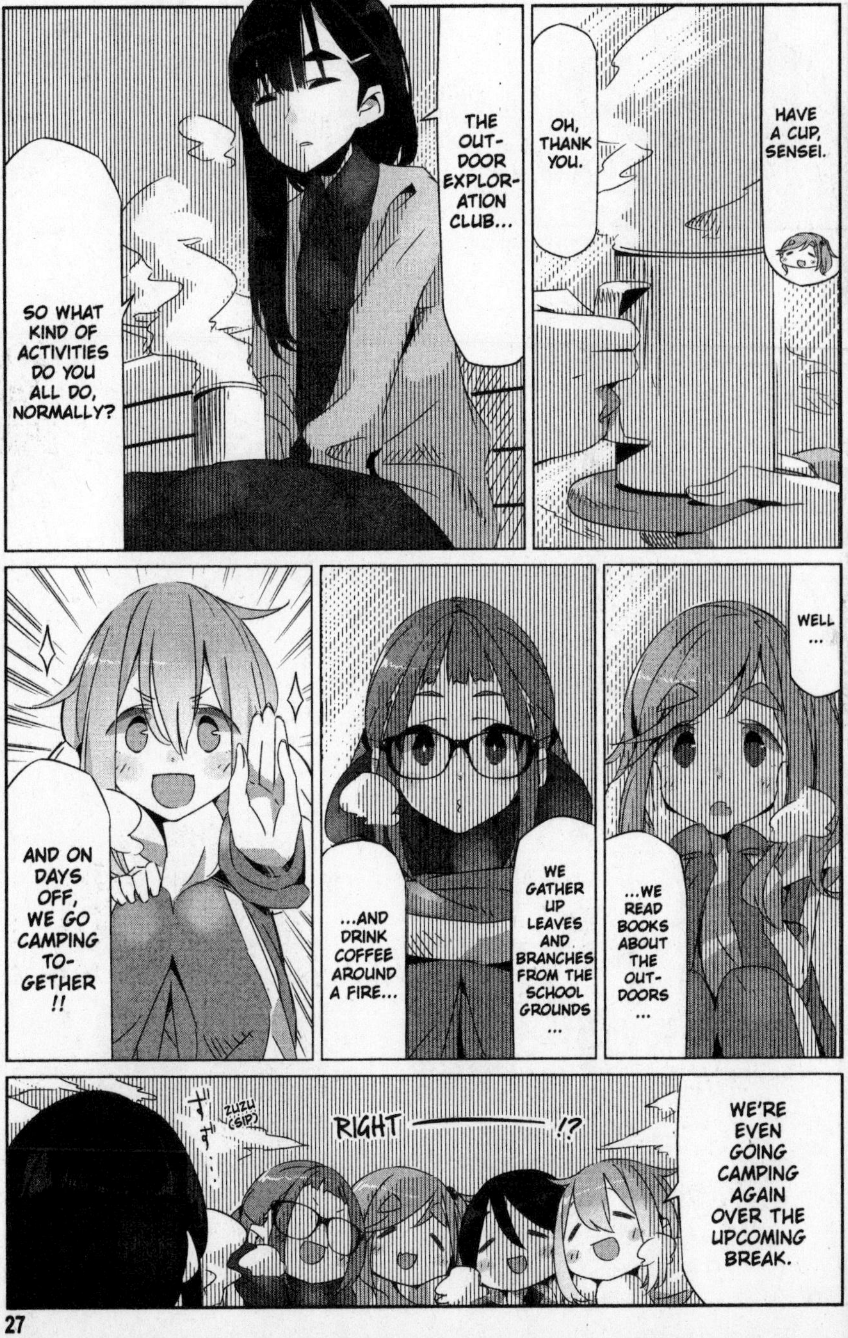
HAVE A CUP, SENSEI.
OH, THANK YOU.
THE OUTDOOR EXPLORATION CLUB...
SO WHAT KIND OF ACTIVITIES DO YOU ALL DO, NORMALLY?
WELL...
...WE READ BOOKS ABOUT THE OUTDOORS...
WE GATHER UP LEAVES AND BRANCHES FROM THE SCHOOL GROUNDS...
...AND DRINK COFFEE AROUND A FIRE...
AND ON DAYS OFF, WE GO CAMPING TOGETHER!!
WE'RE EVEN GOING CAMPING AGAIN OVER THE UPCOMING BREAK.
RIGHT ——— !?
ずず…
ZUZU (SIP)

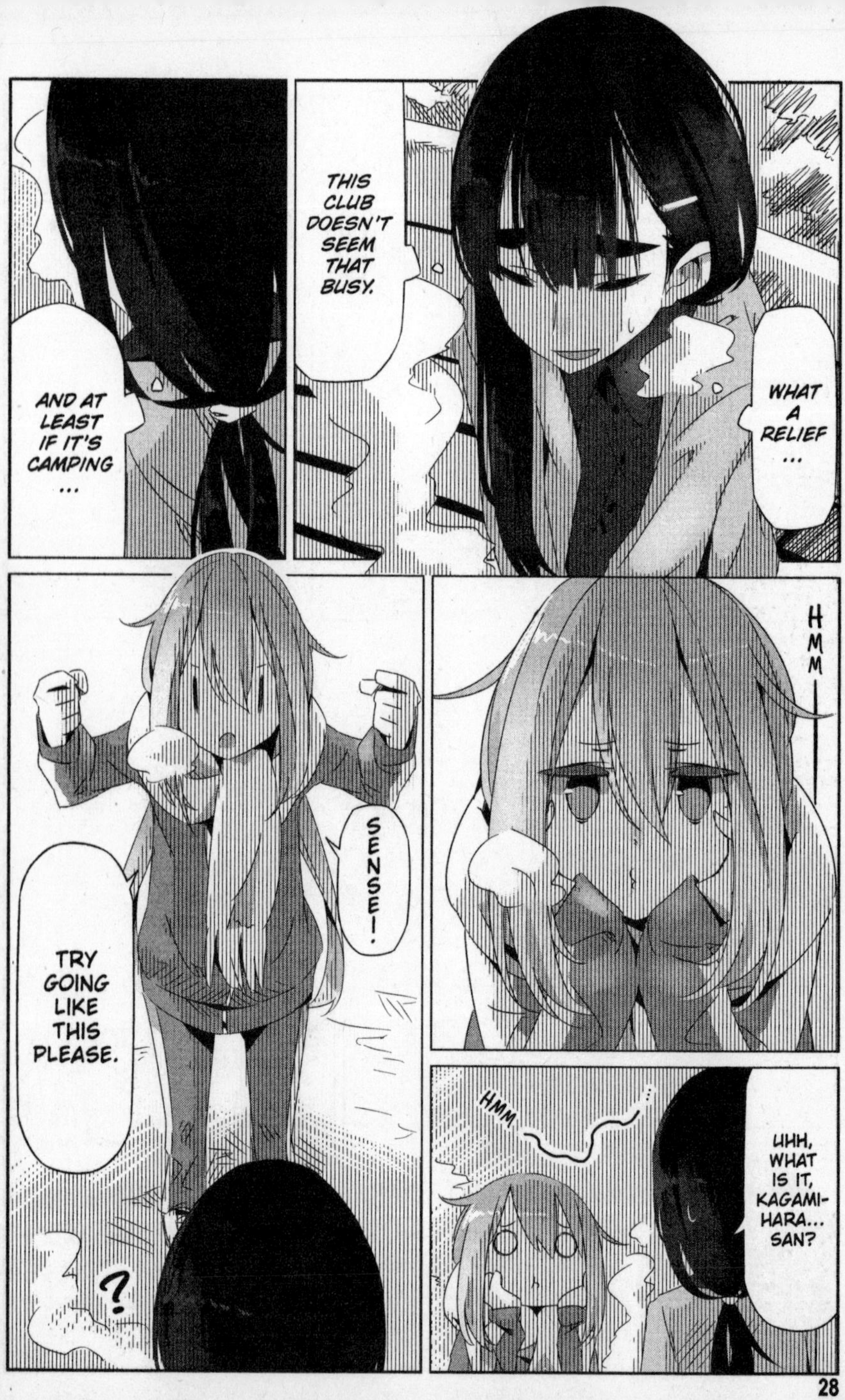
THIS CLUB DOESN'T SEEM THAT BUSY.
WHAT A RELIEF...
AND AT LEAST IF IT'S CAMPING...
HMM—
HMM...
UHH, WHAT IS IT, KAGAMI-HARA... SAN?
SENSE!
TRY GOING LIKE THIS PLEASE.
?

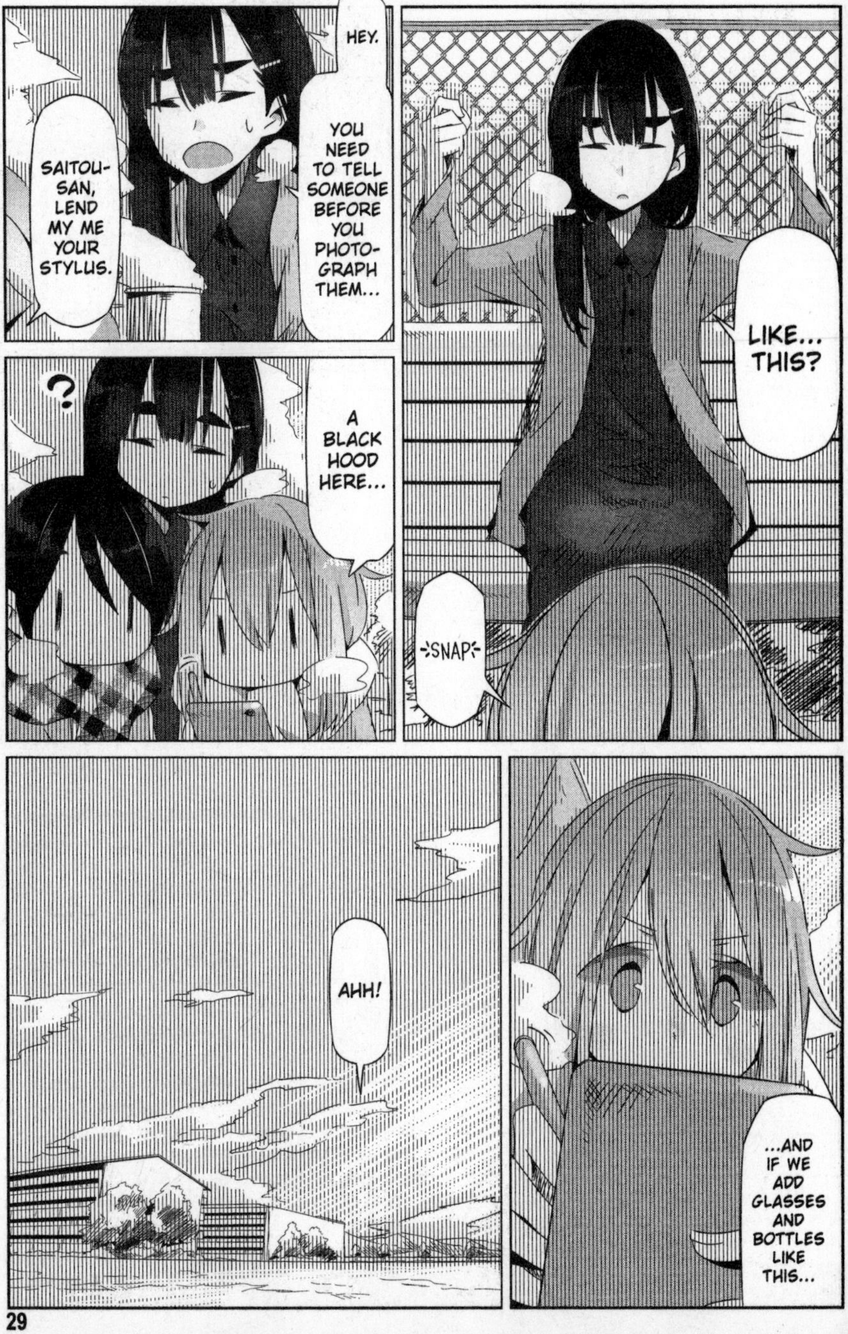
LIKE... THIS?
SNAP
HEY.
YOU NEED TO TELL SOMEONE BEFORE YOU PHOTOGRAPH THEM...
SAITOU-SAN, LEND MY ME YOUR STYLUS.
?
A BLACK HOOD HERE...
...AND IF WE ADD GLASSES AND BOTTLES LIKE THIS...
AHH!

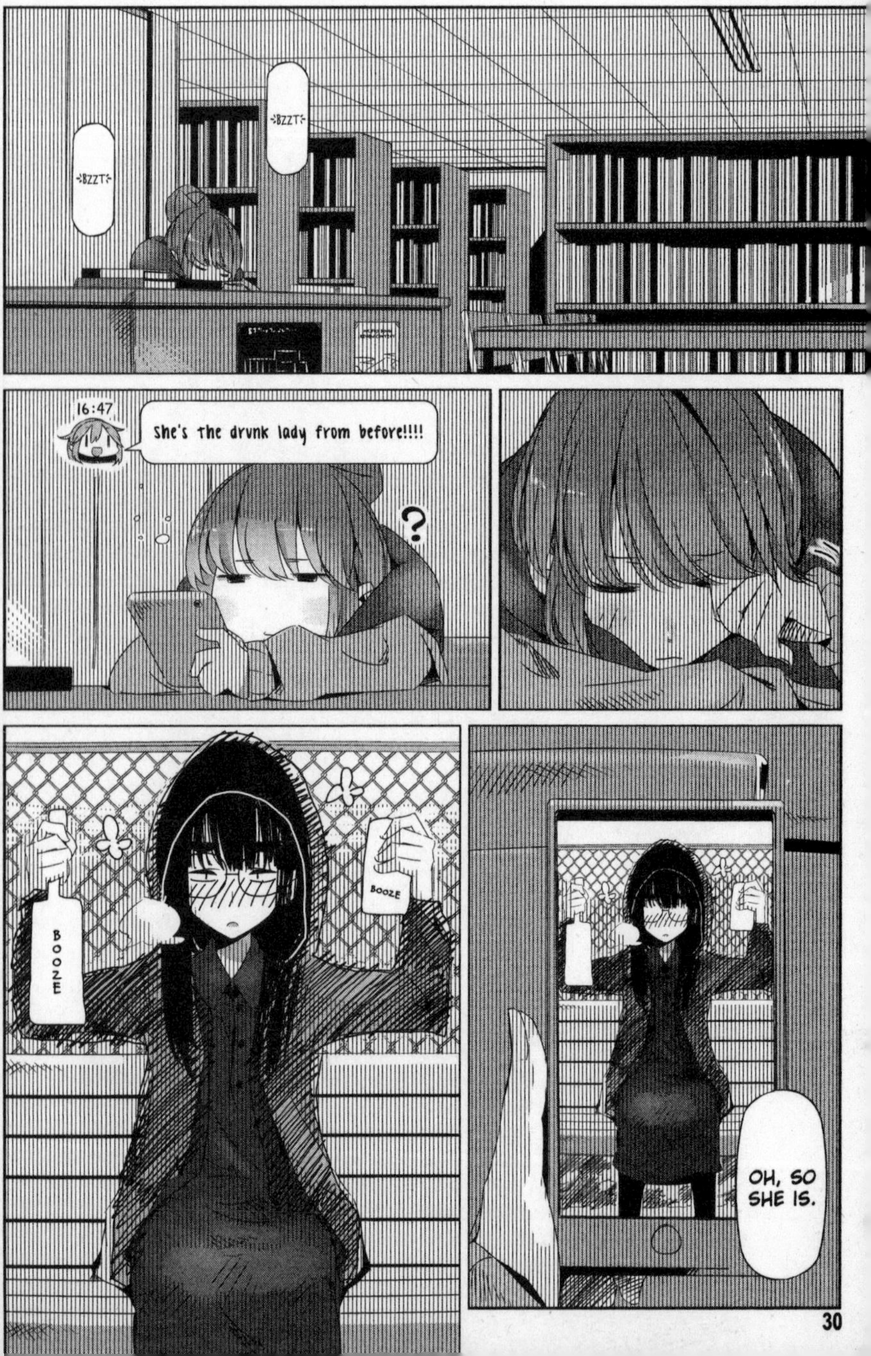
BZZT
BZZT
She's the drunk lady from before!!!!
16:47
?
OH, SO SHE IS.
BOOZE
BOOZE

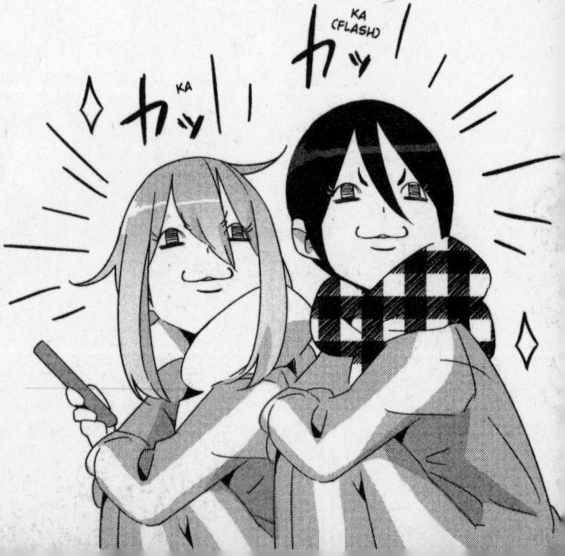
カッ
KA (FLASH)
カッ
KA

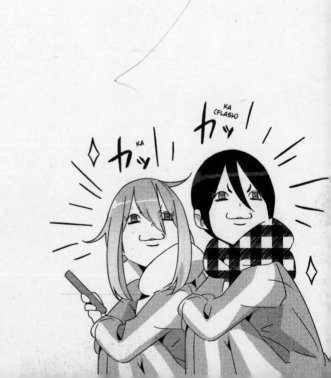

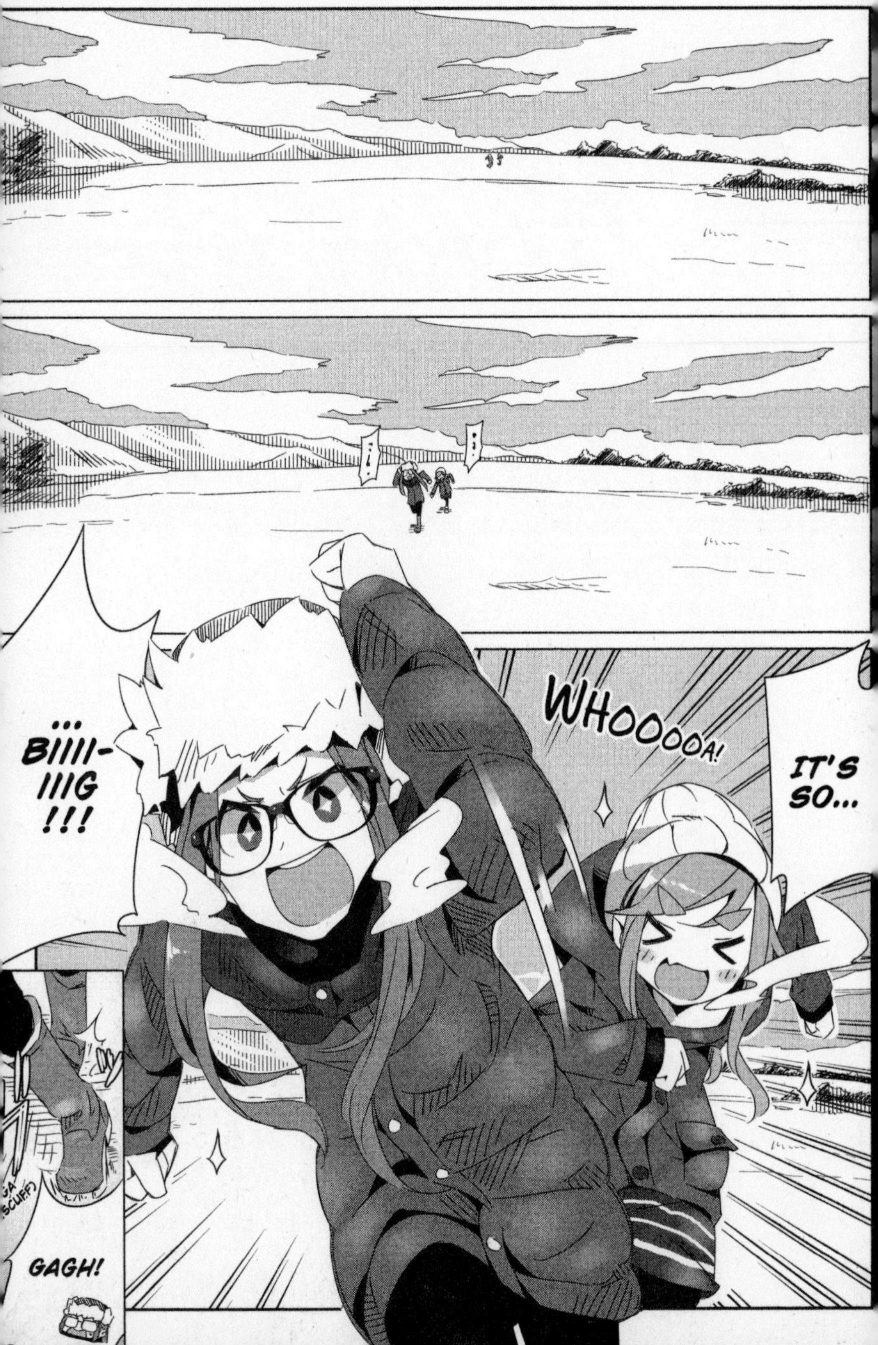
IT'S SO...
WHOOOOOA!
...BIIII-IIIG!!!
GA (SCUFF)
GAGH!

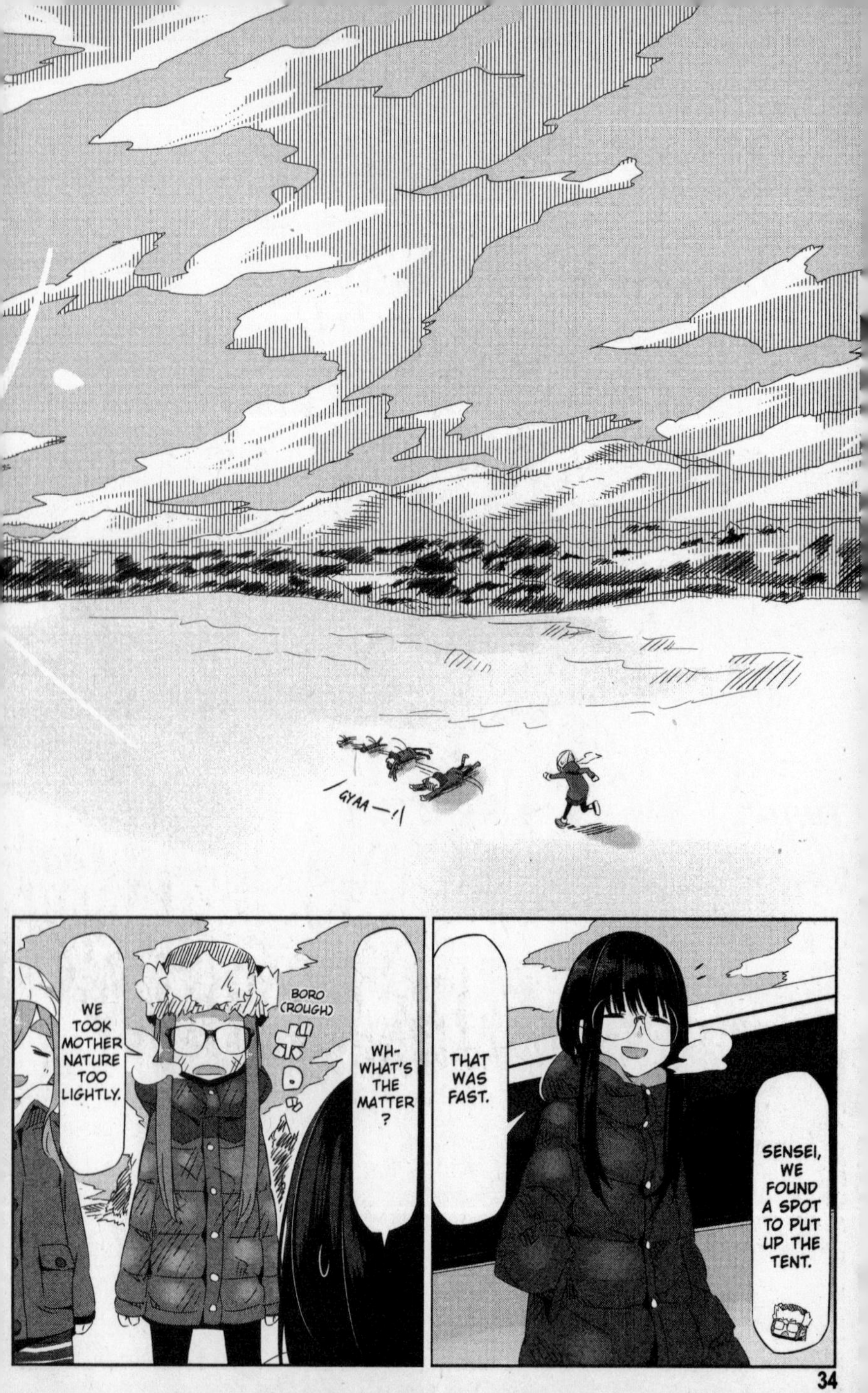
GYAA—!!
SENSEI, WE FOUND A SPOT TO PUT UP THE TENT.
THAT WAS FAST.
WH-WHAT'S THE MATTER?
BORO (ROUGH)
WE TOOK MOTHER NATURE TOO LIGHTLY.

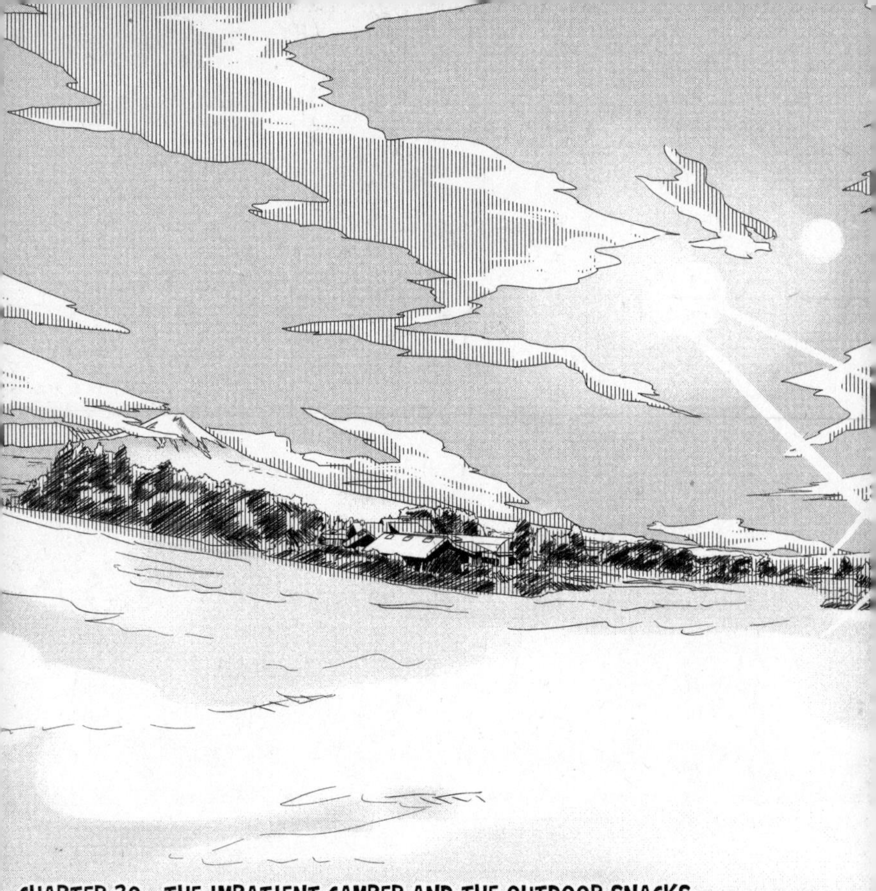

CHAPTER 20 THE IMPATIENT CAMPER AND THE OUTDOOR SNACKS

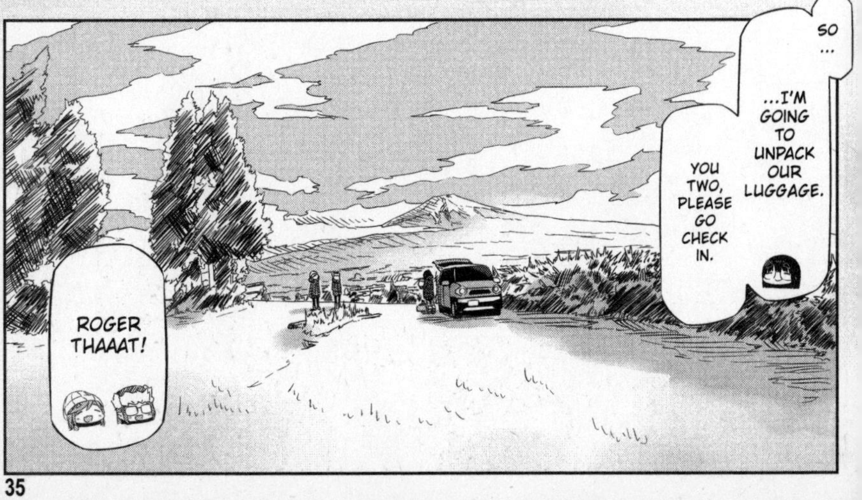
SO...
...I'M GOING TO UNPACK OUR LUGGAGE.
YOU TWO, PLEASE GO CHECK IN.
ROGER THAAAT!

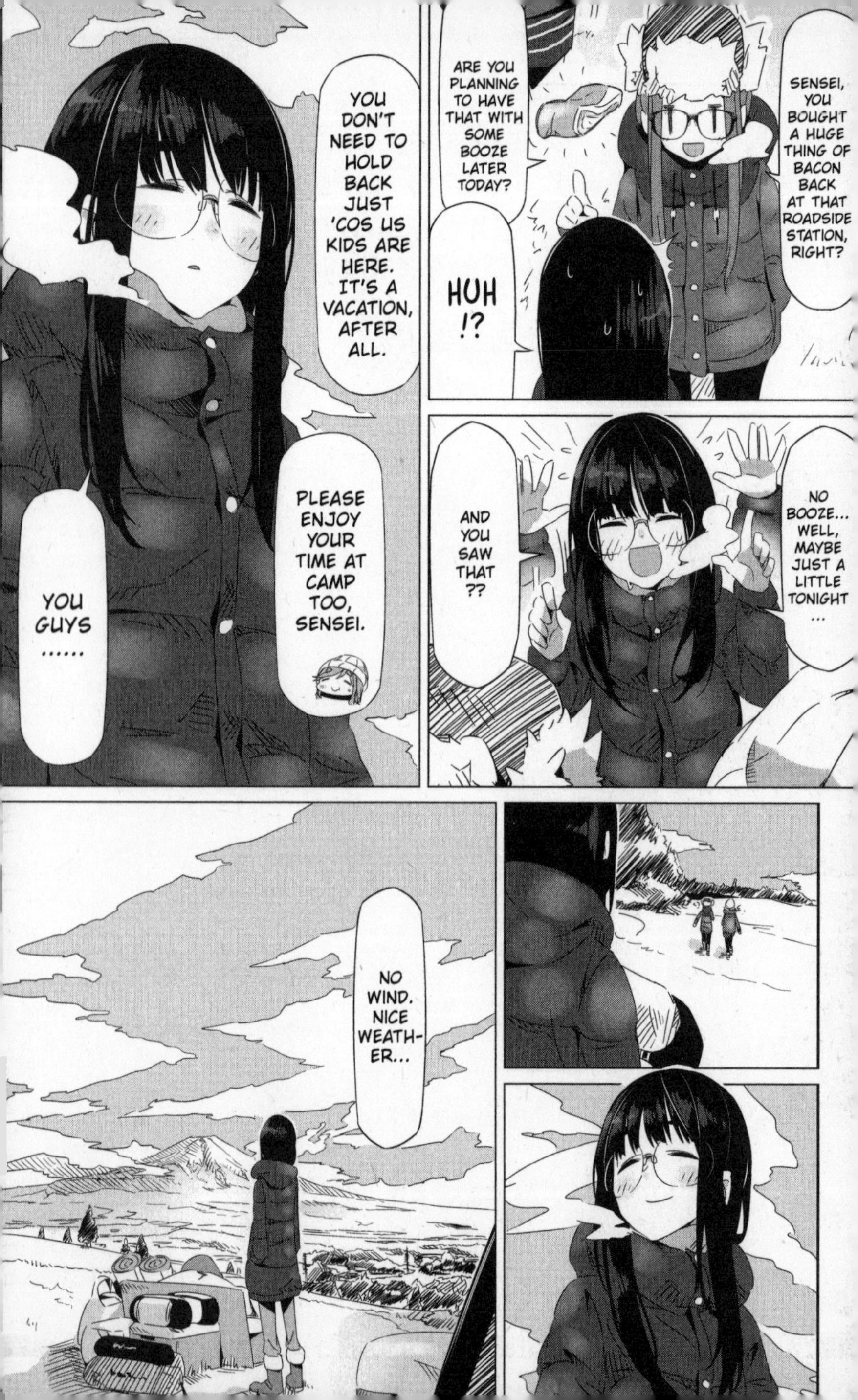
SENSEI, YOU BOUGHT A HUGE THING OF BACON BACK AT THAT ROADSIDE STATION, RIGHT?
ARE YOU PLANNING TO HAVE THAT WITH SOME BOOZE LATER TODAY?
HUH !?
NO BOOZE... WELL, MAYBE JUST A LITTLE TONIGHT ...
AND YOU SAW THAT ??
YOU DON'T NEED TO HOLD BACK JUST 'COS US KIDS ARE HERE. IT'S A VACATION, AFTER ALL.
PLEASE ENJOY YOUR TIME AT CAMP TOO, SENSEI.
YOU GUYS ......
NO WIND. NICE WEATH-ER...

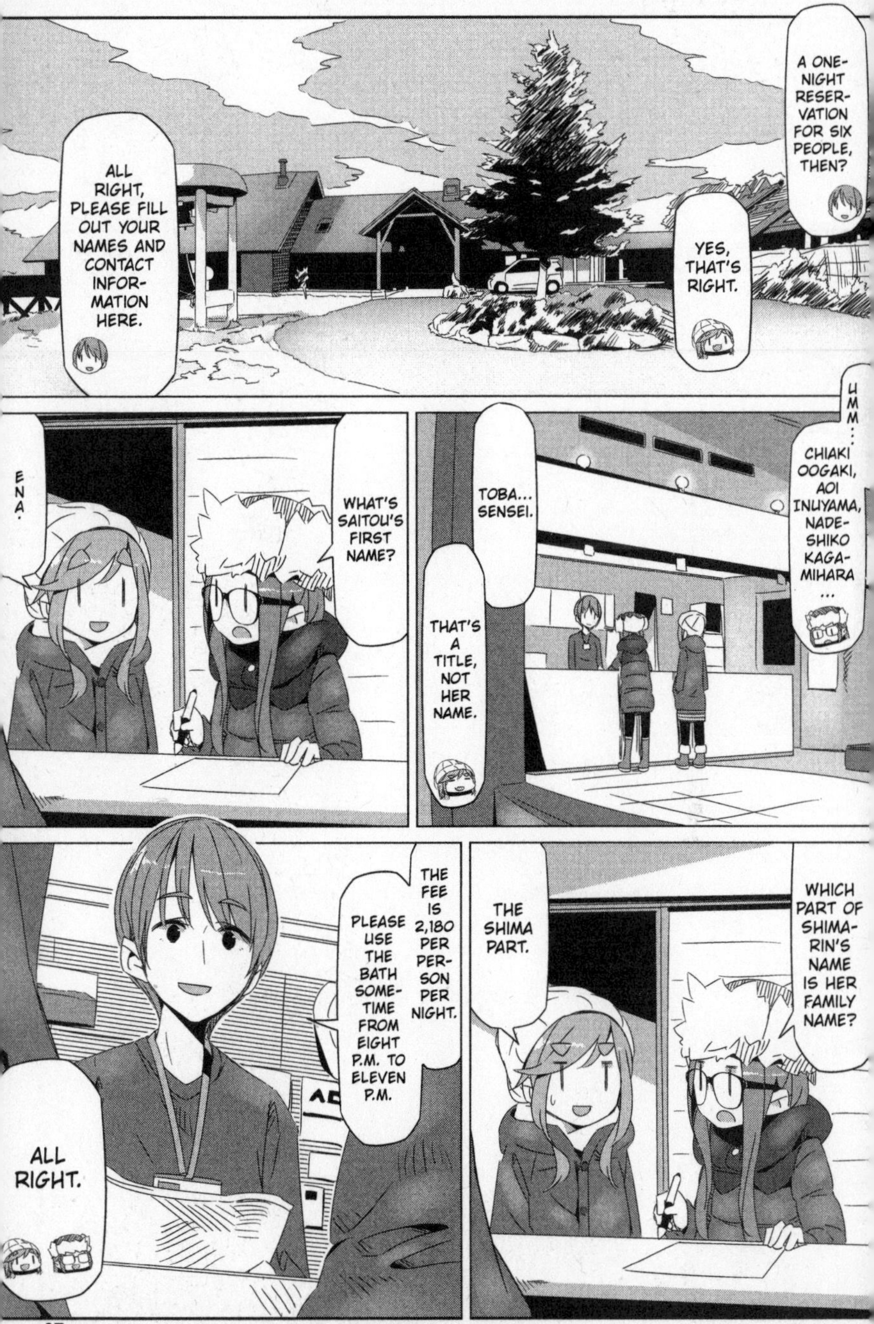
A ONE-NIGHT RESERVATION FOR SIX PEOPLE, THEN?
YES, THAT'S RIGHT.
ALL RIGHT, PLEASE FILL OUT YOUR NAMES AND CONTACT INFORMATION HERE.
UMM...
CHIAKI OOGAKI, AOI INUYAMA, NADESHIKO KAGAMIHARA...
TOBA... SENSEI.
THAT'S A TITLE, NOT HER NAME.
WHAT'S SAITOU'S FIRST NAME?
ENA.
WHICH PART OF SHIMARIN'S NAME IS HER FAMILY NAME?
THE SHIMA PART.
THE FEE IS 2,180 PER PERSON PER NIGHT.
PLEASE USE THE BATH SOMETIME FROM EIGHT P.M. TO ELEVEN P.M.
ALL RIGHT.

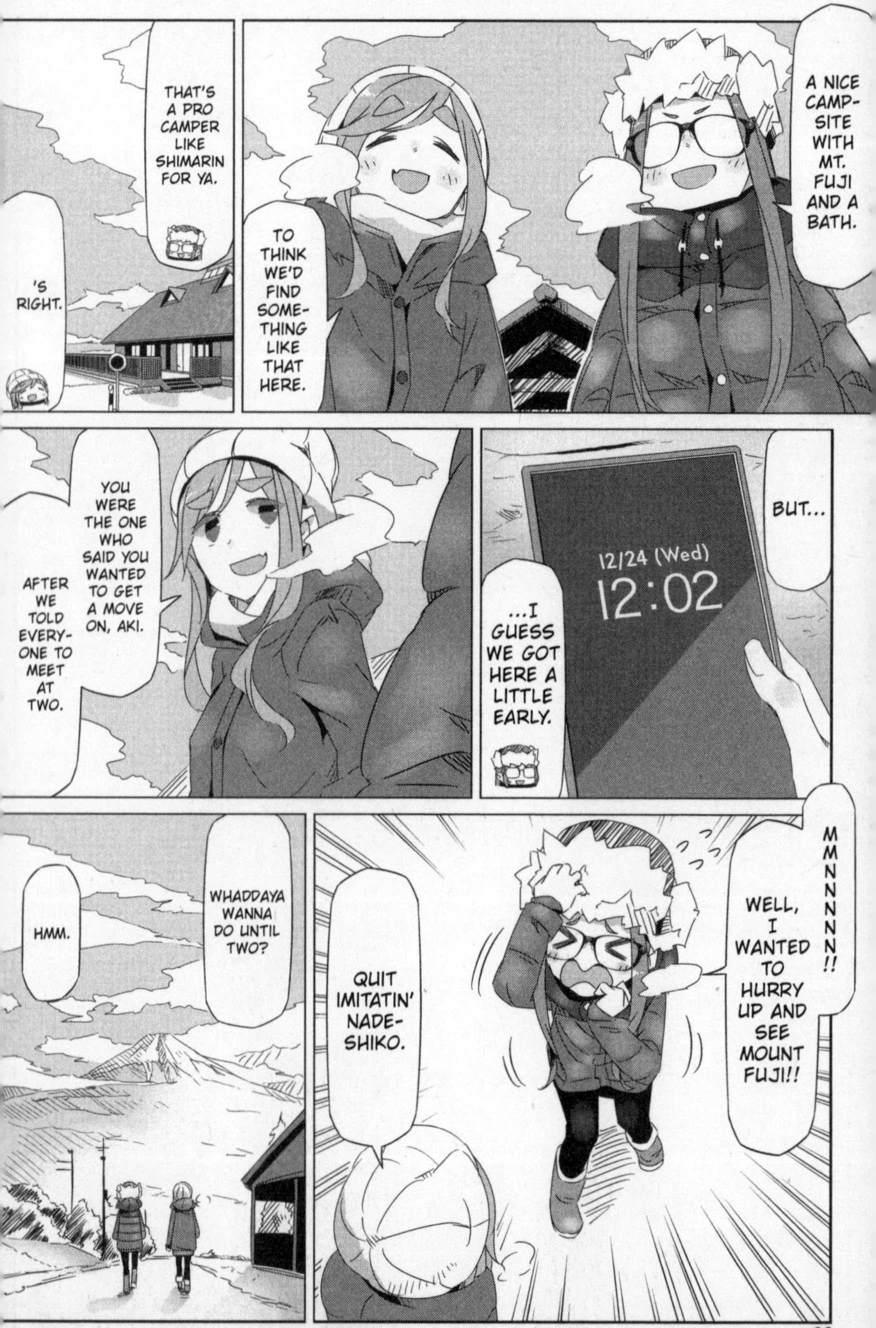
A NICE CAMPSITE WITH MT. FUJI AND A BATH.
TO THINK WE'D FIND SOMETHING LIKE THAT HERE.
THAT'S A PRO CAMPER LIKE SHIMARIN FOR YA.
'S RIGHT.
BUT...
12/24 (Wed)
12:02
...I GUESS WE GOT HERE A LITTLE EARLY.
YOU WERE THE ONE WHO SAID YOU WANTED TO GET A MOVE ON, AKI.
AFTER WE TOLD EVERYONE TO MEET AT TWO.
MMNNNNN!!
WELL, I WANTED TO HURRY UP AND SEE MOUNT FUJI!!
QUIT IMITATIN' NADESHIKO.
WHADDAYA WANNA DO UNTIL TWO?
HMM.

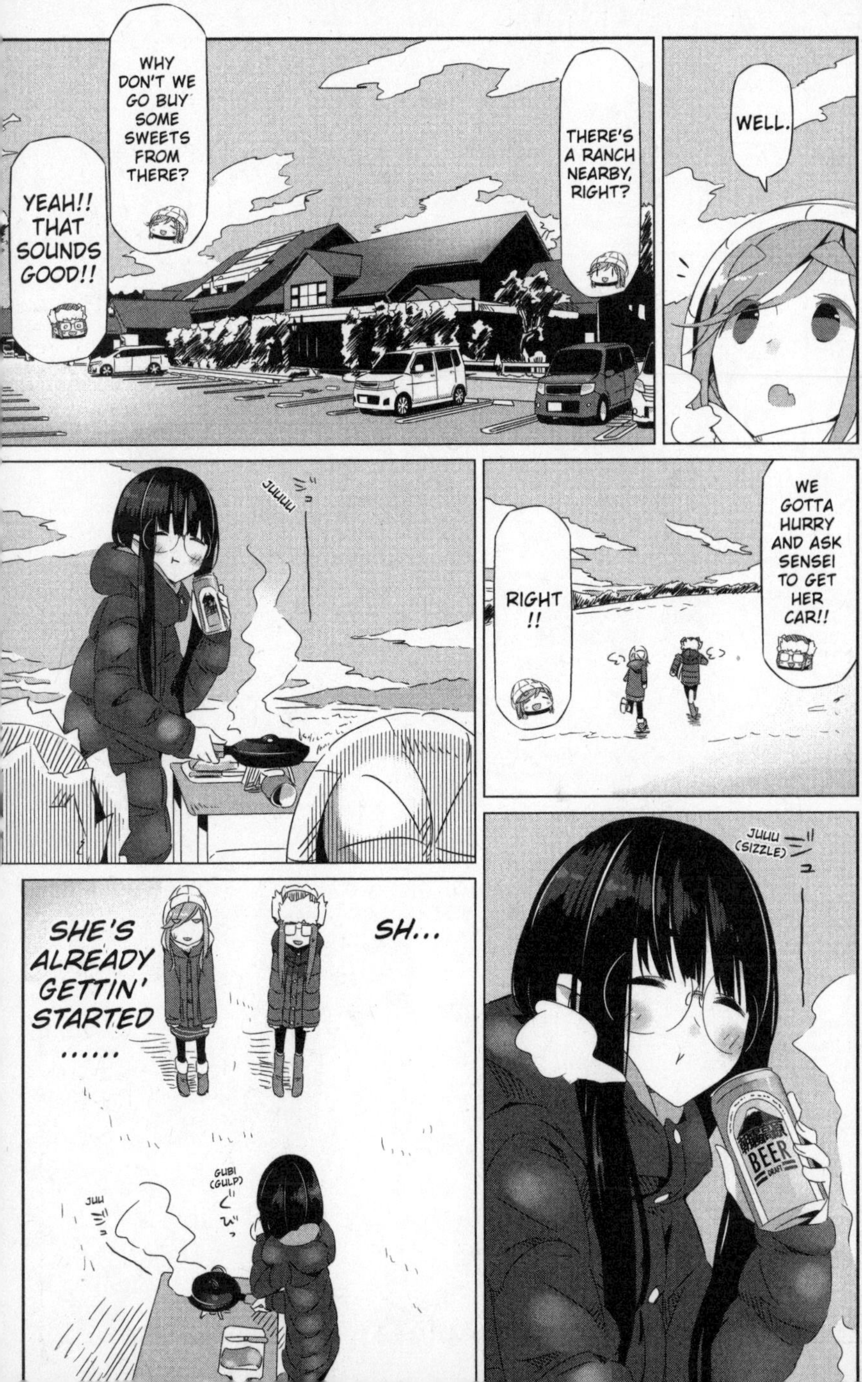
WELL.
THERE'S A RANCH NEARBY, RIGHT?
WHY DON'T WE GO BUY SOME SWEETS FROM THERE?
YEAH!! THAT SOUNDS GOOD!!
WE GOTTA HURRY AND ASK SENSEI TO GET HER CAR!!
RIGHT !!
JUUUU
JUUU (SIZZLE)
SH...
SHE'S ALREADY GETTIN' STARTED ......
GUBI (GULP)
JUU

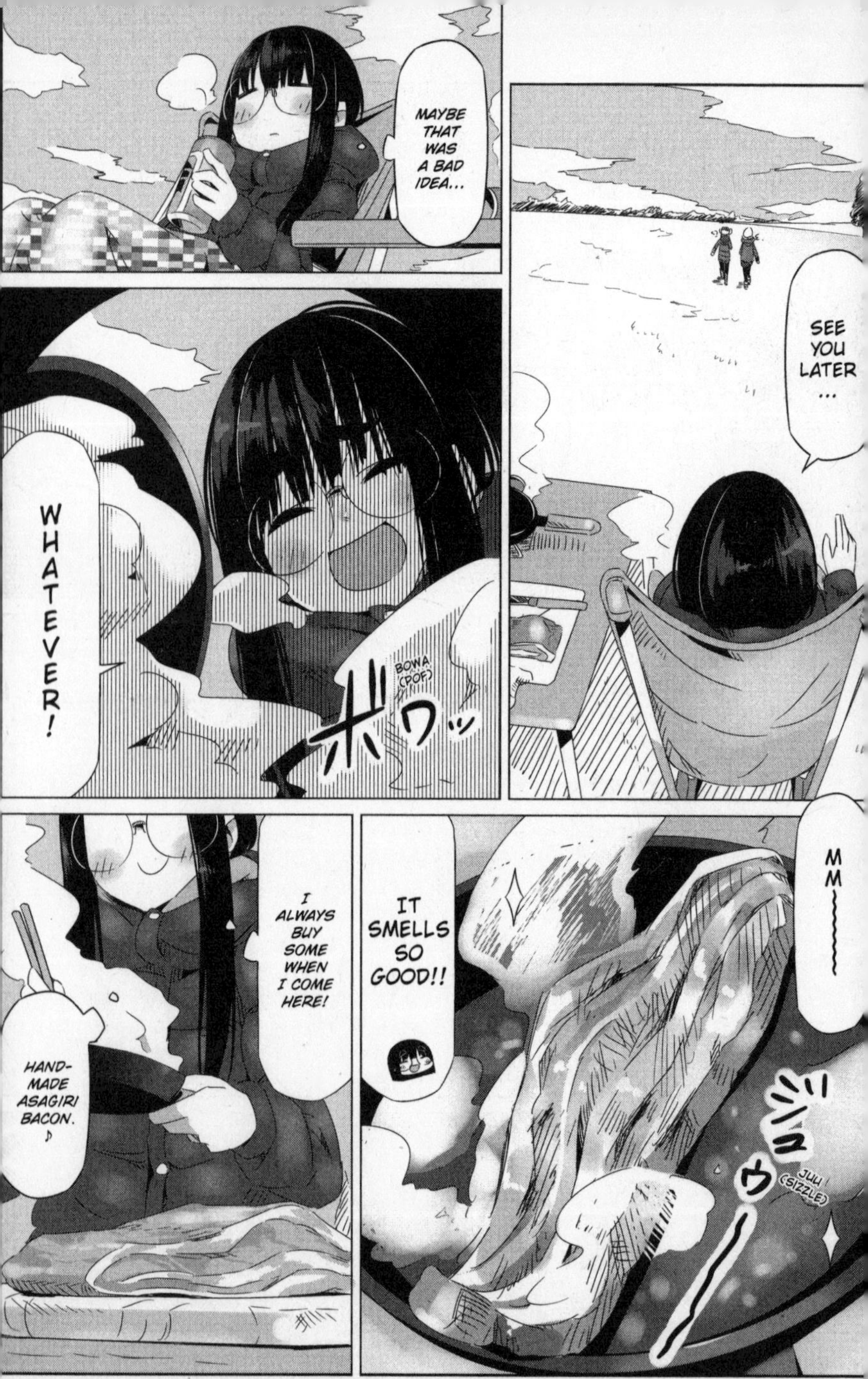
SEE YOU LATER...
MAYBE THAT WAS A BAD IDEA...
WHATEVER!
BOWA (POF)
MM~~~
JUU (SIZZLE)
IT SMELLS SO GOOD!!
I ALWAYS BUY SOME WHEN I COME HERE!
HAND-MADE ASAGIRI BACON. ♪

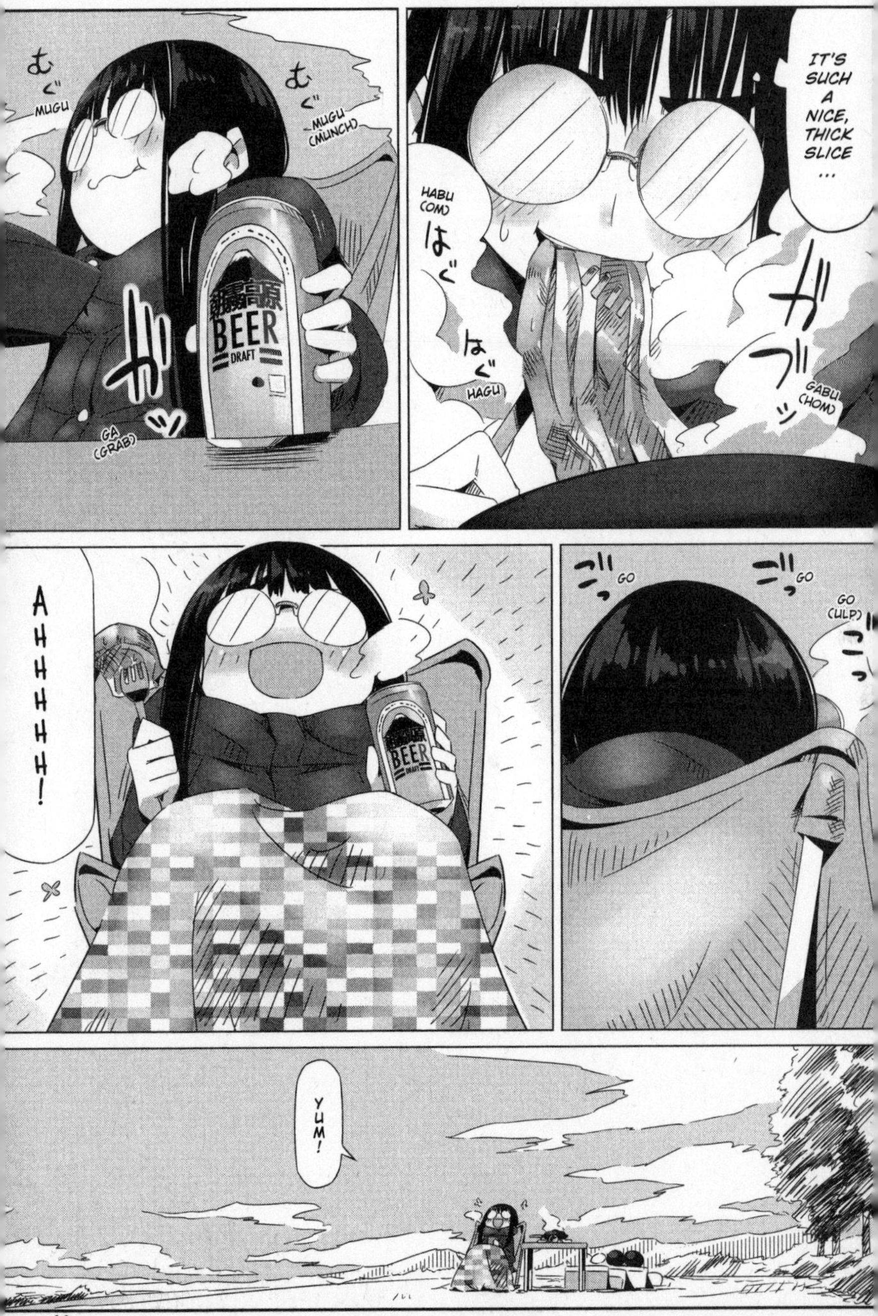

IT'S SUCH A NICE, THICK SLICE...
HABU (OM)
はぐ
はぐ
HAGU
がぶッ
GABU (HOM)
むぐ
MUGU
むぐ
MUGU (MUNCH)
BEER DRAFT
ガッ
GA (GRAB)
ごっ
GO
ごっ
GO
ごっ
GO (ULP)
AHHHHHHH!
BEER DRAFT
YUM!

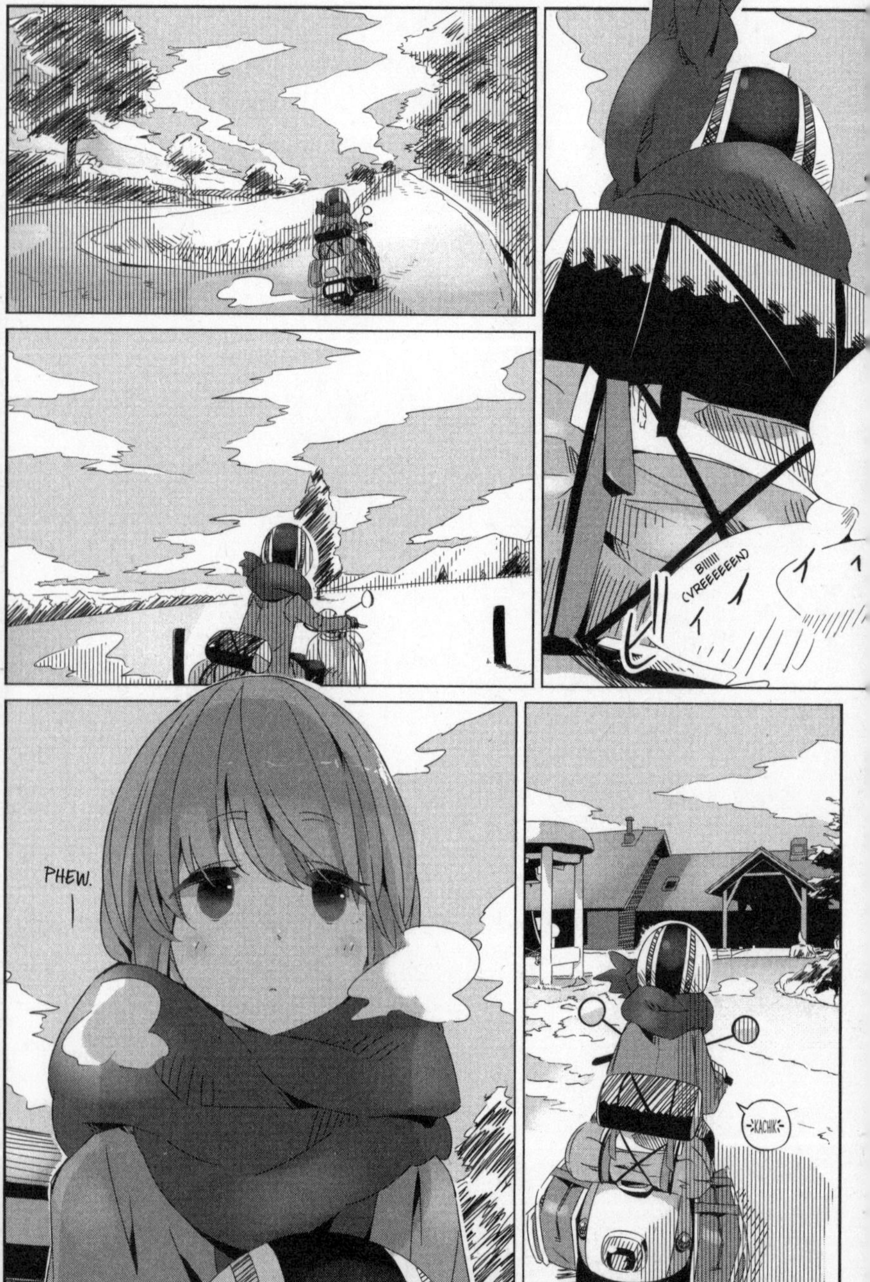
BIIIIIII
(VREEEEEEEN)
KACHIK
PHEW.

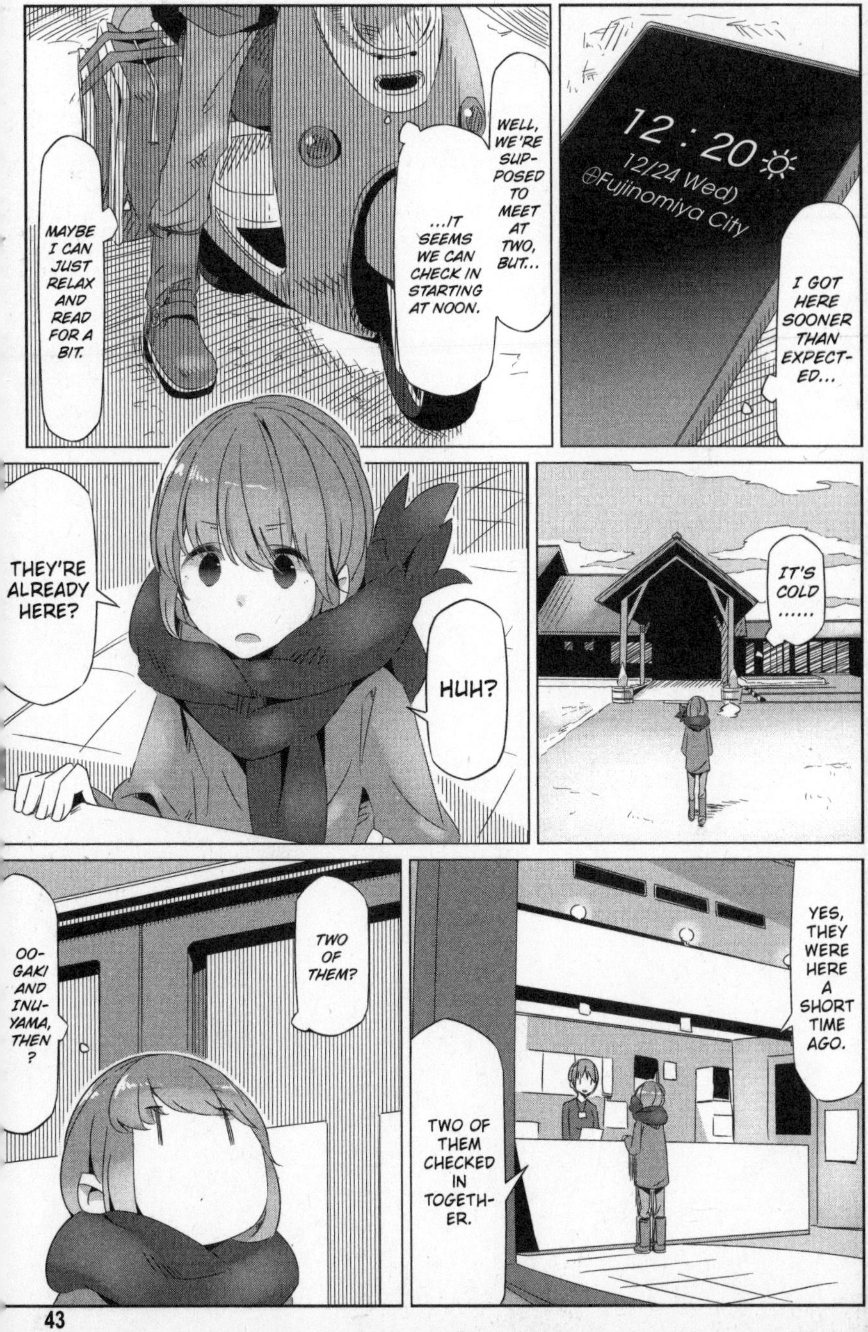
12:20
12/24 Wed)
Fujinomiya City
I GOT HERE SOONER THAN EXPECTED...
WELL, WE'RE SUPPOSED TO MEET AT TWO, BUT...
...IT SEEMS WE CAN CHECK IN STARTING AT NOON.
MAYBE I CAN JUST RELAX AND READ FOR A BIT.
IT'S COLD ......
HUH?
THEY'RE ALREADY HERE?
YES, THEY WERE HERE A SHORT TIME AGO.
TWO OF THEM CHECKED IN TOGETHER.
TWO OF THEM?
OOGAKI AND INUYAMA, THEN?

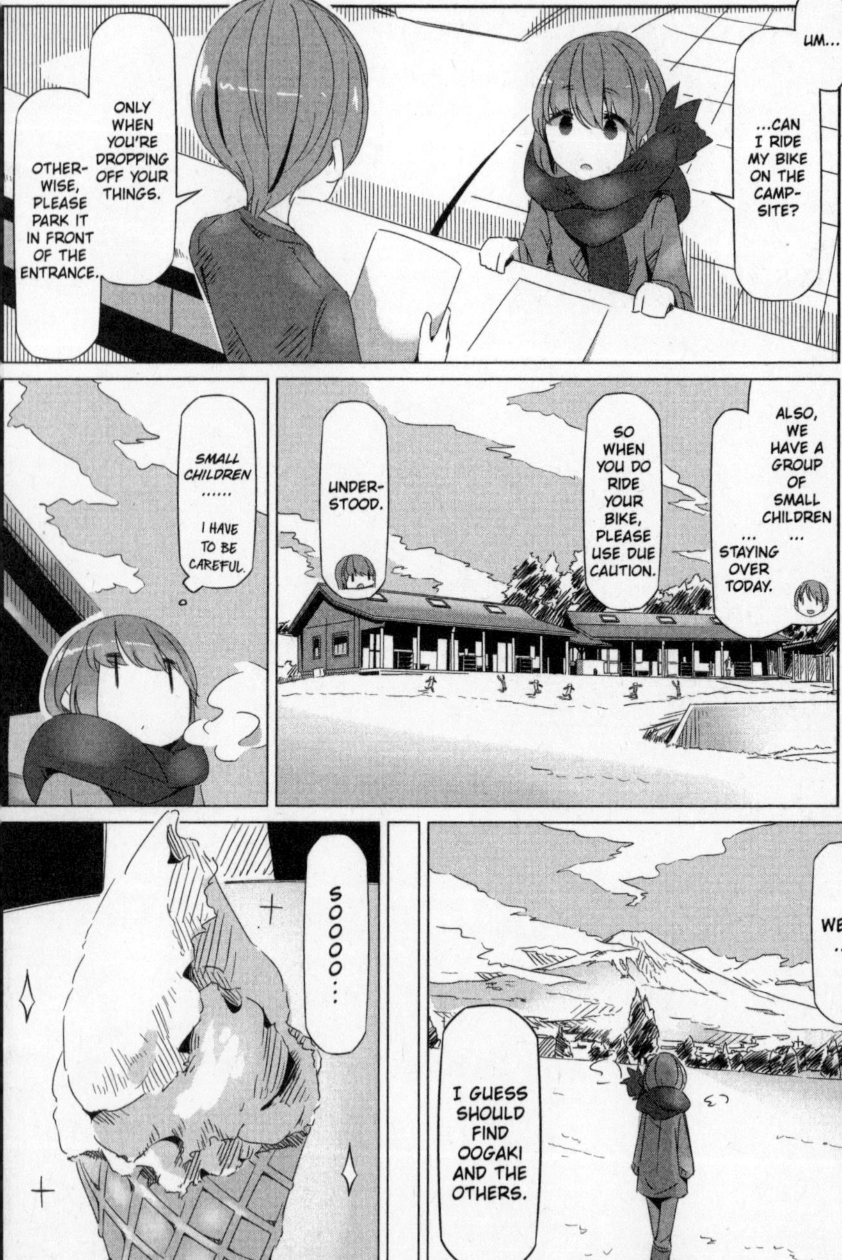
UM...
...CAN I RIDE MY BIKE ON THE CAMPSITE?
ONLY WHEN YOU'RE DROPPING OFF YOUR THINGS.
OTHERWISE, PLEASE PARK IT IN FRONT OF THE ENTRANCE.
ALSO, WE HAVE A GROUP OF SMALL CHILDREN ... ... STAYING OVER TODAY.
SO WHEN YOU DO RIDE YOUR BIKE, PLEASE USE DUE CAUTION.
UNDERSTOOD.
SMALL CHILDREN ...... I HAVE TO BE CAREFUL.
WELL ...
I GUESS SHOULD FIND OOGAKI AND THE OTHERS.
SOOOO...

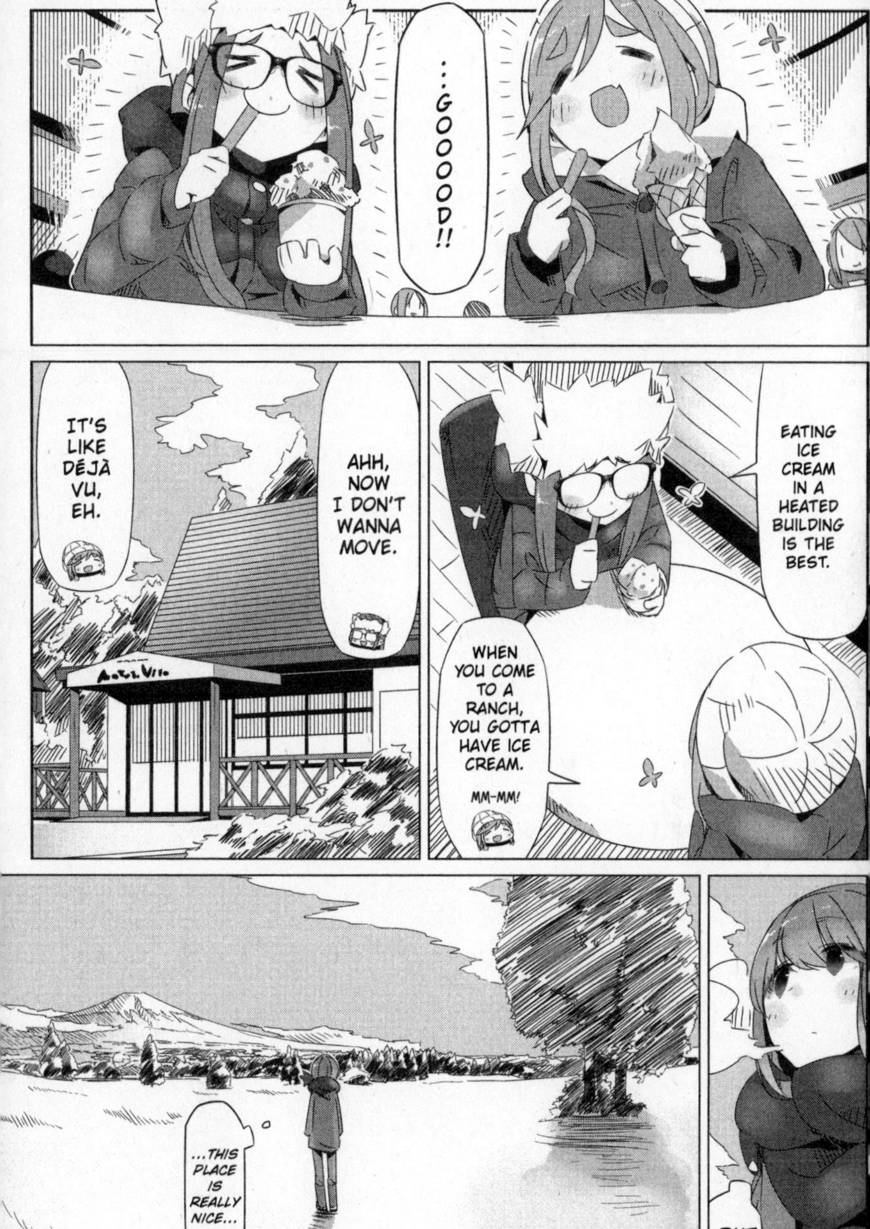
...GOOOOOD!!
EATING ICE CREAM IN A HEATED BUILDING IS THE BEST.
WHEN YOU COME TO A RANCH, YOU GOTTA HAVE ICE CREAM.
MM-MM!
AHH, NOW I DON'T WANNA MOVE.
IT'S LIKE DÉJÀ VU, EH.
BUT MAN...
...THIS PLACE IS REALLY NICE...

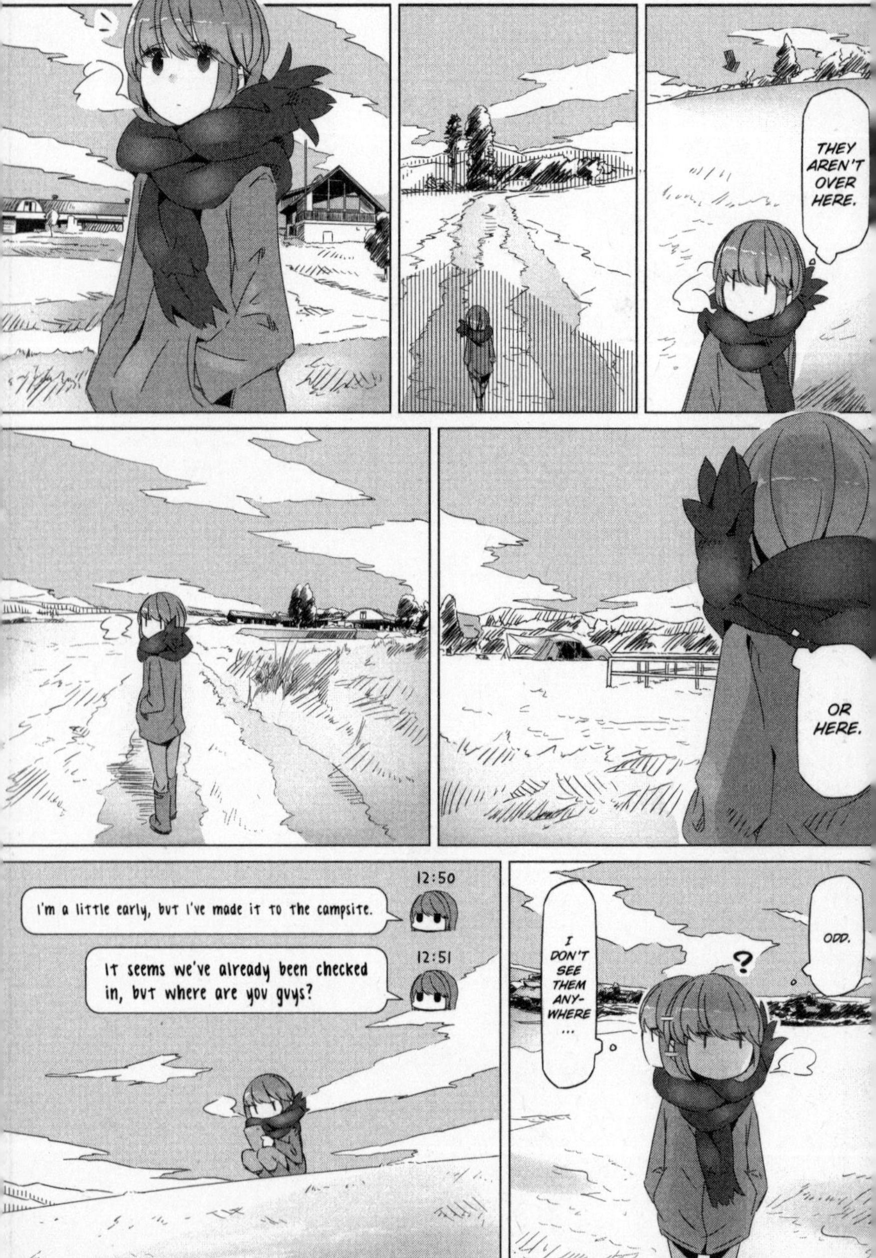
THEY AREN'T OVER HERE.
OR HERE.
ODD.
I DON'T SEE THEM ANYWHERE...
12:50
I'm a little early, but I've made it to the campsite.
12:51
It seems we've already been checked in, but where are you guys?

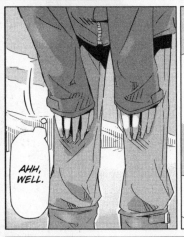

AHH, WELL.

CHILDREN...

GU (STRETCH)

GUESS I'LL PUT THE TENT UP HERE.

IT'S GOT A GOOD VIEW, AFTER ALL.

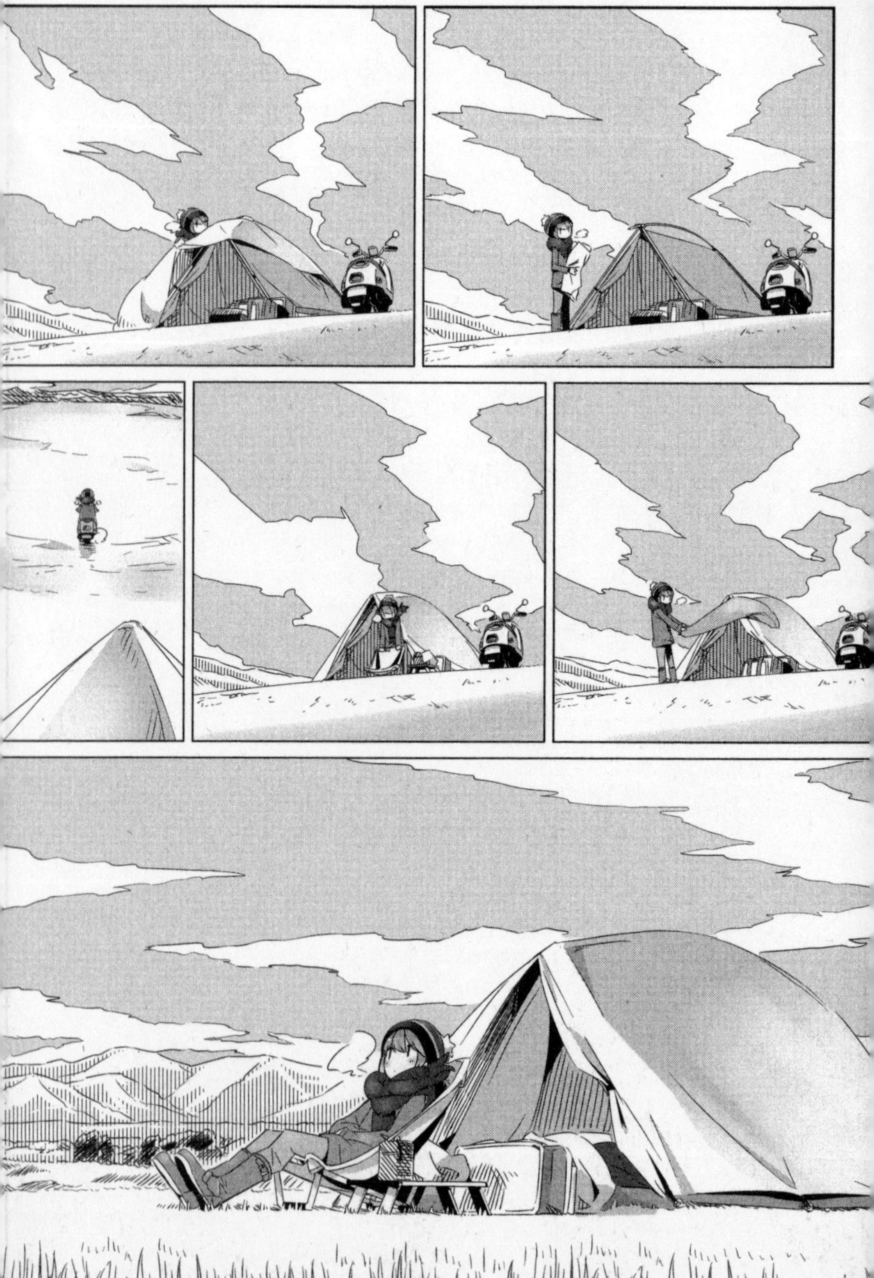

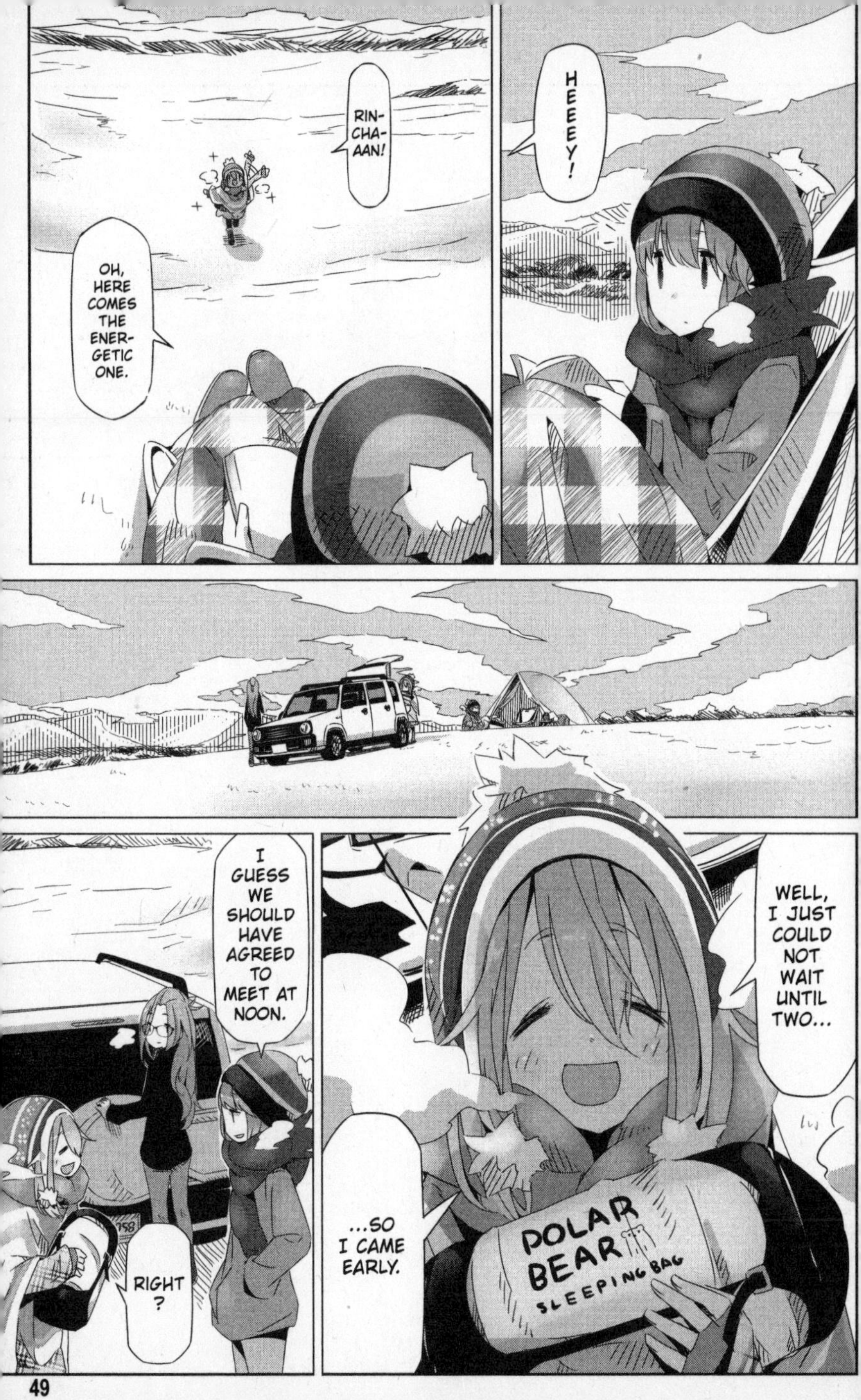
HEEEY!
RIN-CHA-AAN!
OH, HERE COMES THE ENERGETIC ONE.
WELL, I JUST COULD NOT WAIT UNTIL TWO...
...SO I CAME EARLY.
POLAR BEAR SLEEPING BAG
I GUESS WE SHOULD HAVE AGREED TO MEET AT NOON.
RIGHT?

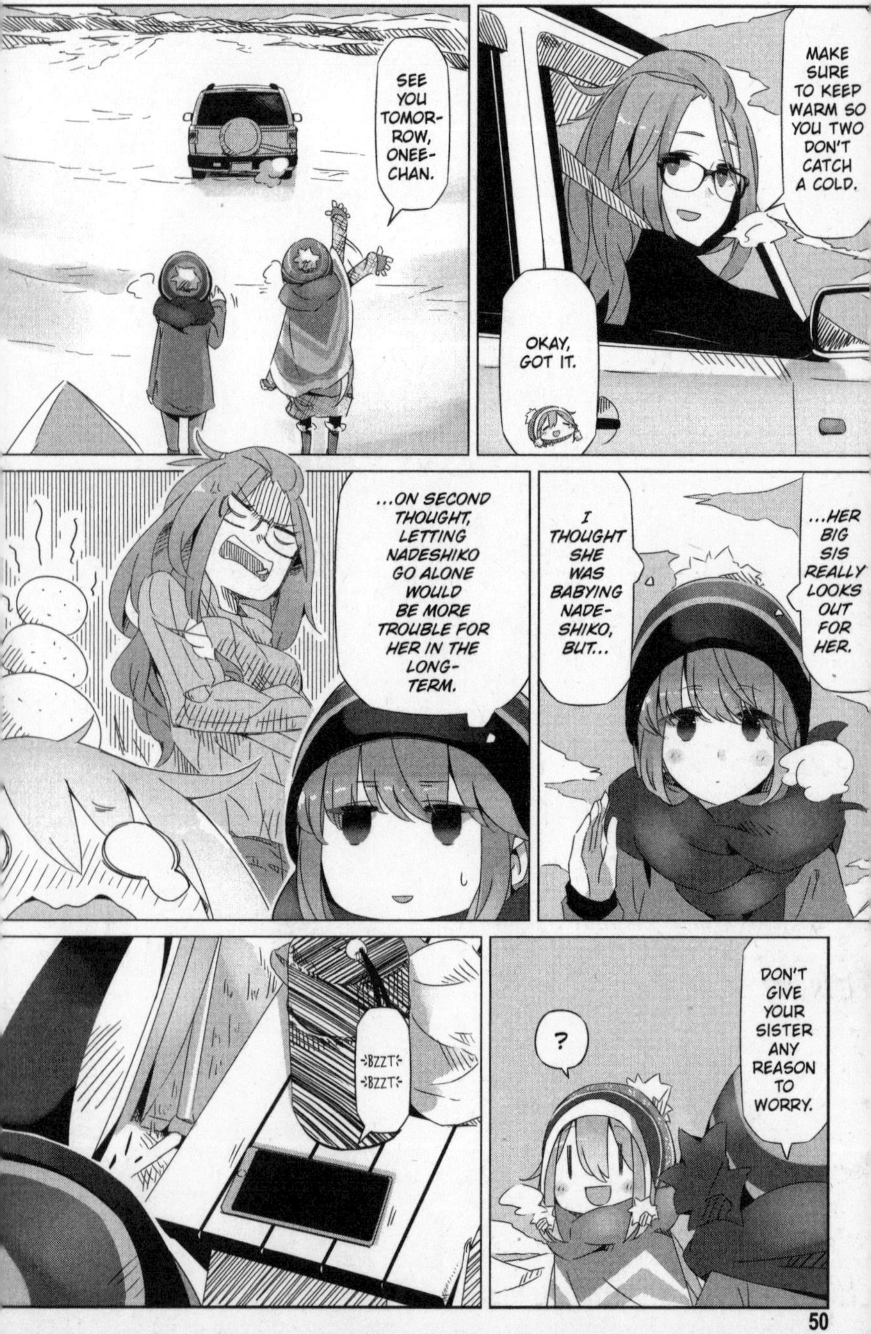
MAKE SURE TO KEEP WARM SO YOU TWO DON'T CATCH A COLD.
OKAY, GOT IT.
SEE YOU TOMORROW, ONEE-CHAN.
...HER BIG SIS REALLY LOOKS OUT FOR HER.
I THOUGHT SHE WAS BABYING NADESHIKO, BUT...
...ON SECOND THOUGHT, LETTING NADESHIKO GO ALONE WOULD BE MORE TROUBLE FOR HER IN THE LONG-TERM.
DON'T GIVE YOUR SISTER ANY REASON TO WORRY.
?
BZZT BZZT

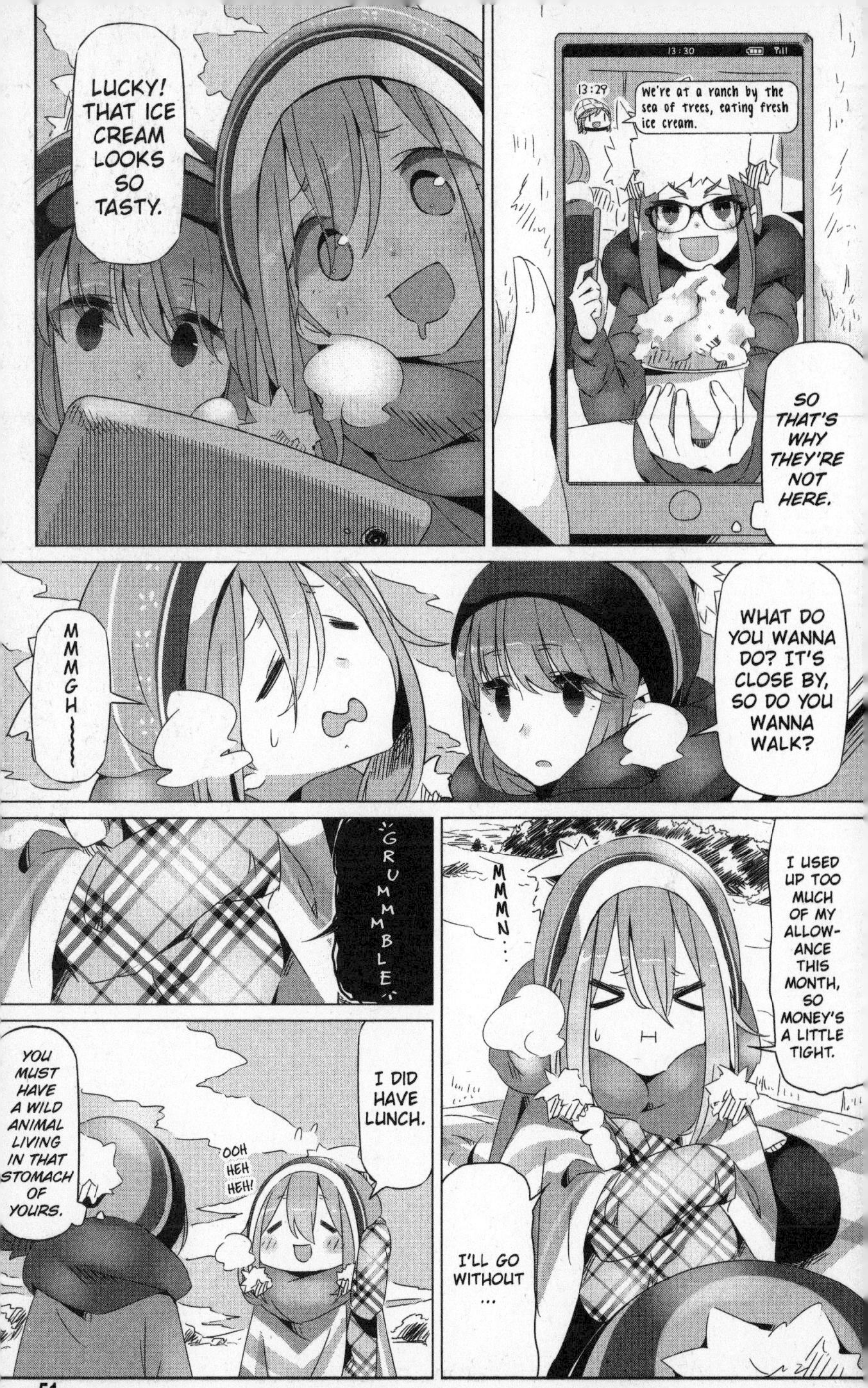
13:30
13:29
We're at a ranch by the sea of trees, eating fresh ice cream.
SO THAT'S WHY THEY'RE NOT HERE.
LUCKY! THAT ICE CREAM LOOKS SO TASTY.
WHAT DO YOU WANNA DO? IT'S CLOSE BY, SO DO YOU WANNA WALK?
MMMGH—
I USED UP TOO MUCH OF MY ALLOW-ANCE THIS MONTH, SO MONEY'S A LITTLE TIGHT.
MMMN...
I'LL GO WITHOUT ...
GRUMMBLE
I DID HAVE LUNCH.
OOH HEH HEH!
YOU MUST HAVE A WILD ANIMAL LIVING IN THAT STOMACH OF YOURS.

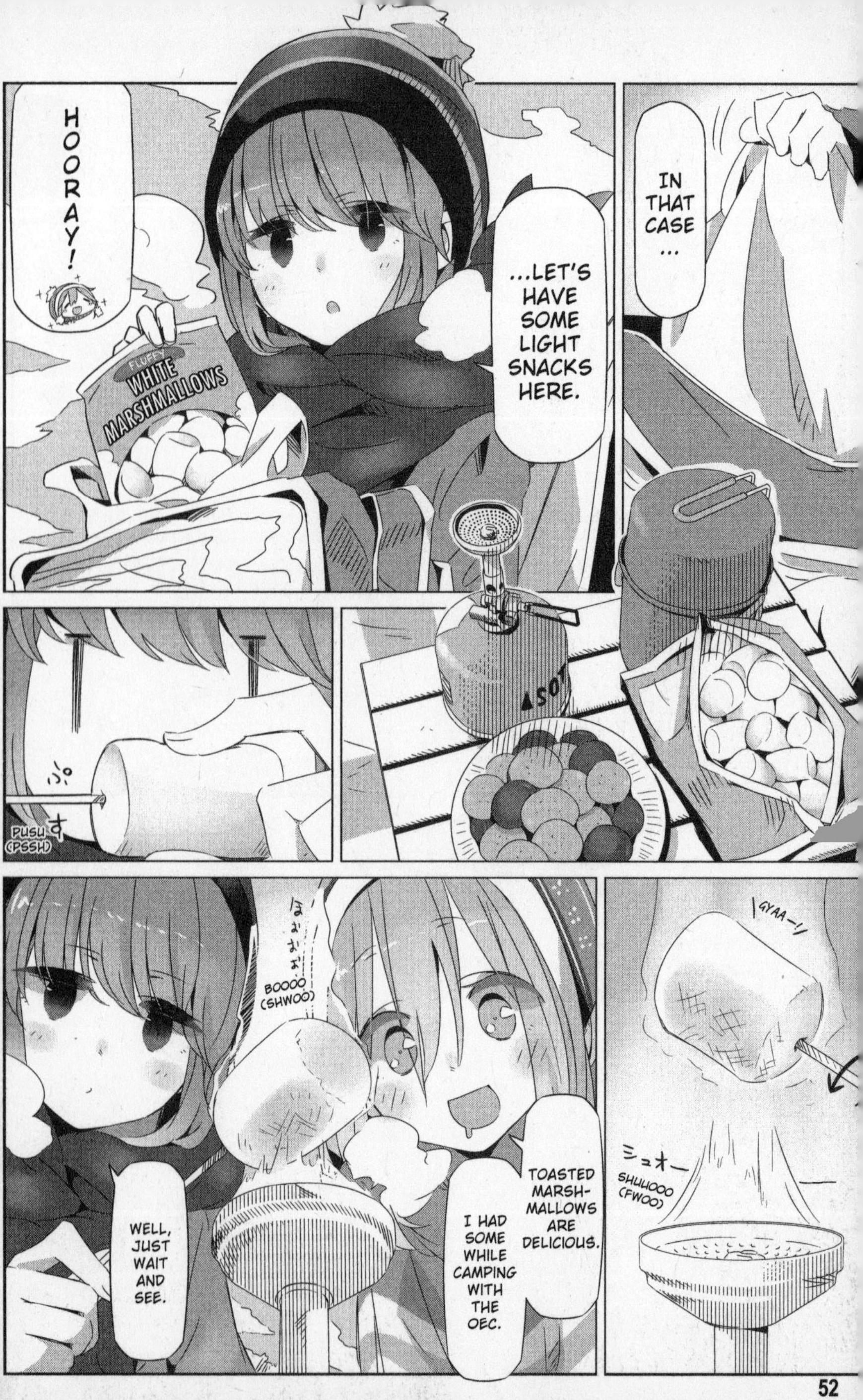
IN THAT CASE ...
...LET'S HAVE SOME LIGHT SNACKS HERE.
HOORAY!
FLUFFY WHITE MARSHMALLOWS
SOT
ぷす
PUSU (PSSH)
GYAA-!
シュオー
SHUOOO (FWOO)
BOOOO (SHWOO)
TOASTED MARSH-MALLOWS ARE DELICIOUS.
I HAD SOME WHILE CAMPING WITH THE OEC.
WELL, JUST WAIT AND SEE.

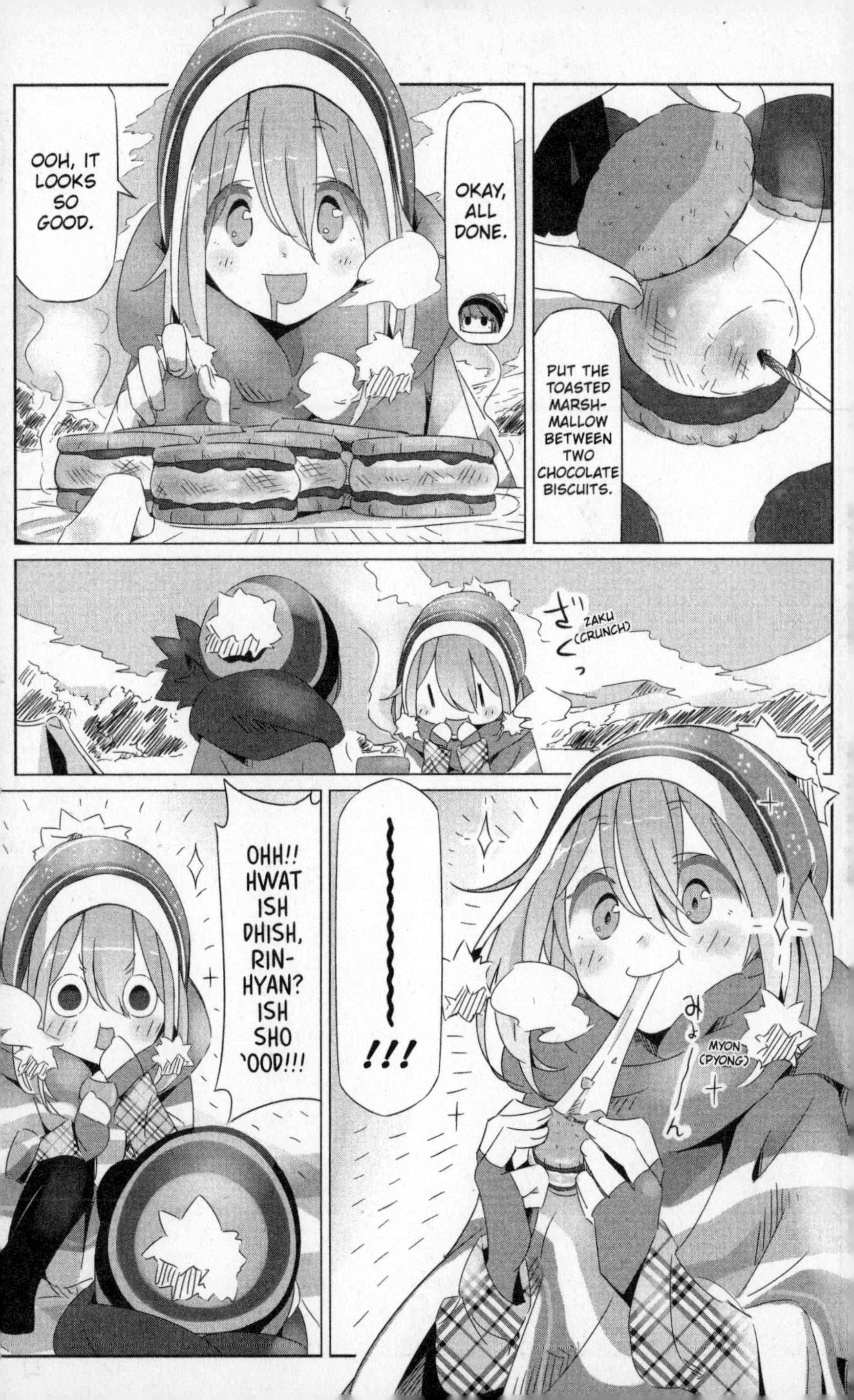
PUT THE TOASTED MARSHMALLOW BETWEEN TWO CHOCOLATE BISCUITS.
OKAY, ALL DONE.
OOH, IT LOOKS SO GOOD.
ざくっ
ZAKU (CRUNCH)
!!!
みょーん
MYON (PYONG)
OHH!! HWAT ISH DHISH, RIN-HYAN? ISH SHO 'OOD!!!

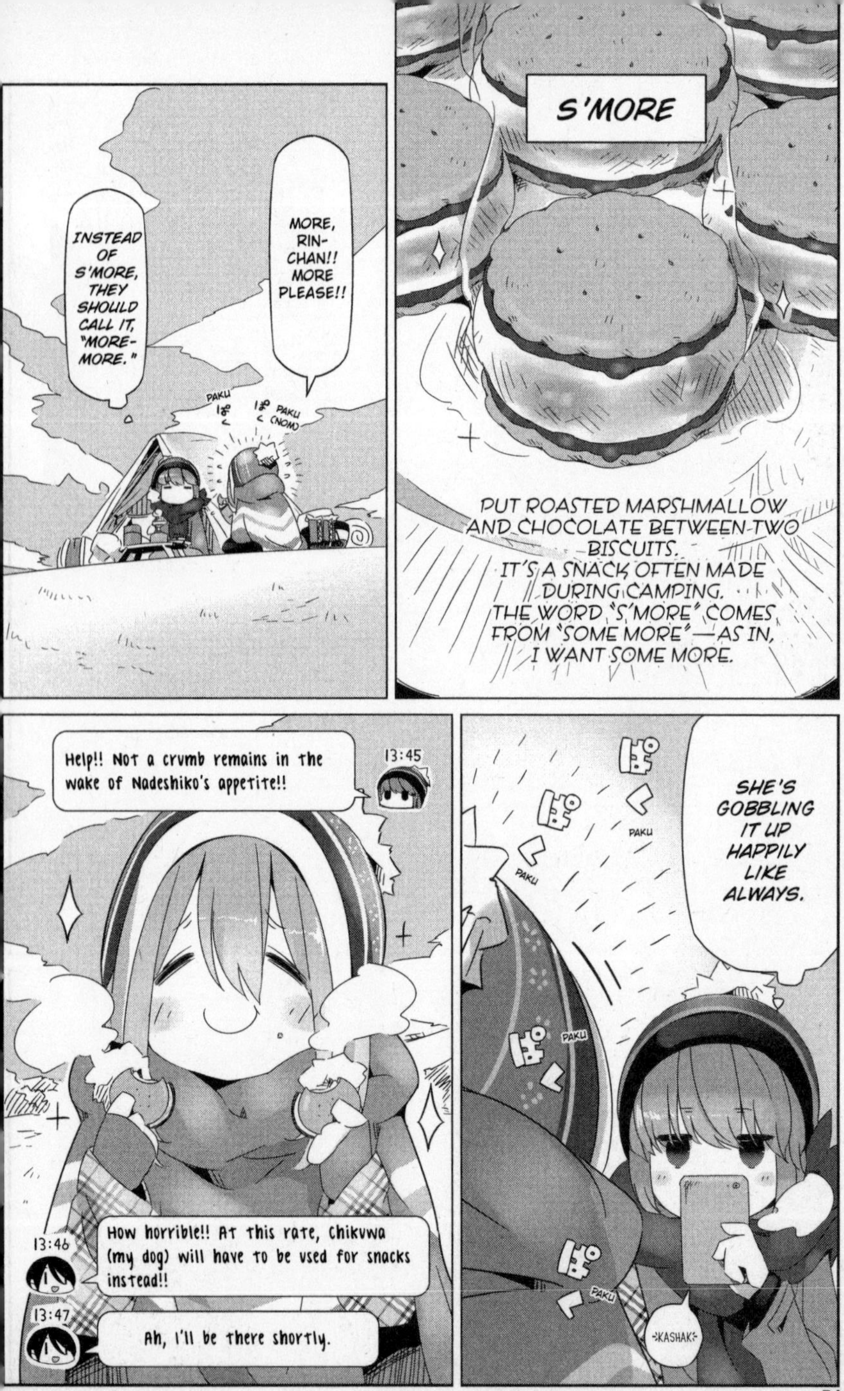
S'MORE
PUT ROASTED MARSHMALLOW AND CHOCOLATE BETWEEN TWO BISCUITS. IT'S A SNACK OFTEN MADE DURING CAMPING. THE WORD "S'MORE" COMES FROM "SOME MORE"—AS IN, I WANT SOME MORE.
MORE, RIN-CHAN!! MORE PLEASE!!
INSTEAD OF S'MORE, THEY SHOULD CALL IT, "MORE-MORE."
PAKU
PAKU (NOM)
SHE'S GOBBLING IT UP HAPPILY LIKE ALWAYS.
PAKU
PAKU
PAKU
PAKU
KASHAK
13:45
Help!! Not a crumb remains in the wake of Nadeshiko's appetite!!
13:46
How horrible!! At this rate, Chikuwa (my dog) will have to be used for snacks instead!!
13:47
Ah, I'll be there shortly.

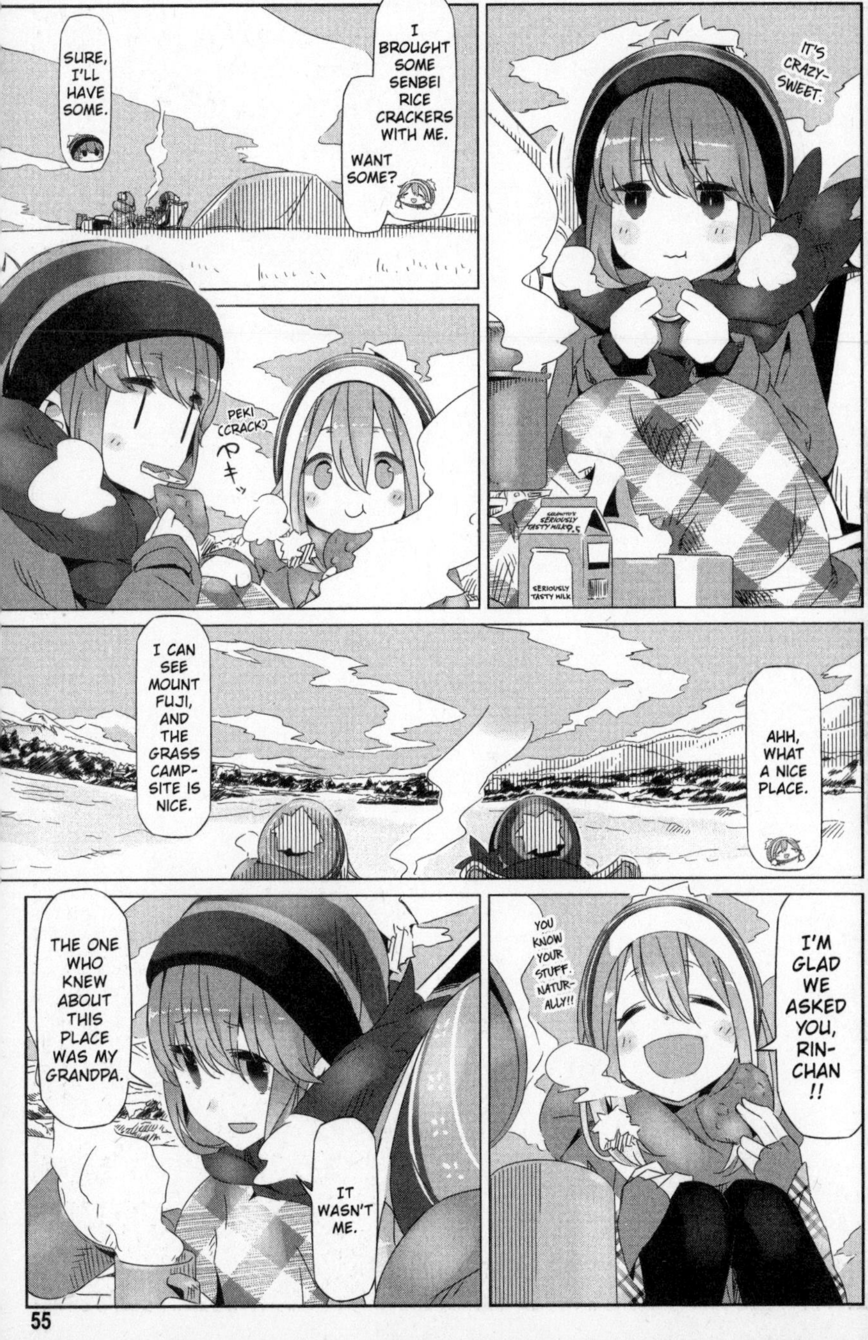
IT'S CRAZY-SWEET.
SERIOUSLY TASTY MILK
SERIOUSLY TASTY MILK
I BROUGHT SOME SENBEI RICE CRACKERS WITH ME.
WANT SOME?
SURE, I'LL HAVE SOME.
PEKI (CRACK)
AHH, WHAT A NICE PLACE.
I CAN SEE MOUNT FUJI, AND THE GRASS CAMP-SITE IS NICE.
I'M GLAD WE ASKED YOU, RIN-CHAN!!
YOU KNOW YOUR STUFF, NATUR-ALLY!!
THE ONE WHO KNEW ABOUT THIS PLACE WAS MY GRANDPA.
IT WASN'T ME.

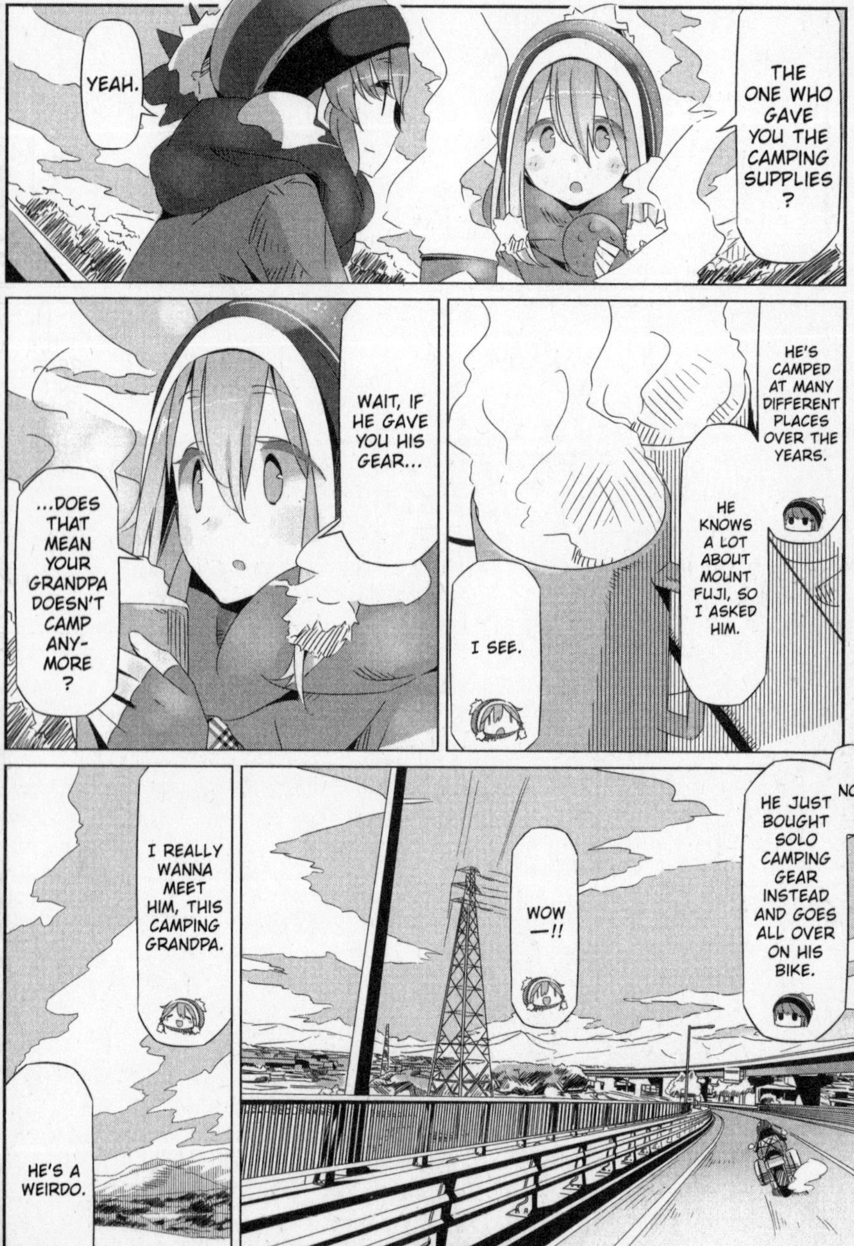
THE ONE WHO GAVE YOU THE CAMPING SUPPLIES?
YEAH.
HE'S CAMPED AT MANY DIFFERENT PLACES OVER THE YEARS.
HE KNOWS A LOT ABOUT MOUNT FUJI, SO I ASKED HIM.
I SEE.
WAIT, IF HE GAVE YOU HIS GEAR...
...DOES THAT MEAN YOUR GRANDPA DOESN'T CAMP ANY-MORE?
NO.
HE JUST BOUGHT SOLO CAMPING GEAR INSTEAD AND GOES ALL OVER ON HIS BIKE.
WOW—!!
I REALLY WANNA MEET HIM, THIS CAMPING GRANDPA.
HE'S A WEIRDO.

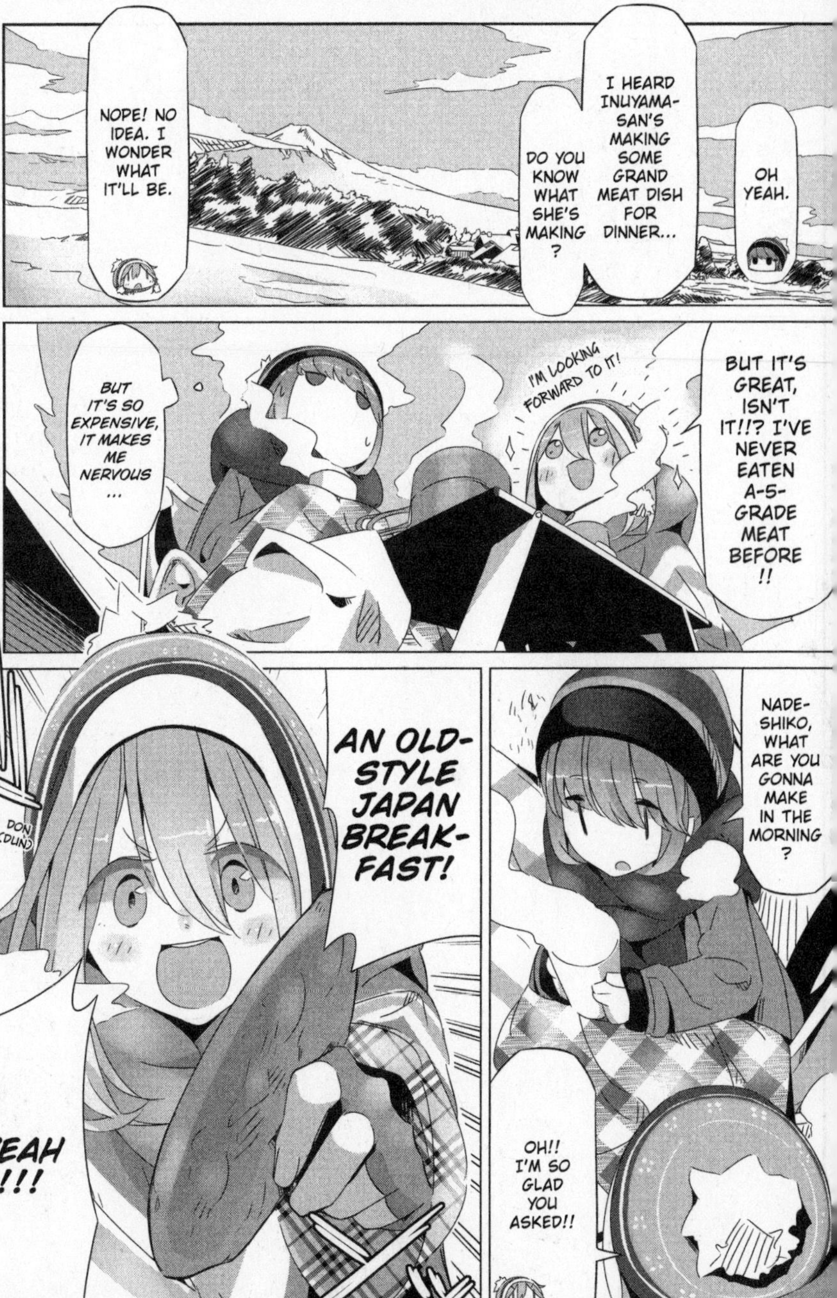
OH YEAH.
I HEARD INUYAMA-SAN'S MAKING SOME GRAND MEAT DISH FOR DINNER...
DO YOU KNOW WHAT SHE'S MAKING?
NOPE! NO IDEA. I WONDER WHAT IT'LL BE.
BUT IT'S GREAT, ISN'T IT!!? I'VE NEVER EATEN A-5-GRADE MEAT BEFORE!!
I'M LOOKING FORWARD TO IT!
BUT IT'S SO EXPENSIVE, IT MAKES ME NERVOUS...
NADESHIKO, WHAT ARE YOU GONNA MAKE IN THE MORNING?
OH!! I'M SO GLAD YOU ASKED!!
AN OLD-STYLE JAPAN BREAKFAST!
DON (DUN)
YEAH!!!

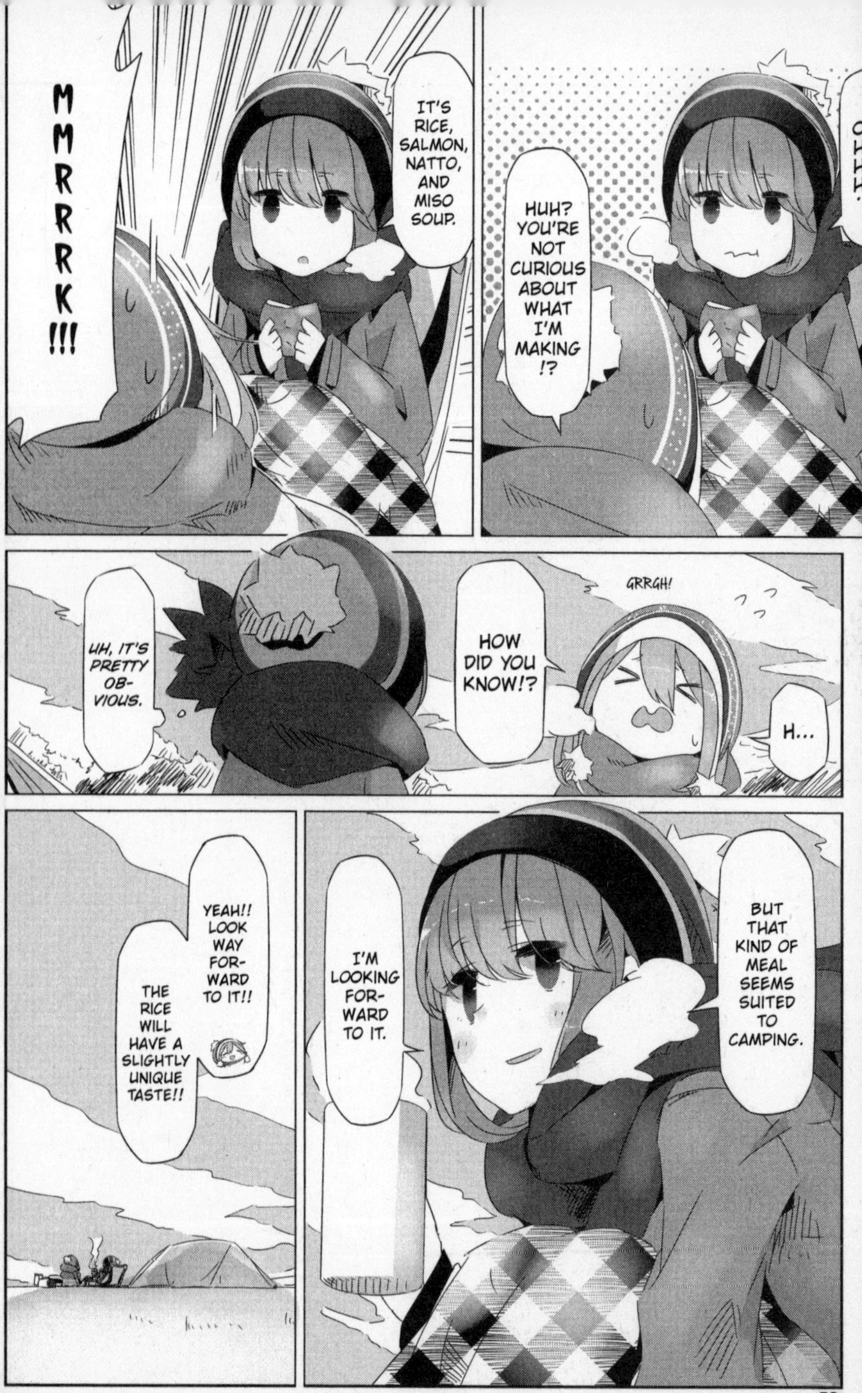
OHHH.
HUH? YOU'RE NOT CURIOUS ABOUT WHAT I'M MAKING!?
IT'S RICE, SALMON, NATTO, AND MISO SOUP.
MMRRRK!!!
GRRGH!
H...
HOW DID YOU KNOW!?
UH, IT'S PRETTY OBVIOUS.
BUT THAT KIND OF MEAL SEEMS SUITED TO CAMPING.
I'M LOOKING FORWARD TO IT.
YEAH!! LOOK WAY FORWARD TO IT!!
THE RICE WILL HAVE A SLIGHTLY UNIQUE TASTE!!

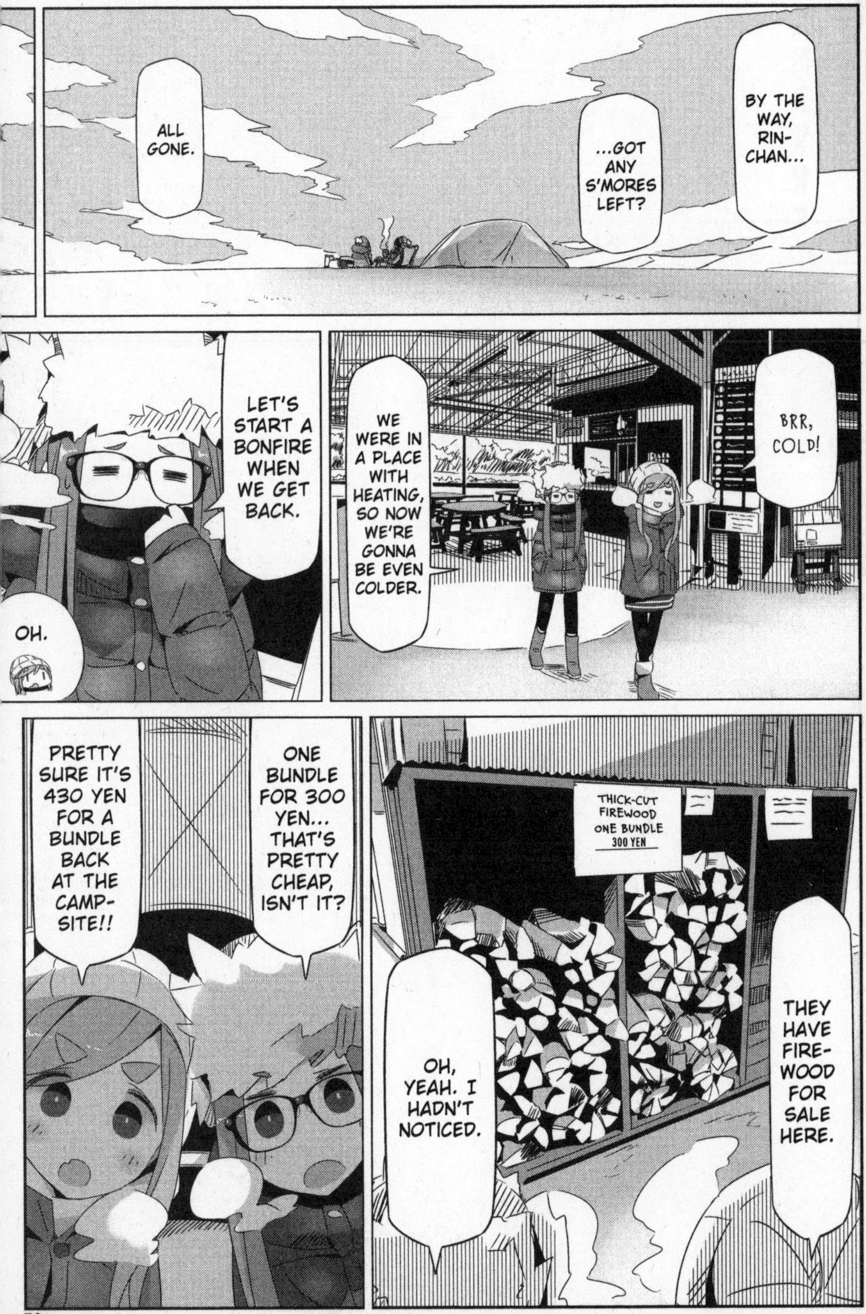

BY THE WAY, RIN-CHAN...
...GOT ANY S'MORES LEFT?
ALL GONE.
BRR, COLD!
WE WERE IN A PLACE WITH HEATING, SO NOW WE'RE GONNA BE EVEN COLDER.
LET'S START A BONFIRE WHEN WE GET BACK.
OH.
THEY HAVE FIREWOOD FOR SALE HERE.
THICK-CUT FIREWOOD ONE BUNDLE 300 YEN
OH, YEAH. I HADN'T NOTICED.
ONE BUNDLE FOR 300 YEN... THAT'S PRETTY CHEAP, ISN'T IT?
PRETTY SURE IT'S 430 YEN FOR A BUNDLE BACK AT THE CAMPSITE!!

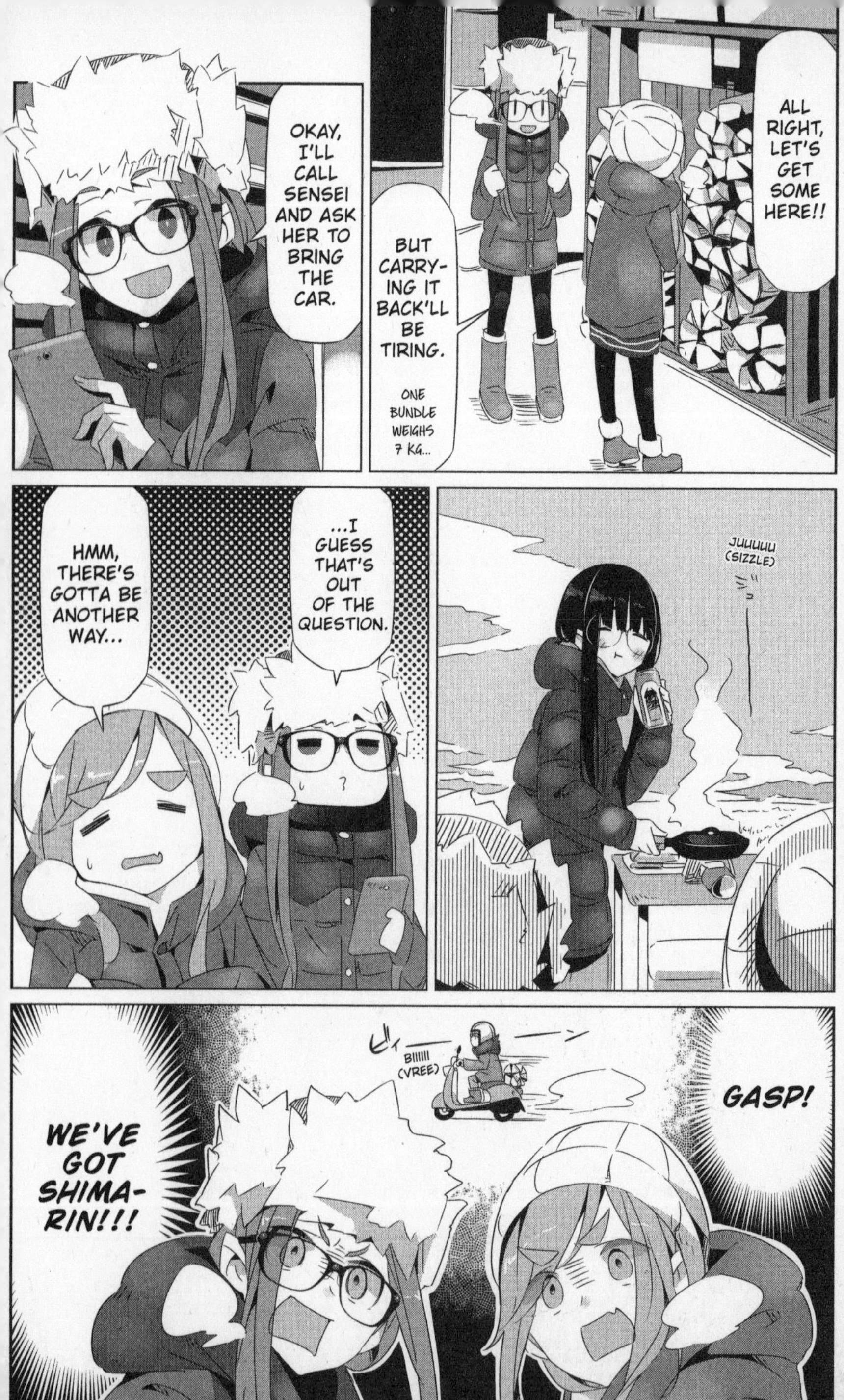
ALL RIGHT, LET'S GET SOME HERE!!
BUT CARRYING IT BACK'LL BE TIRING.
ONE BUNDLE WEIGHS 7 KG...
OKAY, I'LL CALL SENSEI AND ASK HER TO BRING THE CAR.
JUUUUU (SIZZLE)
...I GUESS THAT'S OUT OF THE QUESTION.
HMM, THERE'S GOTTA BE ANOTHER WAY...
BIIIIII (VREE)
GASP!
WE'VE GOT SHIMA-RIN!!!

MYOOOOON (STRETCH)
みょーーーん

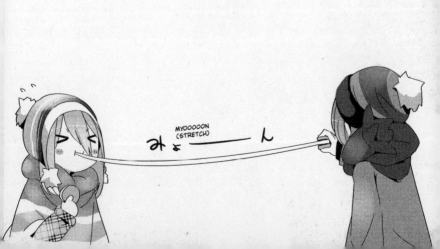

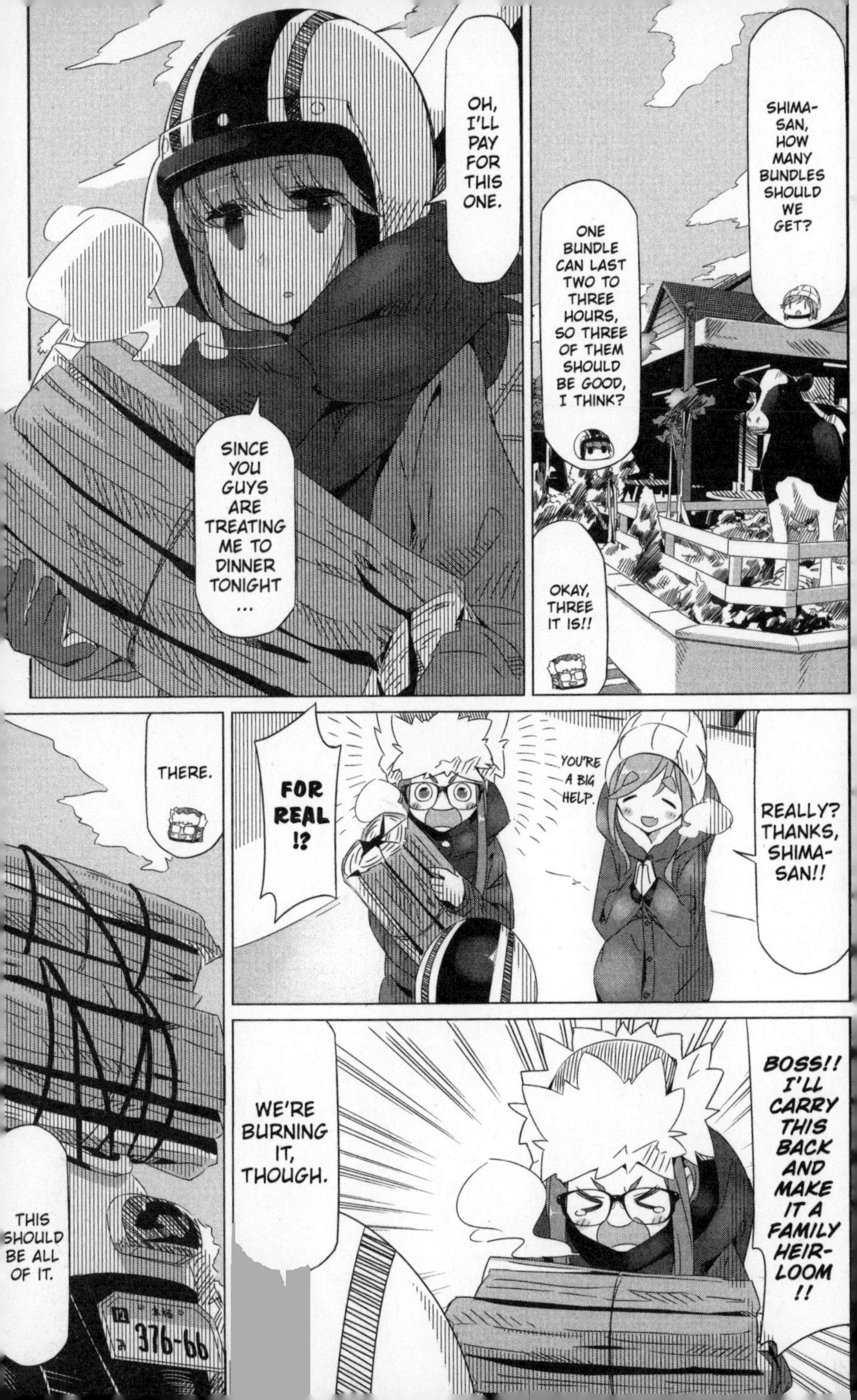
SHIMA-SAN, HOW MANY BUNDLES SHOULD WE GET?
ONE BUNDLE CAN LAST TWO TO THREE HOURS, SO THREE OF THEM SHOULD BE GOOD, I THINK?
OKAY, THREE IT IS!!
OH, I'LL PAY FOR THIS ONE.
SINCE YOU GUYS ARE TREATING ME TO DINNER TONIGHT ...
REALLY? THANKS, SHIMA-SAN!!
YOU'RE A BIG HELP.
FOR REAL!?
BOSS!! I'LL CARRY THIS BACK AND MAKE IT A FAMILY HEIR-LOOM!!
WE'RE BURNING IT, THOUGH.
THERE.
THIS SHOULD BE ALL OF IT.

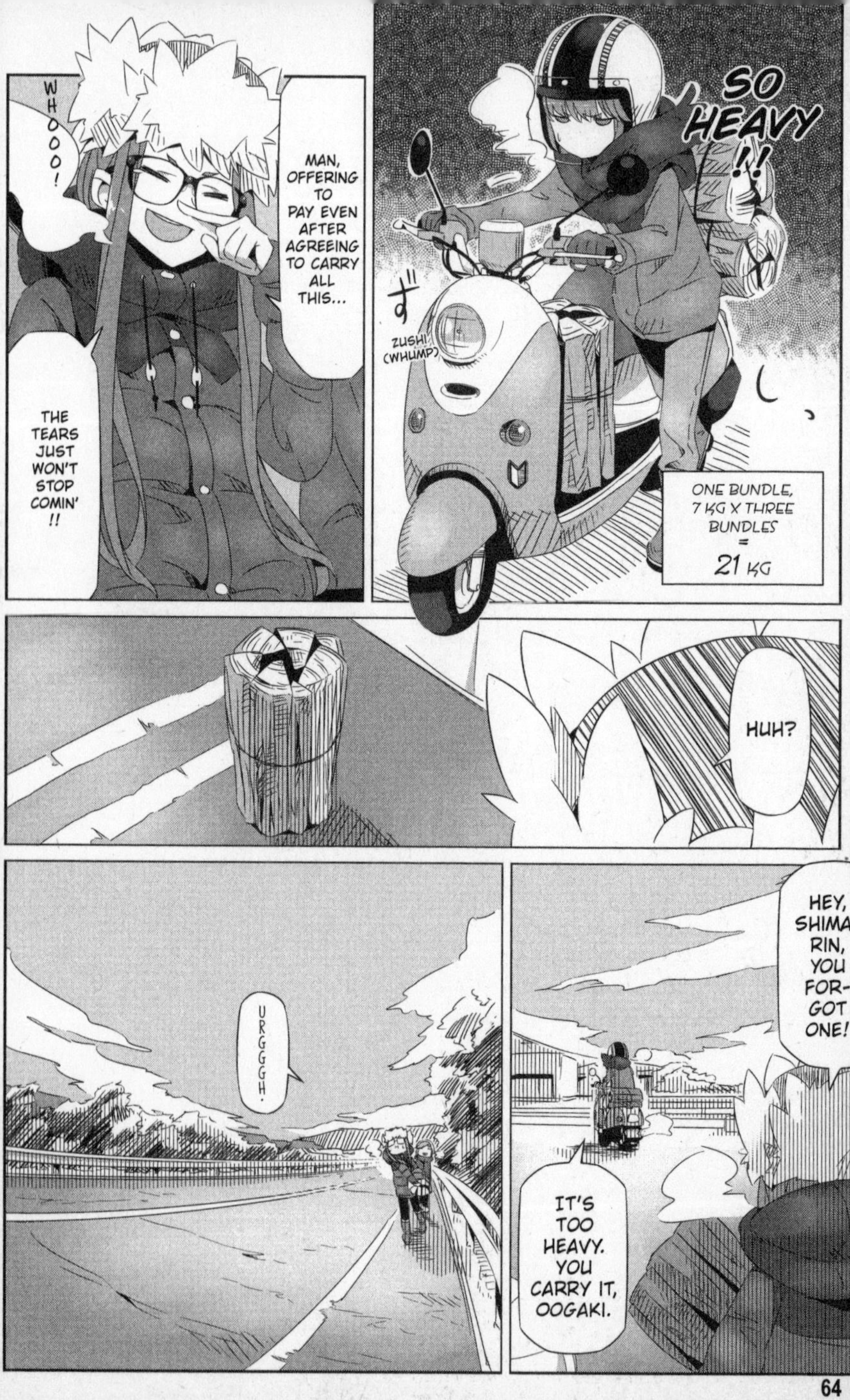
SO HEAVY!!
ず
ZUSHI! (WHUMP)
ONE BUNDLE, 7 KG X THREE BUNDLES = 21 KG
WHOOOO!
MAN, OFFERING TO PAY EVEN AFTER AGREEING TO CARRY ALL THIS...
THE TEARS JUST WON'T STOP COMIN'!!
HUH?
HEY, SHIMA-RIN, YOU FOR-GOT ONE!
IT'S TOO HEAVY. YOU CARRY IT, OOGAKI.
URGGGH.

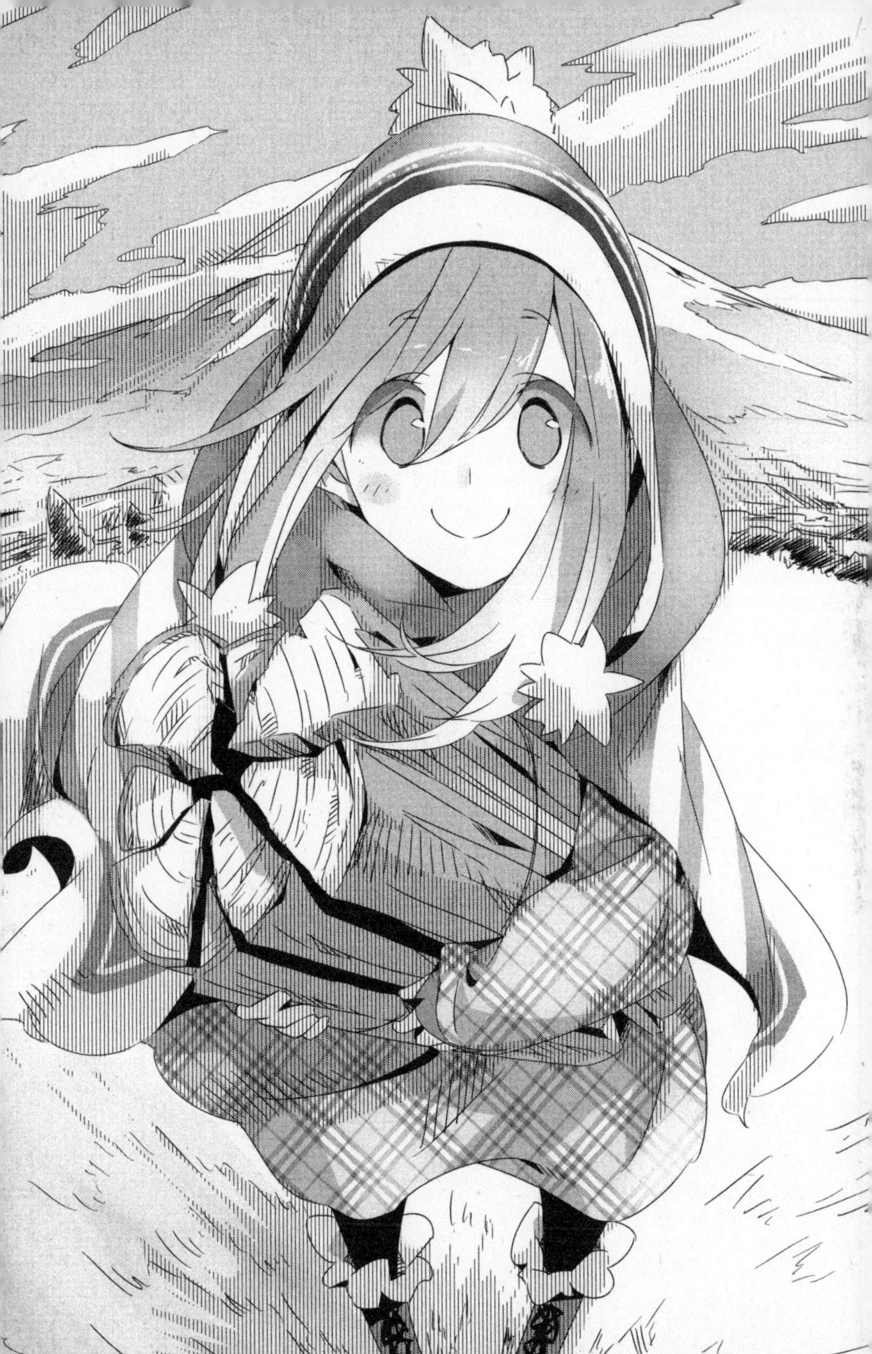

CHAPTER 21 CHRISTMAS CAMP BEGINS!!

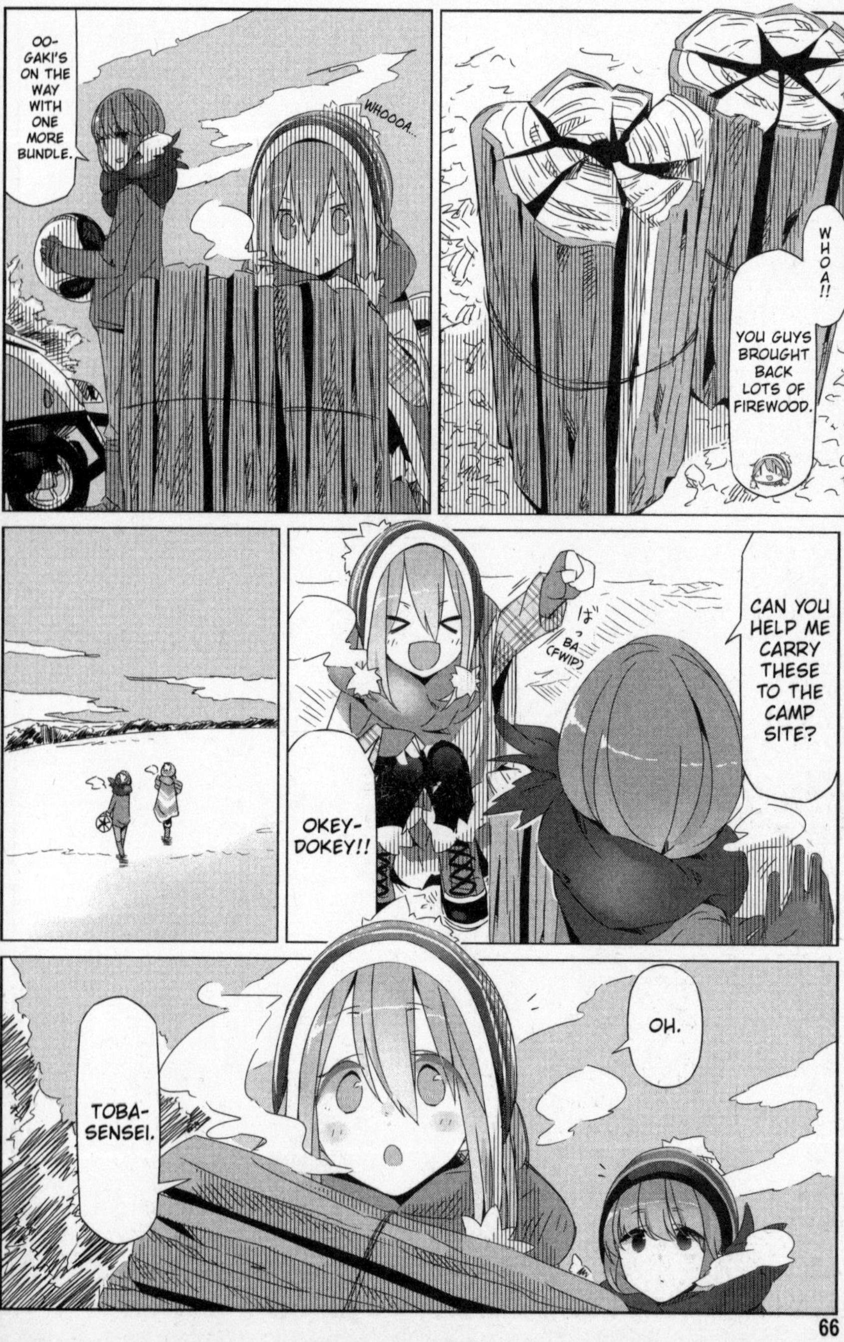
WHOA!!
YOU GUYS BROUGHT BACK LOTS OF FIREWOOD.
WHOOOA...
OO-GAKI'S ON THE WAY WITH ONE MORE BUNDLE.
CAN YOU HELP ME CARRY THESE TO THE CAMP SITE?
ばっ BA (FWIP)
OKEY-DOKEY!!
OH.
TOBA-SENSEI.

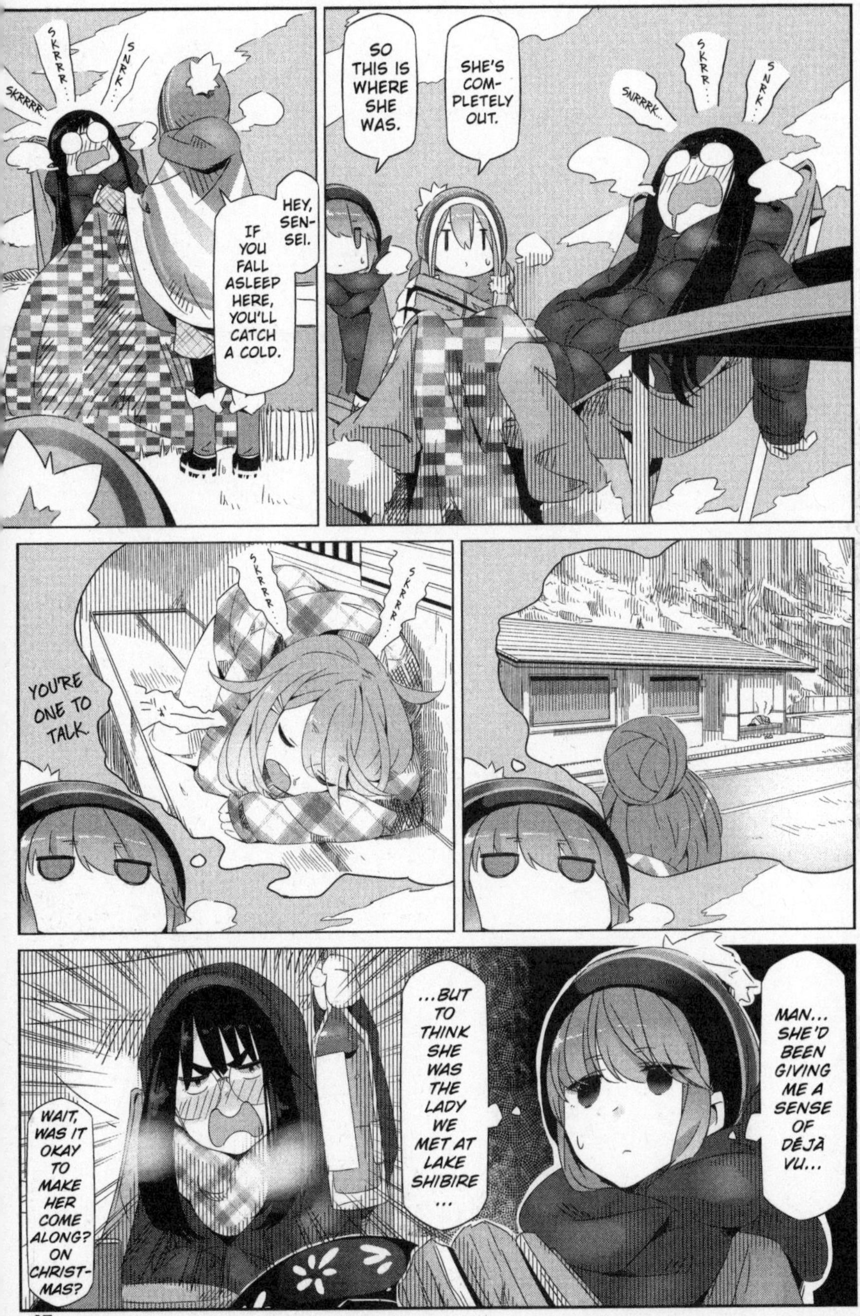
SNRK...
SKRR...
SNRRRK...
SHE'S COM-PLETELY OUT.
SO THIS IS WHERE SHE WAS.
SNRK...
SKRRR...
SKRRRR...
HEY, SEN-SEI.
IF YOU FALL ASLEEP HERE, YOU'LL CATCH A COLD.
SKRRR...
SKRRR...
YOU'RE ONE TO TALK.
MAN... SHE'D BEEN GIVING ME A SENSE OF DÉJÀ VU...
...BUT TO THINK SHE WAS THE LADY WE MET AT LAKE SHIBIRE...
WAIT, WAS IT OKAY TO MAKE HER COME ALONG? ON CHRIST-MAS?

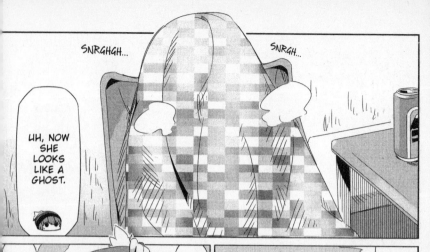

SNRGHGH...

SNRGH...

UH, NOW SHE LOOKS LIKE A GHOST.

IN THAT CASE...

MN...

SNRGH...

SNRGHGH...

BUT IF WE DON'T COVER HER, SHE'LL GET A CHILL EVERY-WHERE ABOVE HER SHOULDERS.

SEEMS HARD TO BREATHE IN.

SNRGH...

SNKHH...

THERE!

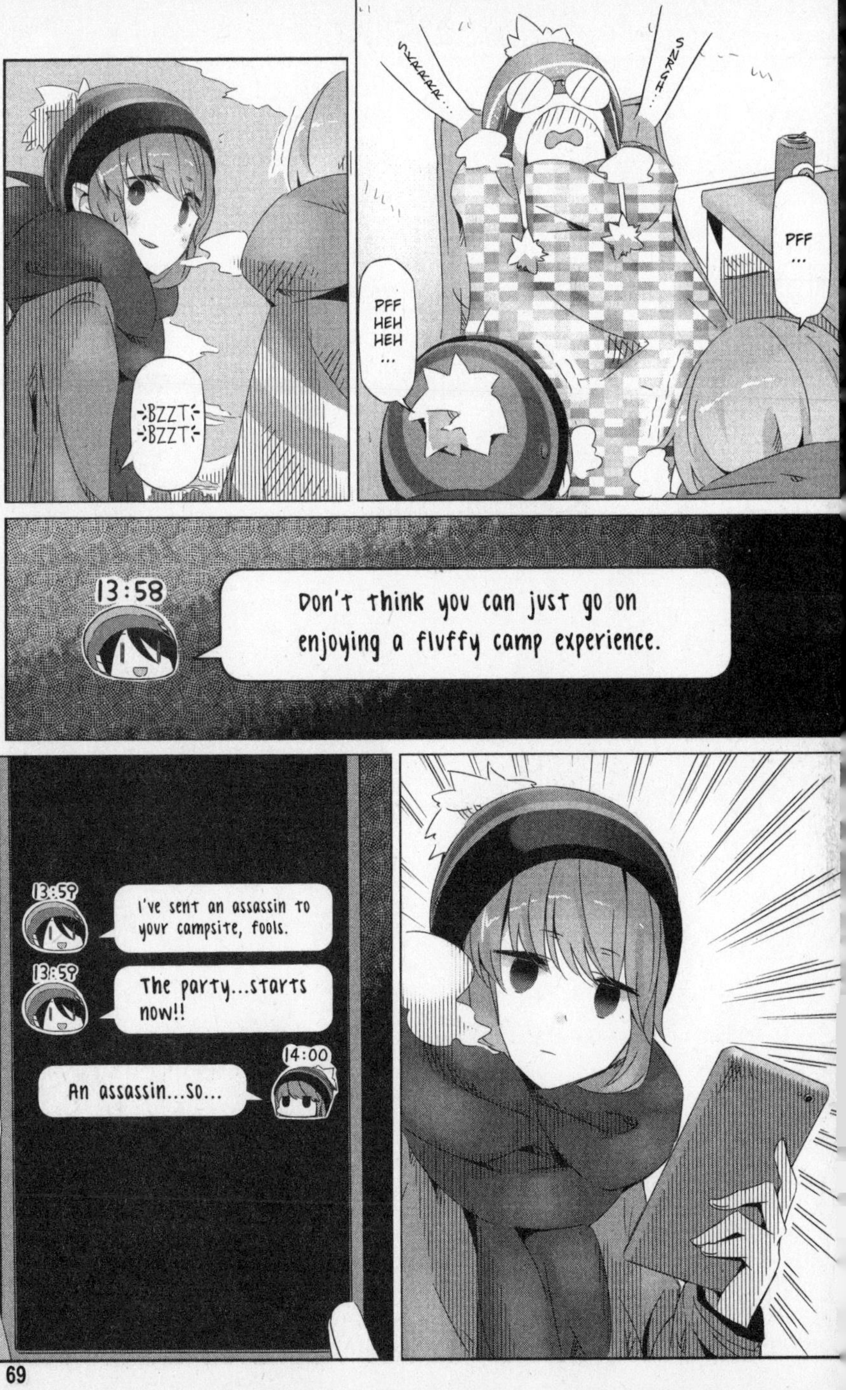
SNRSH...
PFF...
SNRRRK...
PFF HEH HEH...
BZZT BZZT
13:58
Don't think you can just go on enjoying a fluffy camp experience.
13:59
I've sent an assassin to your campsite, fools.
13:59
The party...starts now!!
14:00
An assassin...so...

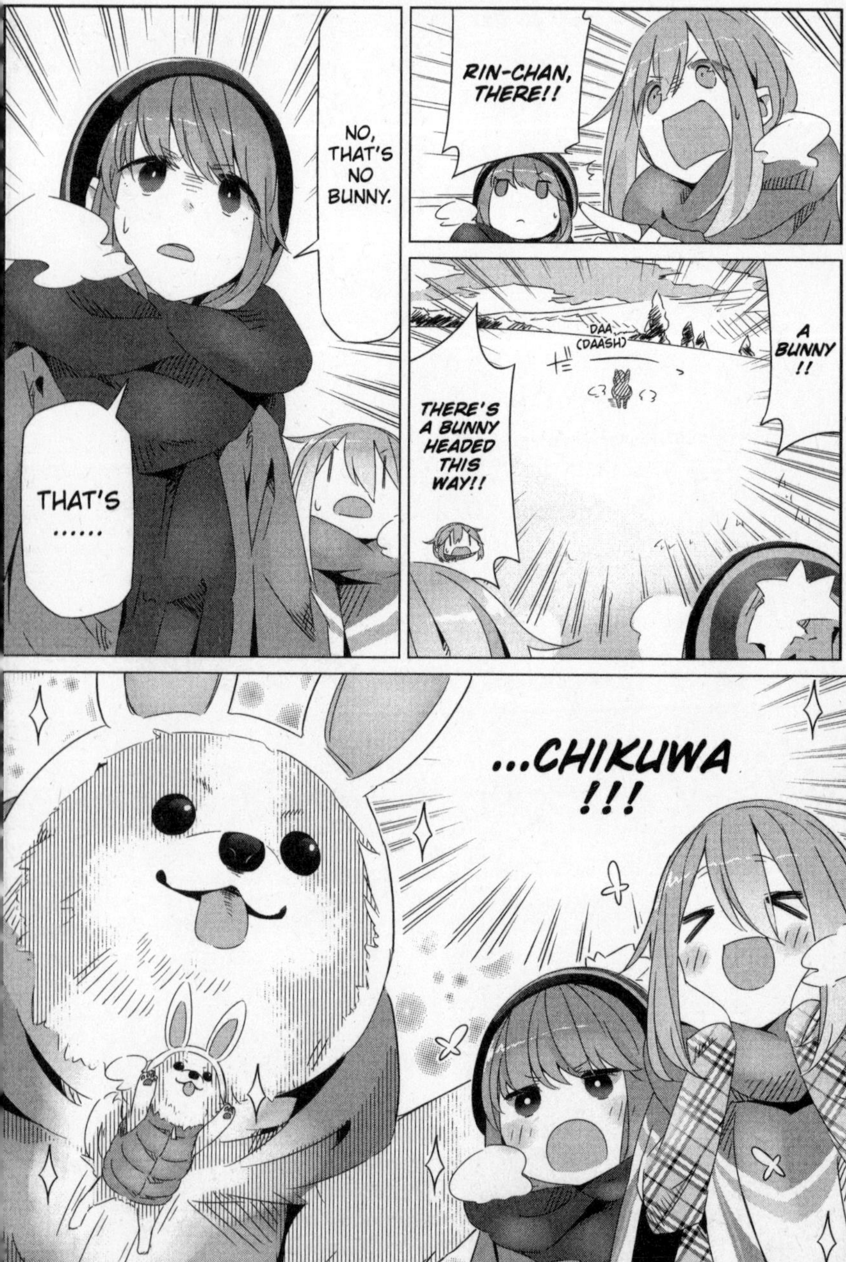
RIN-CHAN, THERE!!
A BUNNY!!
DAA (DAASH)
THERE'S A BUNNY HEADED THIS WAY!!
NO, THAT'S NO BUNNY.
THAT'S ......
...CHIKUWA!!!

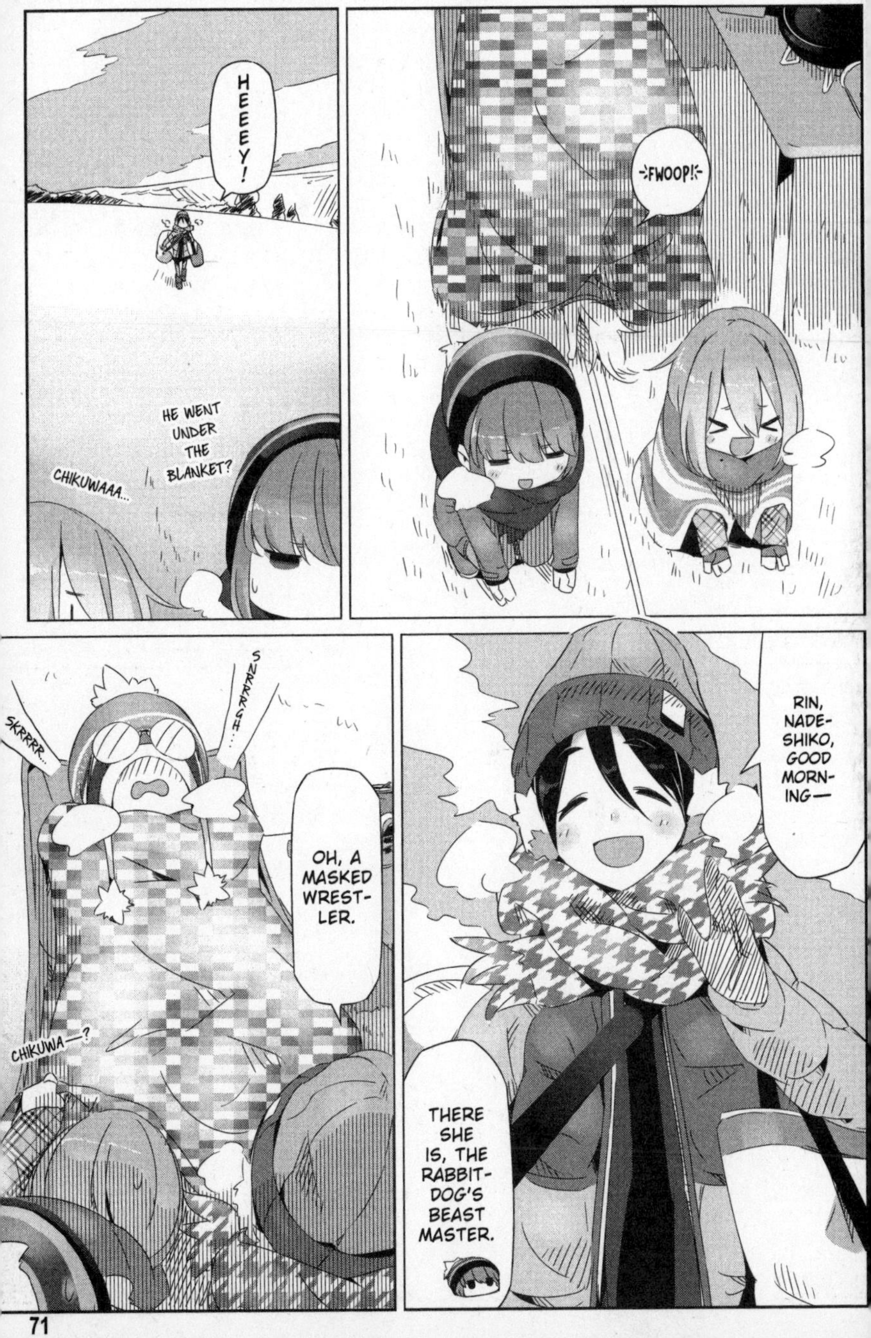

FWOOP!
HEEEEY!
HE WENT UNDER THE BLANKET?
CHIKUWAAA...
RIN, NADE-SHIKO, GOOD MORN-ING—
THERE SHE IS, THE RABBIT-DOG'S BEAST MASTER.
SNRRRSH...
SKRRRR...
OH, A MASKED WREST-LER.
CHIKUWA—?

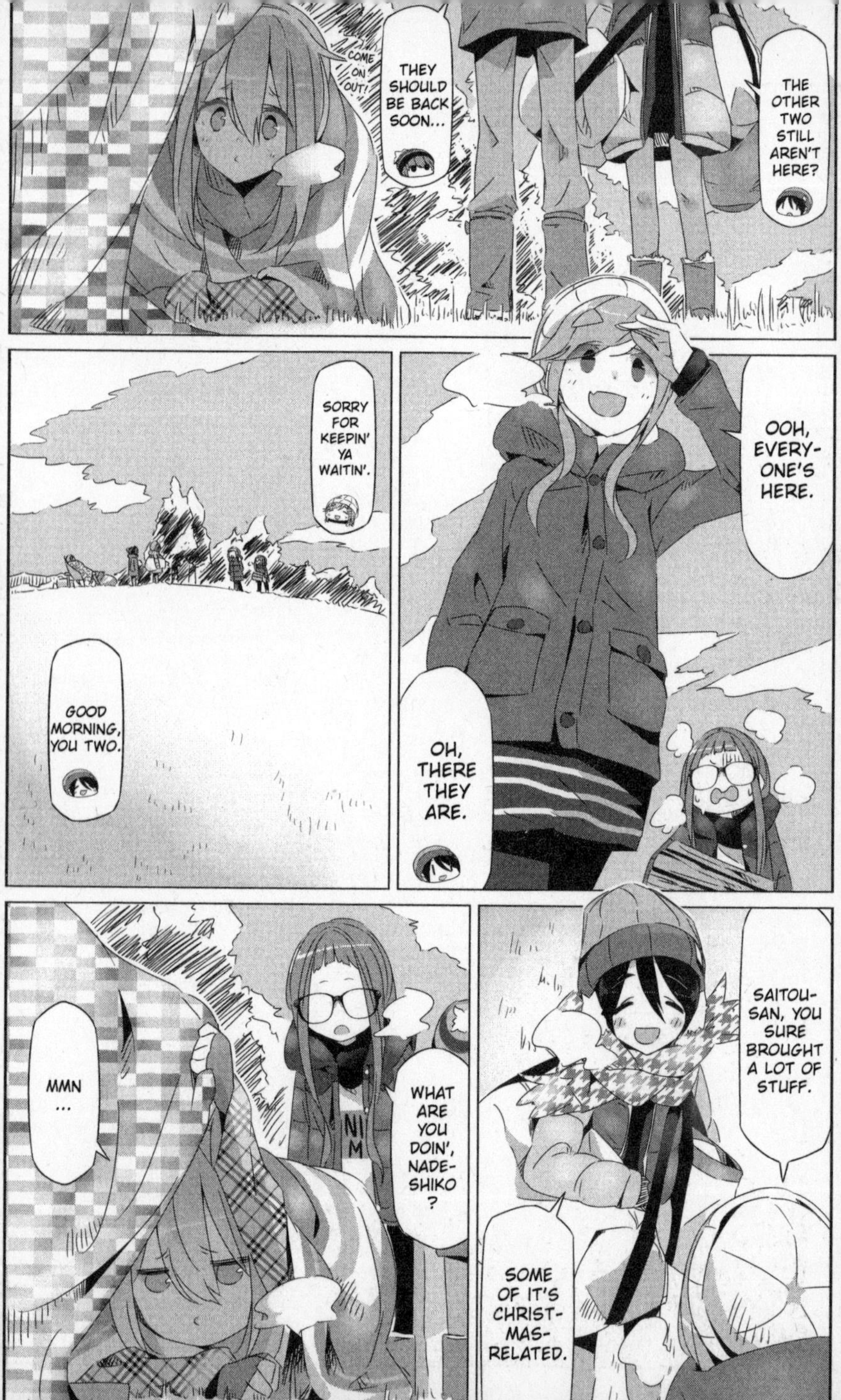
THE OTHER TWO STILL AREN'T HERE?
THEY SHOULD BE BACK SOON...
COME ON OUT!
OOH, EVERY-ONE'S HERE.
OH, THERE THEY ARE.
SORRY FOR KEEPIN' YA WAITIN'.
GOOD MORNING, YOU TWO.
SAITOU-SAN, YOU SURE BROUGHT A LOT OF STUFF.
SOME OF IT'S CHRISTMAS-RELATED.
WHAT ARE YOU DOIN', NADESHIKO?
MMN...

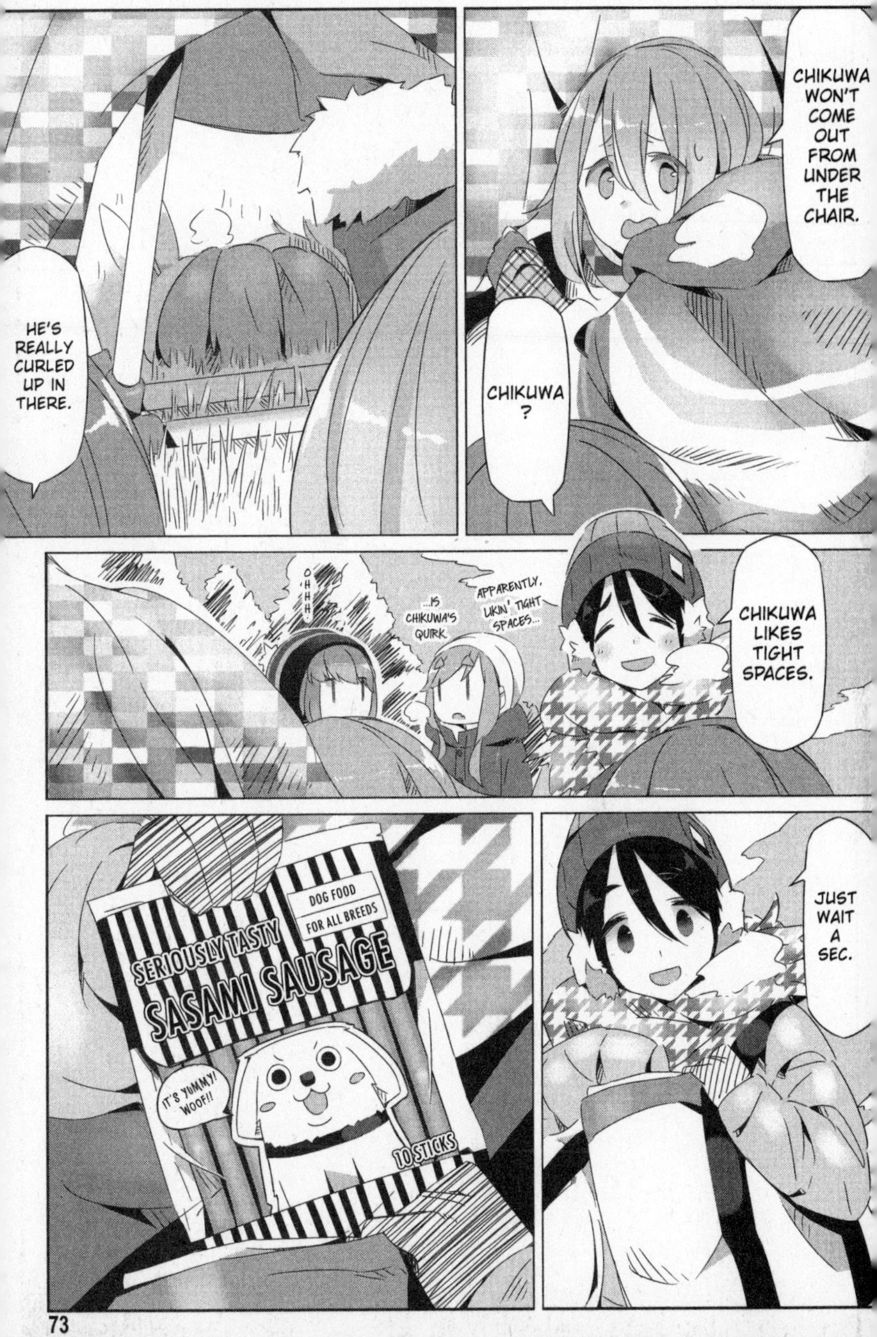
CHIKUWA WON'T COME OUT FROM UNDER THE CHAIR.
CHIKUWA?
HE'S REALLY CURLED UP IN THERE.
CHIKUWA LIKES TIGHT SPACES.
APPARENTLY, LIKIN' TIGHT SPACES...
...IS CHIKUWA'S QUIRK.
OHHH.
JUST WAIT A SEC.
DOG FOOD
FOR ALL BREEDS
SERIOUSLY TASTY
SASAMI SAUSAGE
IT'S YUMMY! WOOF!!
10 STICKS

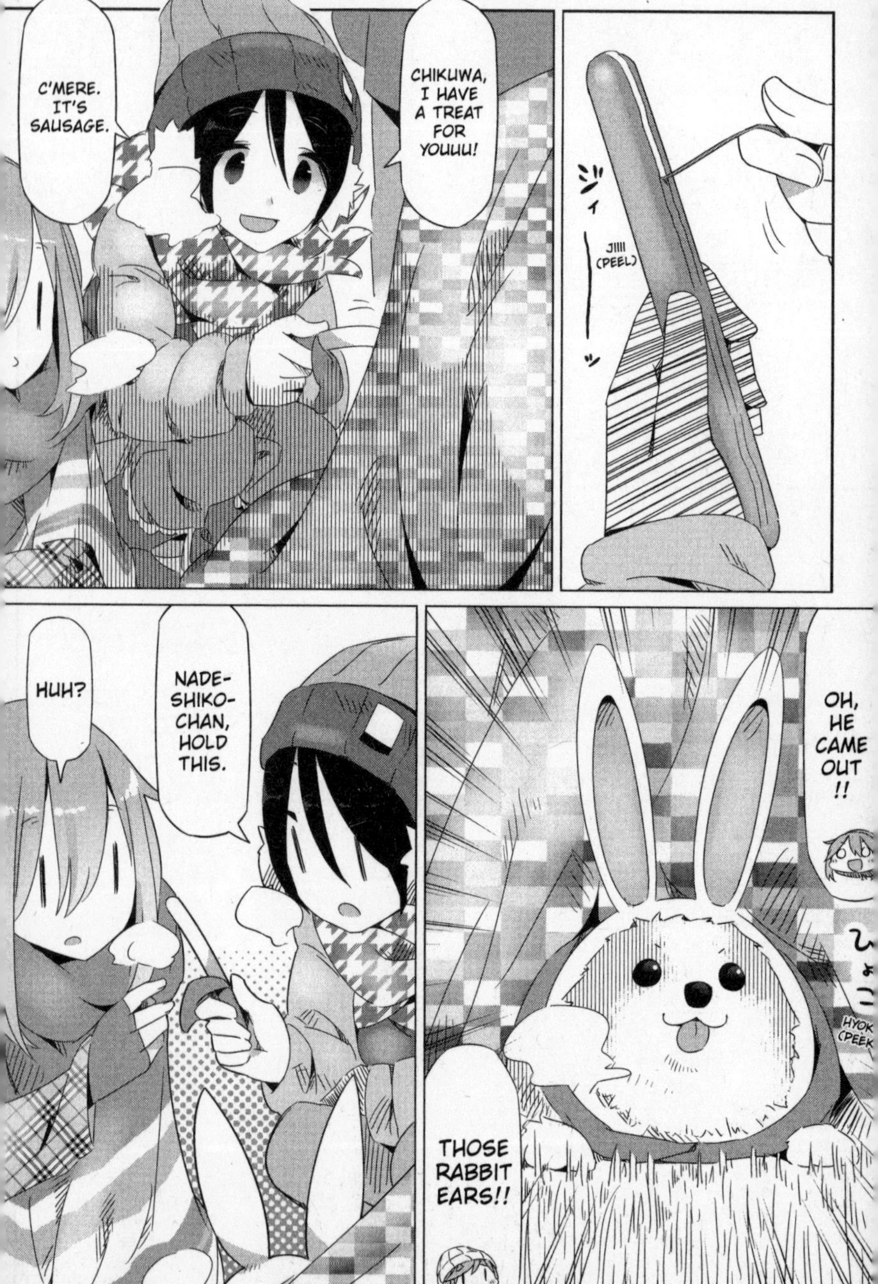
ジィーッ
JIIII (PEEL)
CHIKUWA, I HAVE A TREAT FOR YOUUU!
C'MERE. IT'S SAUSAGE.
OH, HE CAME OUT!!
ひょこ
HYOK (PEEK
THOSE RABBIT EARS!!
NADE-SHIKO-CHAN, HOLD THIS.
HUH?

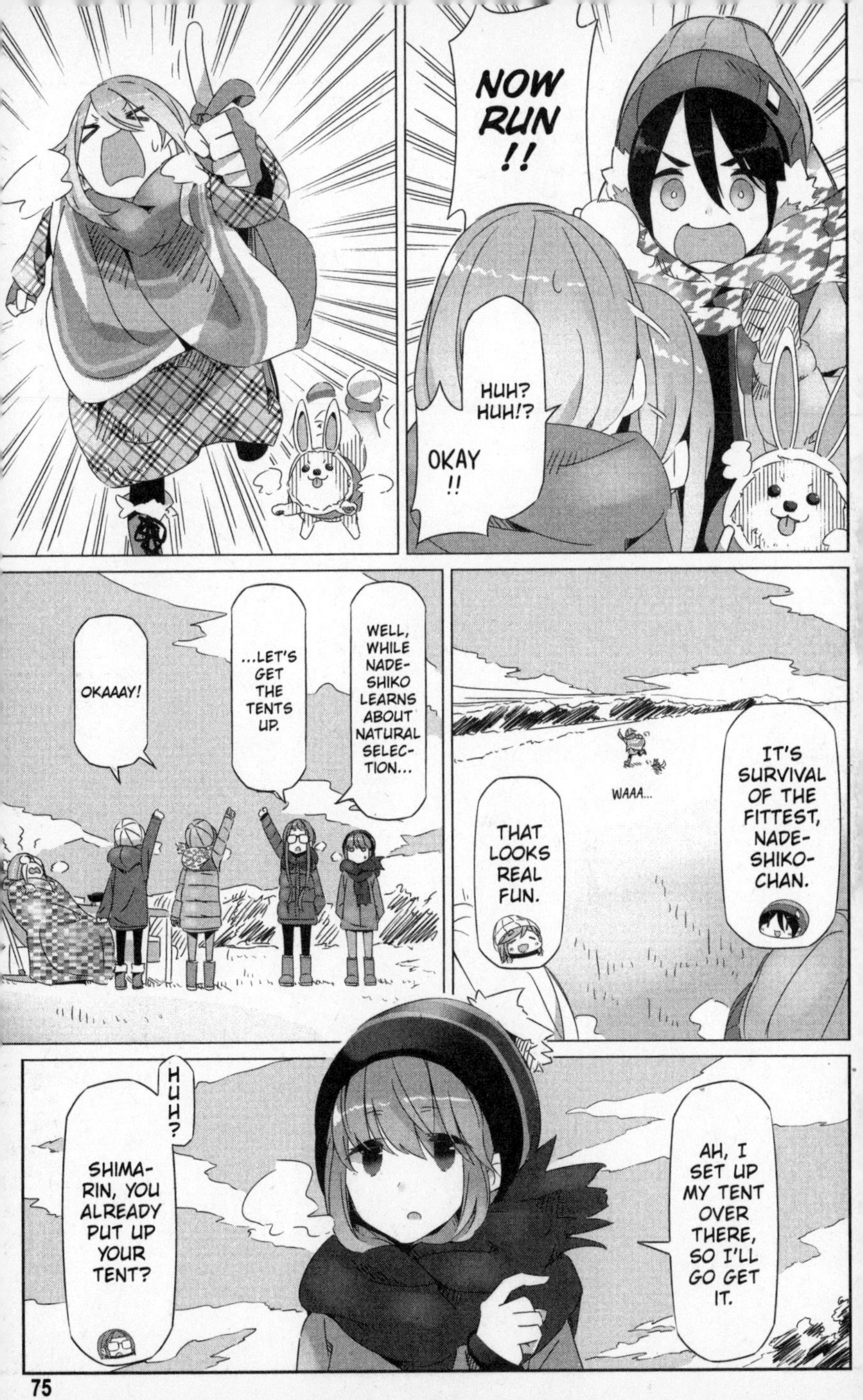
NOW RUN!!
HUH? HUH!?
OKAY!!
IT'S SURVIVAL OF THE FITTEST, NADE-SHIKO-CHAN.
WAAA...
THAT LOOKS REAL FUN.
WELL, WHILE NADE-SHIKO LEARNS ABOUT NATURAL SELEC-TION...
...LET'S GET THE TENTS UP.
OKAAAY!
AH, I SET UP MY TENT OVER THERE, SO I'LL GO GET IT.
HUH?
SHIMA-RIN, YOU ALREADY PUT UP YOUR TENT?

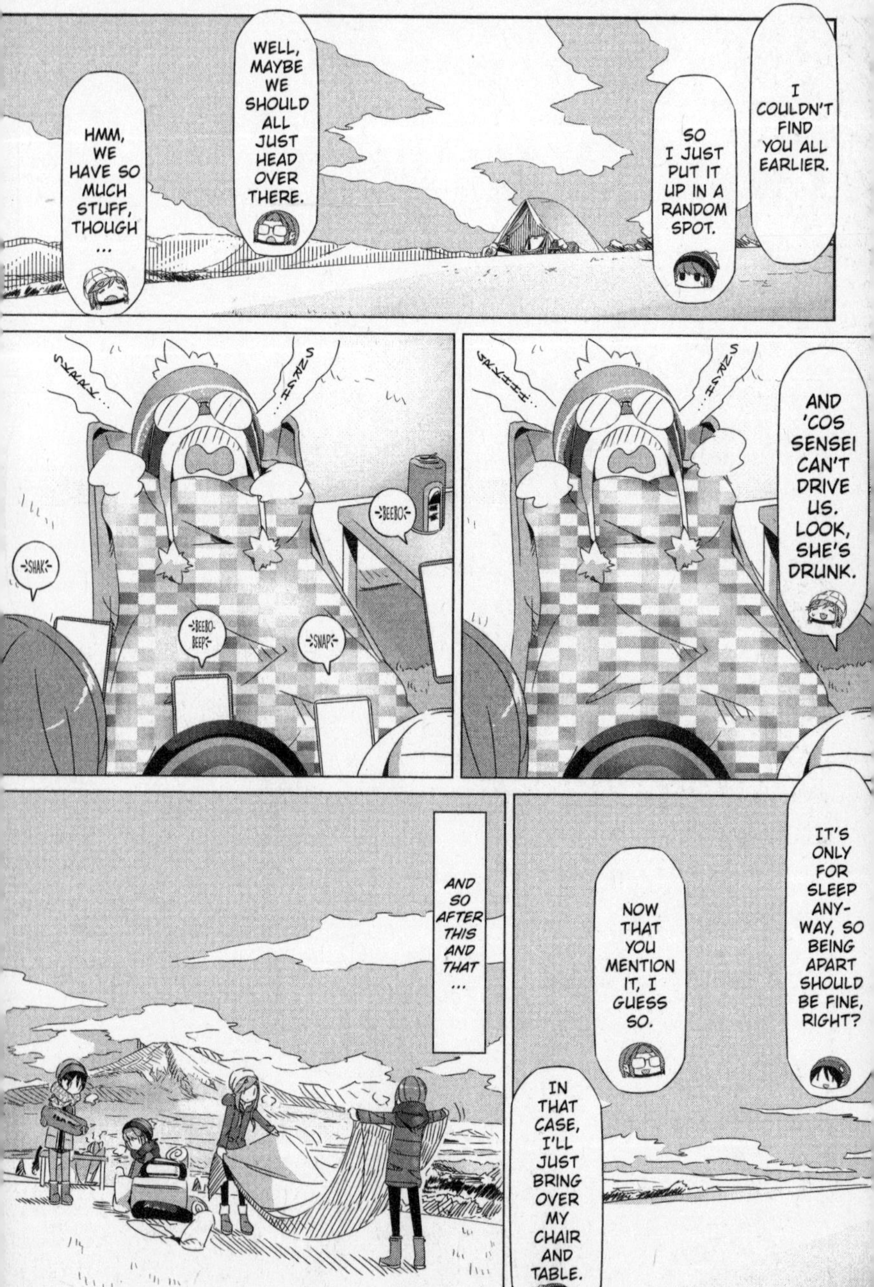
I COULDN'T FIND YOU ALL EARLIER.
SO I JUST PUT IT UP IN A RANDOM SPOT.
WELL, MAYBE WE SHOULD ALL JUST HEAD OVER THERE.
HMM, WE HAVE SO MUCH STUFF, THOUGH ...
AND 'COS SENSEI CAN'T DRIVE US. LOOK, SHE'S DRUNK.
BEEBO
SHAK
BEEBO-BEEP
SNAP
IT'S ONLY FOR SLEEP ANY-WAY, SO BEING APART SHOULD BE FINE, RIGHT?
NOW THAT YOU MENTION IT, I GUESS SO.
IN THAT CASE, I'LL JUST BRING OVER MY CHAIR AND TABLE.
AND SO AFTER THIS AND THAT ...

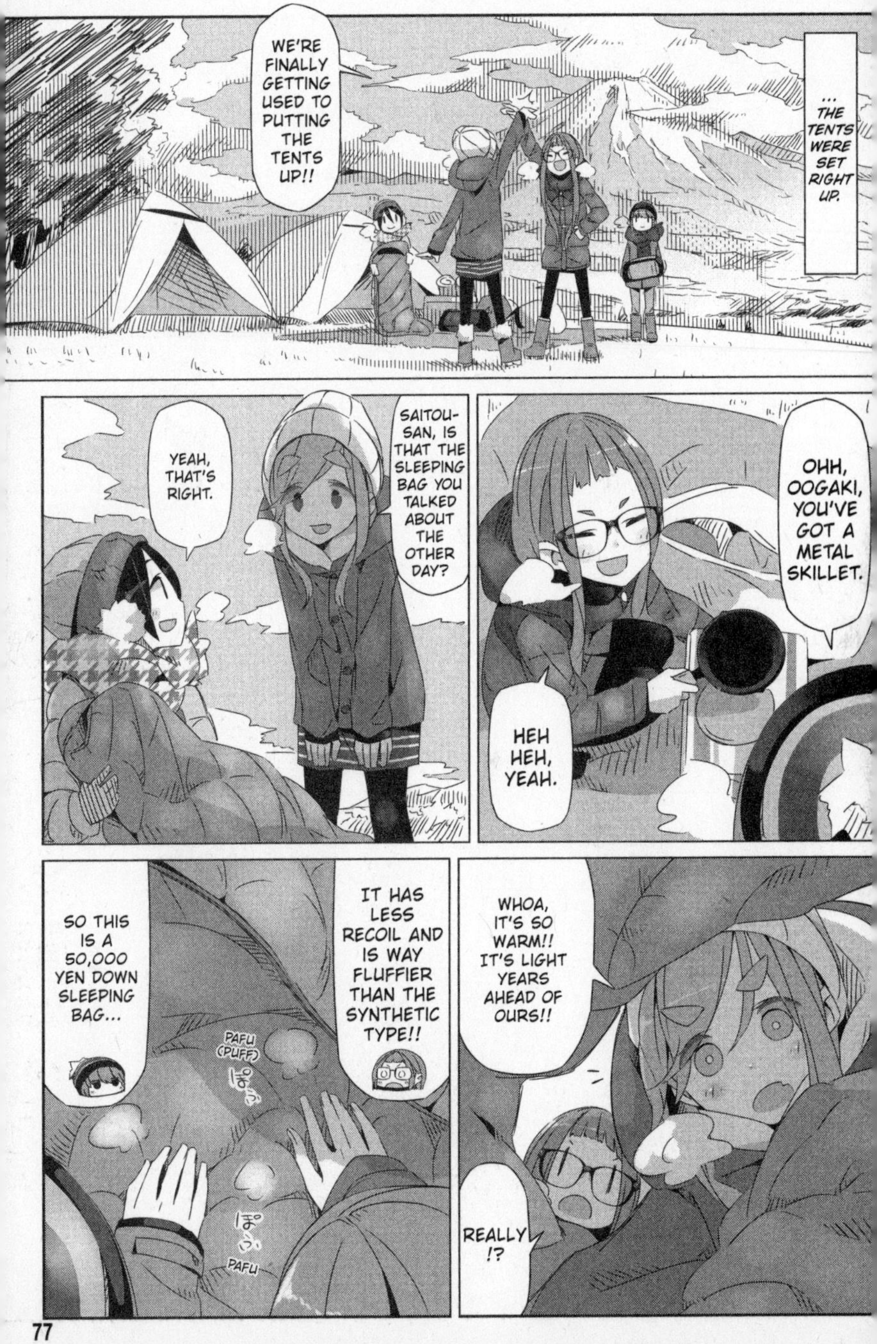
...THE TENTS WERE SET RIGHT UP.
WE'RE FINALLY GETTING USED TO PUTTING THE TENTS UP!!
OHH, OOGAKI, YOU'VE GOT A METAL SKILLET.
HEH HEH, YEAH.
SAITOU-SAN, IS THAT THE SLEEPING BAG YOU TALKED ABOUT THE OTHER DAY?
YEAH, THAT'S RIGHT.
WHOA, IT'S SO WARM!! IT'S LIGHT YEARS AHEAD OF OURS!!
REALLY!?
IT HAS LESS RECOIL AND IS WAY FLUFFIER THAN THE SYNTHETIC TYPE!!
SO THIS IS A 50,000 YEN DOWN SLEEPING BAG...
PAFU (PUFF)
ぽふ
ぽふ
PAFU

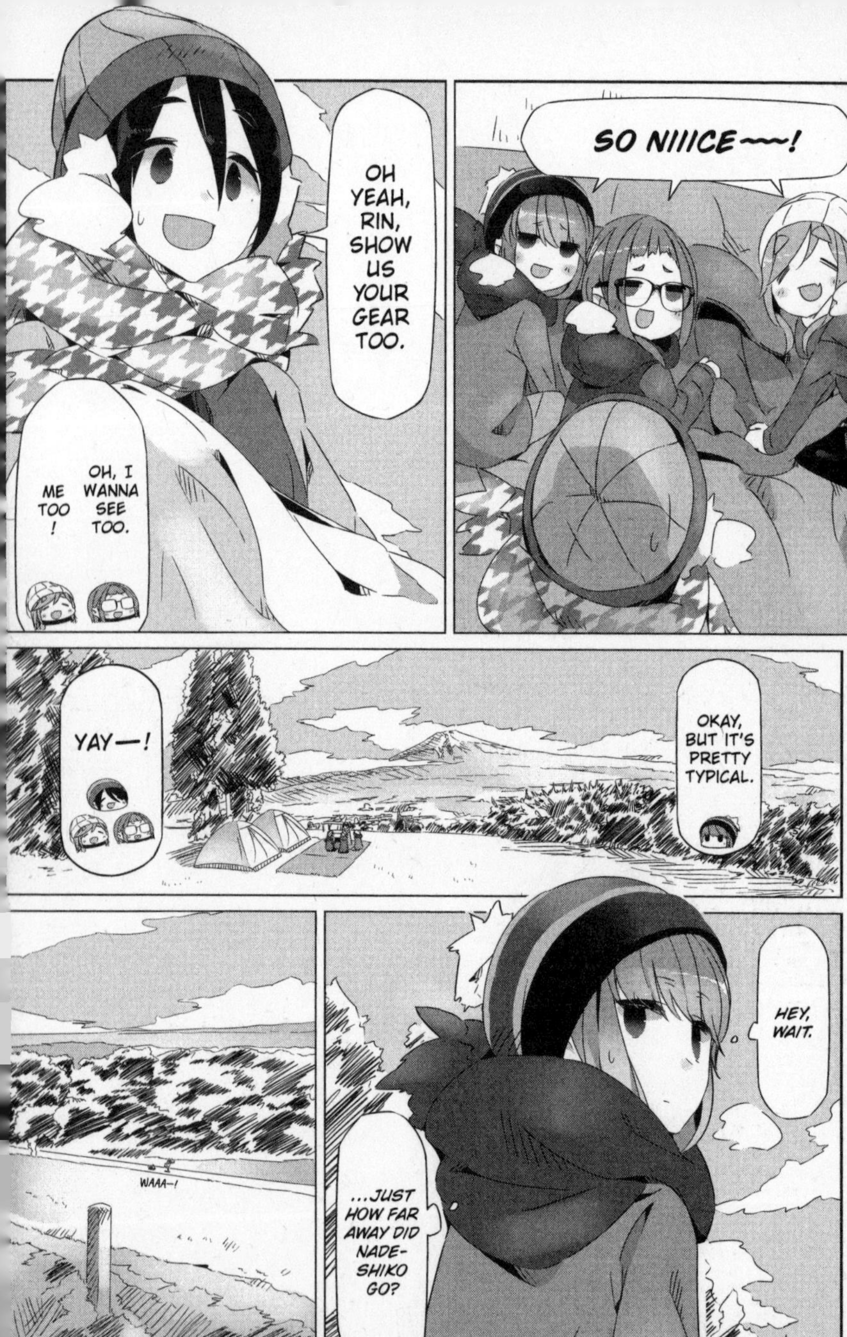
SO NIIICE~~~!
OH YEAH, RIN, SHOW US YOUR GEAR TOO.
OH, I WANNA SEE TOO.
ME TOO!
OKAY, BUT IT'S PRETTY TYPICAL.
YAY—!
HEY, WAIT.
...JUST HOW FAR AWAY DID NADE-SHIKO GO?
WAAA—!

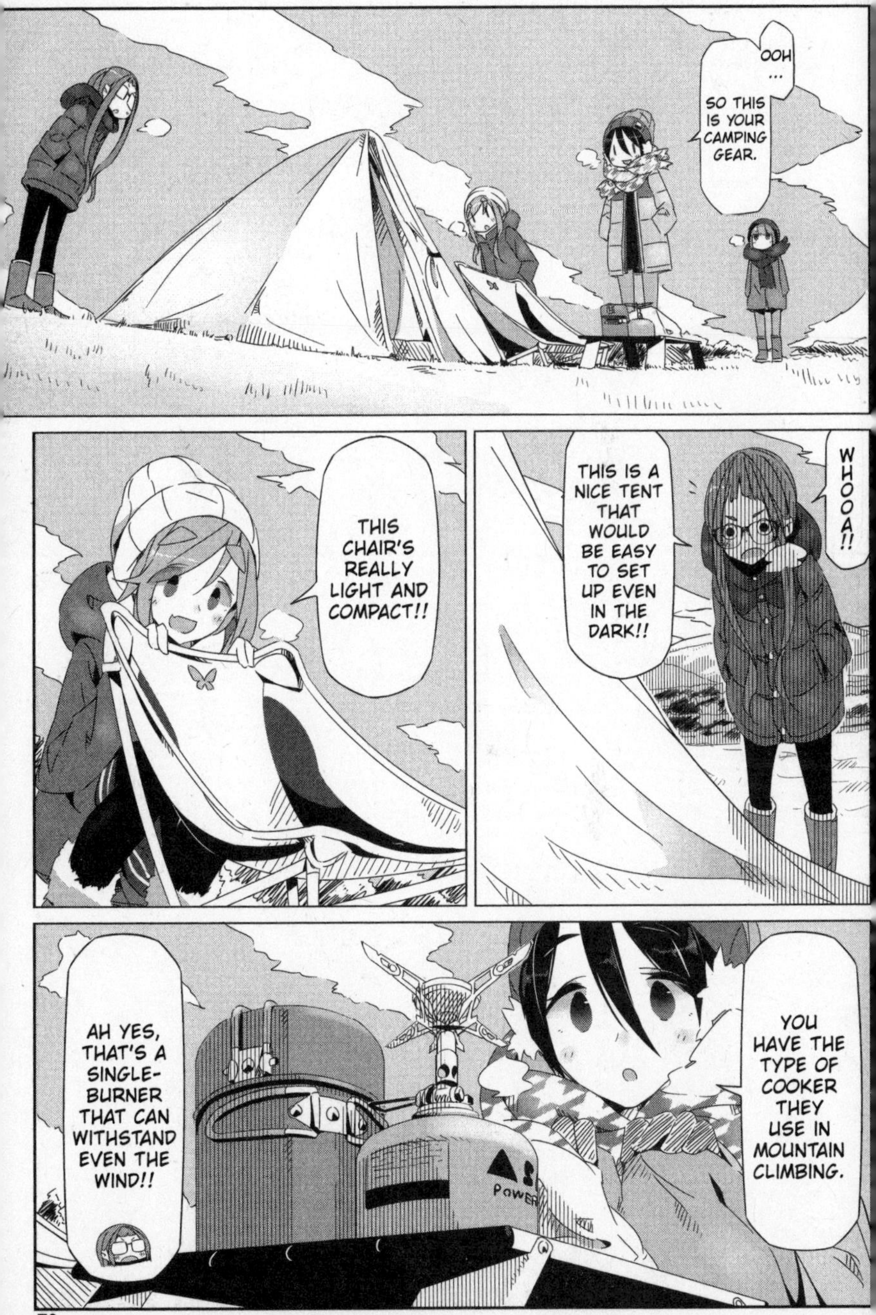
OOH ...
SO THIS IS YOUR CAMPING GEAR.
WHOOA!!
THIS IS A NICE TENT THAT WOULD BE EASY TO SET UP EVEN IN THE DARK!!
THIS CHAIR'S REALLY LIGHT AND COMPACT!!
YOU HAVE THE TYPE OF COOKER THEY USE IN MOUNTAIN CLIMBING.
AH YES, THAT'S A SINGLE-BURNER THAT CAN WITHSTAND EVEN THE WIND!!
POWER

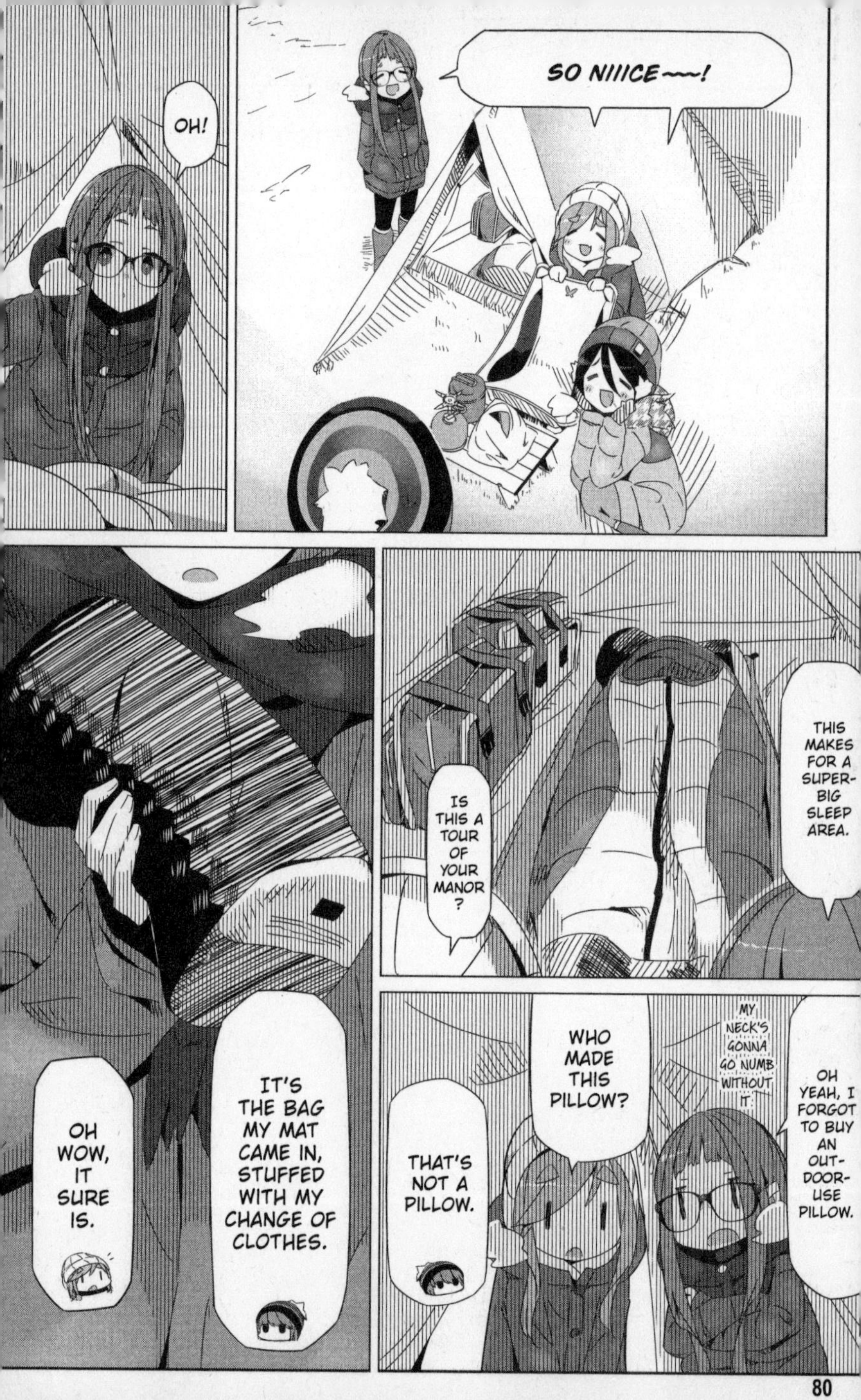
SO NIIICE~~~!
OH!
THIS MAKES FOR A SUPER-BIG SLEEP AREA.
IS THIS A TOUR OF YOUR MANOR?
OH YEAH, I FORGOT TO BUY AN OUT-DOOR-USE PILLOW.
MY NECK'S GONNA GO NUMB WITHOUT IT.
WHO MADE THIS PILLOW?
THAT'S NOT A PILLOW.
IT'S THE BAG MY MAT CAME IN, STUFFED WITH MY CHANGE OF CLOTHES.
OH WOW, IT SURE IS.

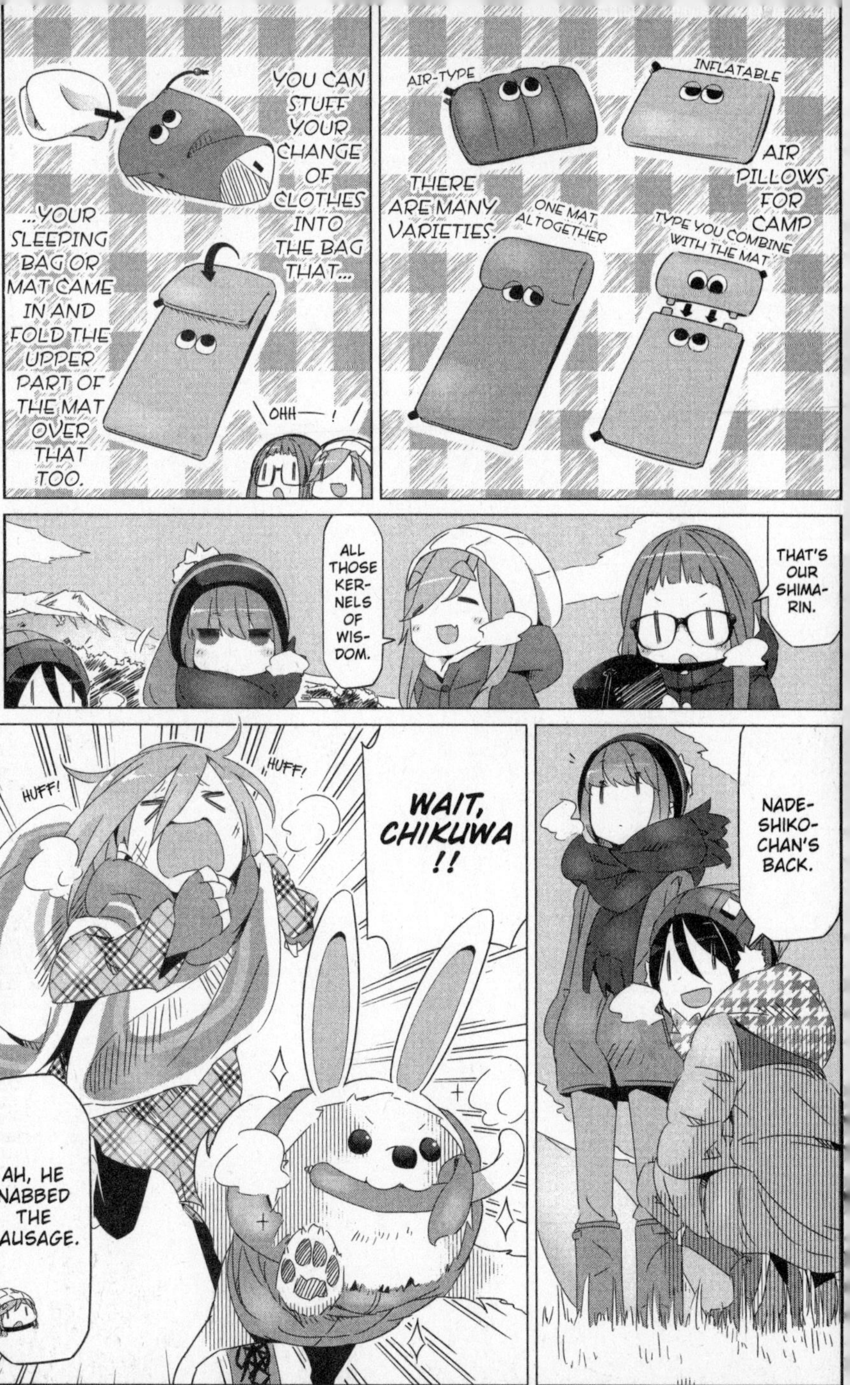
AIR PILLOWS FOR CAMP
INFLATABLE
AIR-TYPE
THERE ARE MANY VARIETIES.
TYPE YOU COMBINE WITH THE MAT
ONE MAT ALTOGETHER
YOU CAN STUFF YOUR CHANGE OF CLOTHES INTO THE BAG THAT...
...YOUR SLEEPING BAG OR MAT CAME IN AND FOLD THE UPPER PART OF THE MAT OVER THAT TOO.
OHH—!
THAT'S OUR SHIMA-RIN.
ALL THOSE KER-NELS OF WIS-DOM.
NADE-SHIKO-CHAN'S BACK.
WAIT, CHIKUWA!!
HUFF!
HUFF!
AH, HE NABBED THE SAUSAGE.

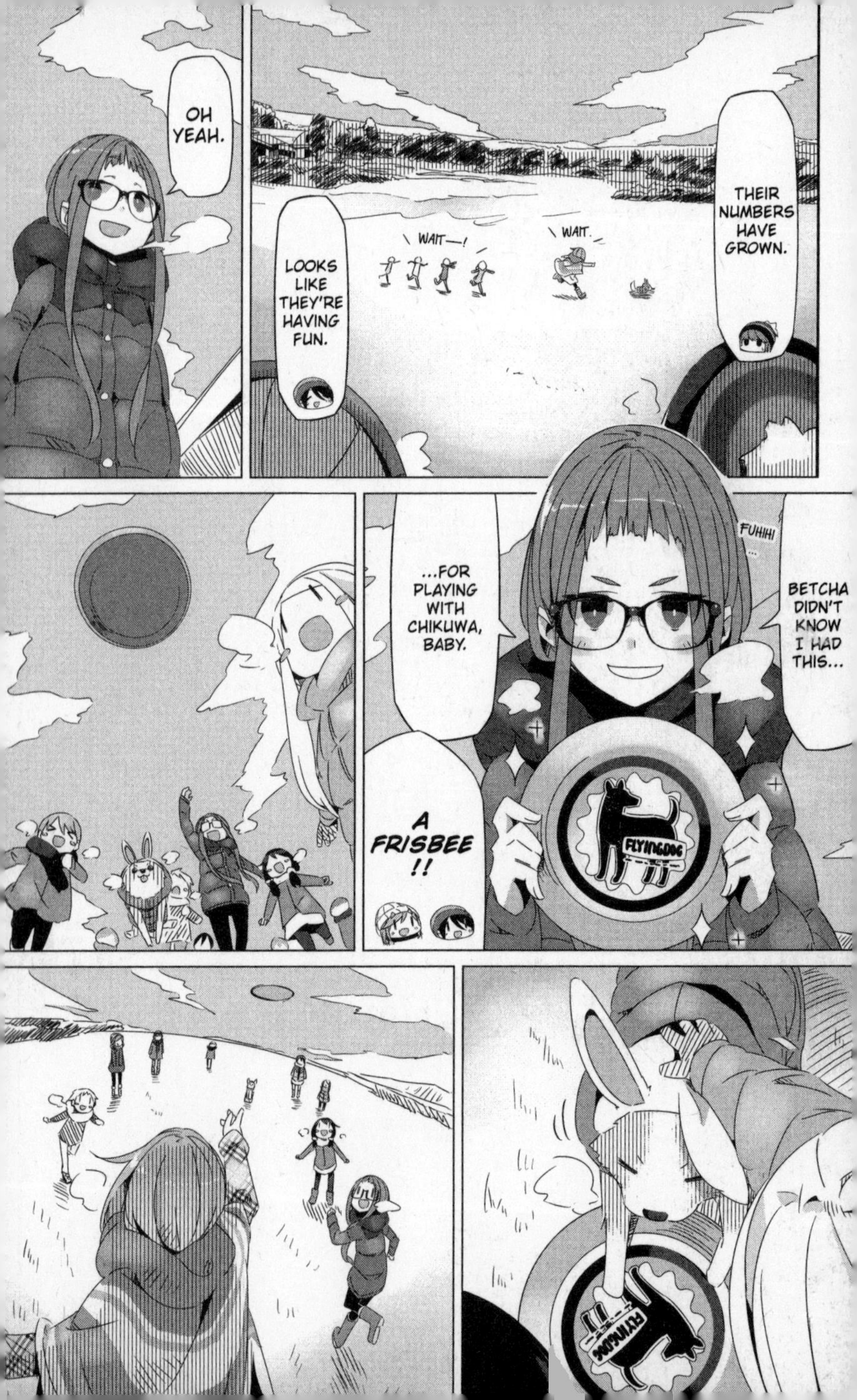
THEIR NUMBERS HAVE GROWN.
WAIT.
WAIT—!
LOOKS LIKE THEY'RE HAVING FUN.
OH YEAH.
FUHIHI ...
BETCHA DIDN'T KNOW I HAD THIS...
...FOR PLAYING WITH CHIKUWA, BABY.
A FRISBEE !!
FLYINGDOG
FLYINGDOG

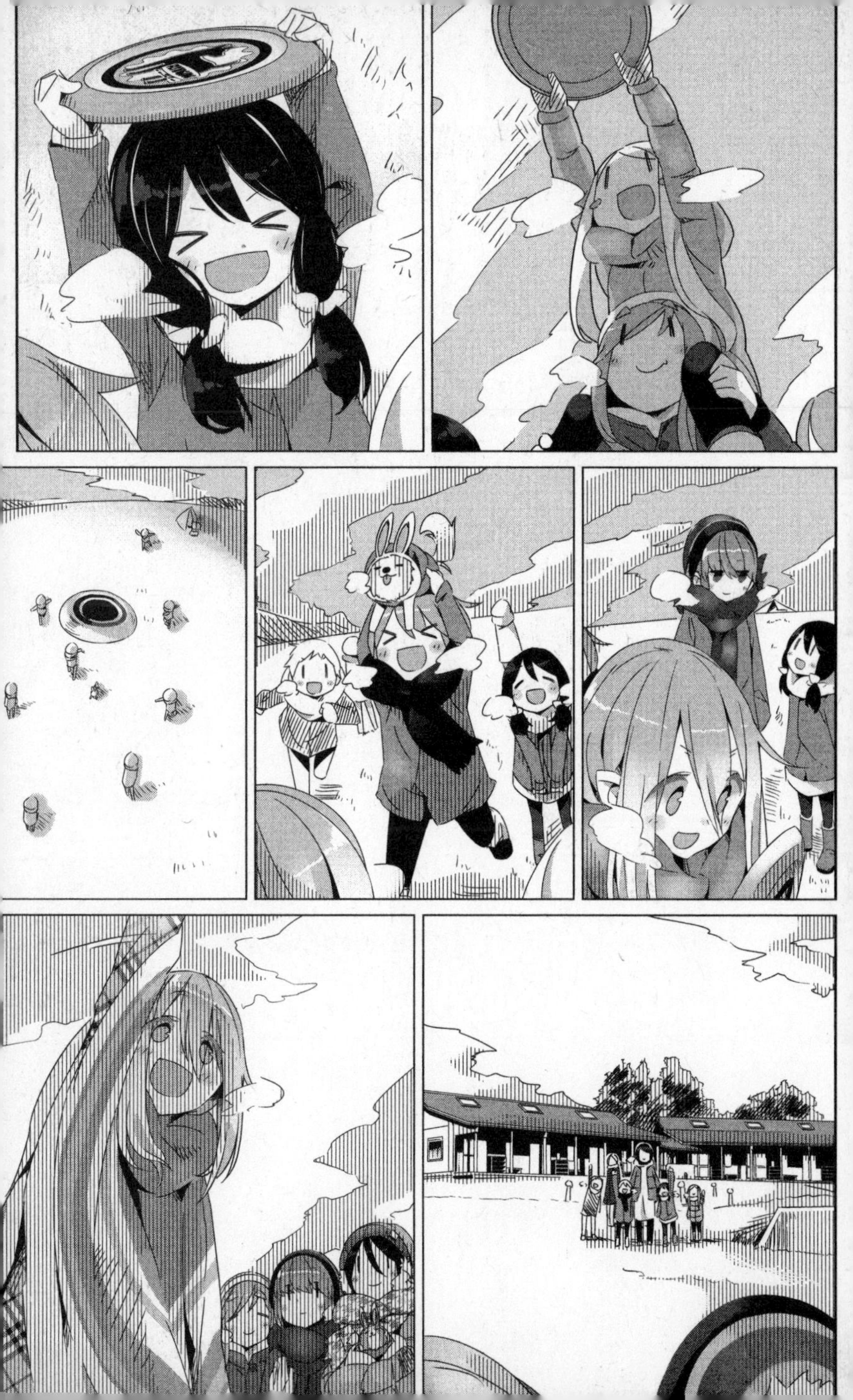

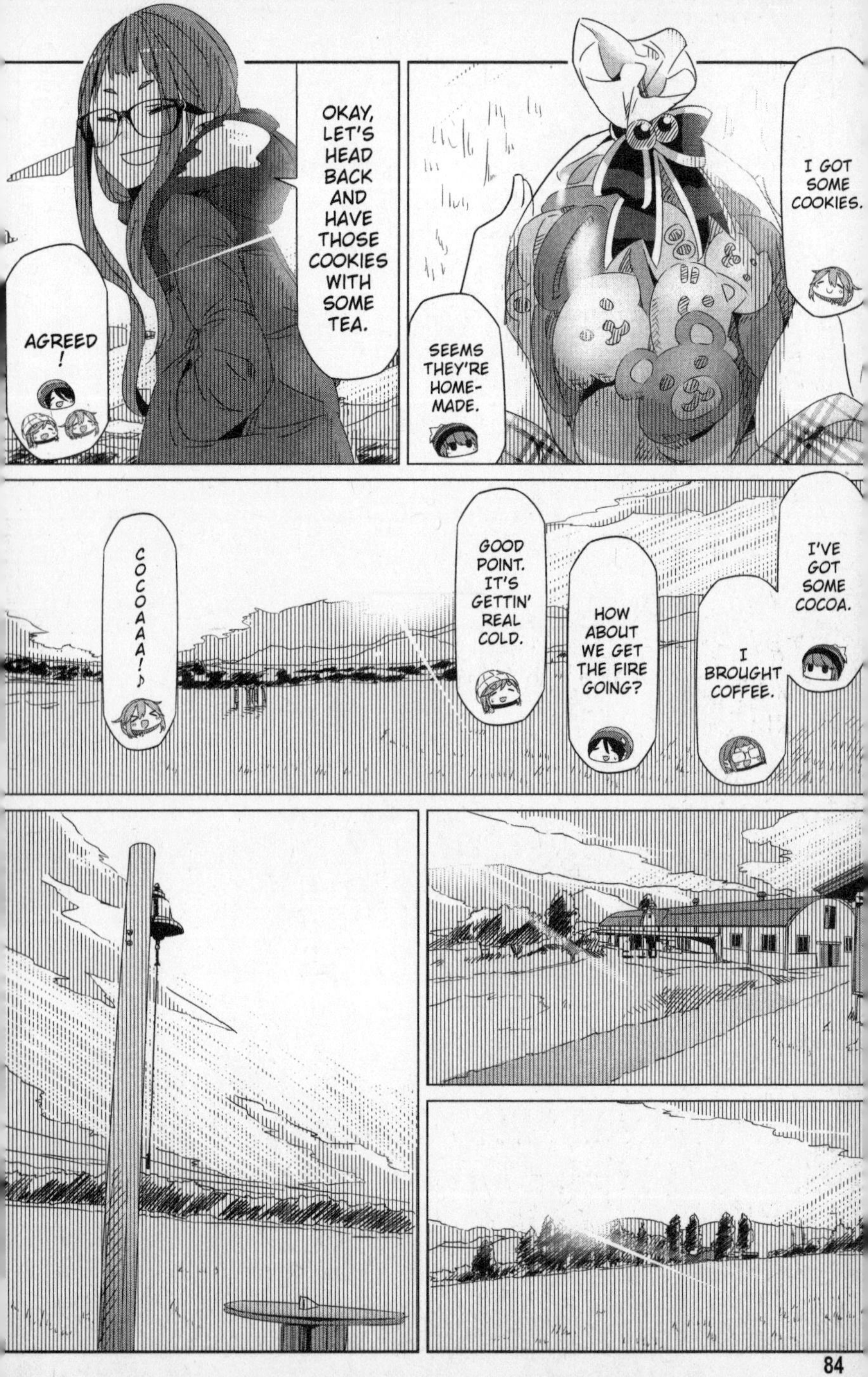
I GOT SOME COOKIES.
SEEMS THEY'RE HOME-MADE.
OKAY, LET'S HEAD BACK AND HAVE THOSE COOKIES WITH SOME TEA.
AGREED!
I'VE GOT SOME COCOA.
I BROUGHT COFFEE.
HOW ABOUT WE GET THE FIRE GOING?
GOOD POINT. IT'S GETTIN' REAL COLD.
COCOAAA!♪

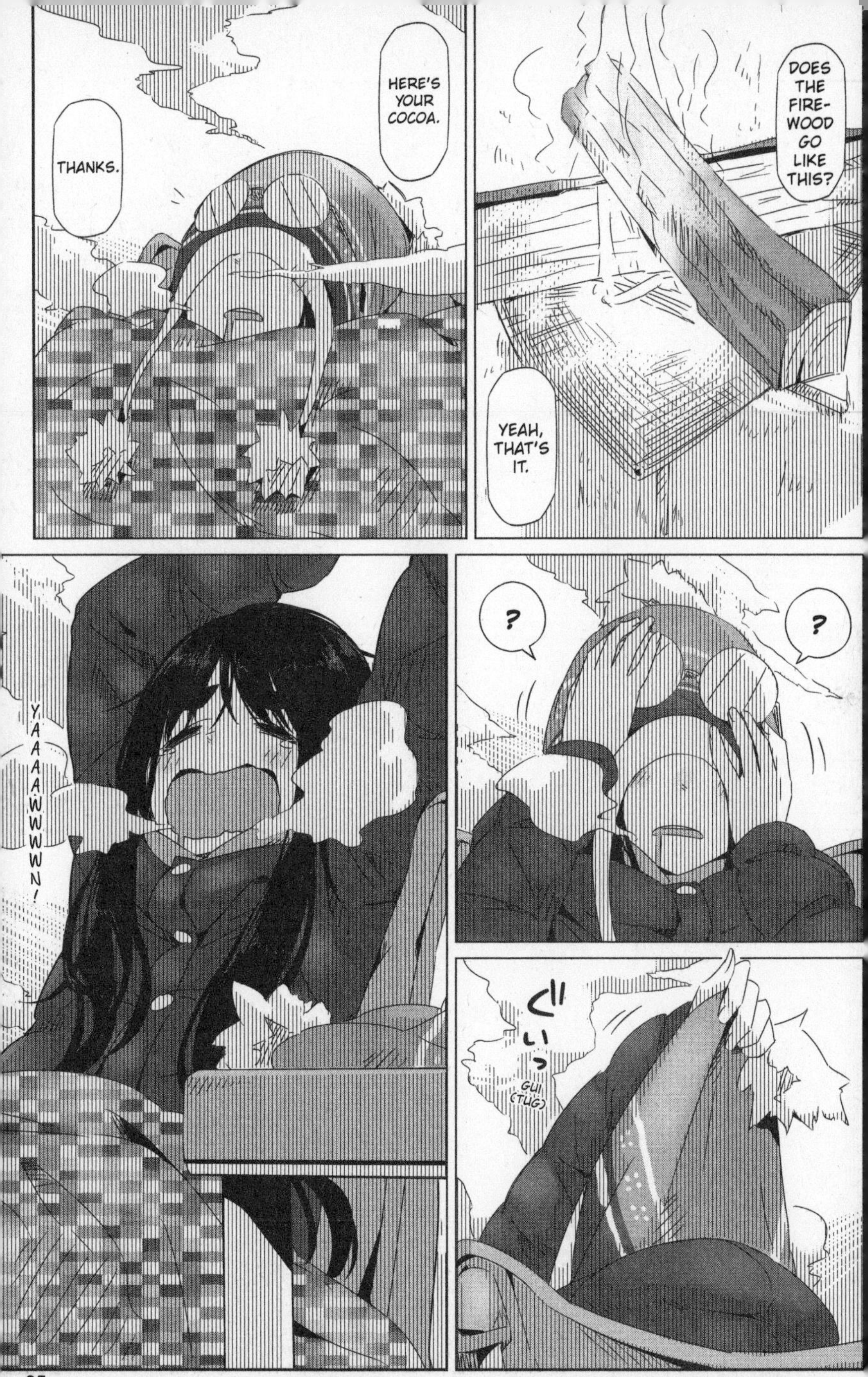
DOES THE FIRE-WOOD GO LIKE THIS?
YEAH, THAT'S IT.
HERE'S YOUR COCOA.
THANKS.
?
?
ぐいっ
GUI (TUG)
YAAAAAWWWWN!

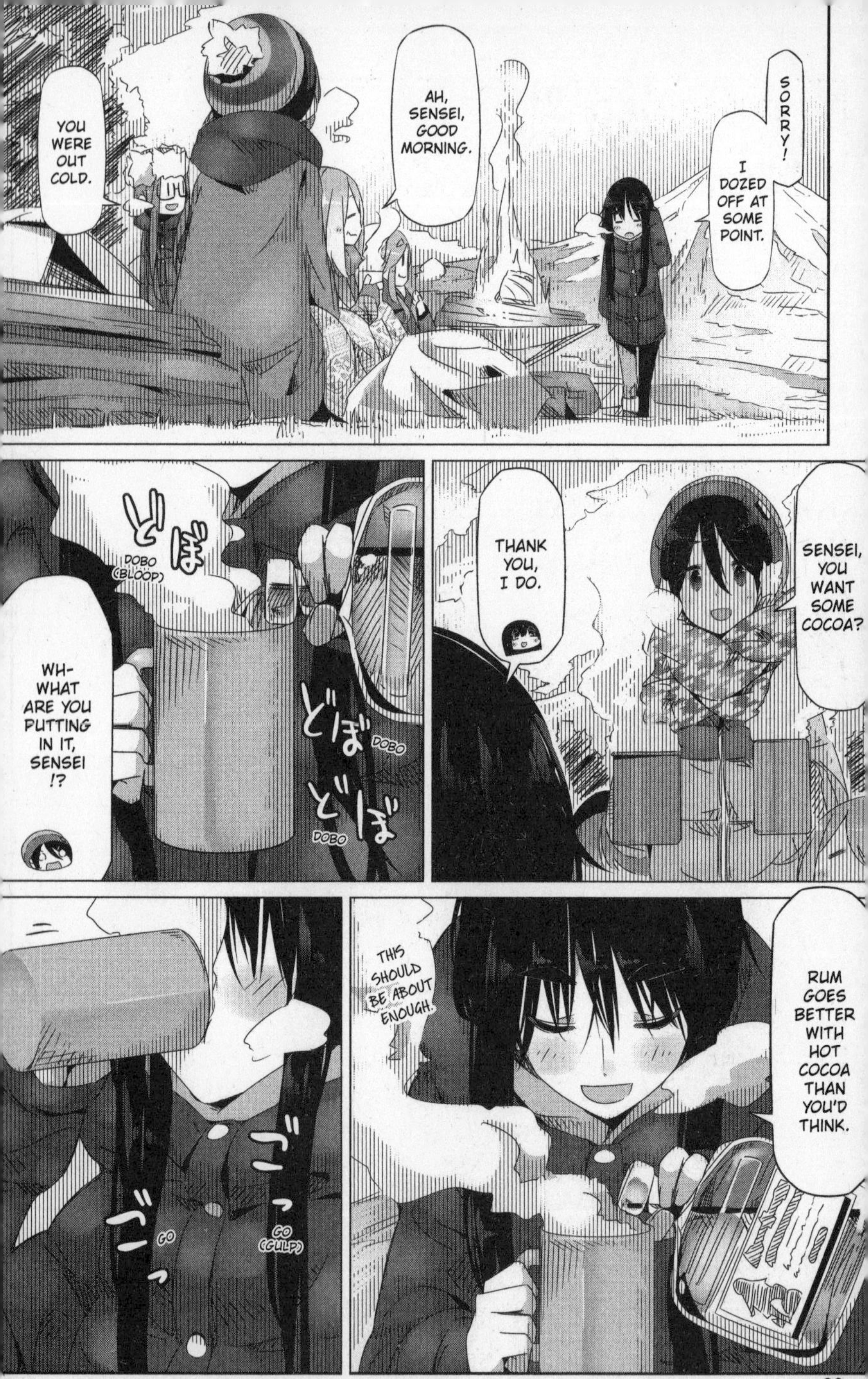
SORRY! I DOZED OFF AT SOME POINT.
AH, SENSEI, GOOD MORNING.
YOU WERE OUT COLD.
SENSEI, YOU WANT SOME COCOA?
THANK YOU, I DO.
どぼ DOBO (BLOOP)
どぼ DOBO
どぼ DOBO
WH-WHAT ARE YOU PUTTING IN IT, SENSEI!?
RUM GOES BETTER WITH HOT COCOA THAN YOU'D THINK.
THIS SHOULD BE ABOUT ENOUGH.
ごっ GO (GULP)
ごっ GO

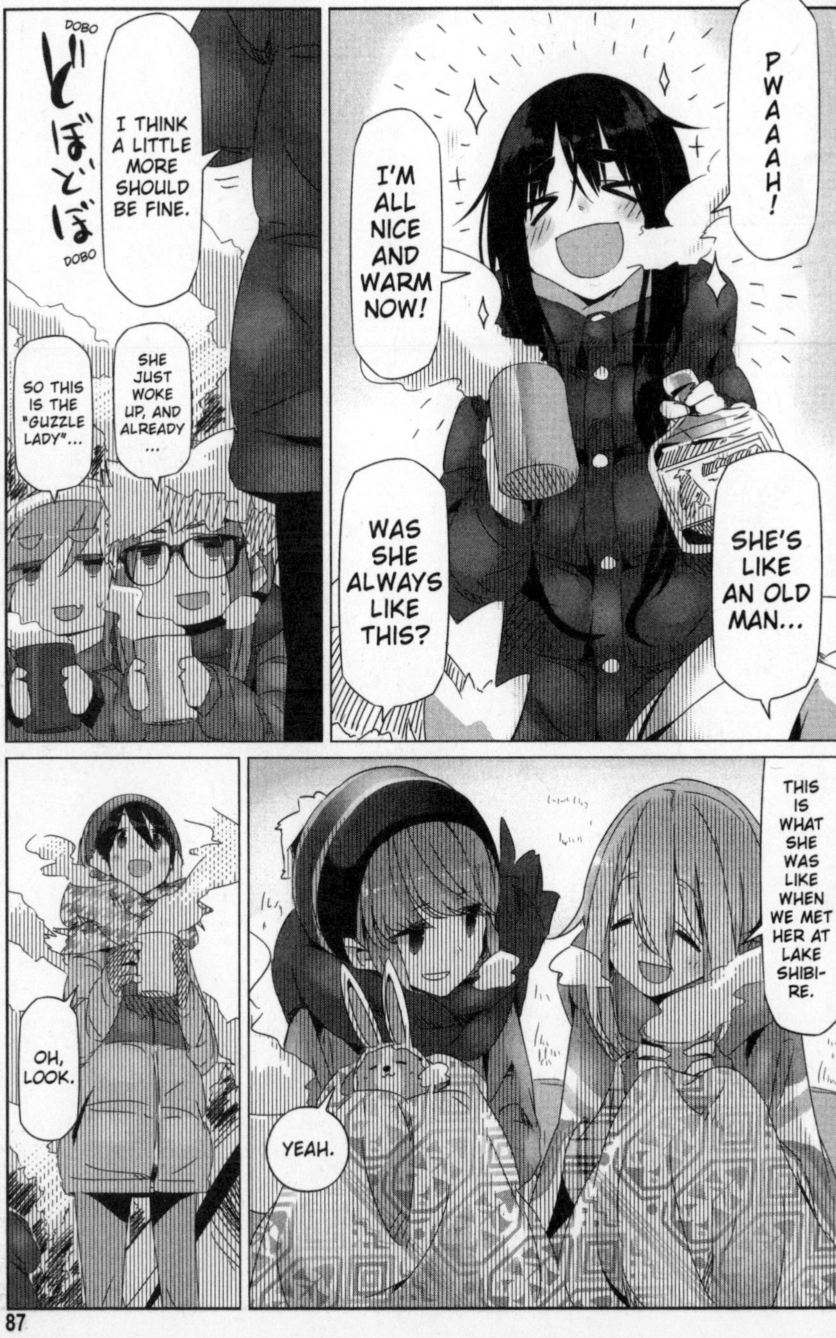
PWAAAH!
I'M ALL NICE AND WARM NOW!
SHE'S LIKE AN OLD MAN...
WAS SHE ALWAYS LIKE THIS?
I THINK A LITTLE MORE SHOULD BE FINE.
どぼどぼ
DOBO DOBO
SHE JUST WOKE UP, AND ALREADY ...
SO THIS IS THE "GUZZLE LADY"...
THIS IS WHAT SHE WAS LIKE WHEN WE MET HER AT LAKE SHIBI-RE.
YEAH.
OH, LOOK.

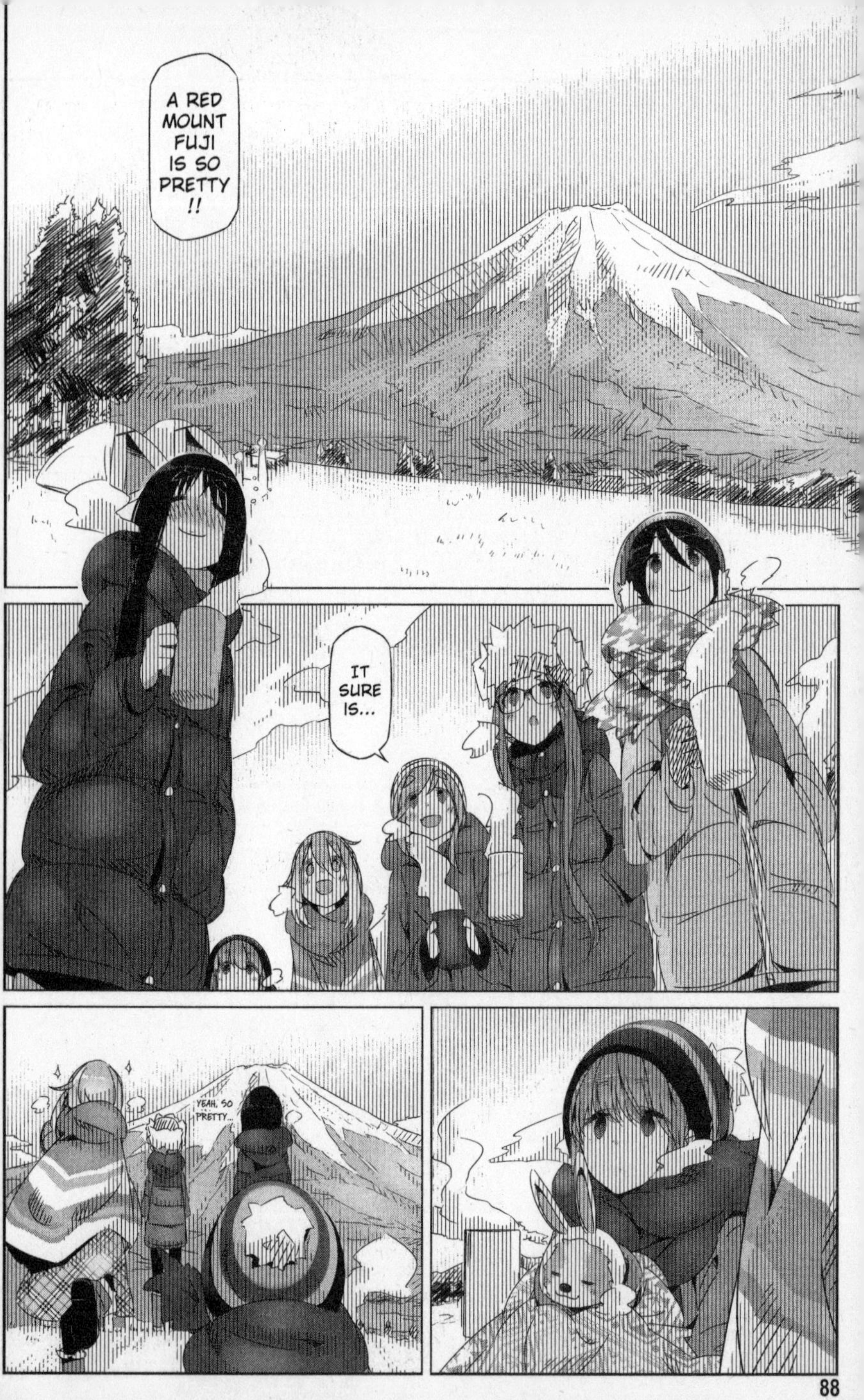
A RED MOUNT FUJI IS SO PRETTY!!
IT SURE IS...
YEAH, SO PRETTY...

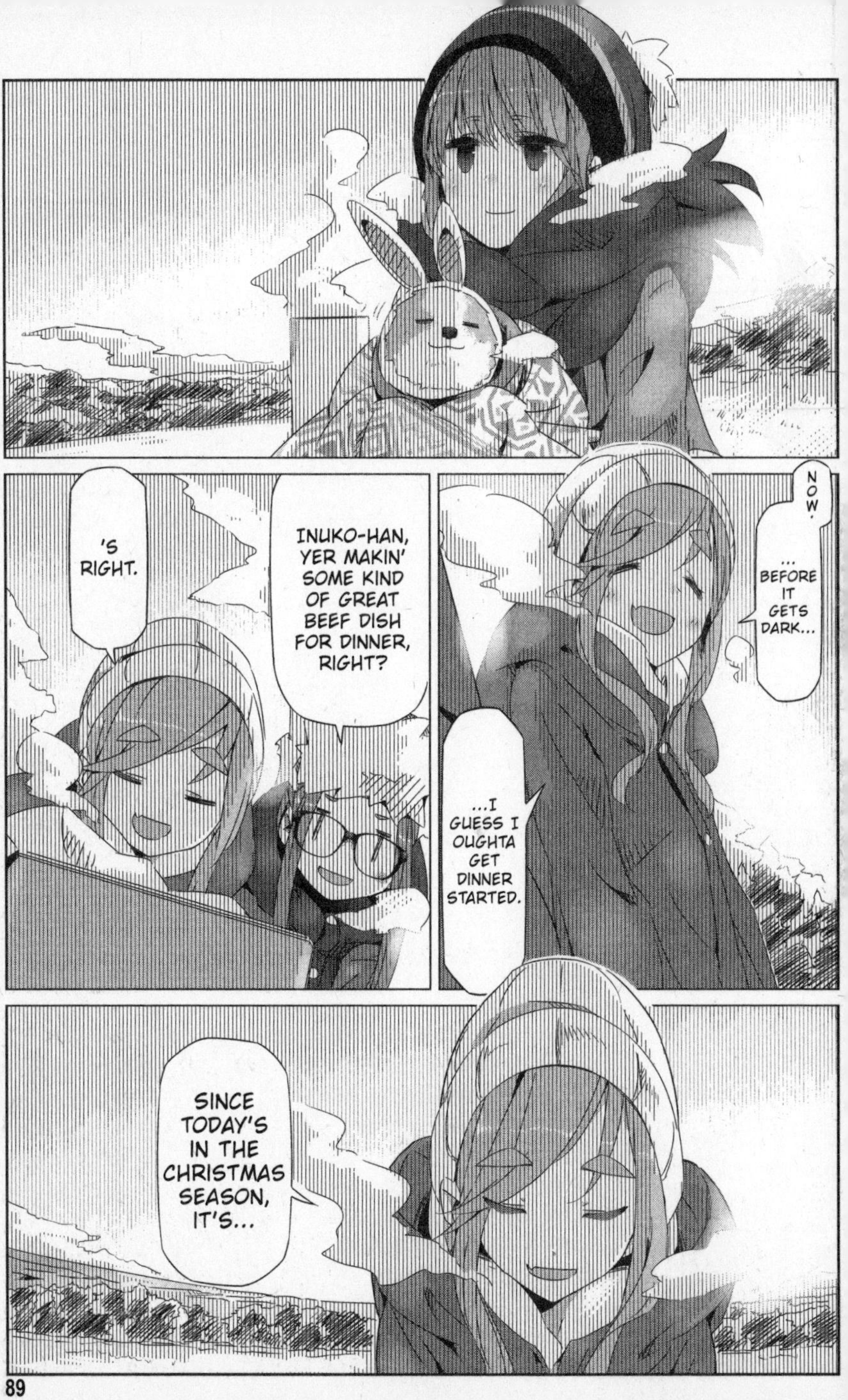
NOW.
...BEFORE IT GETS DARK...
...I GUESS I OUGHTA GET DINNER STARTED.
INUKO-HAN, YER MAKIN' SOME KIND OF GREAT BEEF DISH FOR DINNER, RIGHT?
'S RIGHT.
SINCE TODAY'S IN THE CHRISTMAS SEASON, IT'S...

...SUKIYAKI!
SEARED TOFU
SUKIYAKI...
SUKIYAKI......
SUKIYAKI......
SUKIYAKI ......?
EVEN THOUGH IT'S FOR CHRISTMAS?
WHY SUKIYAKI???
IT IS GOOD, BUT...
HF-CHOO !!

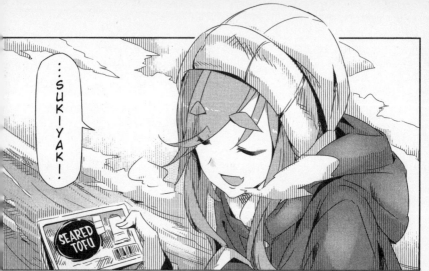

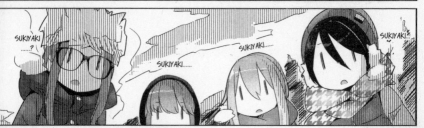

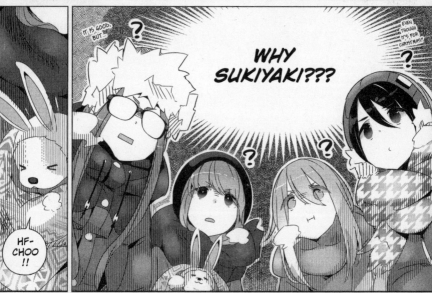

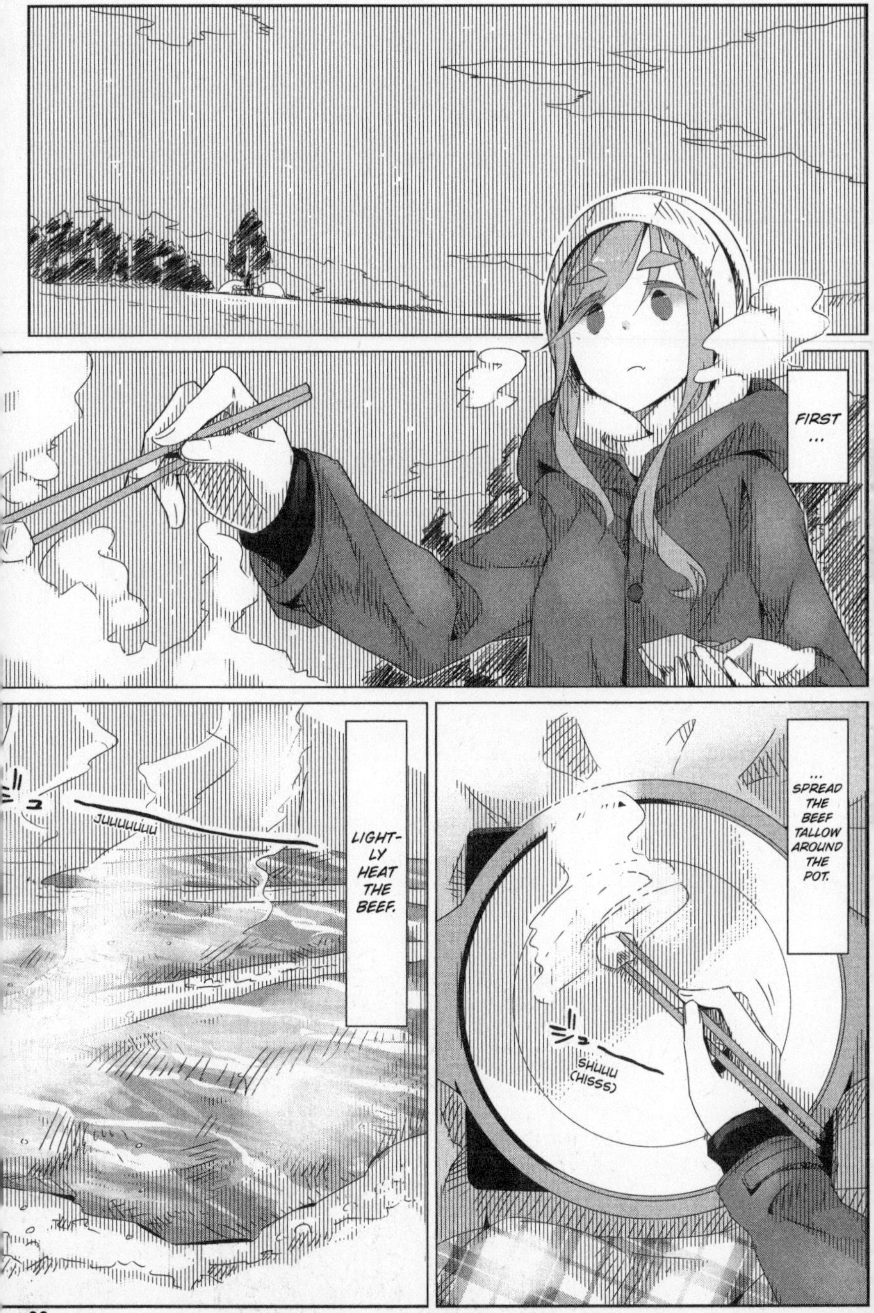
FIRST...
... SPREAD THE BEEF TALLOW AROUND THE POT.
SHUUU (HISSS)
LIGHT-LY HEAT THE BEEF.
JUUUUUUU

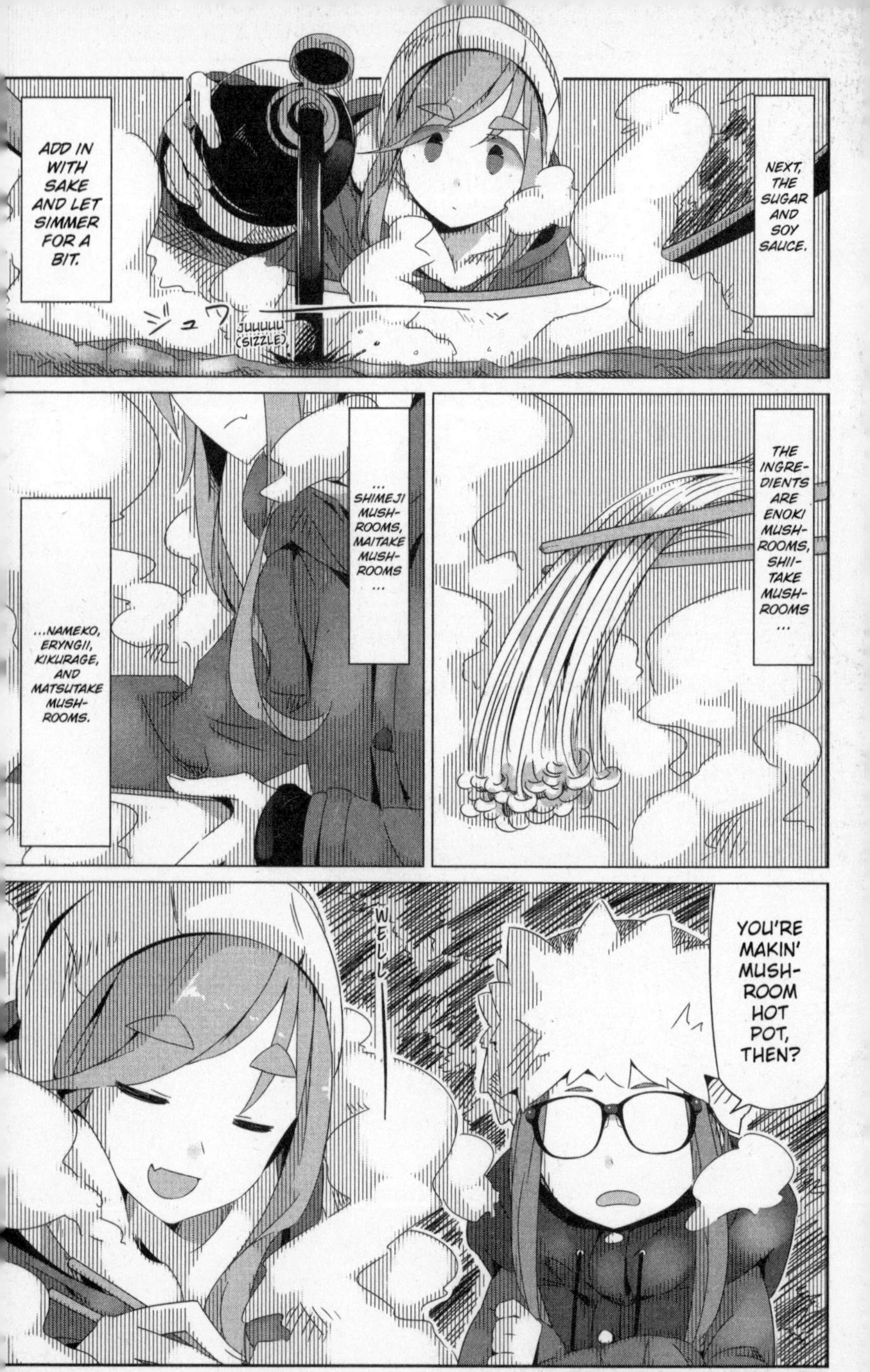
NEXT, THE SUGAR AND SOY SAUCE.
ADD IN WITH SAKE AND LET SIMMER FOR A BIT.
JUUUUU (SIZZLE)
THE INGREDIENTS ARE ENOKI MUSHROOMS, SHIITAKE MUSHROOMS...
...SHIMEJI MUSHROOMS, MAITAKE MUSHROOMS...
...NAMEKO, ERYNGII, KIKURAGE, AND MATSUTAKE MUSHROOMS.
YOU'RE MAKIN' MUSHROOM HOT POT, THEN?
WELL

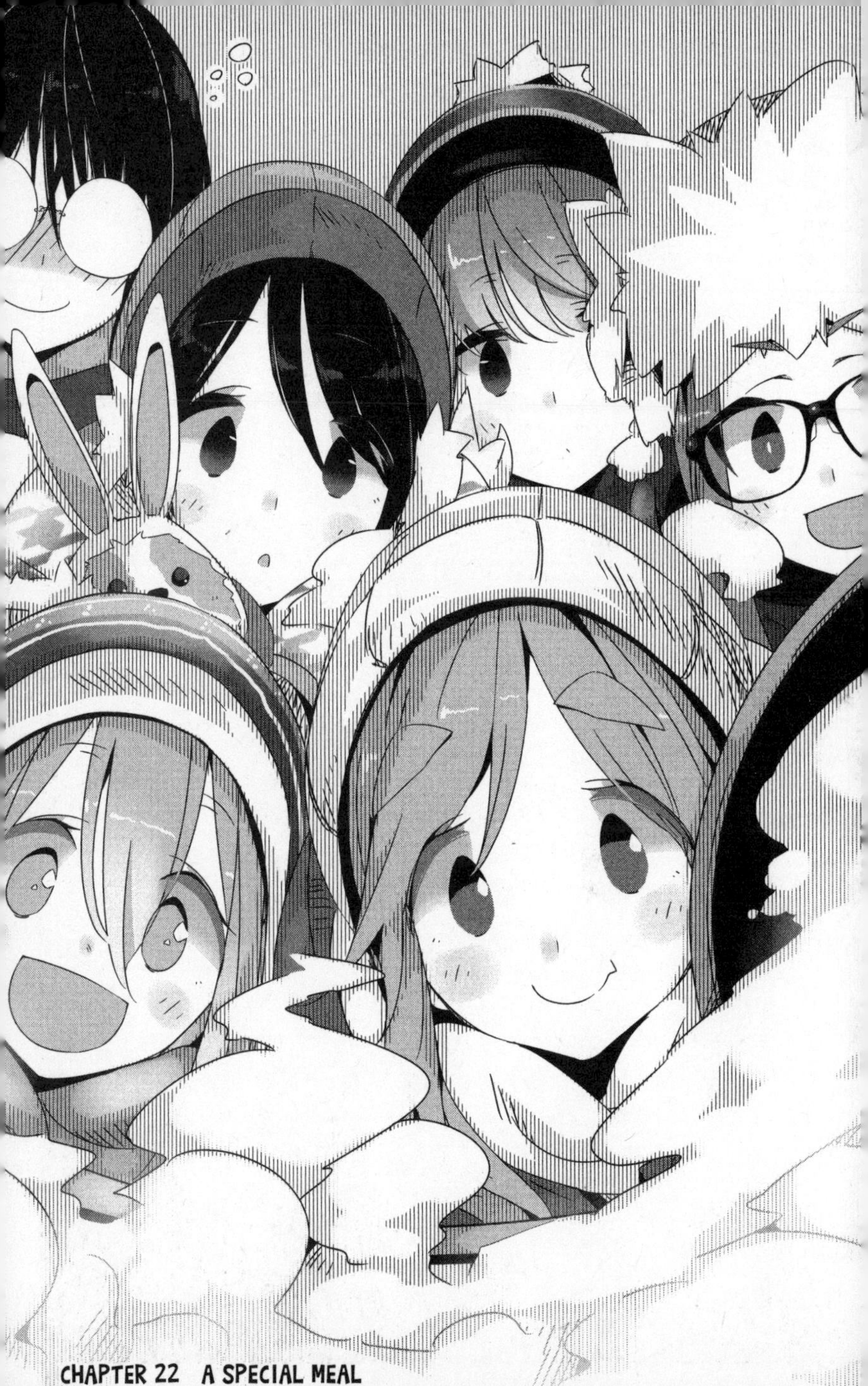

CHAPTER 22 A SPECIAL MEAL

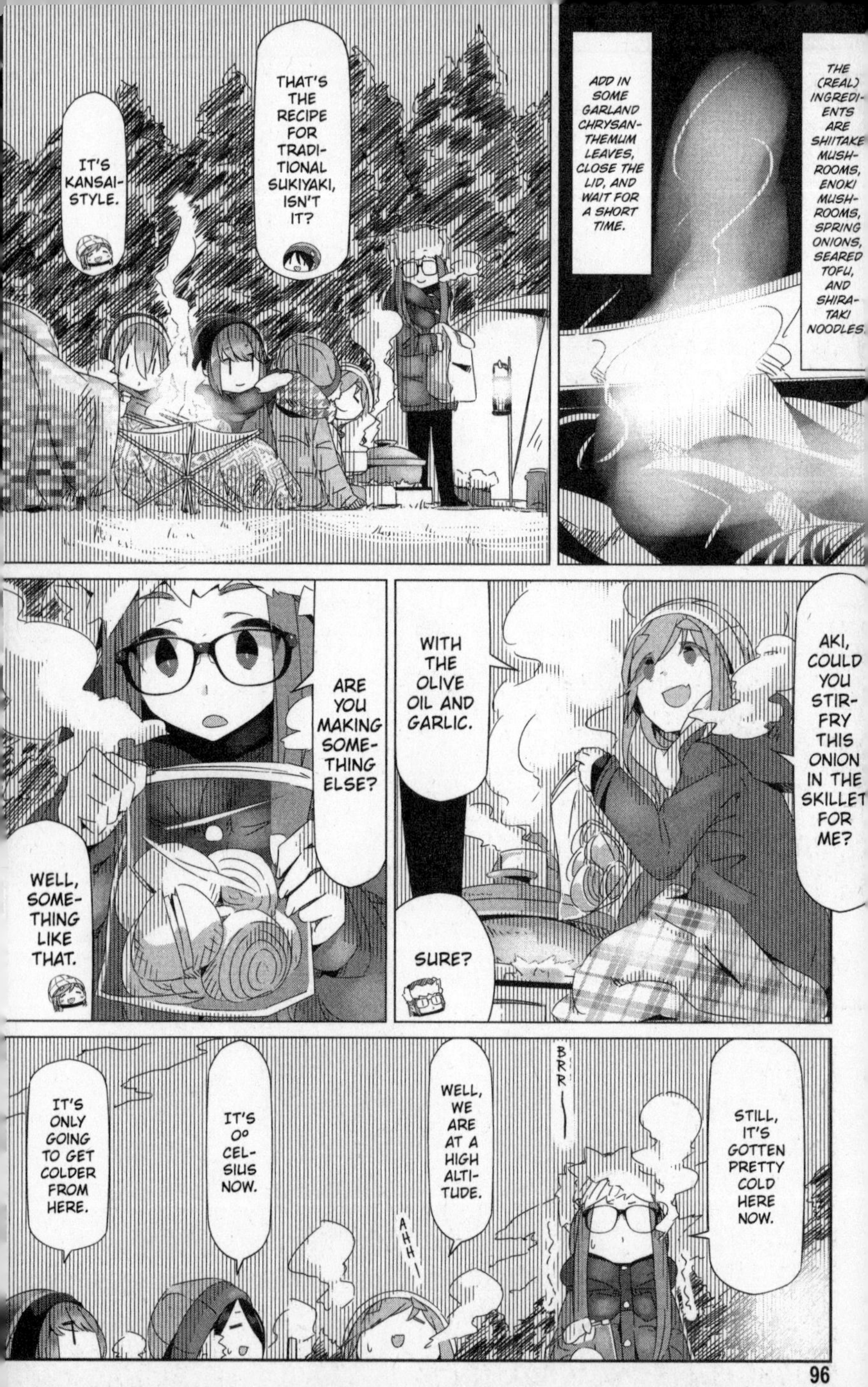
THE (REAL) INGREDIENTS ARE SHIITAKE MUSHROOMS, ENOKI MUSHROOMS, SPRING ONIONS, SEARED TOFU, AND SHIRATAKI NOODLES.
ADD IN SOME GARLAND CHRYSANTHEMUM LEAVES, CLOSE THE LID, AND WAIT FOR A SHORT TIME.
THAT'S THE RECIPE FOR TRADITIONAL SUKIYAKI, ISN'T IT?
IT'S KANSAI-STYLE.
AKI, COULD YOU STIR-FRY THIS ONION IN THE SKILLET FOR ME?
WITH THE OLIVE OIL AND GARLIC.
SURE?
ARE YOU MAKING SOMETHING ELSE?
WELL, SOMETHING LIKE THAT.
STILL, IT'S GOTTEN PRETTY COLD HERE NOW.
BRR
WELL, WE ARE AT A HIGH ALTITUDE.
AHH
IT'S 0° CELSIUS NOW.
IT'S ONLY GOING TO GET COLDER FROM HERE.

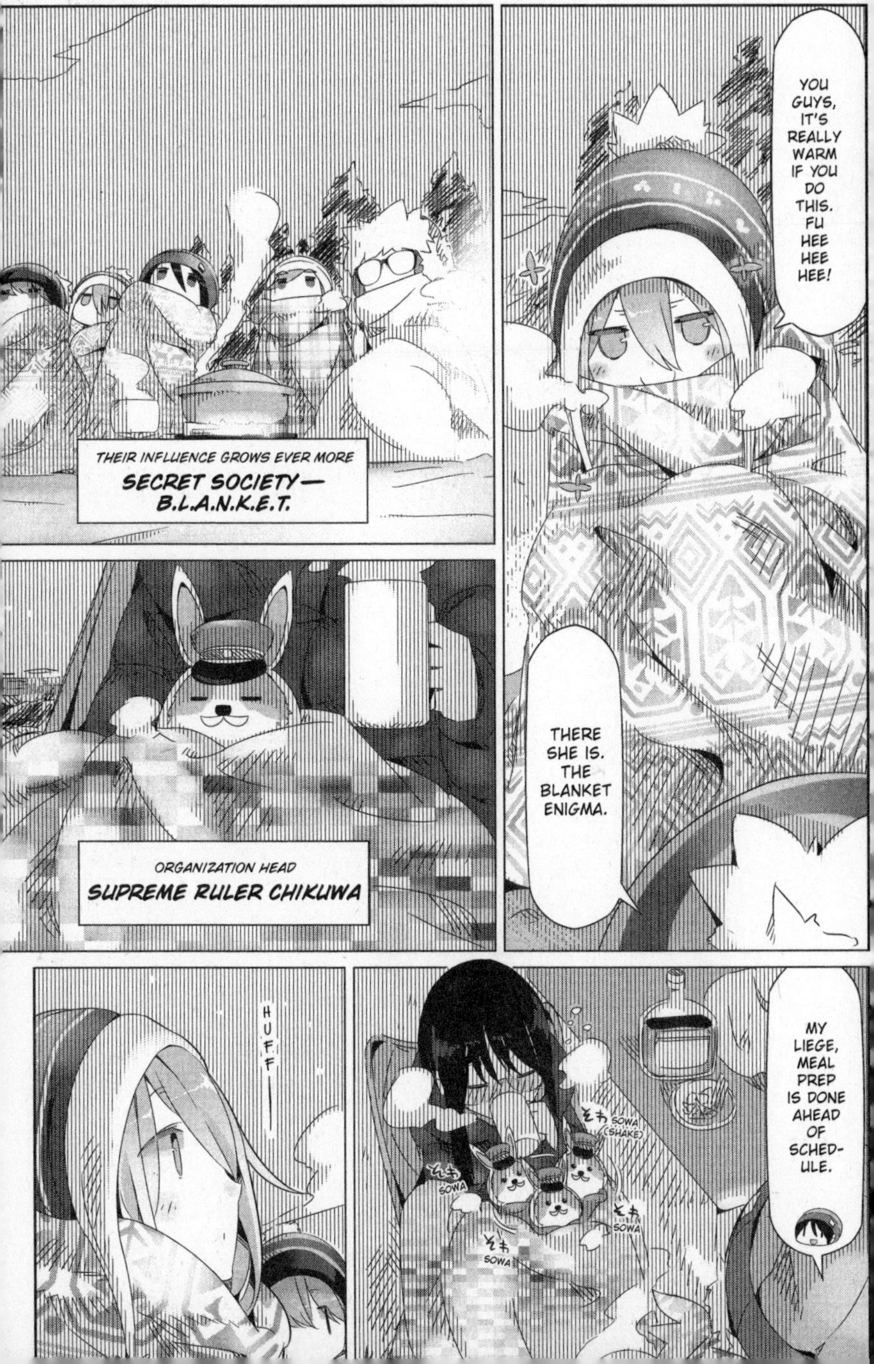
YOU GUYS, IT'S REALLY WARM IF YOU DO THIS. FU HEE HEE HEE!
THERE SHE IS. THE BLANKET ENIGMA.
THEIR INFLUENCE GROWS EVER MORE
SECRET SOCIETY— B.L.A.N.K.E.T.
ORGANIZATION HEAD
SUPREME RULER CHIKUWA
MY LIEGE, MEAL PREP IS DONE AHEAD OF SCHED-ULE.
SOWA (SHAKE)
SOWA
SOWA
SOWA
HUFF—

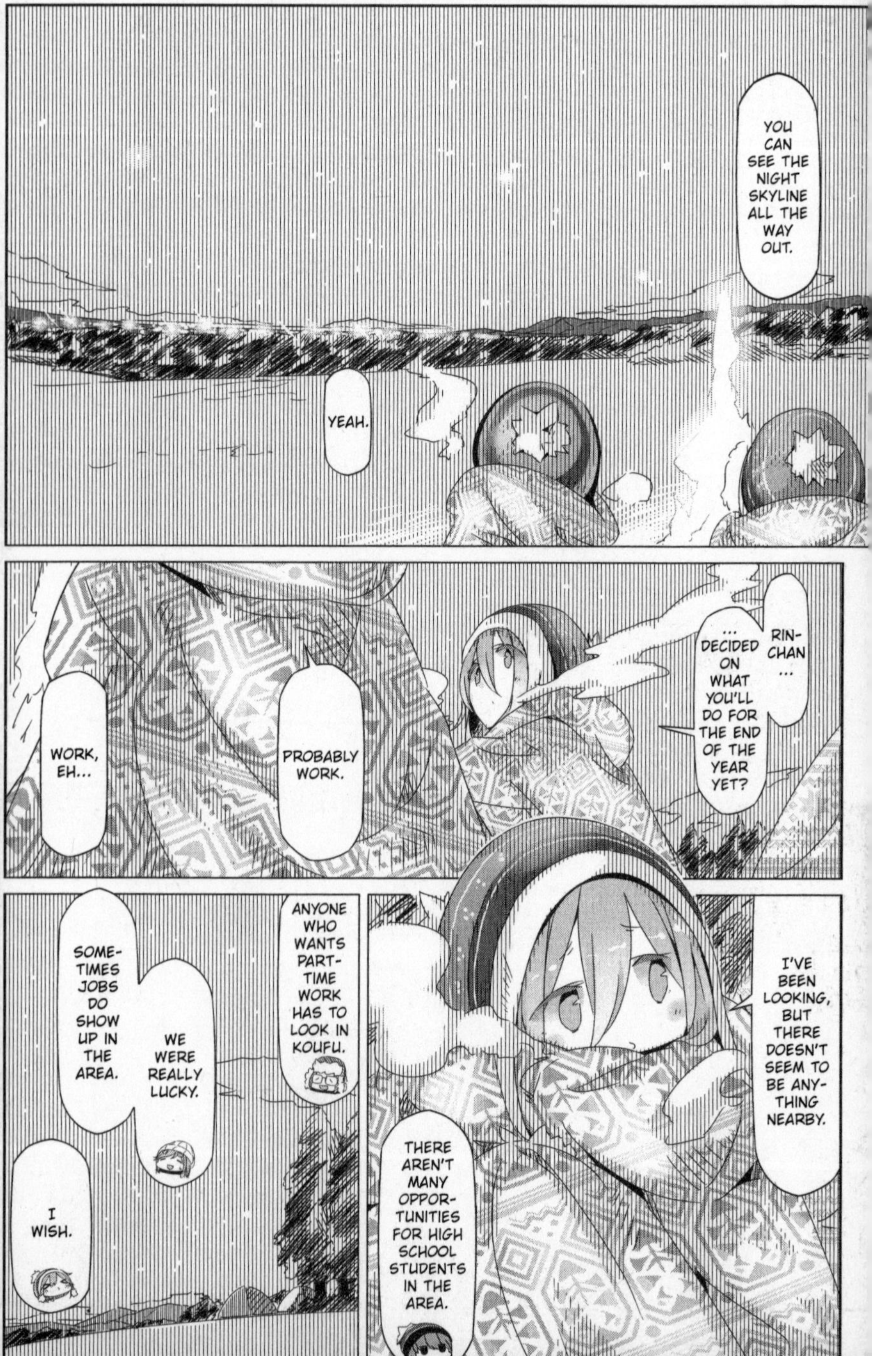
YOU CAN SEE THE NIGHT SKYLINE ALL THE WAY OUT.
YEAH.
RIN-CHAN...
...DECIDED ON WHAT YOU'LL DO FOR THE END OF THE YEAR YET?
PROBABLY WORK.
WORK, EH...
I'VE BEEN LOOKING, BUT THERE DOESN'T SEEM TO BE ANY-THING NEARBY.
THERE AREN'T MANY OPPOR-TUNITIES FOR HIGH SCHOOL STUDENTS IN THE AREA.
ANYONE WHO WANTS PART-TIME WORK HAS TO LOOK IN KOUFU.
SOME-TIMES JOBS DO SHOW UP IN THE AREA.
WE WERE REALLY LUCKY.
I WISH.

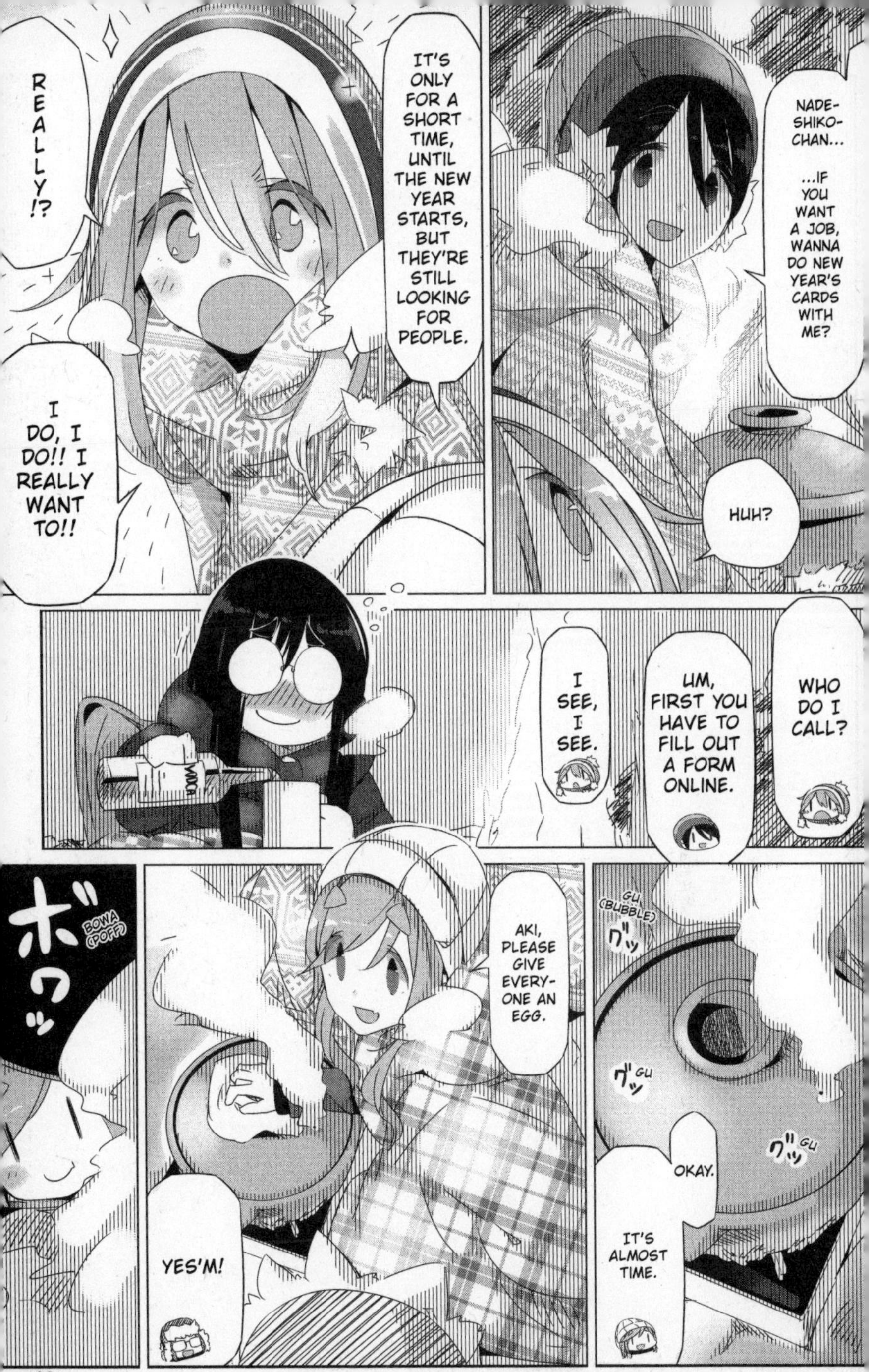
NADE-SHIKO-CHAN...
...IF YOU WANT A JOB, WANNA DO NEW YEAR'S CARDS WITH ME?
HUH?
IT'S ONLY FOR A SHORT TIME, UNTIL THE NEW YEAR STARTS, BUT THEY'RE STILL LOOKING FOR PEOPLE.
REALLY!?
I DO, I DO!! I REALLY WANT TO!!
WHO DO I CALL?
UM, FIRST YOU HAVE TO FILL OUT A FORM ONLINE.
I SEE, I SEE.
グッ GU (BUBBLE)
グッ GU
グッ GU
OKAY.
IT'S ALMOST TIME.
AKI, PLEASE GIVE EVERY-ONE AN EGG.
YES'M!
ボワッ BOWA (POFF)

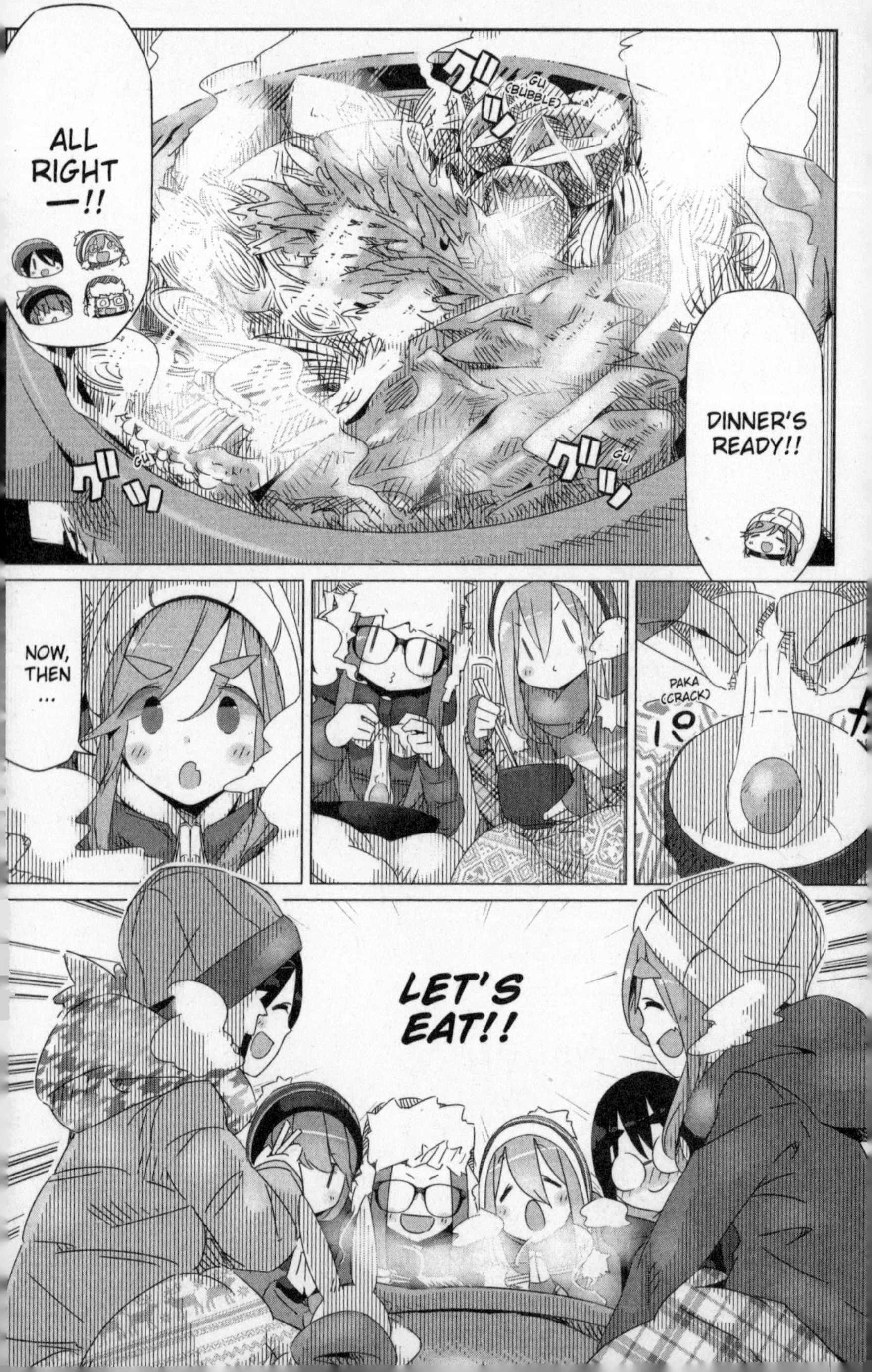
DINNER'S READY!!
GU (BUBBLE)
GU
GU
ALL RIGHT—!!
PAKA (CRACK)
NOW, THEN ...
LET'S EAT!!

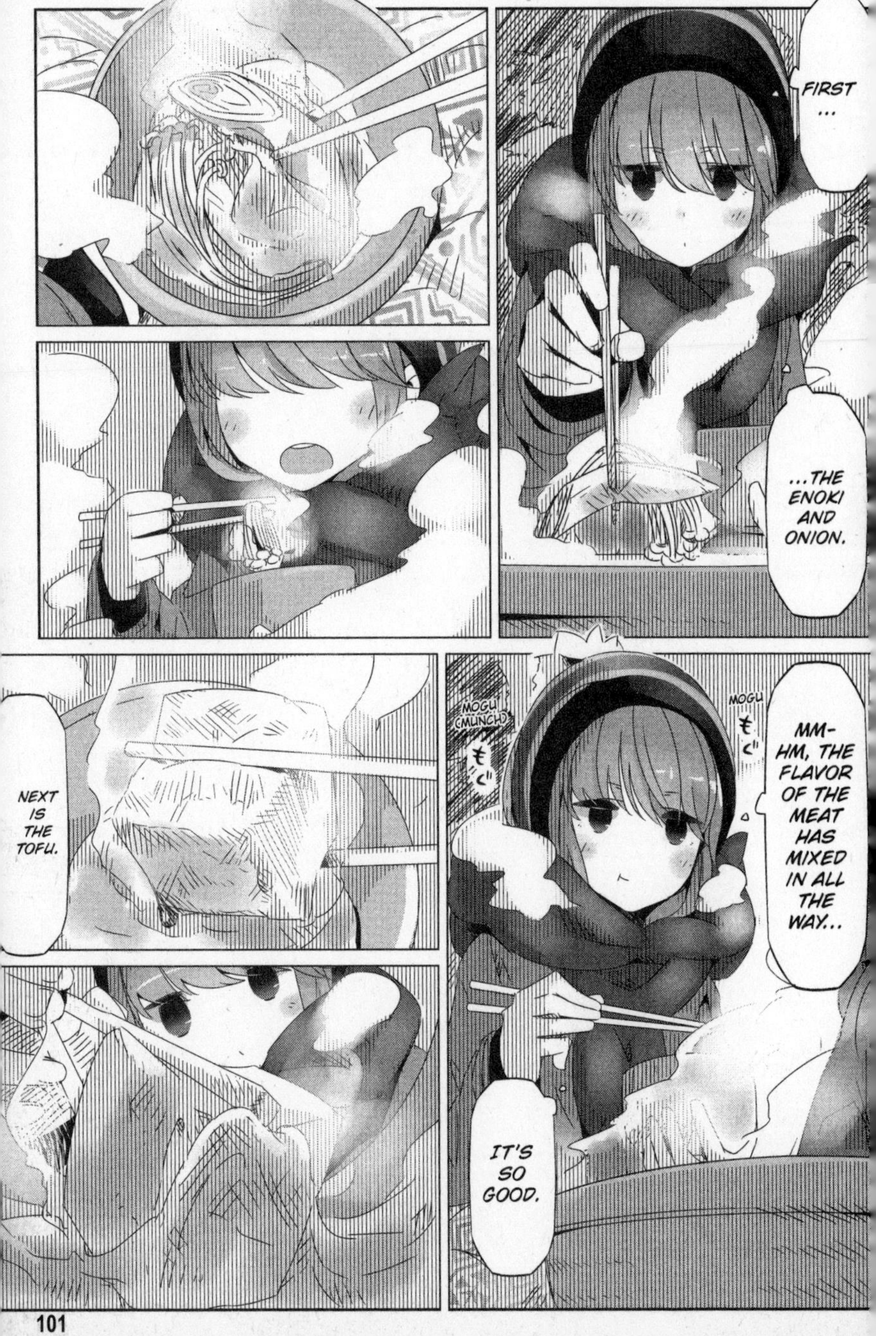
FIRST ...
...THE ENOKI AND ONION.
MM-HM, THE FLAVOR OF THE MEAT HAS MIXED IN ALL THE WAY...
MOGU もぐ
MOGU (MUNCH) もぐ
IT'S SO GOOD.
NEXT IS THE TOFU.

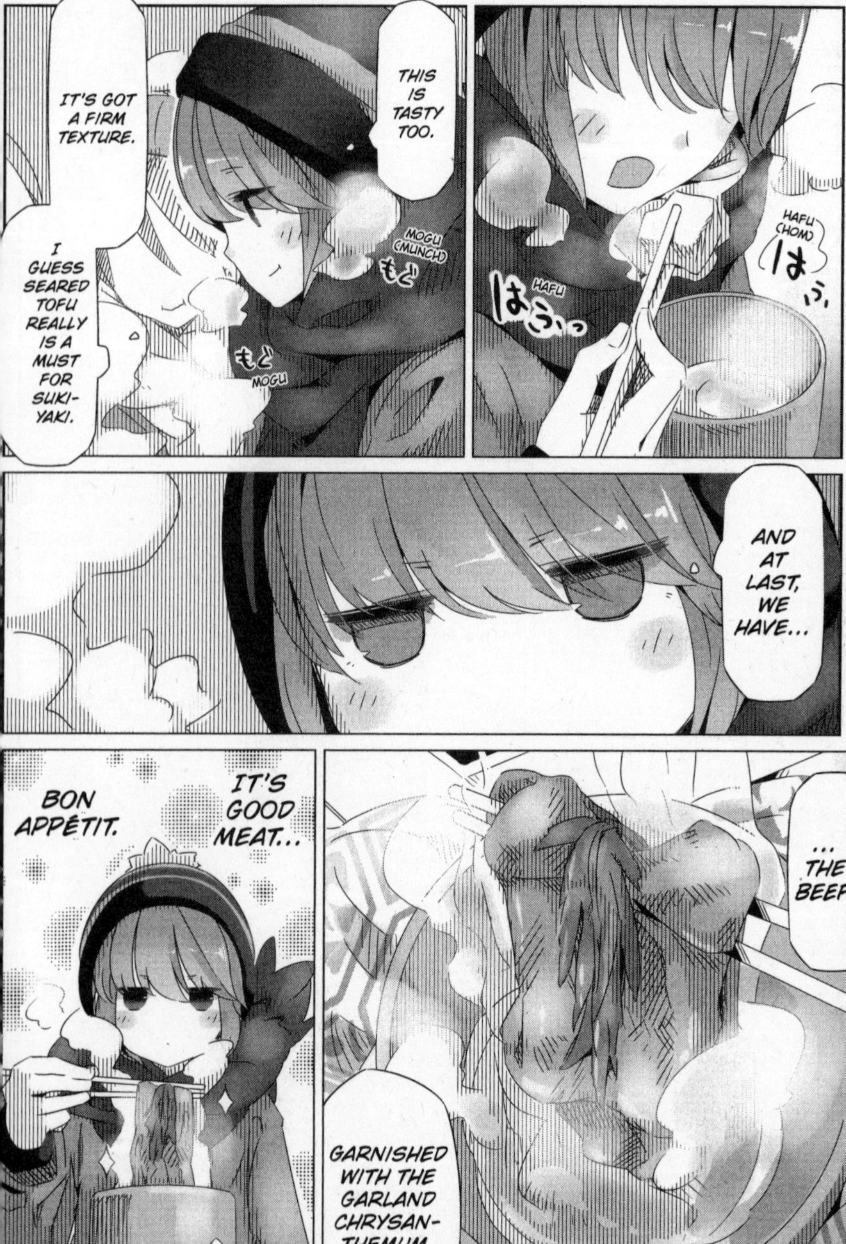
HAFU (CHOM)
はふ
HAFU
はふっ
THIS IS TASTY TOO.
IT'S GOT A FIRM TEXTURE.
I GUESS SEARED TOFU REALLY IS A MUST FOR SUKI-YAKI.
MOGU (MUNCH)
もぐ
もぐ
MOGU
AND AT LAST, WE HAVE...
... THE BEEF.
GARNISHED WITH THE GARLAND CHRYSAN-THEMUM.
IT'S GOOD MEAT...
BON APPÉTIT.

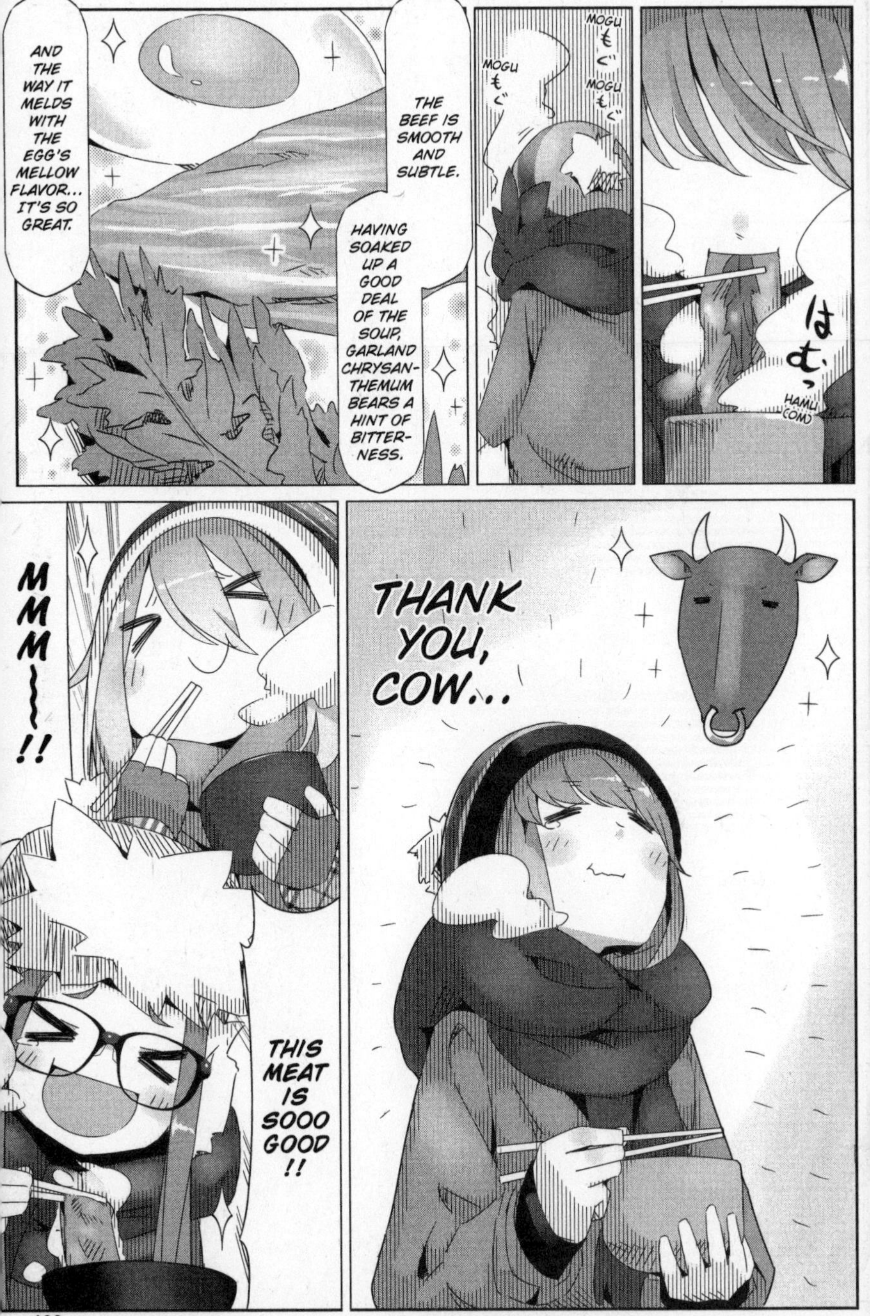
はむっ
HAMU
(OM)
もぐ もぐ もぐ
MOGU MOGU MOGU
THE BEEF IS SMOOTH AND SUBTLE.
HAVING SOAKED UP A GOOD DEAL OF THE SOUP, GARLAND CHRYSANTHEMUM BEARS A HINT OF BITTERNESS.
AND THE WAY IT MELDS WITH THE EGG'S MELLOW FLAVOR... IT'S SO GREAT.
THANK YOU, COW...
MMM~~!!
THIS MEAT IS SOOO GOOD!!

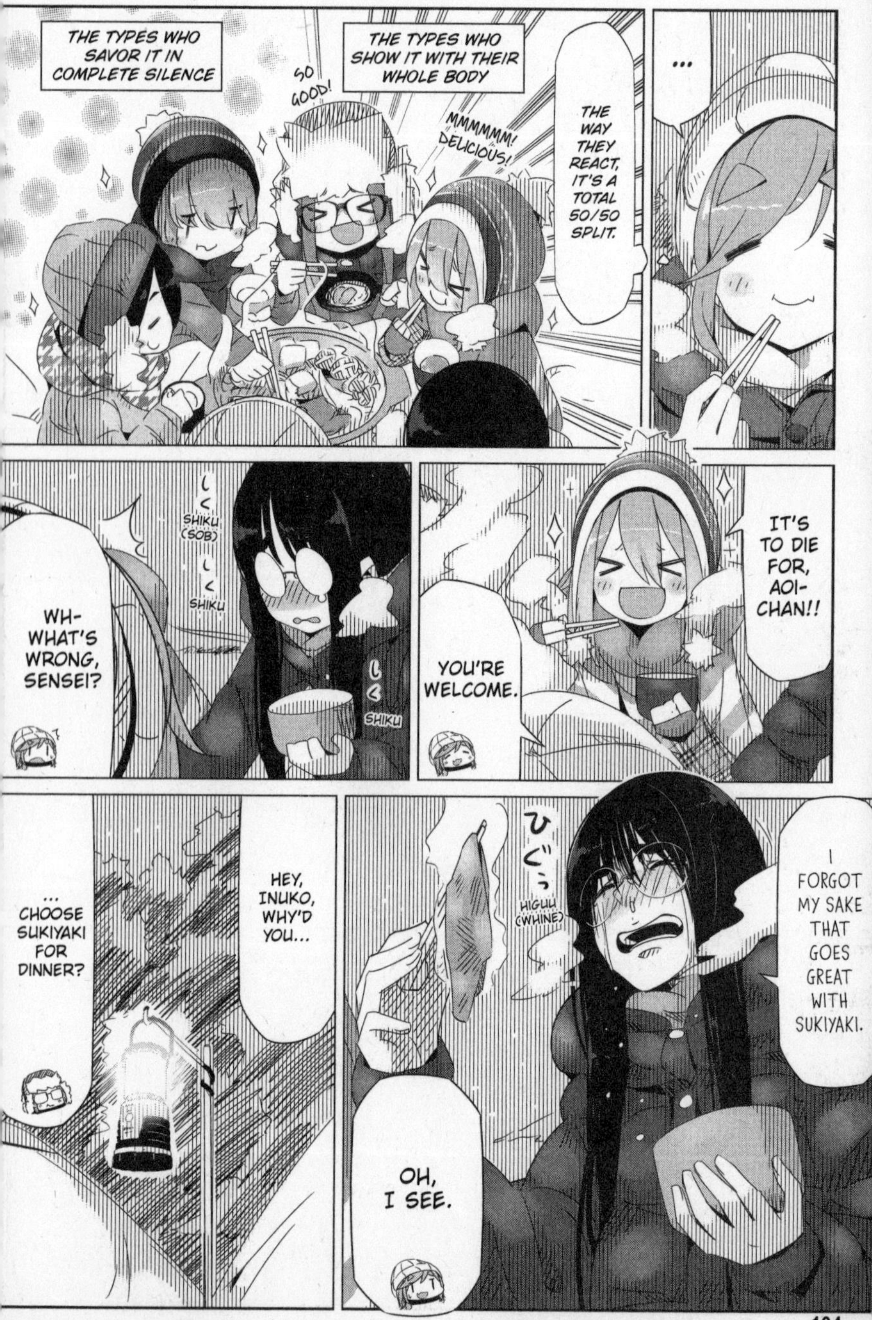
...
THE WAY THEY REACT, IT'S A TOTAL 50/50 SPLIT.
THE TYPES WHO SHOW IT WITH THEIR WHOLE BODY
MMMMMM! DELICIOUS!
SO GOOD!
THE TYPES WHO SAVOR IT IN COMPLETE SILENCE
IT'S TO DIE FOR, AOI-CHAN!!
YOU'RE WELCOME.
しく
SHIKU (SOB)
しく
SHIKU
しく
SHIKU
WH-WHAT'S WRONG, SENSEI?
I FORGOT MY SAKE THAT GOES GREAT WITH SUKIYAKI.
ひぐっ
HIGUU (WHINE)
OH, I SEE.
HEY, INUKO, WHY'D YOU...
...CHOOSE SUKIYAKI FOR DINNER?

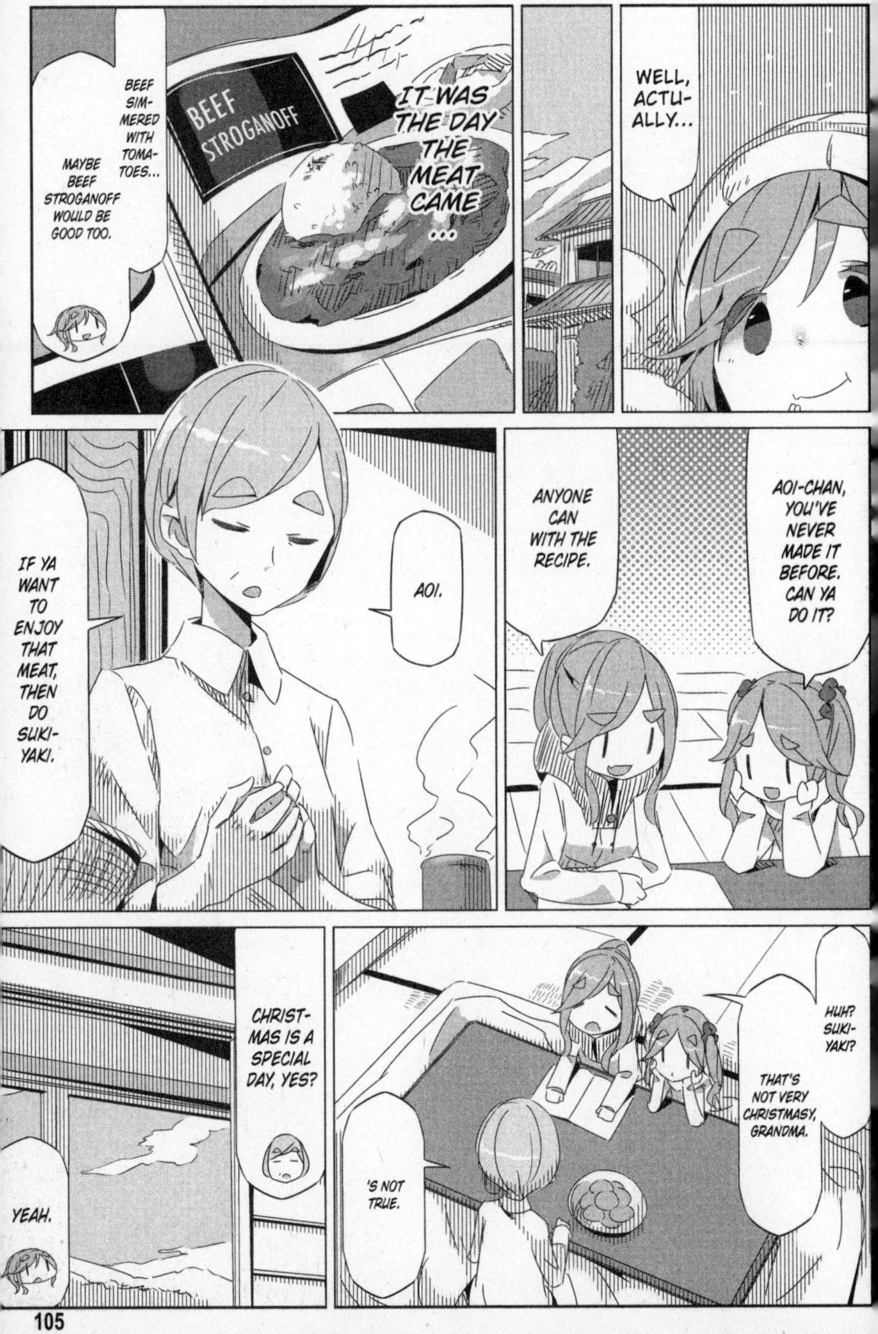
WELL, ACTUALLY...
IT WAS THE DAY THE MEAT CAME...
BEEF STROGANOFF
BEEF SIMMERED WITH TOMATOES...
MAYBE BEEF STROGANOFF WOULD BE GOOD TOO.
AOI-CHAN, YOU'VE NEVER MADE IT BEFORE. CAN YA DO IT?
ANYONE CAN WITH THE RECIPE.
AOI.
IF YA WANT TO ENJOY THAT MEAT, THEN DO SUKIYAKI.
HUH? SUKIYAKI?
THAT'S NOT VERY CHRISTMASY, GRANDMA.
'S NOT TRUE.
CHRISTMAS IS A SPECIAL DAY, YES?
YEAH.

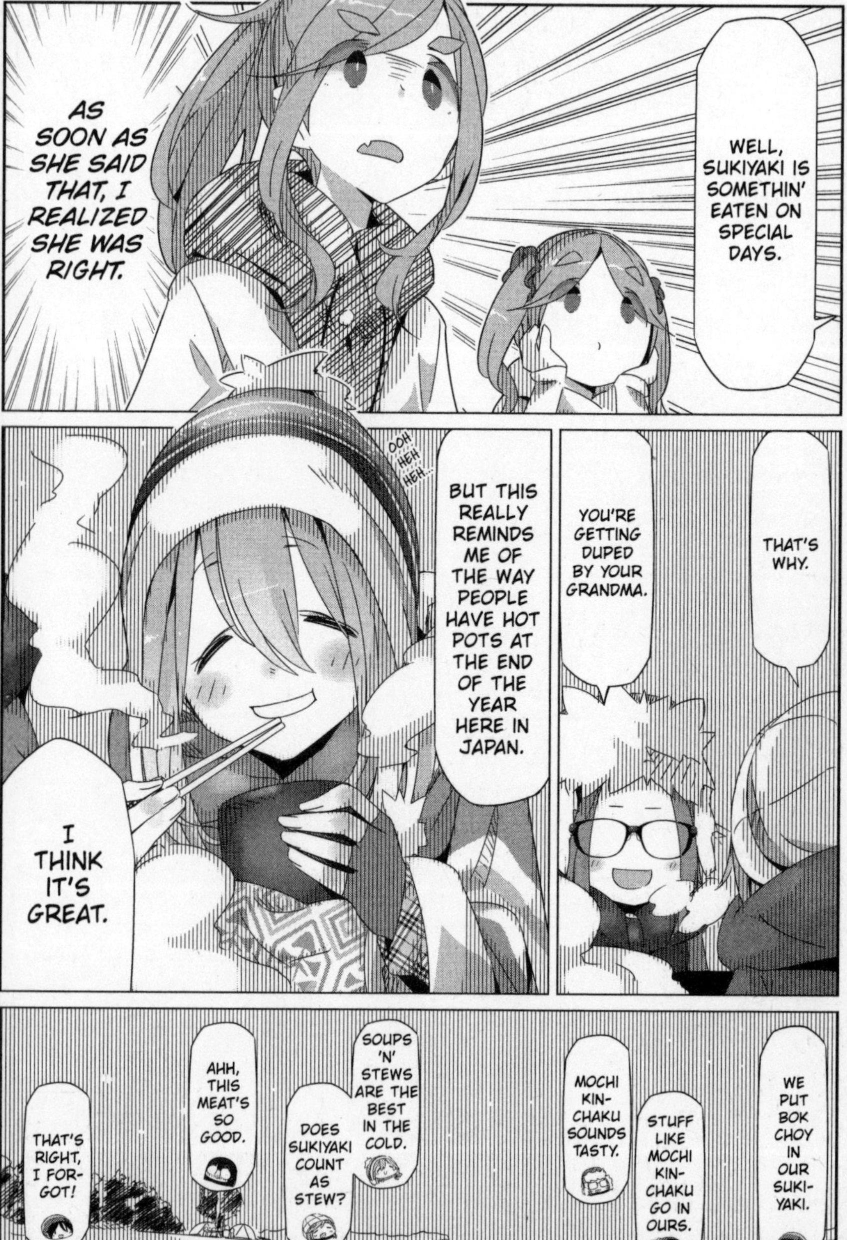
WELL, SUKIYAKI IS SOMETHIN' EATEN ON SPECIAL DAYS.
AS SOON AS SHE SAID THAT, I REALIZED SHE WAS RIGHT.
THAT'S WHY.
YOU'RE GETTING DUPED BY YOUR GRANDMA.
OOH HEH HEH...
BUT THIS REALLY REMINDS ME OF THE WAY PEOPLE HAVE HOT POTS AT THE END OF THE YEAR HERE IN JAPAN.
I THINK IT'S GREAT.
WE PUT BOK CHOY IN OUR SUKI-YAKI.
STUFF LIKE MOCHI KIN-CHAKU GO IN OURS.
MOCHI KIN-CHAKU SOUNDS TASTY.
SOUPS 'N' STEWS ARE THE BEST IN THE COLD.
DOES SUKIYAKI COUNT AS STEW?
AHH, THIS MEAT'S SO GOOD.
THAT'S RIGHT, I FOR-GOT!

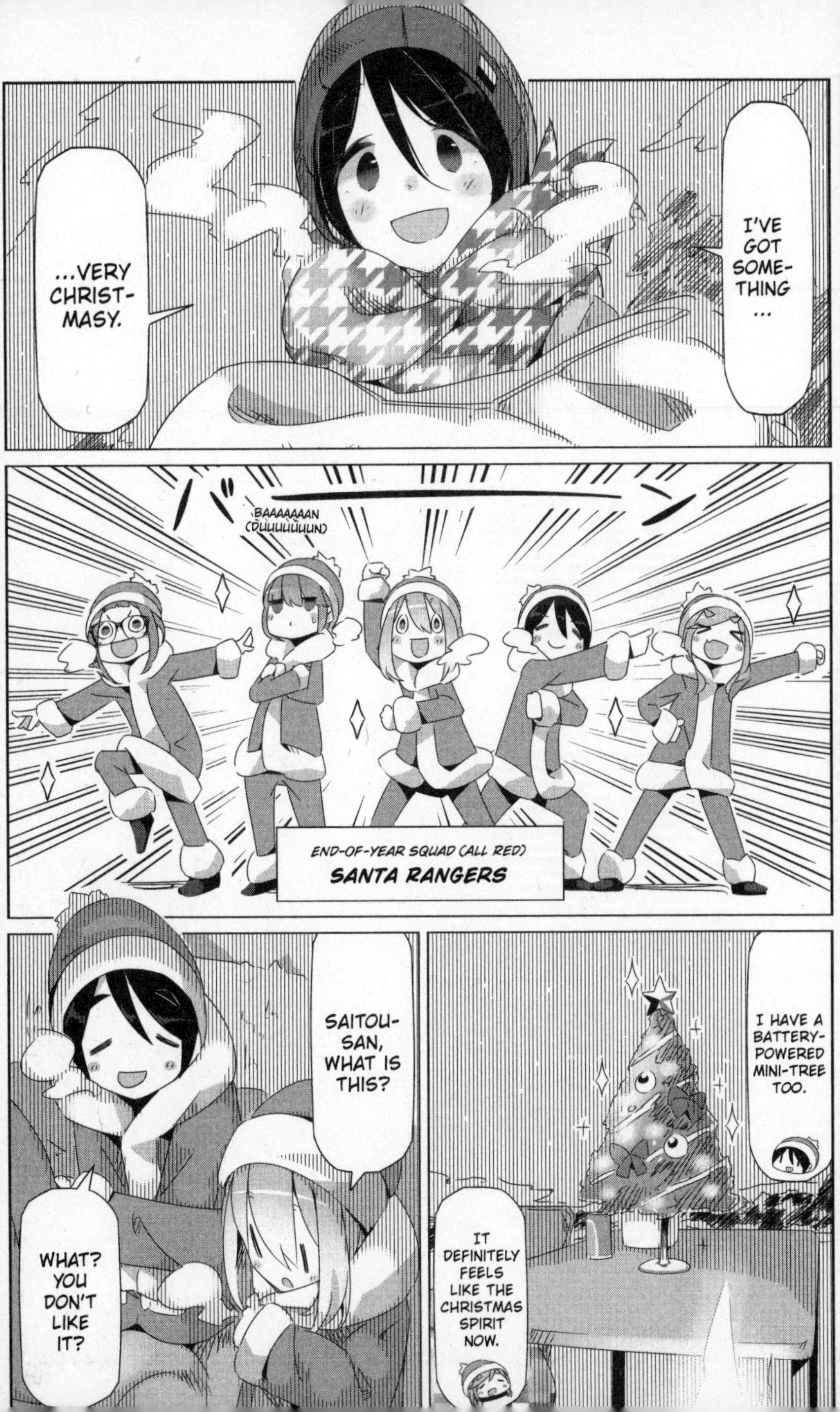
I'VE GOT SOMETHING...
...VERY CHRISTMASY.
BAAAAAAAN (DUUUUUUUN)
END-OF-YEAR SQUAD (ALL RED)
SANTA RANGERS
I HAVE A BATTERY-POWERED MINI-TREE TOO.
IT DEFINITELY FEELS LIKE THE CHRISTMAS SPIRIT NOW.
SAITOU-SAN, WHAT IS THIS?
WHAT? YOU DON'T LIKE IT?

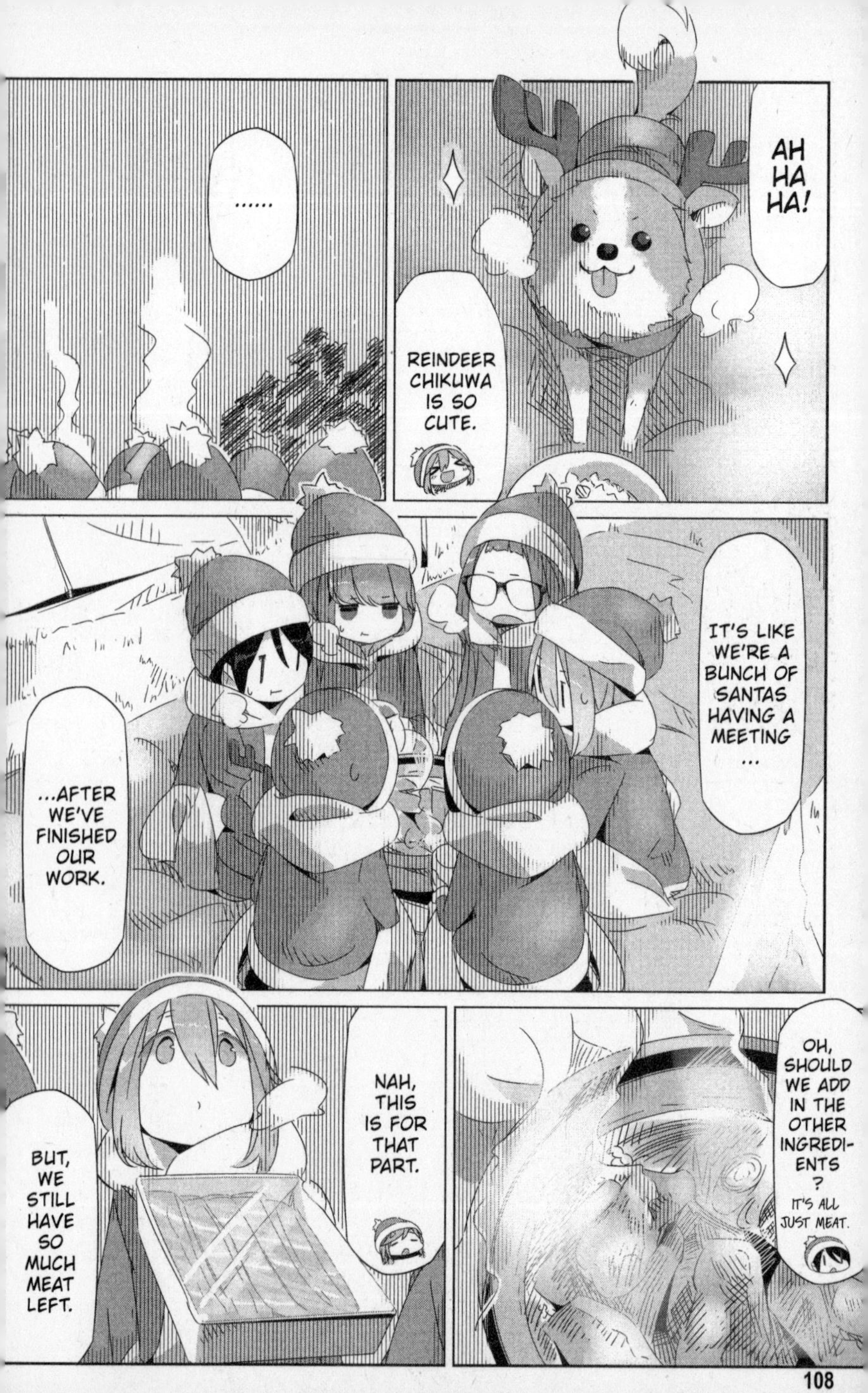
AH HA HA!
REINDEER CHIKUWA IS SO CUTE.
......
IT'S LIKE WE'RE A BUNCH OF SANTAS HAVING A MEETING ...
...AFTER WE'VE FINISHED OUR WORK.
OH, SHOULD WE ADD IN THE OTHER INGREDI-ENTS ?
IT'S ALL JUST MEAT.
NAH, THIS IS FOR THAT PART.
BUT, WE STILL HAVE SO MUCH MEAT LEFT.

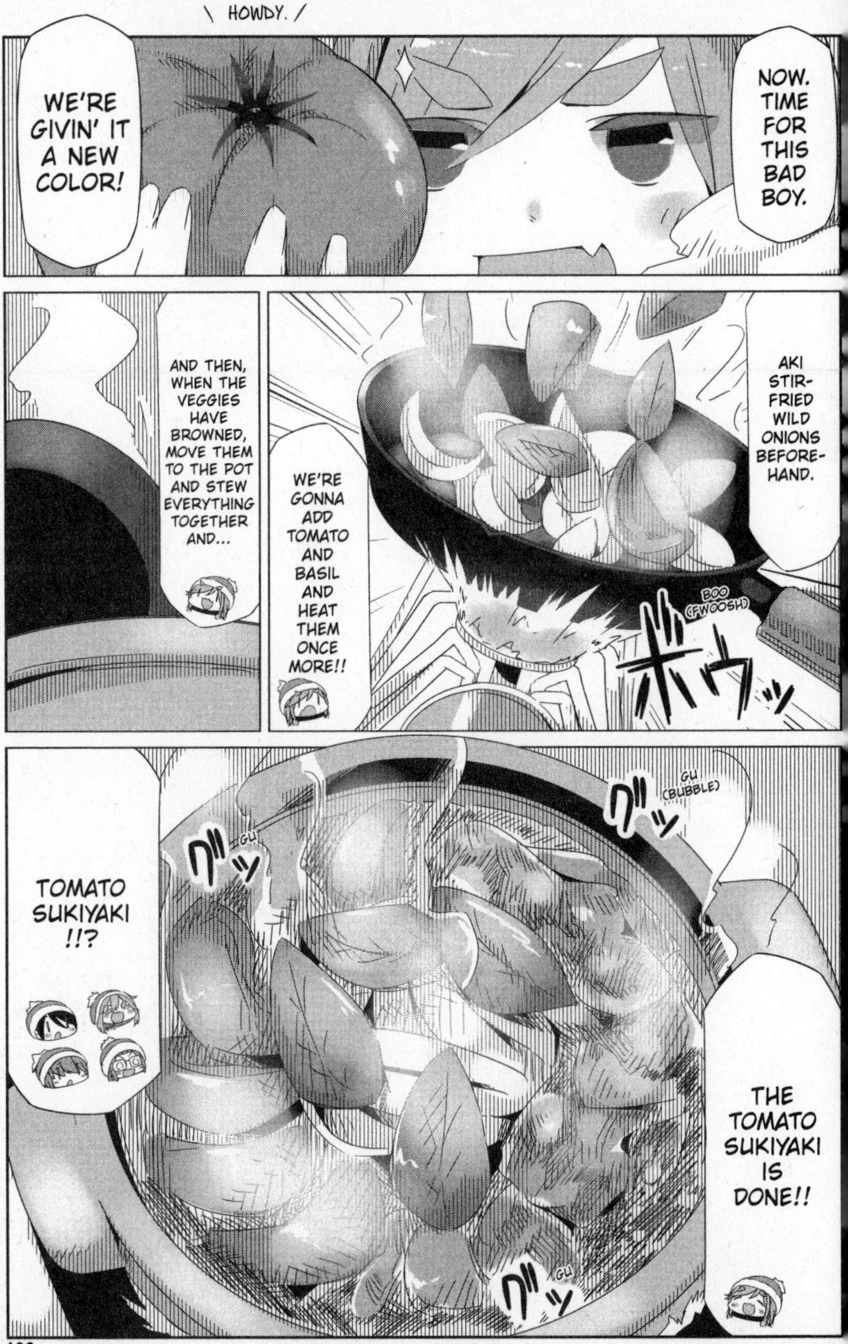
\ HOWDY. /
NOW. TIME FOR THIS BAD BOY.
WE'RE GIVIN' IT A NEW COLOR!
AKI STIR-FRIED WILD ONIONS BEFORE-HAND.
WE'RE GONNA ADD TOMATO AND BASIL AND HEAT THEM ONCE MORE!!
BOO (FWOOSH)
ボウッ
AND THEN, WHEN THE VEGGIES HAVE BROWNED, MOVE THEM TO THE POT AND STEW EVERYTHING TOGETHER AND...
GU (BUBBLE)
グッ
THE TOMATO SUKIYAKI IS DONE!!
GU
グッ
TOMATO SUKIYAKI!!?
GU
グッ

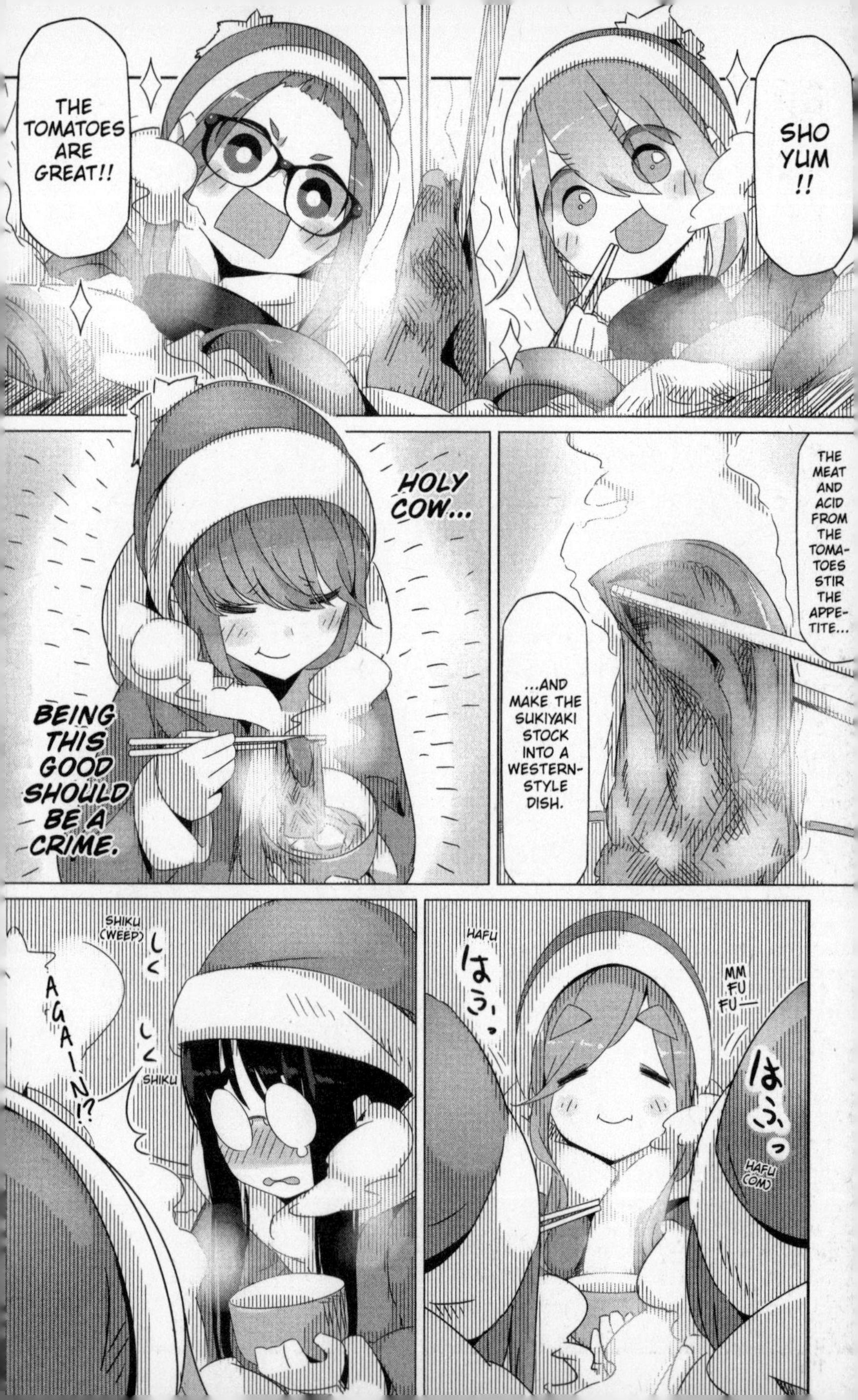
SHO YUM !!
THE TOMATOES ARE GREAT!!
THE MEAT AND ACID FROM THE TOMA-TOES STIR THE APPE-TITE...
...AND MAKE THE SUKIYAKI STOCK INTO A WESTERN-STYLE DISH.
HOLY COW...
BEING THIS GOOD SHOULD BE A CRIME.
HAFU
はふっ
MM FU FU—
はふっ
HAFU (OM)
SHIKU (WEEP)
しく
しく
SHIKU
AGAIN!?

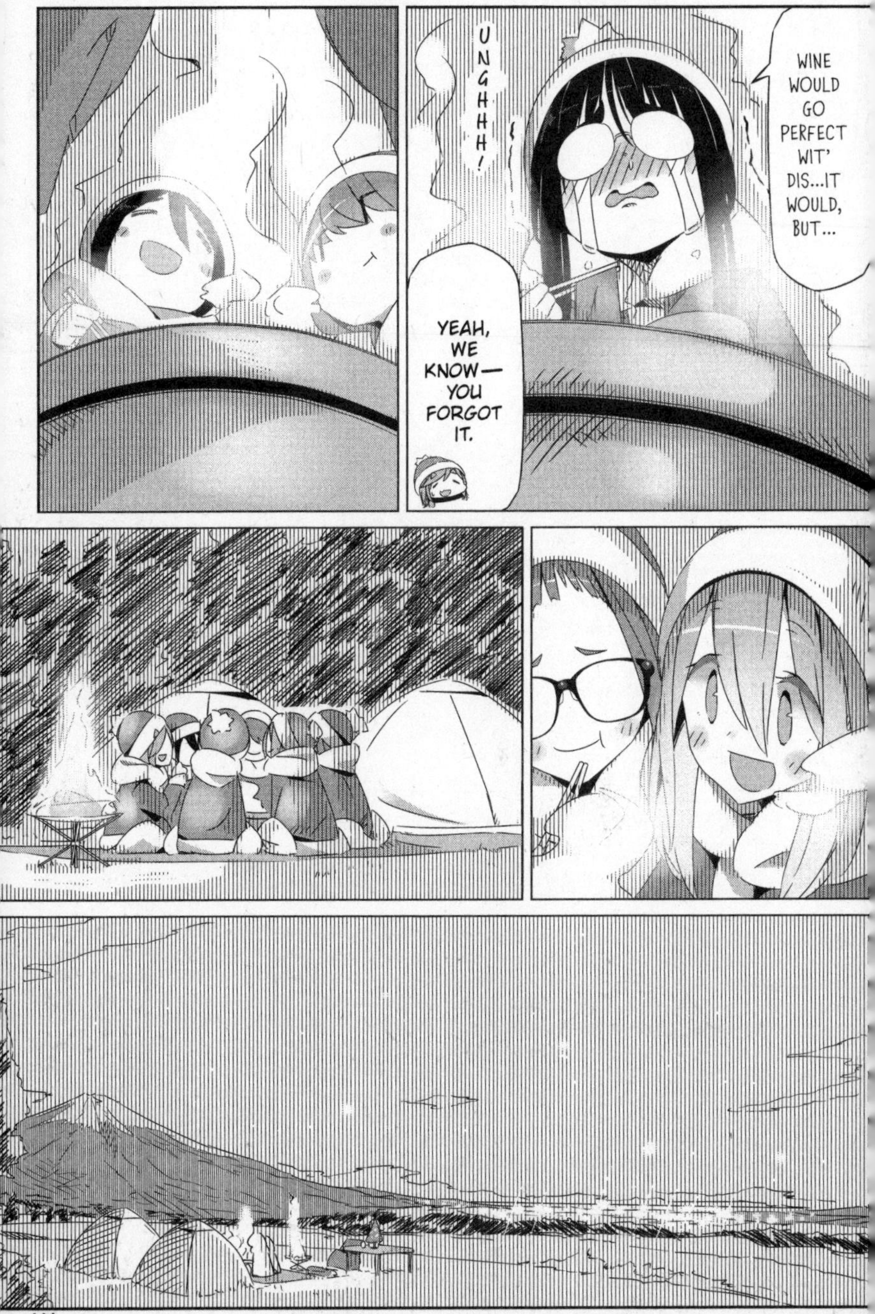
WINE WOULD GO PERFECT WIT' DIS...IT WOULD, BUT...
UNGHHH!
YEAH, WE KNOW— YOU FORGOT IT.

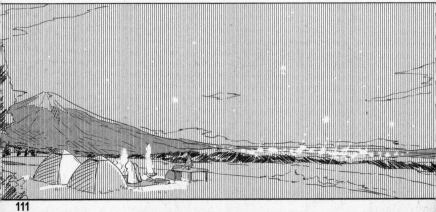

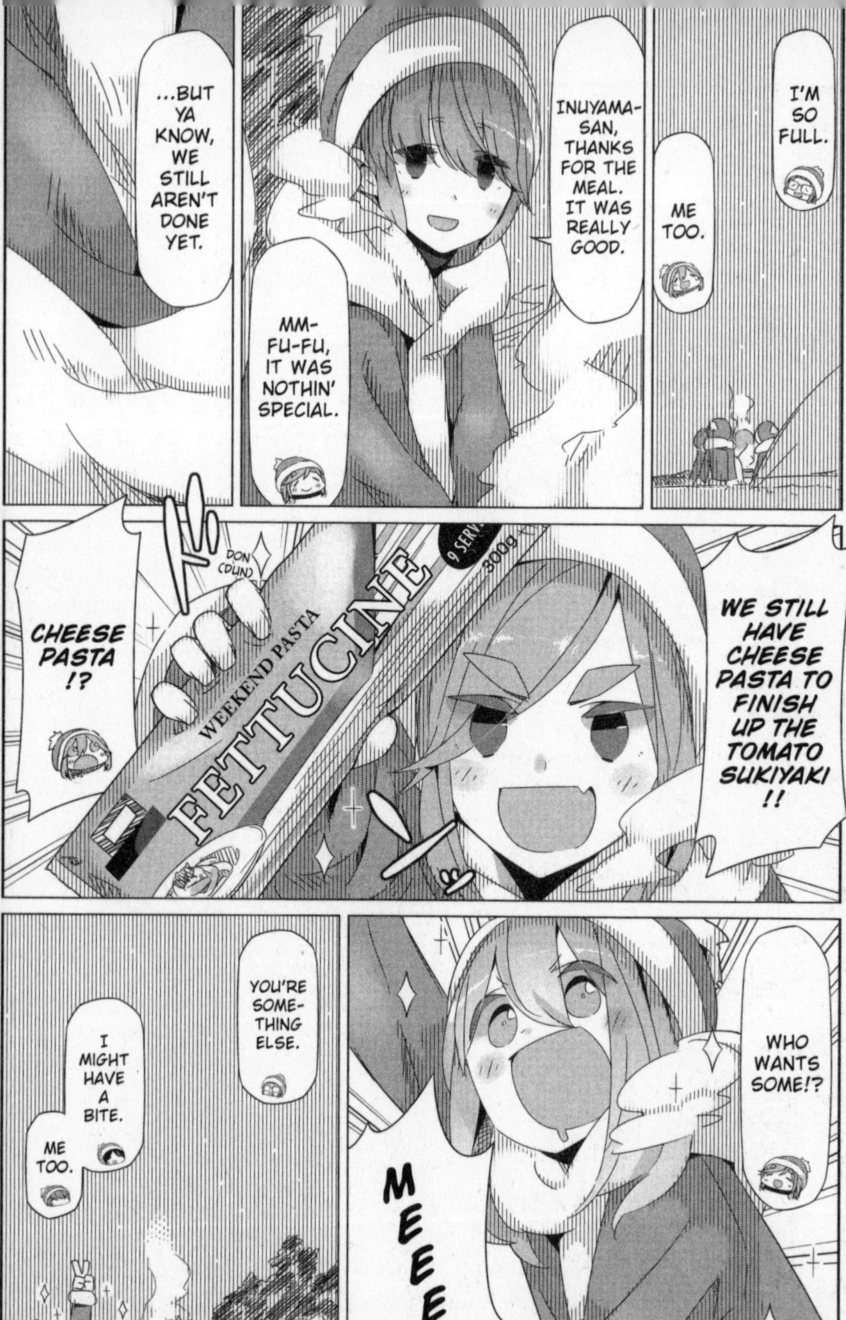
I'M SO FULL.
ME TOO.
INUYAMA-SAN, THANKS FOR THE MEAL. IT WAS REALLY GOOD.
MM-FU-FU, IT WAS NOTHIN' SPECIAL.
...BUT YA KNOW, WE STILL AREN'T DONE YET.
WE STILL HAVE CHEESE PASTA TO FINISH UP THE TOMATO SUKIYAKI!!
DON (DUN)
WEEKEND PASTA
FETTUCINE
300g
CHEESE PASTA!?
WHO WANTS SOME!?
MEEE!!
YOU'RE SOME-THING ELSE.
I MIGHT HAVE A BITE.
ME TOO.

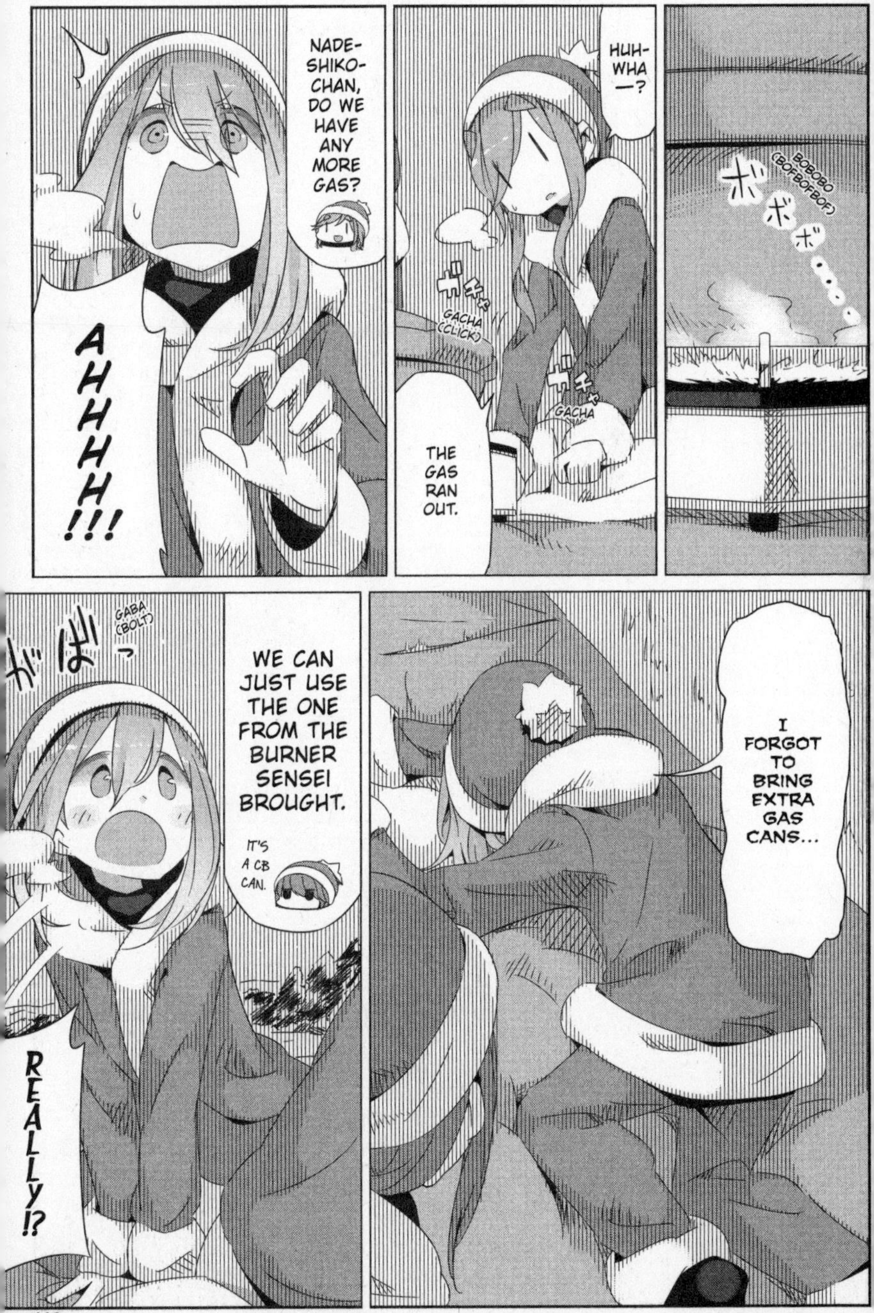
BOBOBO (BOFBOFBOF)
ボボボ・・・
HUH-WHA—?
GACHA (CLICK)
GACHA
THE GAS RAN OUT.
NADE-SHIKO-CHAN, DO WE HAVE ANY MORE GAS?
AHHHHH!!!
I FORGOT TO BRING EXTRA GAS CANS...
GABA (BOLT)
WE CAN JUST USE THE ONE FROM THE BURNER SENSEI BROUGHT.
IT'S A CB CAN.
REALLY!?

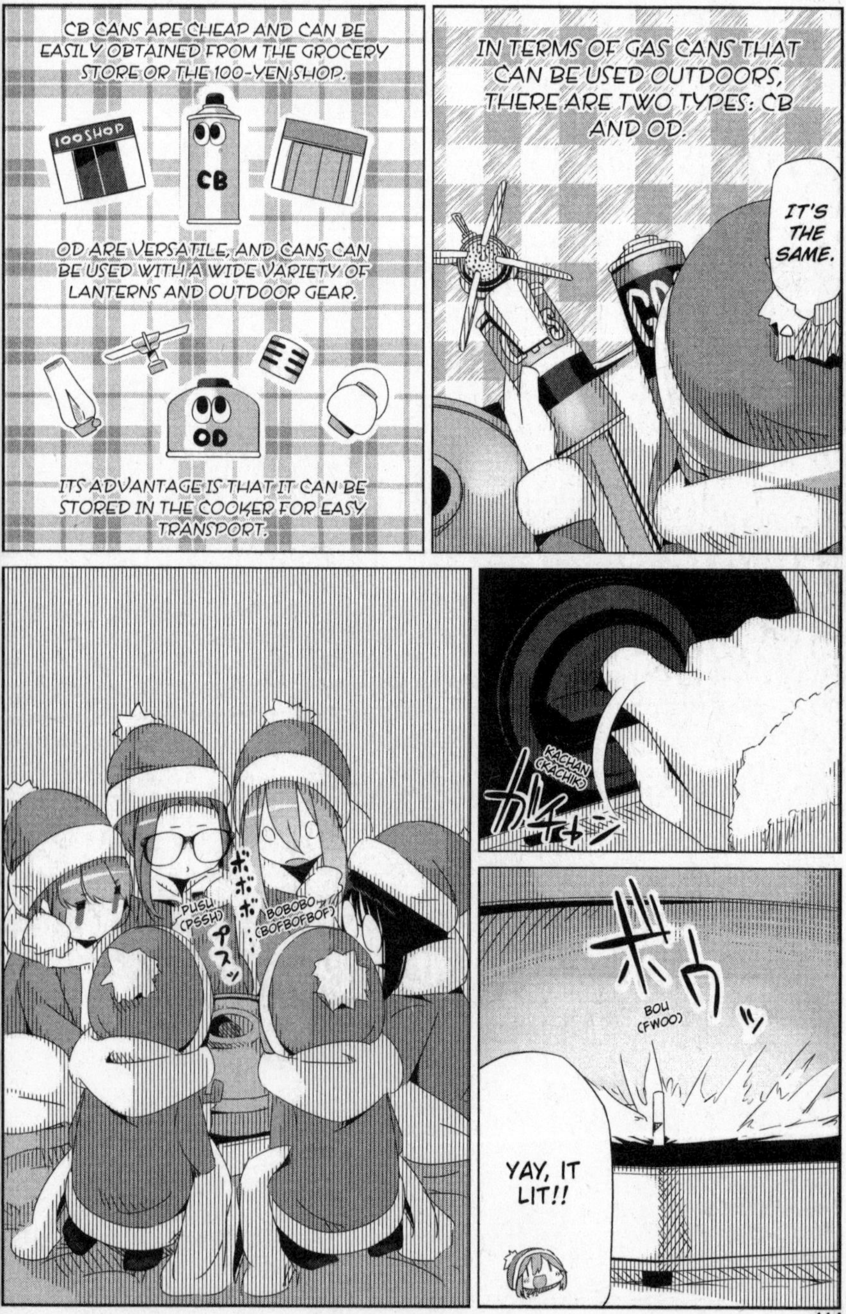
IN TERMS OF GAS CANS THAT CAN BE USED OUTDOORS, THERE ARE TWO TYPES: CB AND OD.
IT'S THE SAME.
CB CANS ARE CHEAP AND CAN BE EASILY OBTAINED FROM THE GROCERY STORE OR THE 100-YEN SHOP.
100 SHOP
CB
OD ARE VERSATILE, AND CANS CAN BE USED WITH A WIDE VARIETY OF LANTERNS AND OUTDOOR GEAR.
OD
ITS ADVANTAGE IS THAT IT CAN BE STORED IN THE COOKER FOR EASY TRANSPORT.
KACHAN (KACHIK)
カチャン
ボウッ
BOU (FWOO)
YAY, IT LIT!!
ボボボ…
プスッ
PUSU (PSSH)
BOBOBO (BOFBOFBOF)

DEVICES WITH SIMILAR FORMS MIGHT HAVE DIFFERENT SPECIFICATIONS FOR THEIR GAS CYLINDERS, SO PLEASE CAREFULLY READ AND FOLLOW PRODUCT-SPECIFIC INSTRUCTIONS.

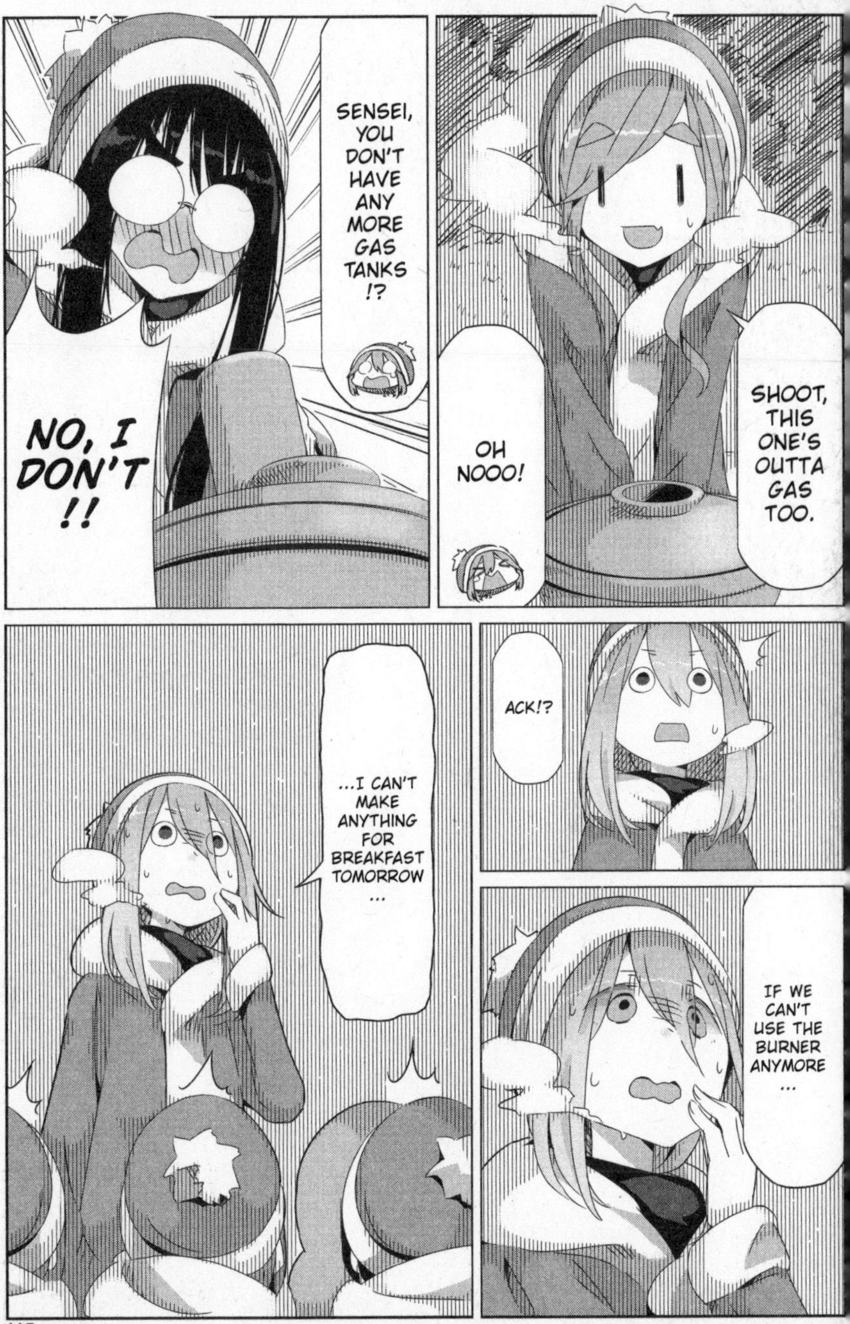
SHOOT, THIS ONE'S OUTTA GAS TOO.
OH NOOO!
SENSEI, YOU DON'T HAVE ANY MORE GAS TANKS !?
NO, I DON'T !!
ACK!?
IF WE CAN'T USE THE BURNER ANYMORE ...
...I CAN'T MAKE ANYTHING FOR BREAKFAST TOMORROW ...

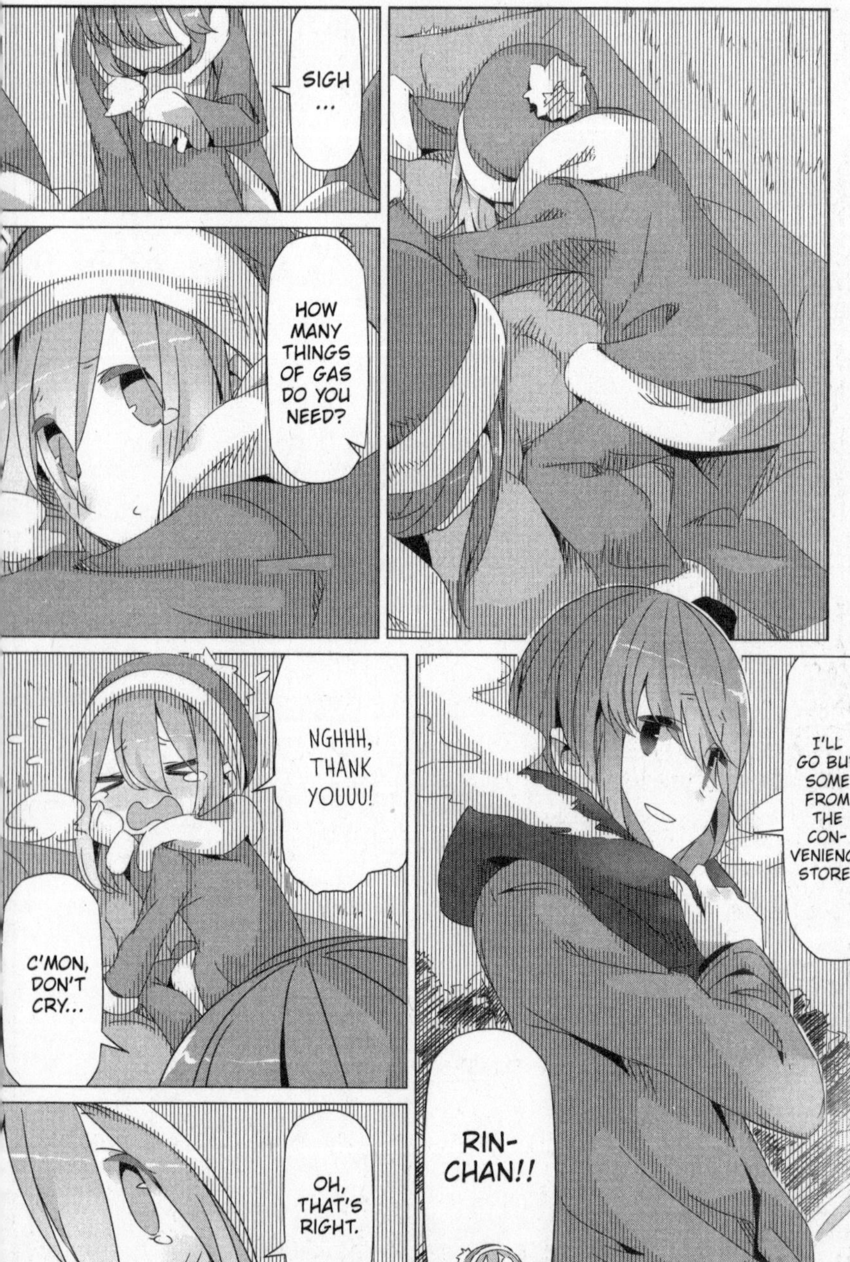
SIGH...
HOW MANY THINGS OF GAS DO YOU NEED?
I'LL GO BUY SOME FROM THE CON-VENIENCE STORE.
RIN-CHAN!!
NGHHH, THANK YOUUU!
C'MON, DON'T CRY...
OH, THAT'S RIGHT.

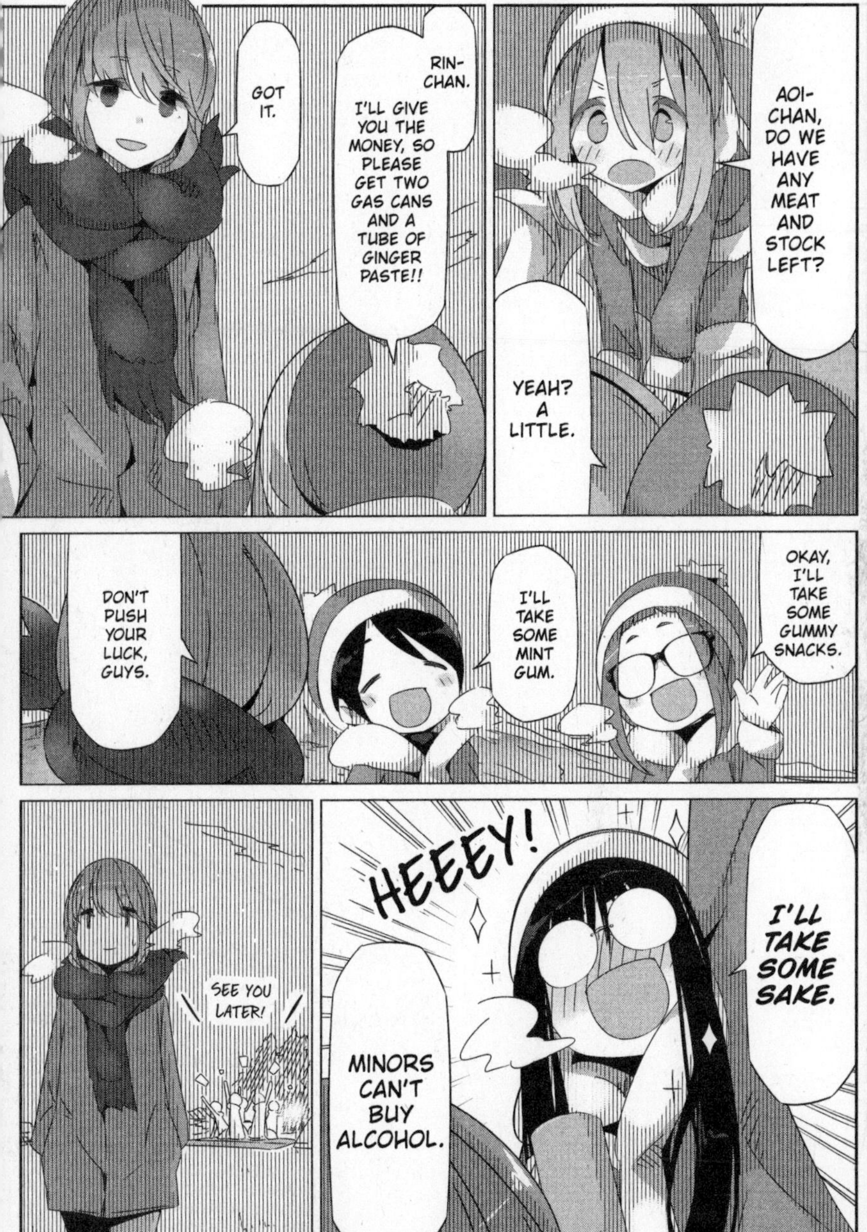
AOI-CHAN, DO WE HAVE ANY MEAT AND STOCK LEFT?
YEAH? A LITTLE.
RIN-CHAN.
I'LL GIVE YOU THE MONEY, SO PLEASE GET TWO GAS CANS AND A TUBE OF GINGER PASTE!!
GOT IT.
OKAY, I'LL TAKE SOME GUMMY SNACKS.
I'LL TAKE SOME MINT GUM.
DON'T PUSH YOUR LUCK, GUYS.
HEEEY!
I'LL TAKE SOME SAKE.
MINORS CAN'T BUY ALCOHOL.
SEE YOU LATER!

IT'S TWENTY MINUTES TO THE STORE AND BACK.

IT'LL TAKE A LITTLE TIME...

-RRRUMBLE-

ベンベン
(VRRVRRN)

BEBEN
(VRRVRRN)

バビ ウゴォォォ
(VROOOOOOO)

ウォォォ
オー

WHOA.

THIS COLD IS BAD NEWS.

オオ

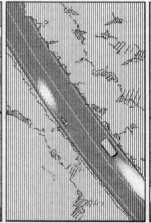

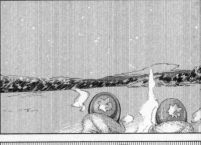

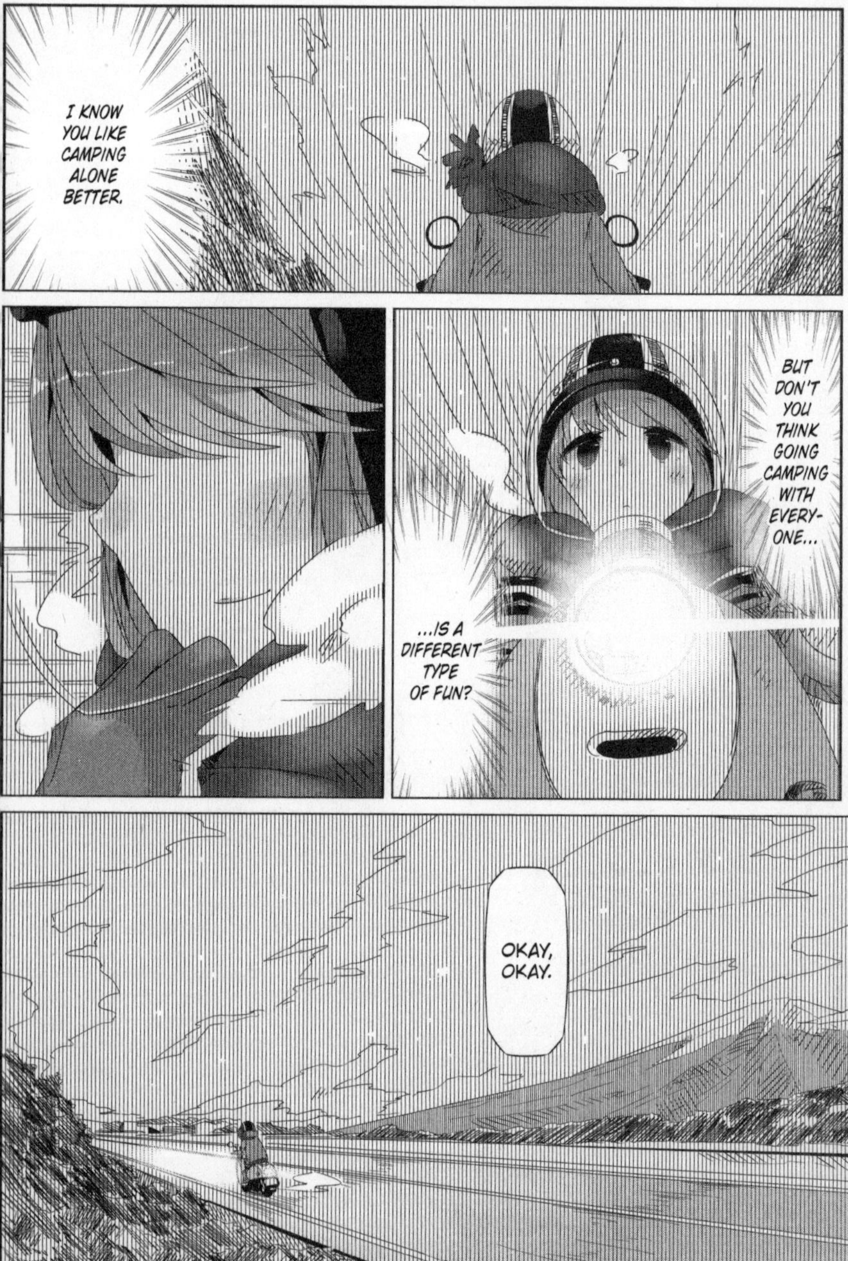
I KNOW YOU LIKE CAMPING ALONE BETTER.
BUT DON'T YOU THINK GOING CAMPING WITH EVERY-ONE...
...IS A DIFFERENT TYPE OF FUN?
OKAY, OKAY.

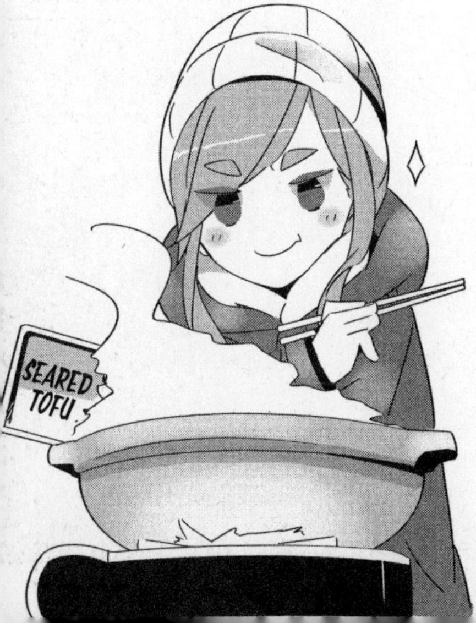
SEARED TOFU

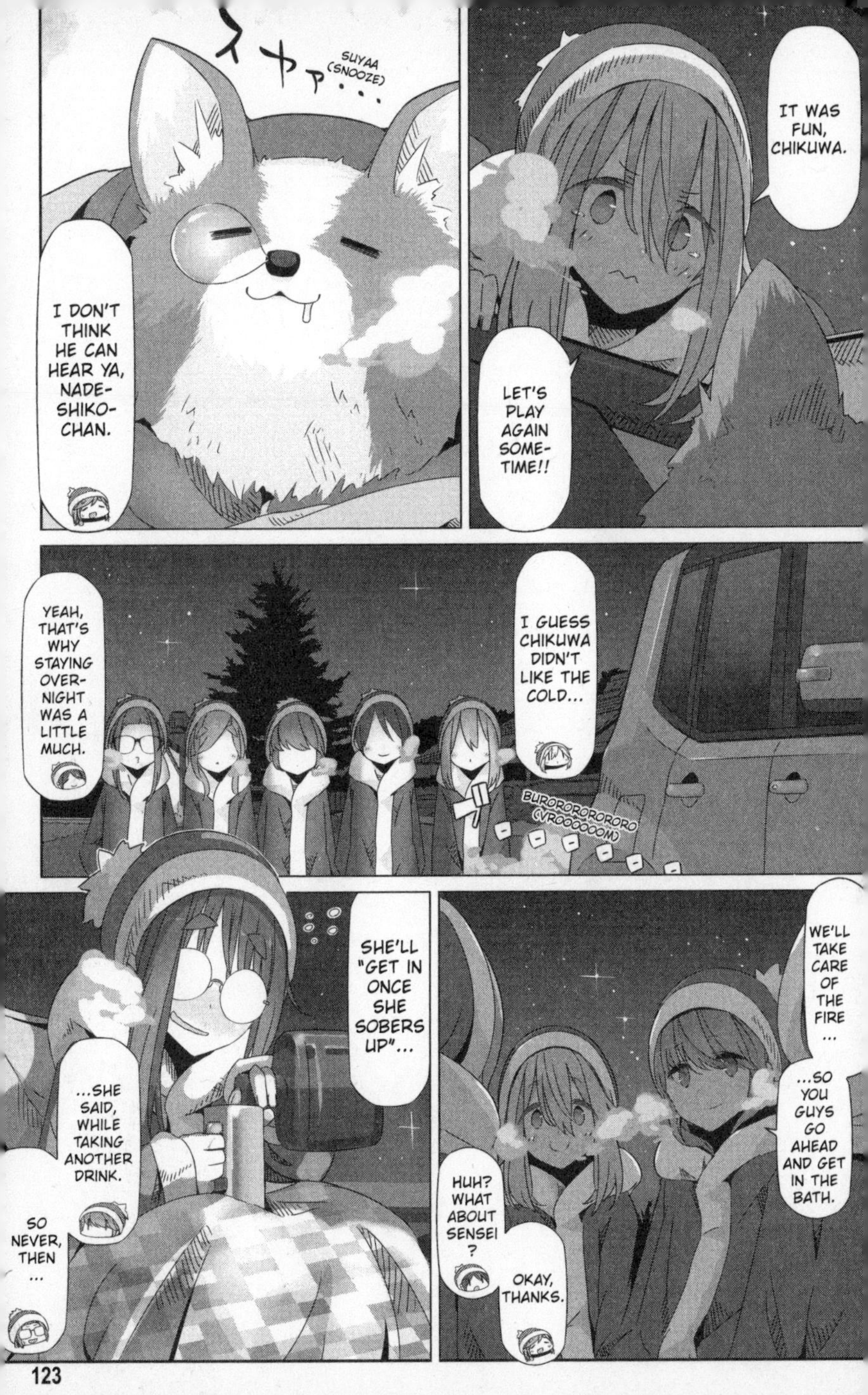
IT WAS FUN, CHIKUWA.
LET'S PLAY AGAIN SOME-TIME!!
スヤァ...
SUYAA (SNOOZE)
I DON'T THINK HE CAN HEAR YA, NADE-SHIKO-CHAN.
I GUESS CHIKUWA DIDN'T LIKE THE COLD...
BURORORORORORO (VROOOOOOM)
YEAH, THAT'S WHY STAYING OVER-NIGHT WAS A LITTLE MUCH.
WE'LL TAKE CARE OF THE FIRE...
...SO YOU GUYS GO AHEAD AND GET IN THE BATH.
OKAY, THANKS.
HUH? WHAT ABOUT SENSEI?
SHE'LL "GET IN ONCE SHE SOBERS UP"...
...SHE SAID, WHILE TAKING ANOTHER DRINK.
SO NEVER, THEN...

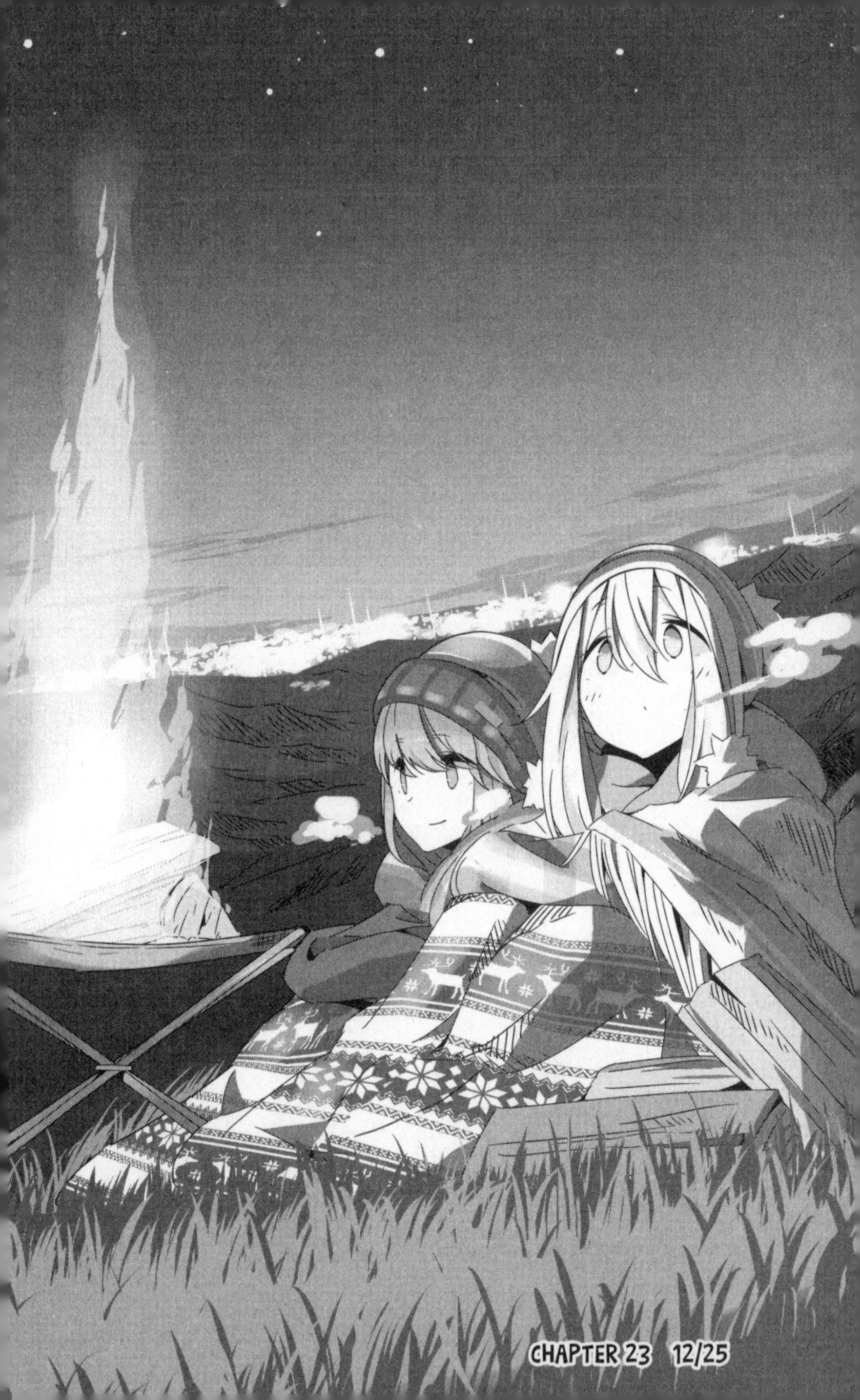
CHAPTER 23 12/25

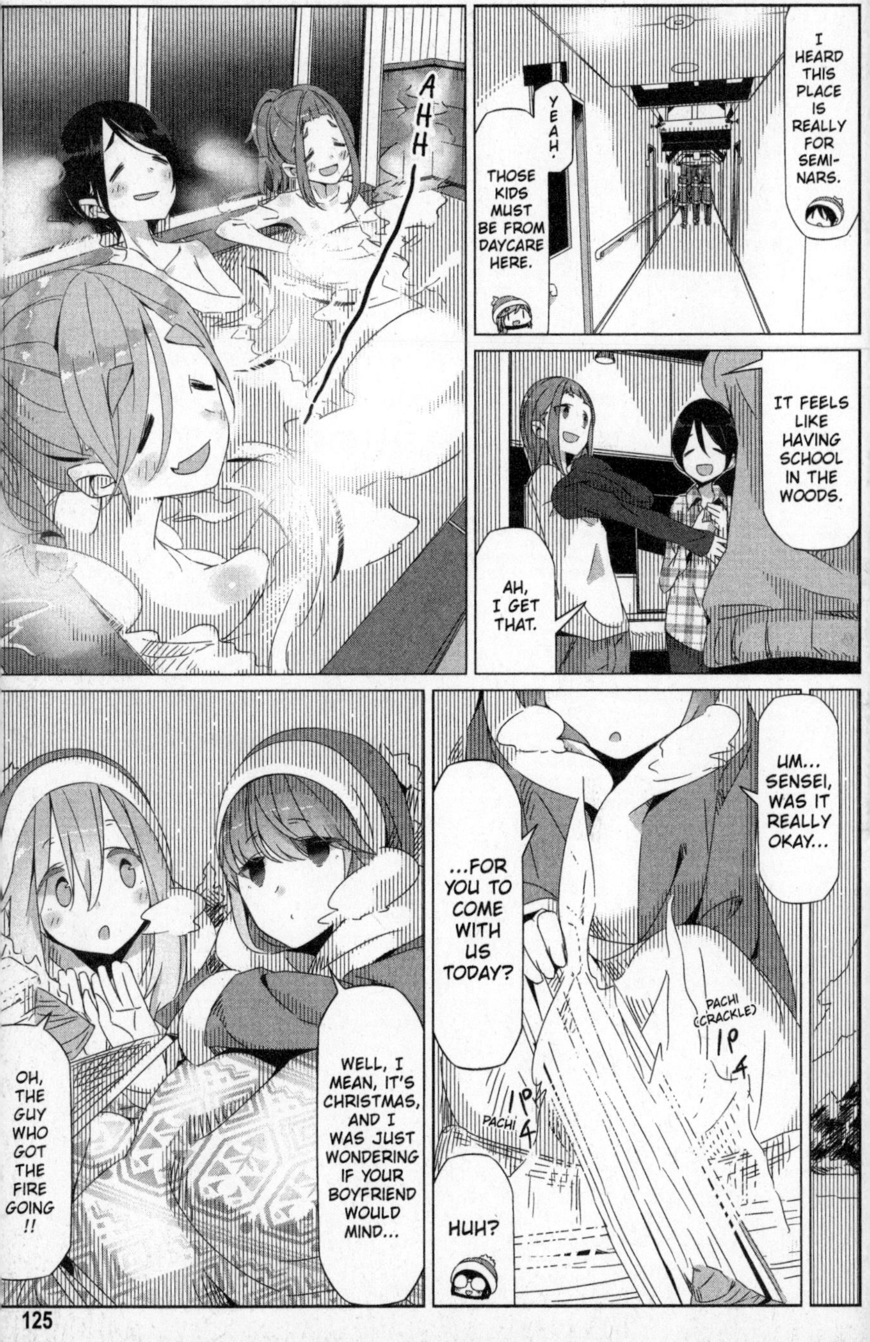
I HEARD THIS PLACE IS REALLY FOR SEMI-NARS.
YEAH.
THOSE KIDS MUST BE FROM DAYCARE HERE.
IT FEELS LIKE HAVING SCHOOL IN THE WOODS.
AH, I GET THAT.
AHH
UM... SENSEI, WAS IT REALLY OKAY...
...FOR YOU TO COME WITH US TODAY?
PACHI (CRACKLE)
PACHI
HUH?
WELL, I MEAN, IT'S CHRISTMAS, AND I WAS JUST WONDERING IF YOUR BOYFRIEND WOULD MIND...
OH, THE GUY WHO GOT THE FIRE GOING!!

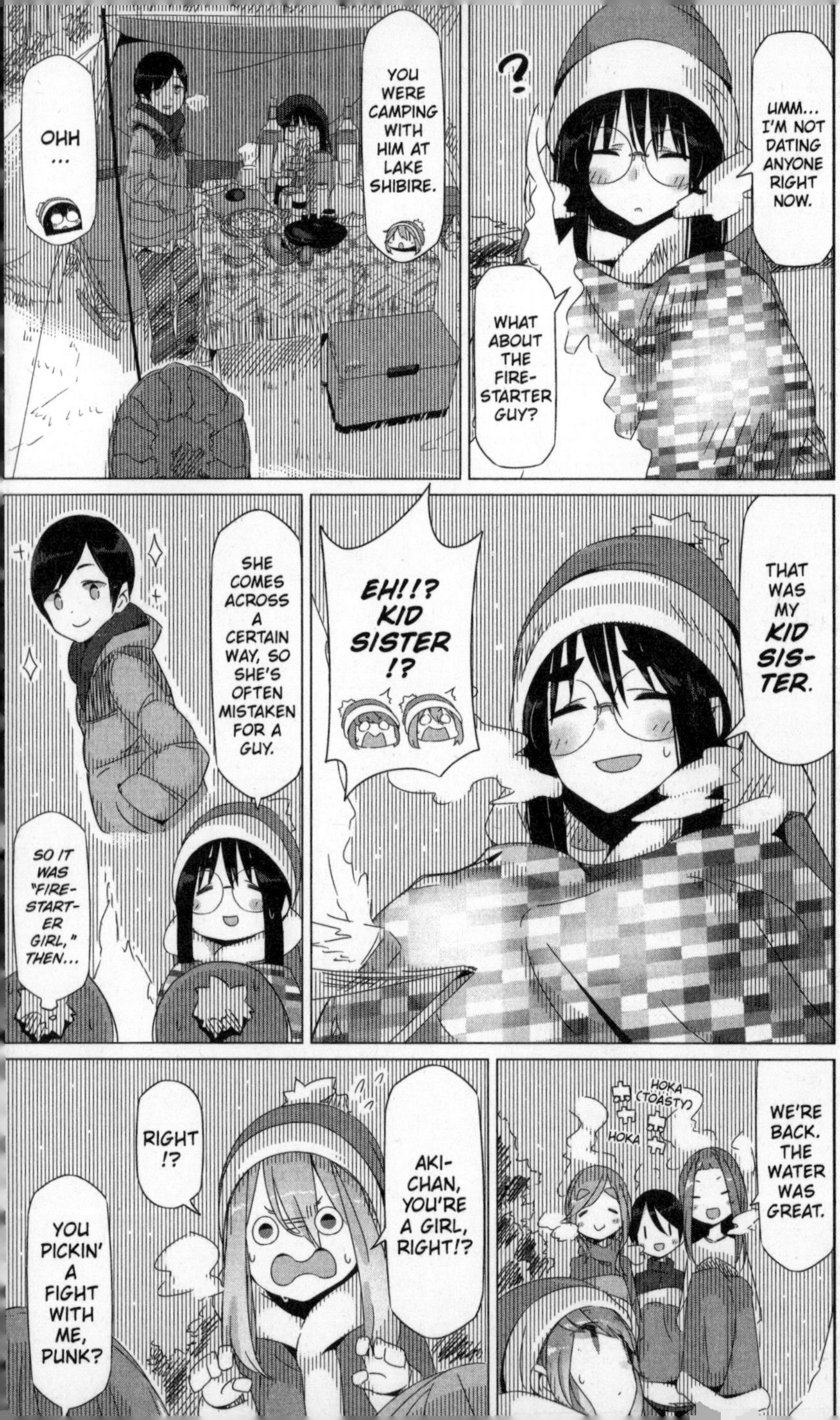
?
UMM... I'M NOT DATING ANYONE RIGHT NOW.
WHAT ABOUT THE FIRE-STARTER GUY?
YOU WERE CAMPING WITH HIM AT LAKE SHIBIRE.
OHH ...
THAT WAS MY KID SISTER.
EH!!? KID SISTER !?
SHE COMES ACROSS A CERTAIN WAY, SO SHE'S OFTEN MISTAKEN FOR A GUY.
SO IT WAS "FIRE-STARTER GIRL," THEN...
WE'RE BACK. THE WATER WAS GREAT.
HOKA (TOASTY)
HOKA
AKI-CHAN, YOU'RE A GIRL, RIGHT!?
RIGHT !?
YOU PICKIN' A FIGHT WITH ME, PUNK?

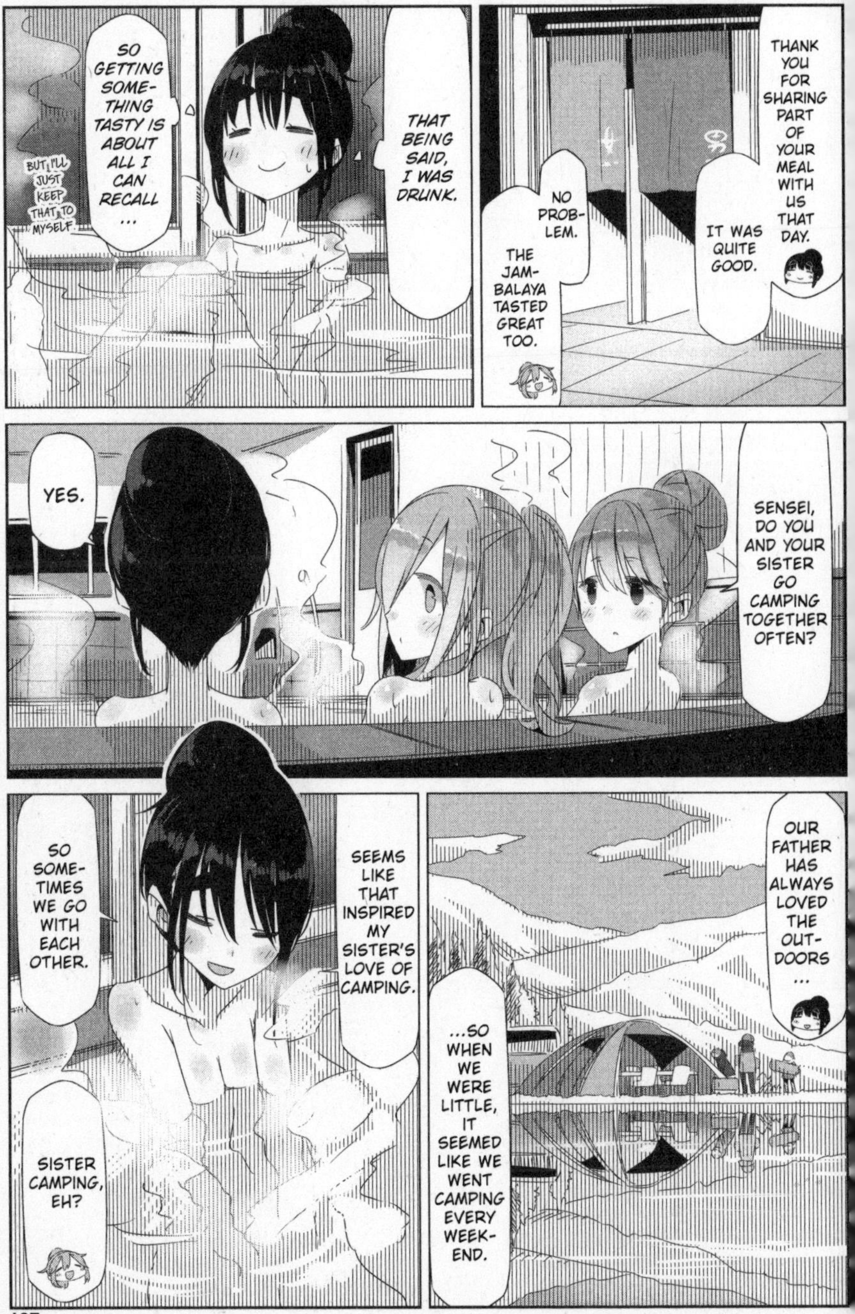
THANK YOU FOR SHARING PART OF YOUR MEAL WITH US THAT DAY.
IT WAS QUITE GOOD.
NO PROBLEM.
THE JAMBALAYA TASTED GREAT TOO.
THAT BEING SAID, I WAS DRUNK.
SO GETTING SOMETHING TASTY IS ABOUT ALL I CAN RECALL...
BUT I'LL JUST KEEP THAT TO MYSELF.
SENSEI, DO YOU AND YOUR SISTER GO CAMPING TOGETHER OFTEN?
YES.
OUR FATHER HAS ALWAYS LOVED THE OUTDOORS...
...SO WHEN WE WERE LITTLE, IT SEEMED LIKE WE WENT CAMPING EVERY WEEKEND.
SEEMS LIKE THAT INSPIRED MY SISTER'S LOVE OF CAMPING.
SO SOMETIMES WE GO WITH EACH OTHER.
SISTER CAMPING, EH?

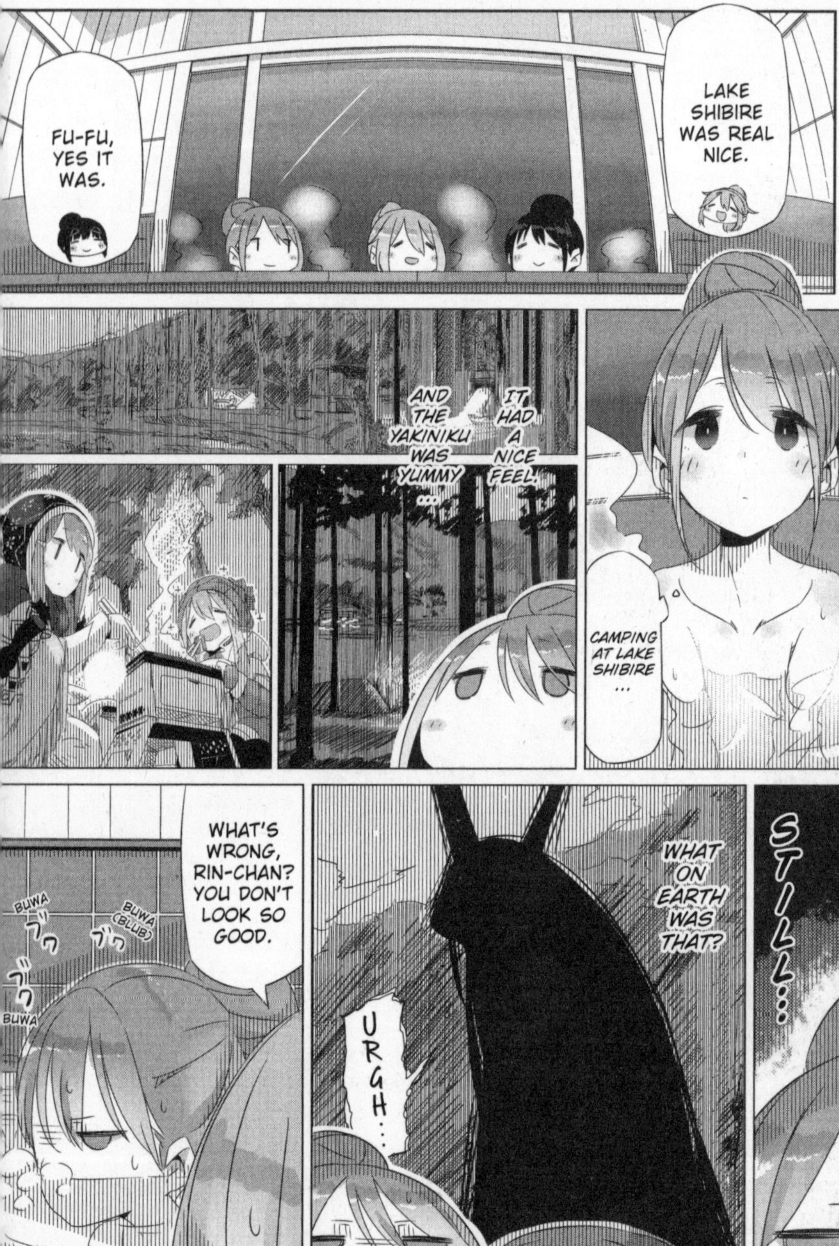
LAKE SHIBIRE WAS REAL NICE.
FU-FU, YES IT WAS.
CAMPING AT LAKE SHIBIRE...
IT HAD A NICE FEEL.
AND THE YAKINIKU WAS YUMMY...
STILL...
WHAT ON EARTH WAS THAT?
URGH...
WHAT'S WRONG, RIN-CHAN? YOU DON'T LOOK SO GOOD.
BUWA (BLUB)
BUWA
BUWA

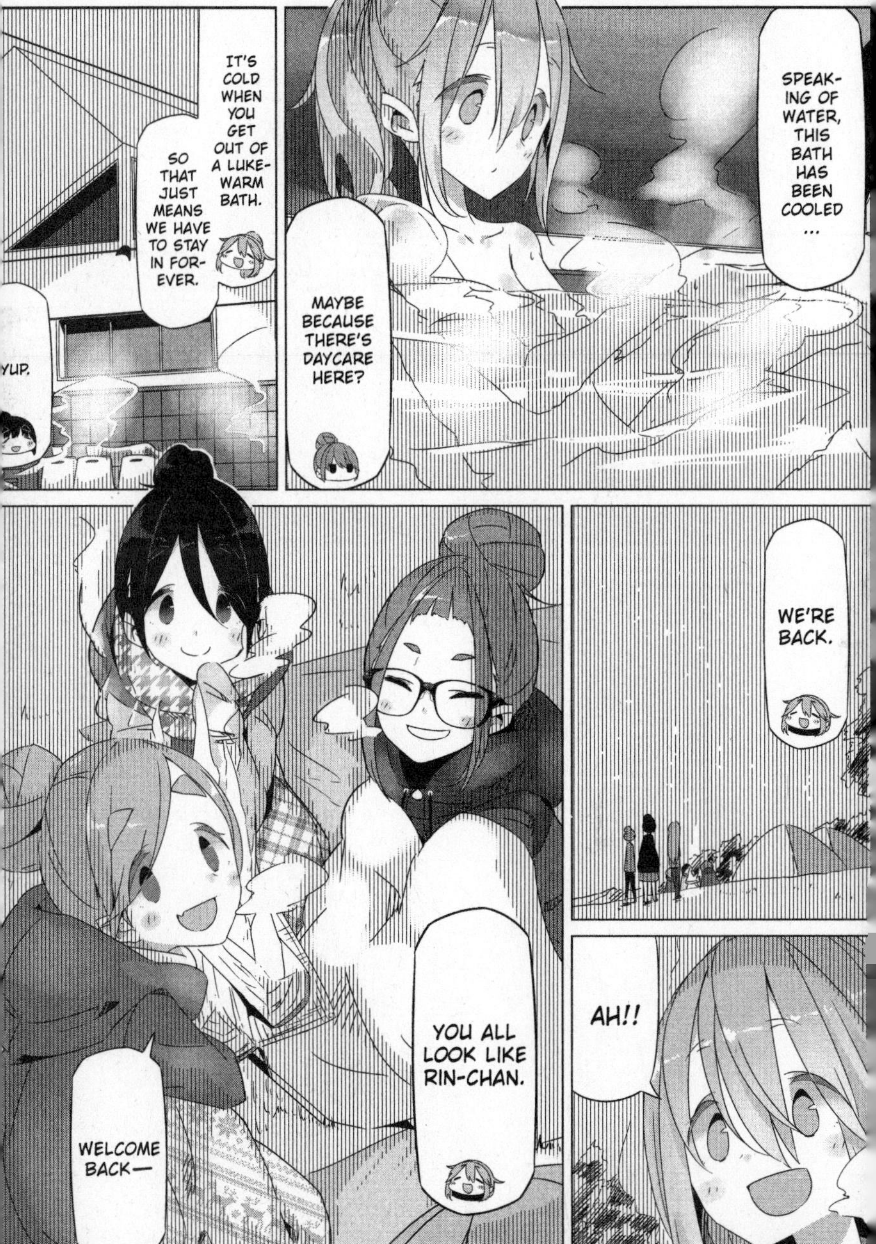
SPEAK-ING OF WATER, THIS BATH HAS BEEN COOLED ...
MAYBE BECAUSE THERE'S DAYCARE HERE?
IT'S COLD WHEN YOU GET OUT OF A LUKE-WARM BATH.
SO THAT JUST MEANS WE HAVE TO STAY IN FOR-EVER.
YUP.
WE'RE BACK.
AH!!
YOU ALL LOOK LIKE RIN-CHAN.
WELCOME BACK—

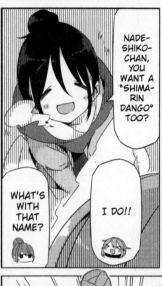

OOH!
LUCKY!
NADE-SHIKO-CHAN, YOU WANT A "SHIMARIN DANGO" TOO?
I DO!!
WHAT'S WITH THAT NAME?
POPULAR TREAT
SHIMARIN DANGO
SHIMARIN DANGO...
THERE. ALL DONE.
HMPH...
HOW DO I LOOK?
PF...
PF...
PFF...
PFF...

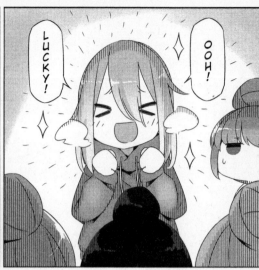

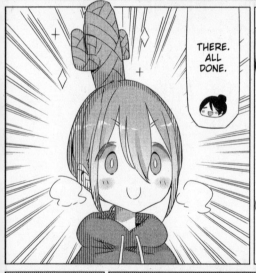

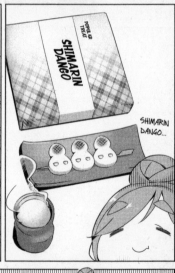

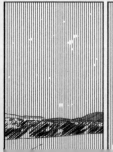

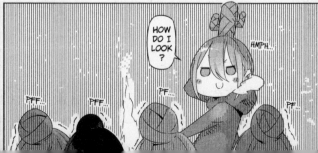

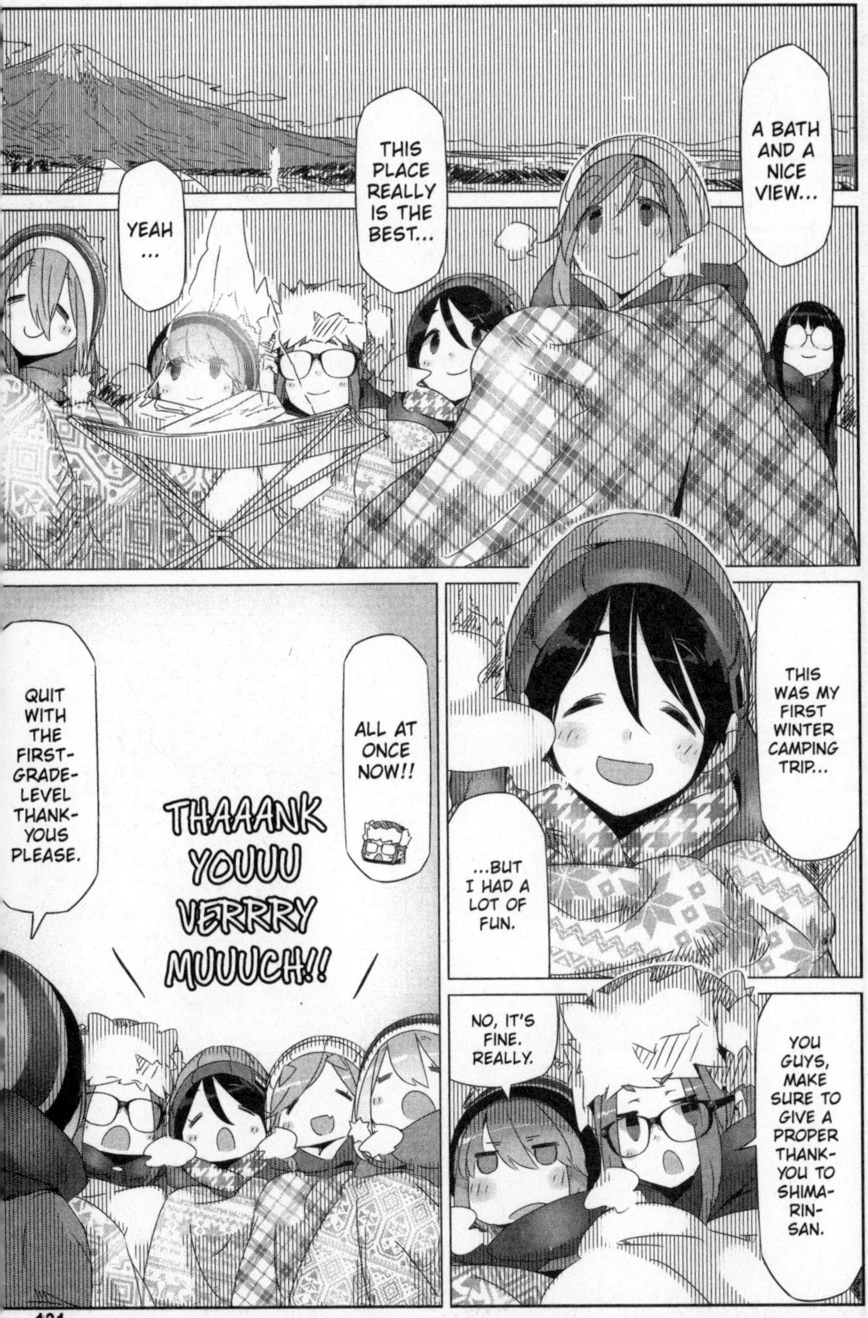
A BATH AND A NICE VIEW...
THIS PLACE REALLY IS THE BEST...
YEAH ...
THIS WAS MY FIRST WINTER CAMPING TRIP...
...BUT I HAD A LOT OF FUN.
YOU GUYS, MAKE SURE TO GIVE A PROPER THANK-YOU TO SHIMA-RIN-SAN.
NO, IT'S FINE. REALLY.
ALL AT ONCE NOW!!
THAAANK YOUUU VERRRY MUUUCH!!
QUIT WITH THE FIRST-GRADE-LEVEL THANK-YOUS PLEASE.

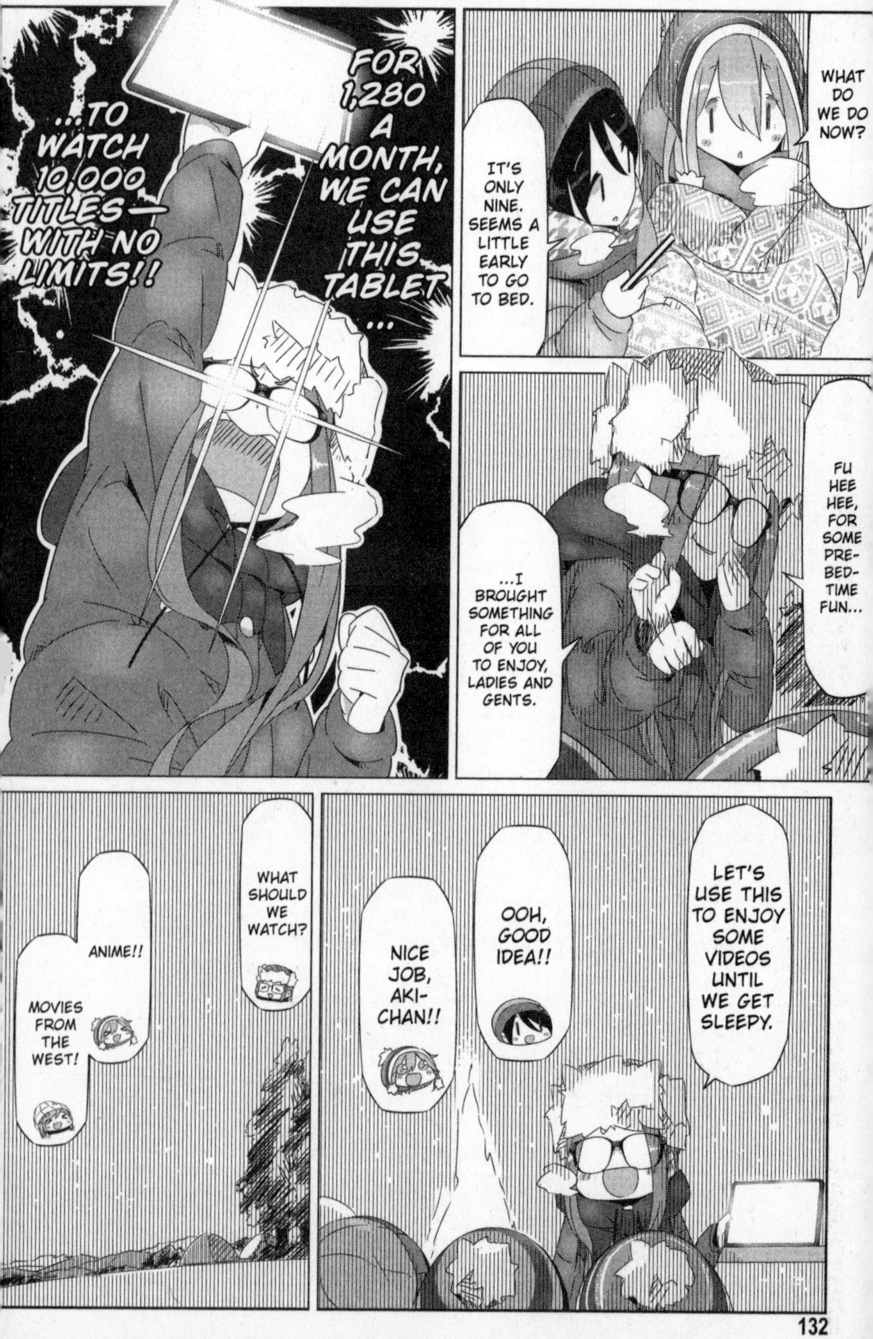
WHAT DO WE DO NOW?
IT'S ONLY NINE. SEEMS A LITTLE EARLY TO GO TO BED.
FU HEE HEE, FOR SOME PRE-BED-TIME FUN...
...I BROUGHT SOMETHING FOR ALL OF YOU TO ENJOY, LADIES AND GENTS.
FOR 1,280 A MONTH, WE CAN USE THIS TABLET...
...TO WATCH 10,000 TITLES—WITH NO LIMITS!!
LET'S USE THIS TO ENJOY SOME VIDEOS UNTIL WE GET SLEEPY.
OOH, GOOD IDEA!!
NICE JOB, AKI-CHAN!!
WHAT SHOULD WE WATCH?
ANIME!!
MOVIES FROM THE WEST!

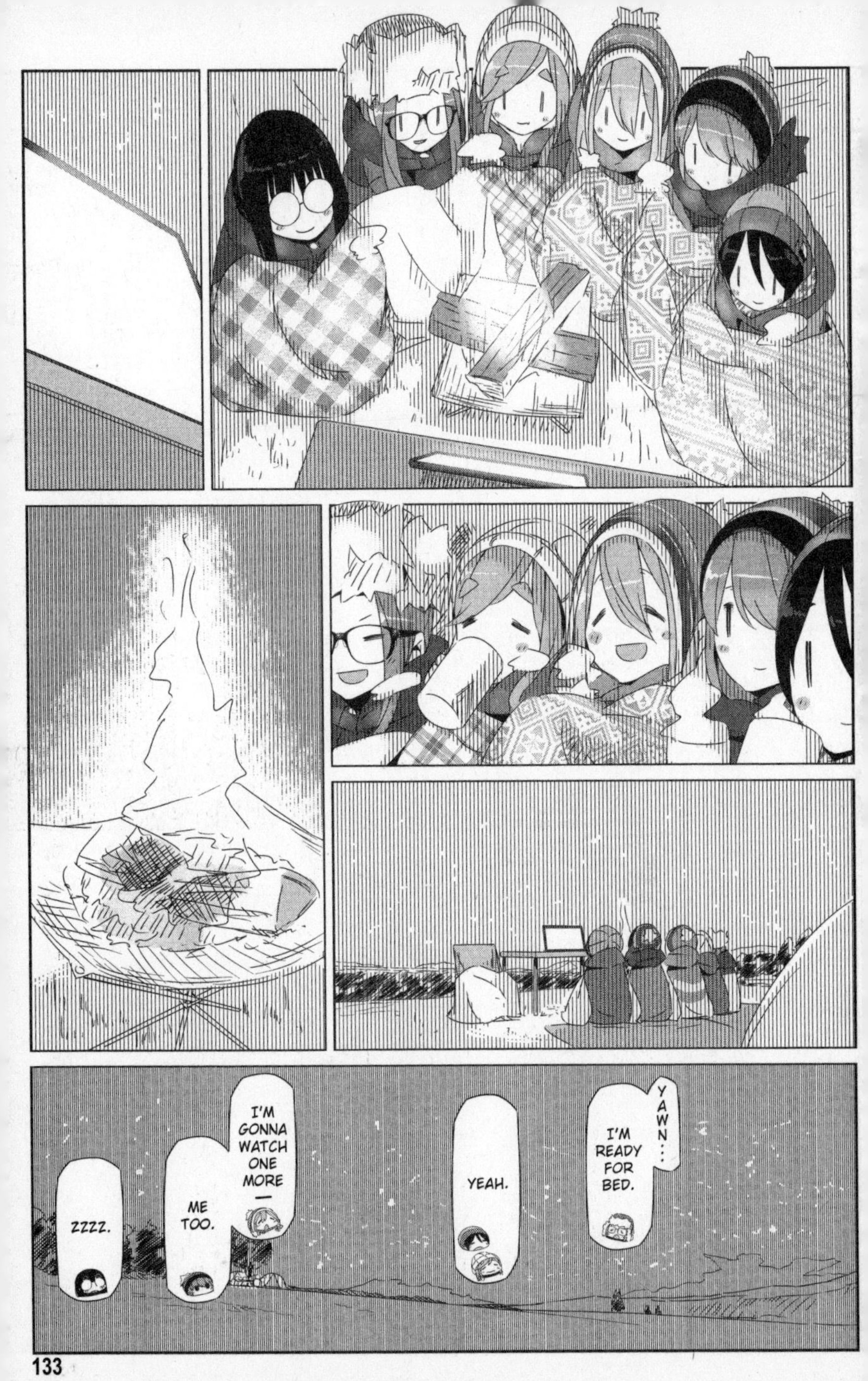
YAWN...
I'M READY FOR BED.
YEAH.
I'M GONNA WATCH ONE MORE—
ME TOO.
ZZZZ.

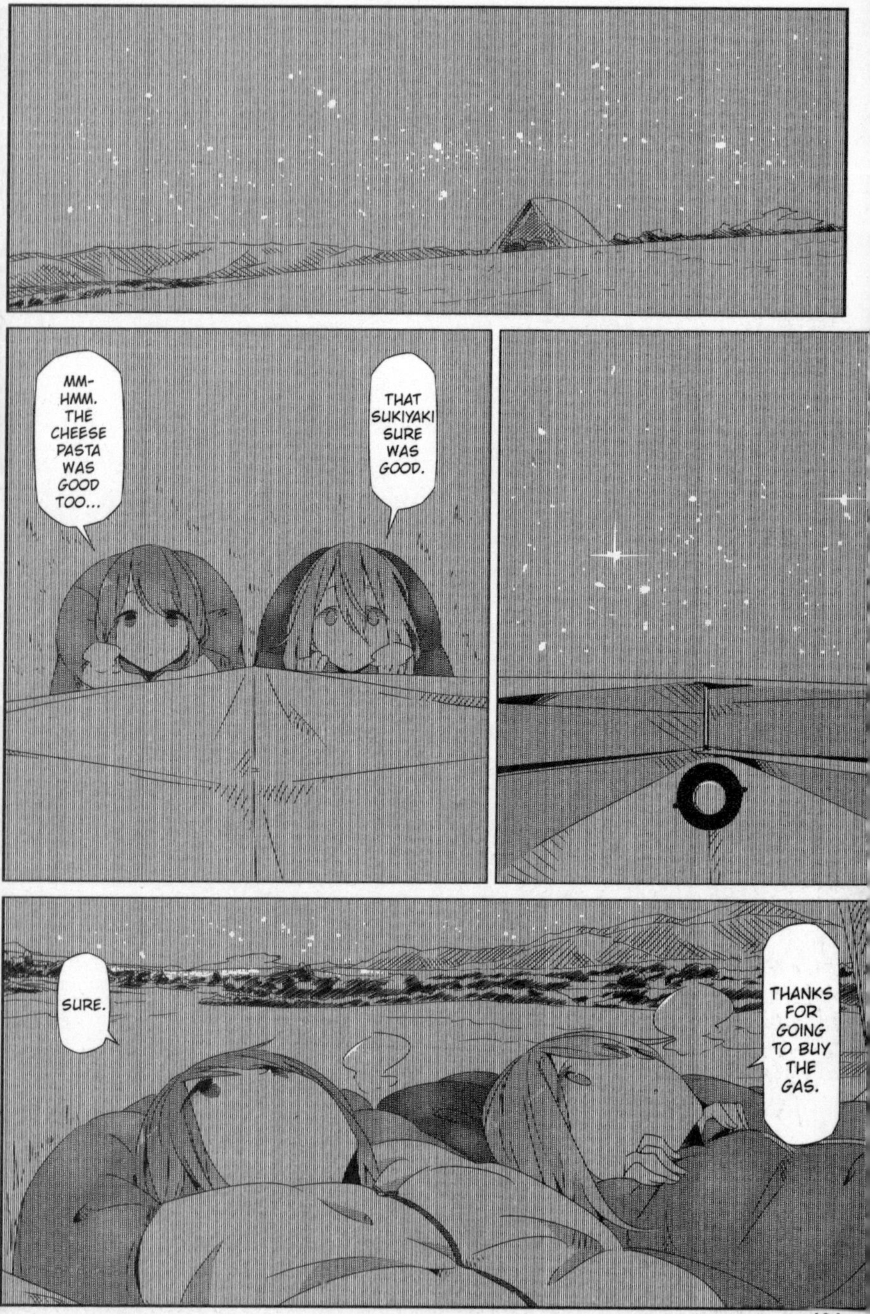
THAT SUKIYAKI SURE WAS GOOD.
MM-HMM. THE CHEESE PASTA WAS GOOD TOO...
THANKS FOR GOING TO BUY THE GAS.
SURE.

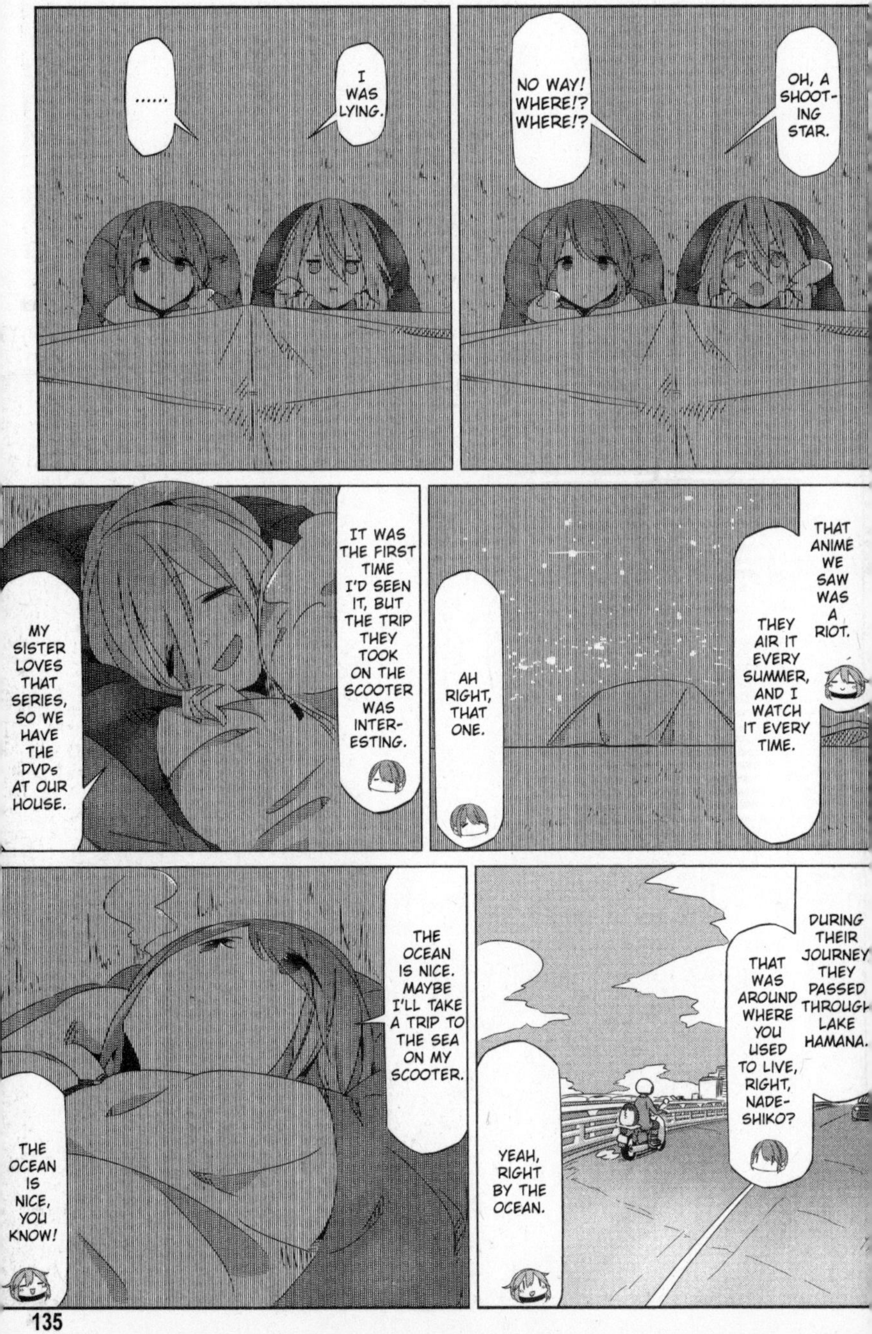
OH, A SHOOTING STAR.
NO WAY! WHERE!? WHERE!?
I WAS LYING.
......
THAT ANIME WE SAW WAS A RIOT.
THEY AIR IT EVERY SUMMER, AND I WATCH IT EVERY TIME.
AH RIGHT, THAT ONE.
IT WAS THE FIRST TIME I'D SEEN IT, BUT THE TRIP THEY TOOK ON THE SCOOTER WAS INTERESTING.
MY SISTER LOVES THAT SERIES, SO WE HAVE THE DVDs AT OUR HOUSE.
DURING THEIR JOURNEY THEY PASSED THROUGH LAKE HAMANA.
THAT WAS AROUND WHERE YOU USED TO LIVE, RIGHT, NADESHIKO?
YEAH, RIGHT BY THE OCEAN.
THE OCEAN IS NICE. MAYBE I'LL TAKE A TRIP TO THE SEA ON MY SCOOTER.
THE OCEAN IS NICE, YOU KNOW!

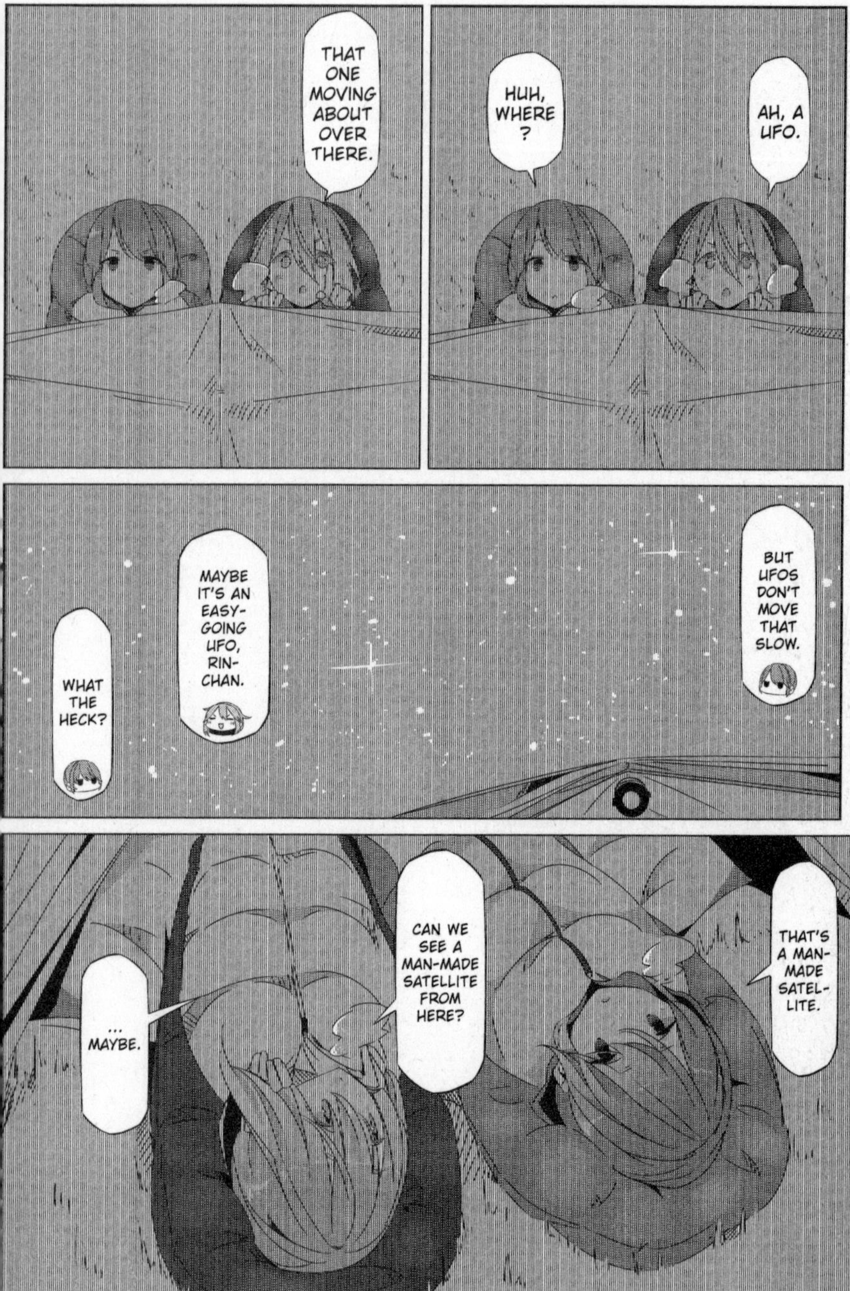
AH, A UFO.
HUH, WHERE?
THAT ONE MOVING ABOUT OVER THERE.
BUT UFOS DON'T MOVE THAT SLOW.
MAYBE IT'S AN EASY-GOING UFO, RIN-CHAN.
WHAT THE HECK?
THAT'S A MAN-MADE SATELLITE.
CAN WE SEE A MAN-MADE SATELLITE FROM HERE?
... MAYBE.

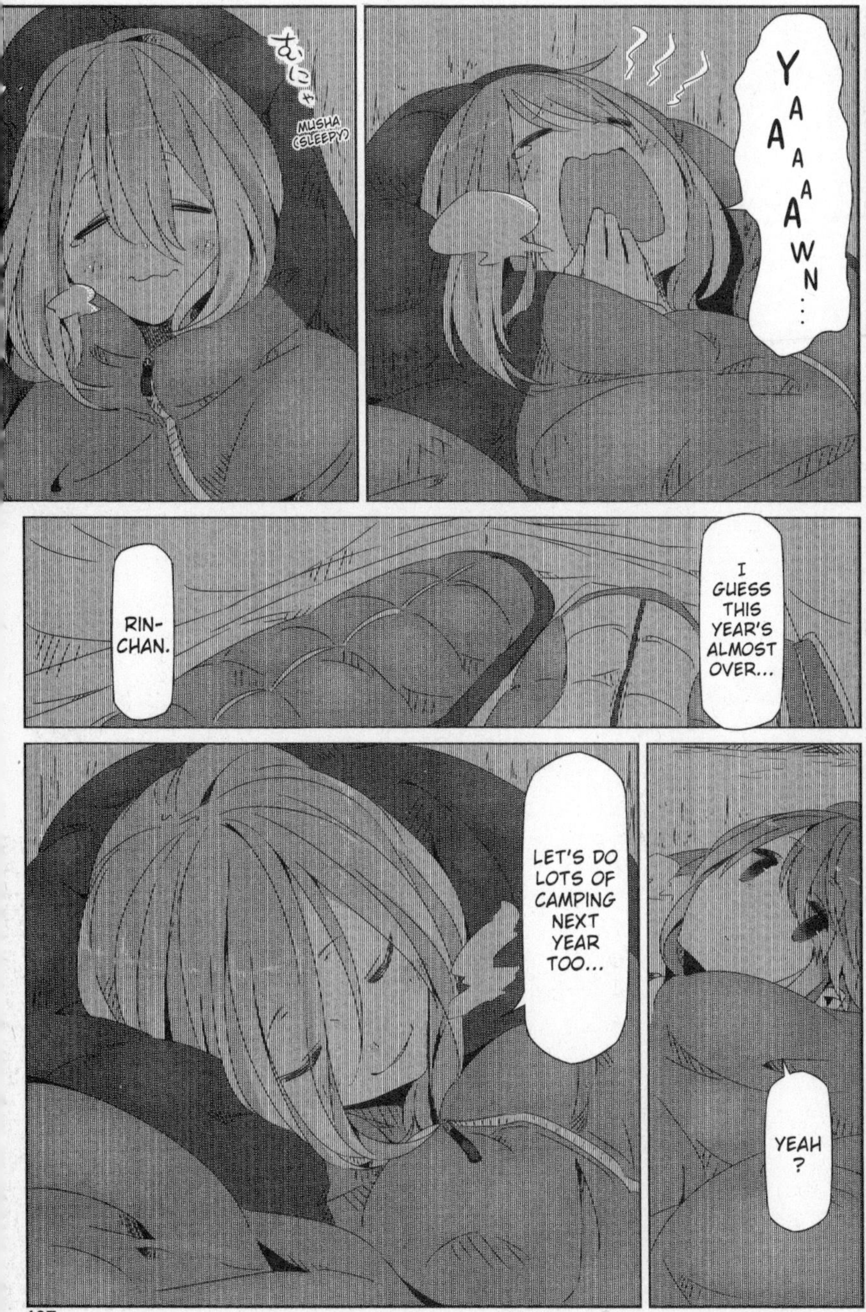
YAAAAAWN...
むにゃ
MUSHA (SLEEPY)
I GUESS THIS YEAR'S ALMOST OVER...
RIN-CHAN.
YEAH?
LET'S DO LOTS OF CAMPING NEXT YEAR TOO...

YEAH.

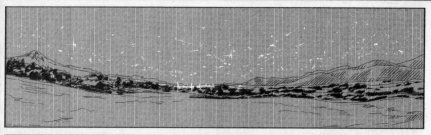

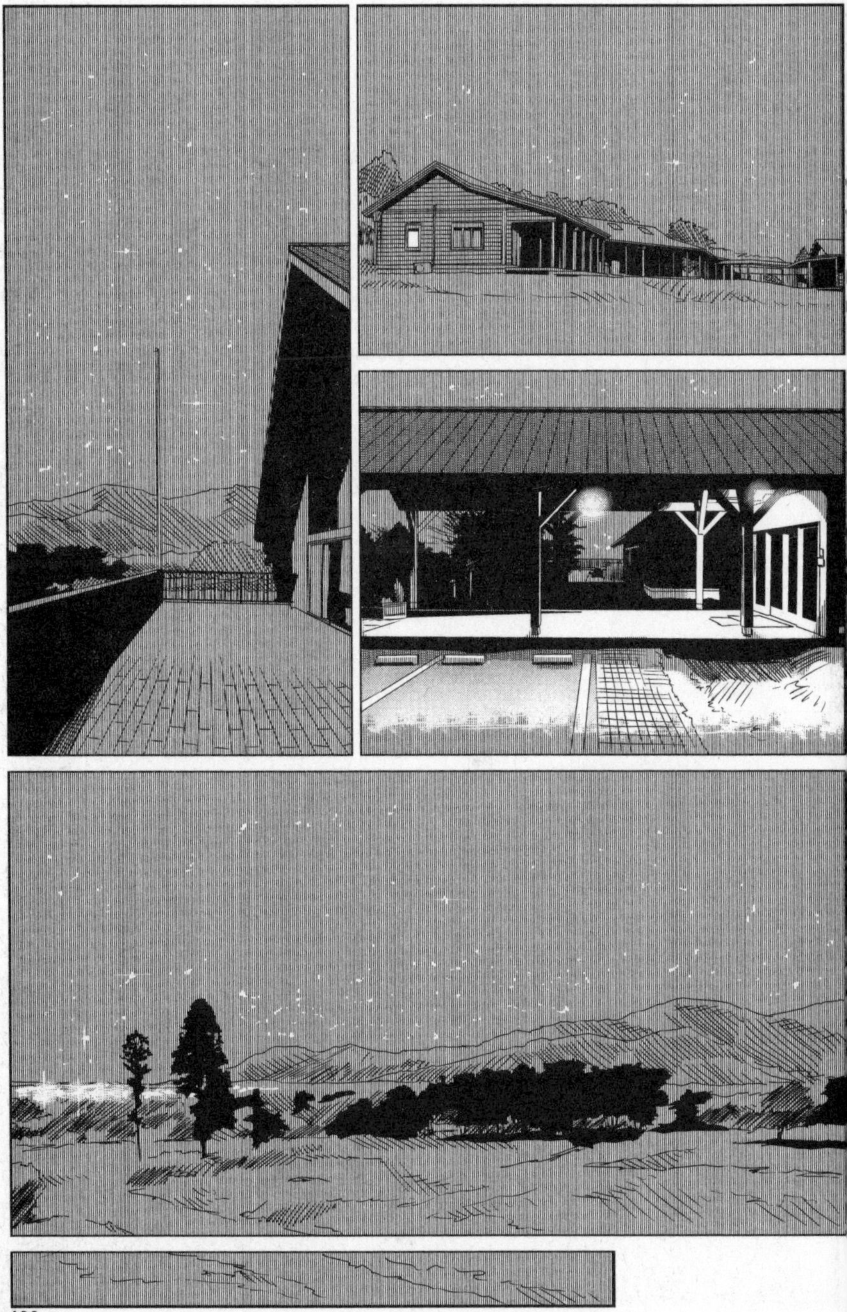

BEE BEE BEE BEEP BEE BEE BEE BEEP
5:00
ALARM
STOP
BEE BEE BEE BEEP BEE BEE BEE BEEP
BEE BEE BEE BEEP BEE BEE BEE BEEP
BZZZ- BZZT
......
IT'S COLD ...

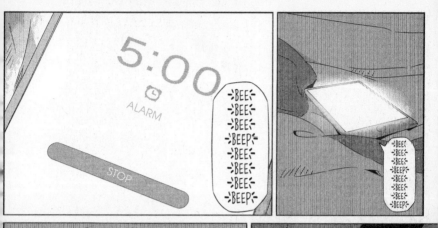

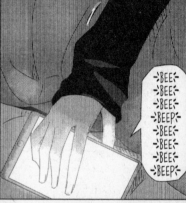

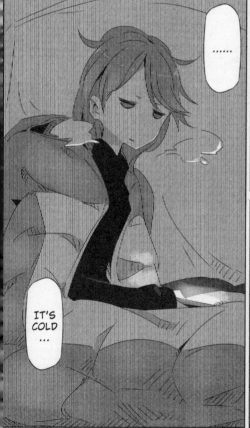

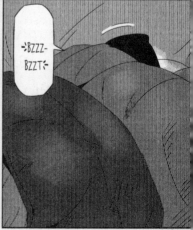

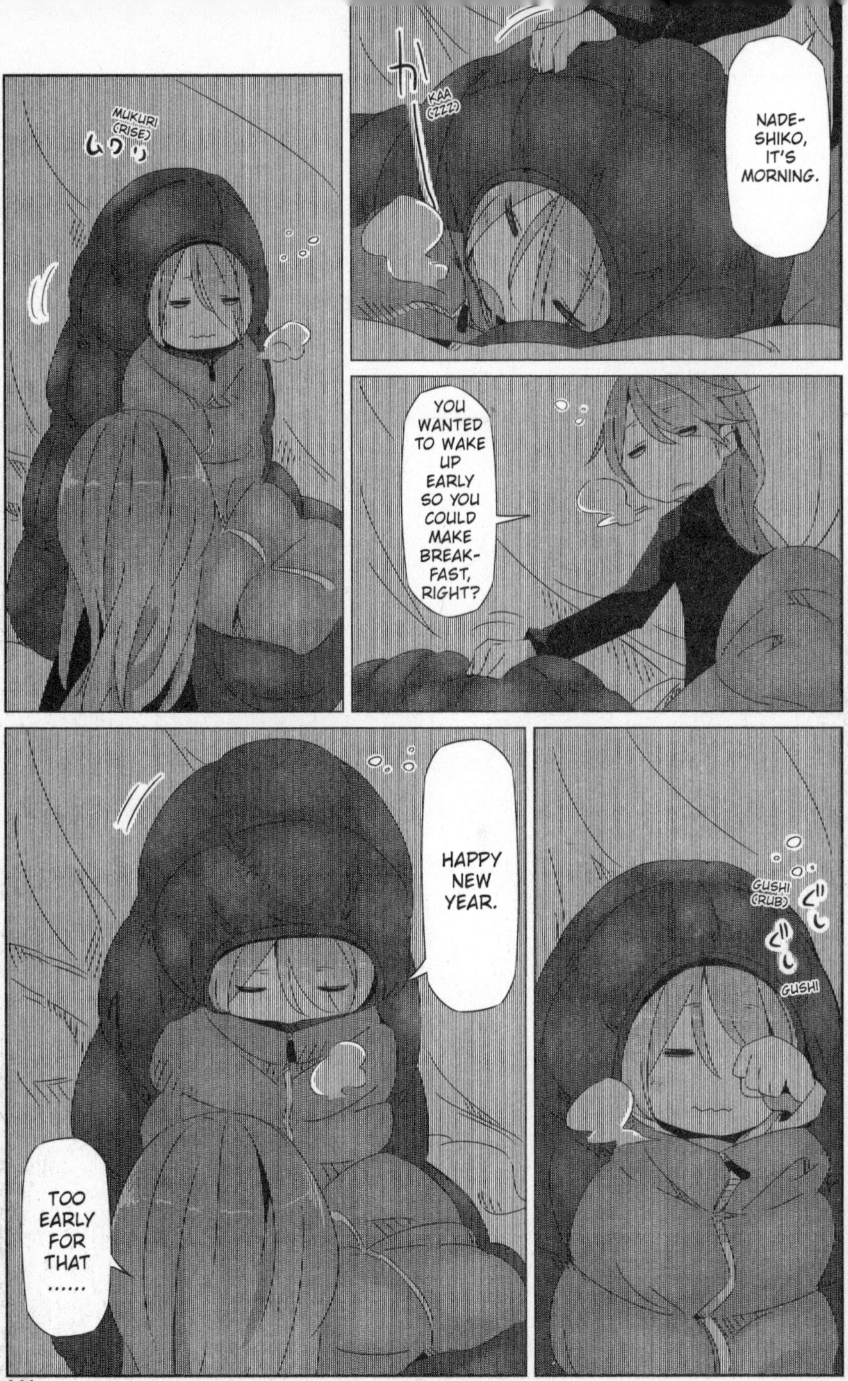
NADE-SHIKO, IT'S MORNING.
KAA (ZZZ)
かー
YOU WANTED TO WAKE UP EARLY SO YOU COULD MAKE BREAK-FAST, RIGHT?
MUKURI (RISE)
ムクり
GUSHI (RUB)
ぐし
ぐし
GUSHI
HAPPY NEW YEAR.
TOO EARLY FOR THAT ......

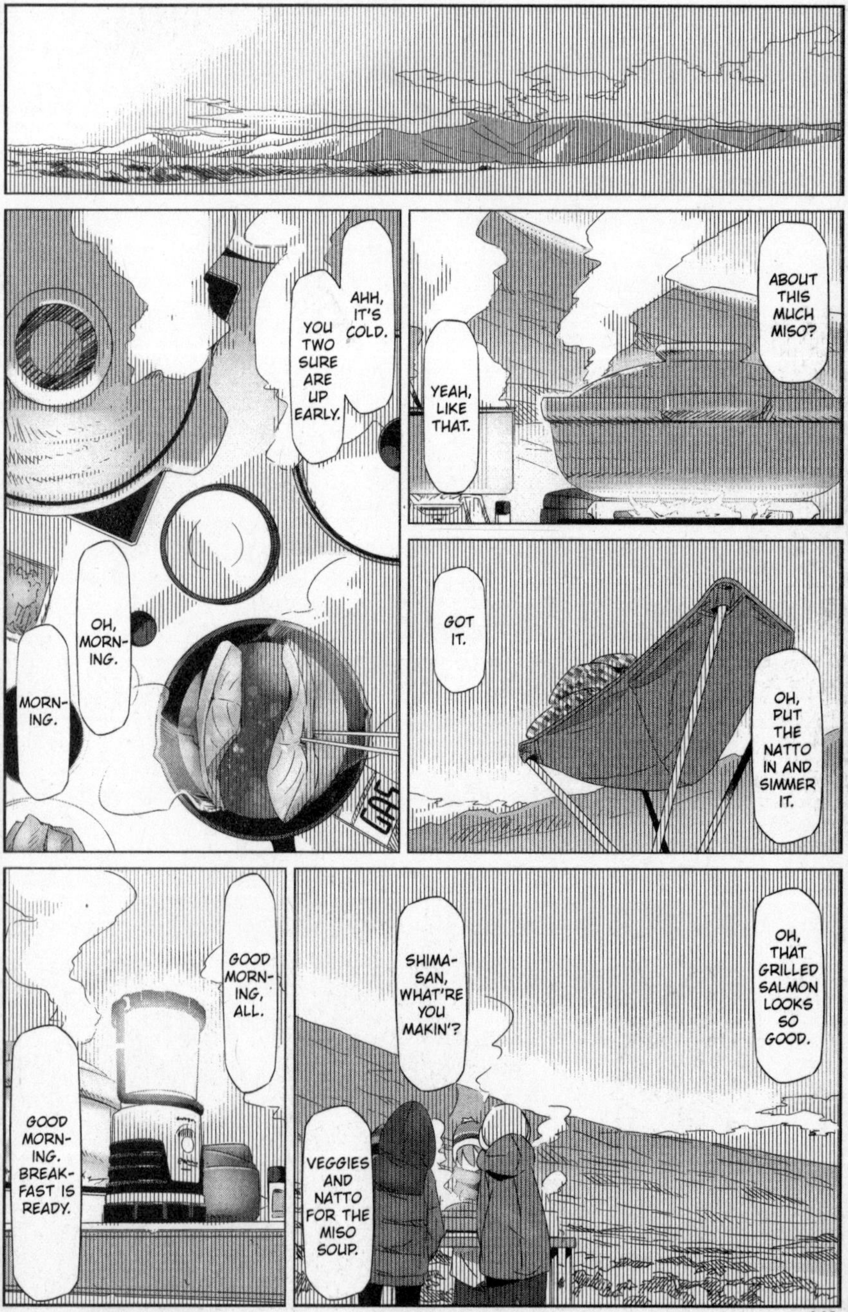
ABOUT THIS MUCH MISO?
YEAH, LIKE THAT.
OH, PUT THE NATTO IN AND SIMMER IT.
GOT IT.
AHH, IT'S COLD.
YOU TWO SURE ARE UP EARLY.
OH, MORNING.
MORNING.
GAS
OH, THAT GRILLED SALMON LOOKS SO GOOD.
SHIMA-SAN, WHAT'RE YOU MAKIN'?
VEGGIES AND NATTO FOR THE MISO SOUP.
GOOD MORNING, ALL.
GOOD MORNING. BREAKFAST IS READY.

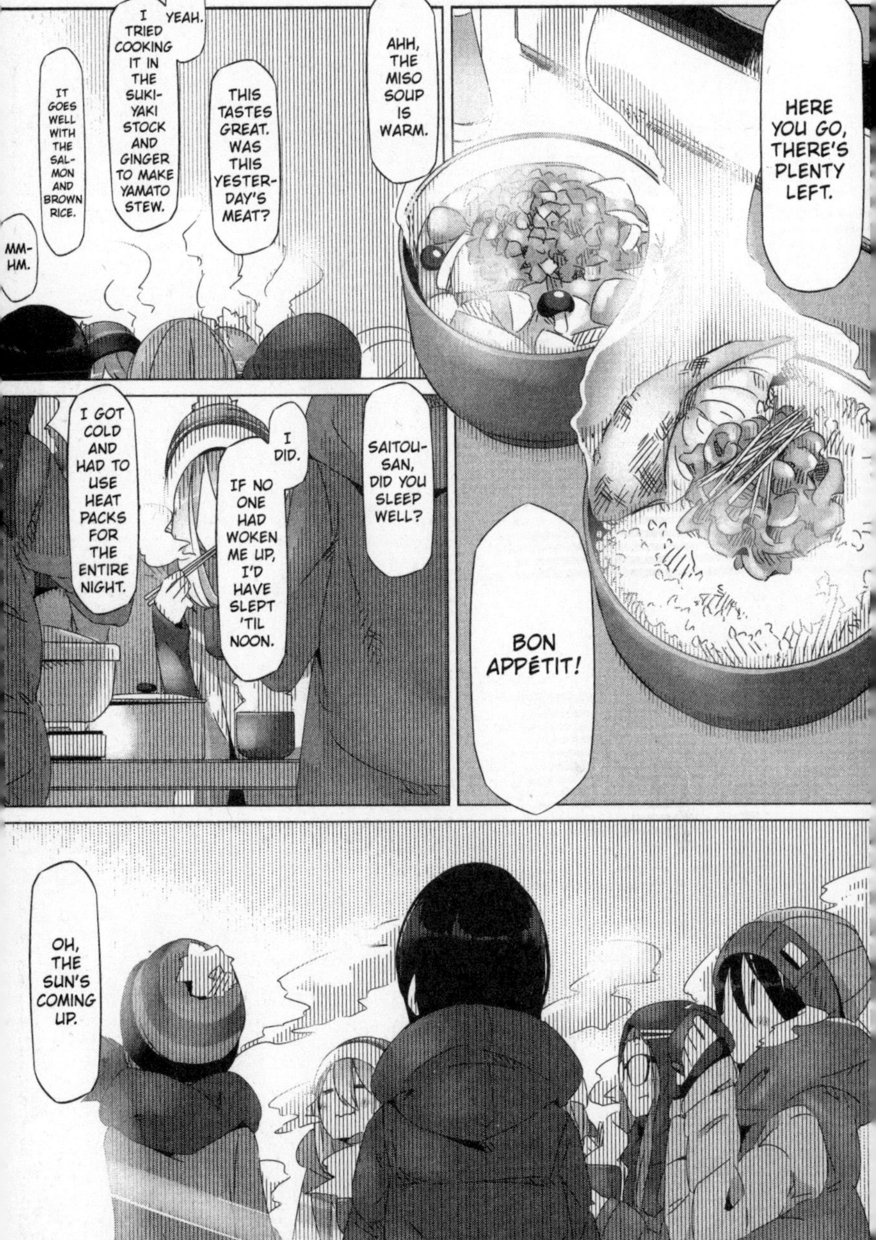
HERE YOU GO, THERE'S PLENTY LEFT.
BON APPÉTIT!
AHH, THE MISO SOUP IS WARM.
THIS TASTES GREAT. WAS THIS YESTERDAY'S MEAT?
YEAH.
I TRIED COOKING IT IN THE SUKIYAKI STOCK AND GINGER TO MAKE YAMATO STEW.
IT GOES WELL WITH THE SALMON AND BROWN RICE.
MM-HM.
SAITOU-SAN, DID YOU SLEEP WELL?
I DID.
IF NO ONE HAD WOKEN ME UP, I'D HAVE SLEPT 'TIL NOON.
I GOT COLD AND HAD TO USE HEAT PACKS FOR THE ENTIRE NIGHT.
OH, THE SUN'S COMING UP.

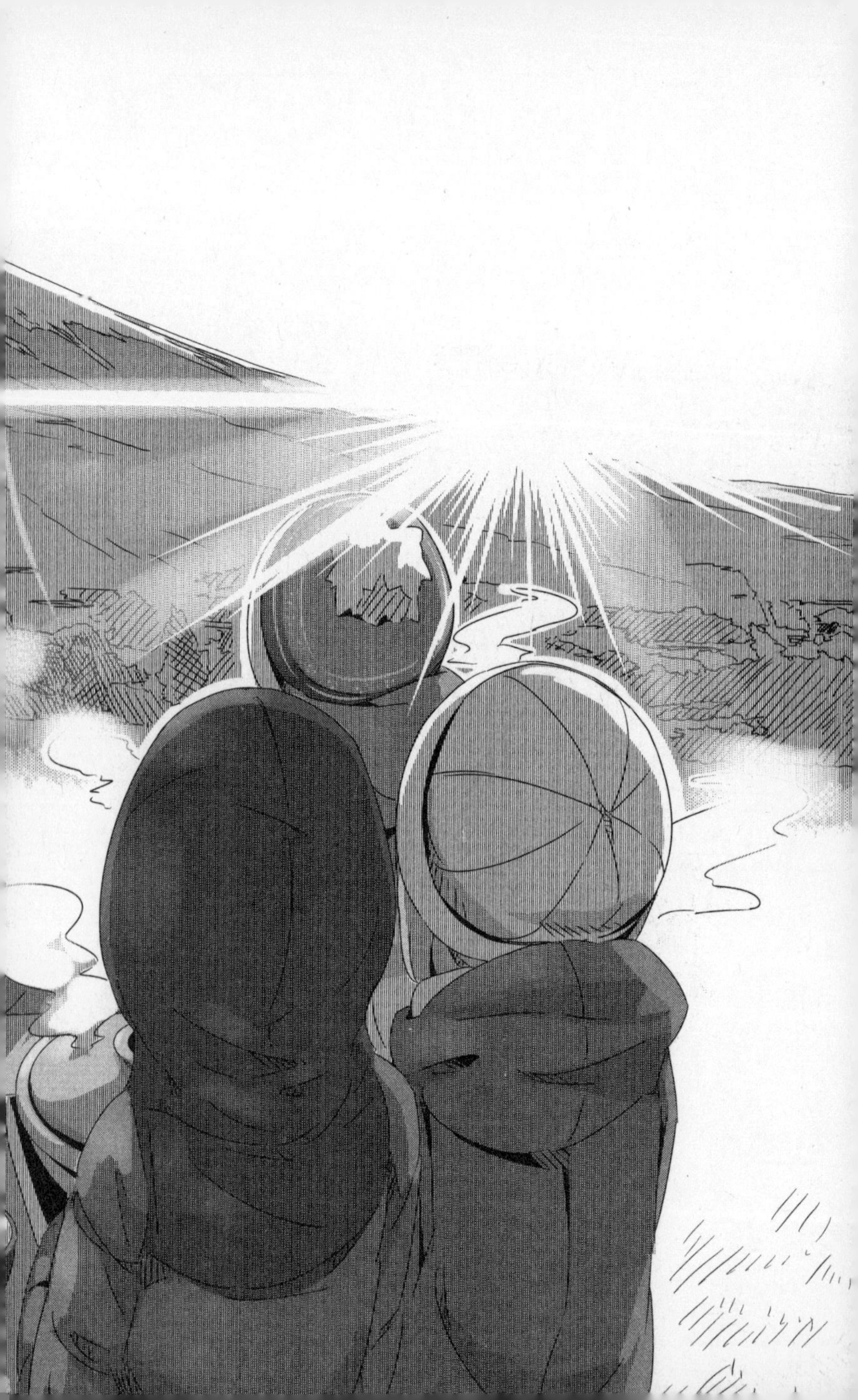

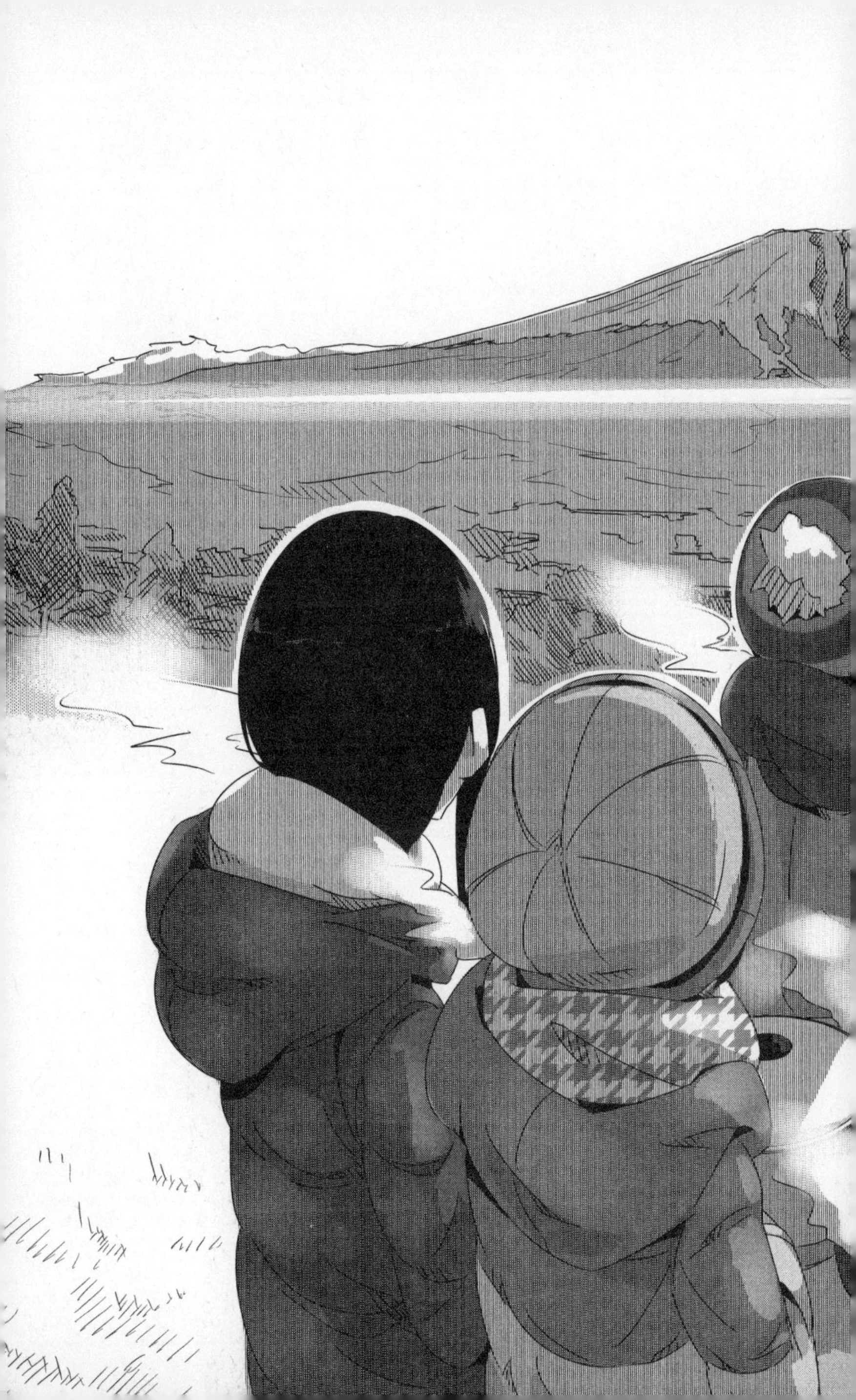

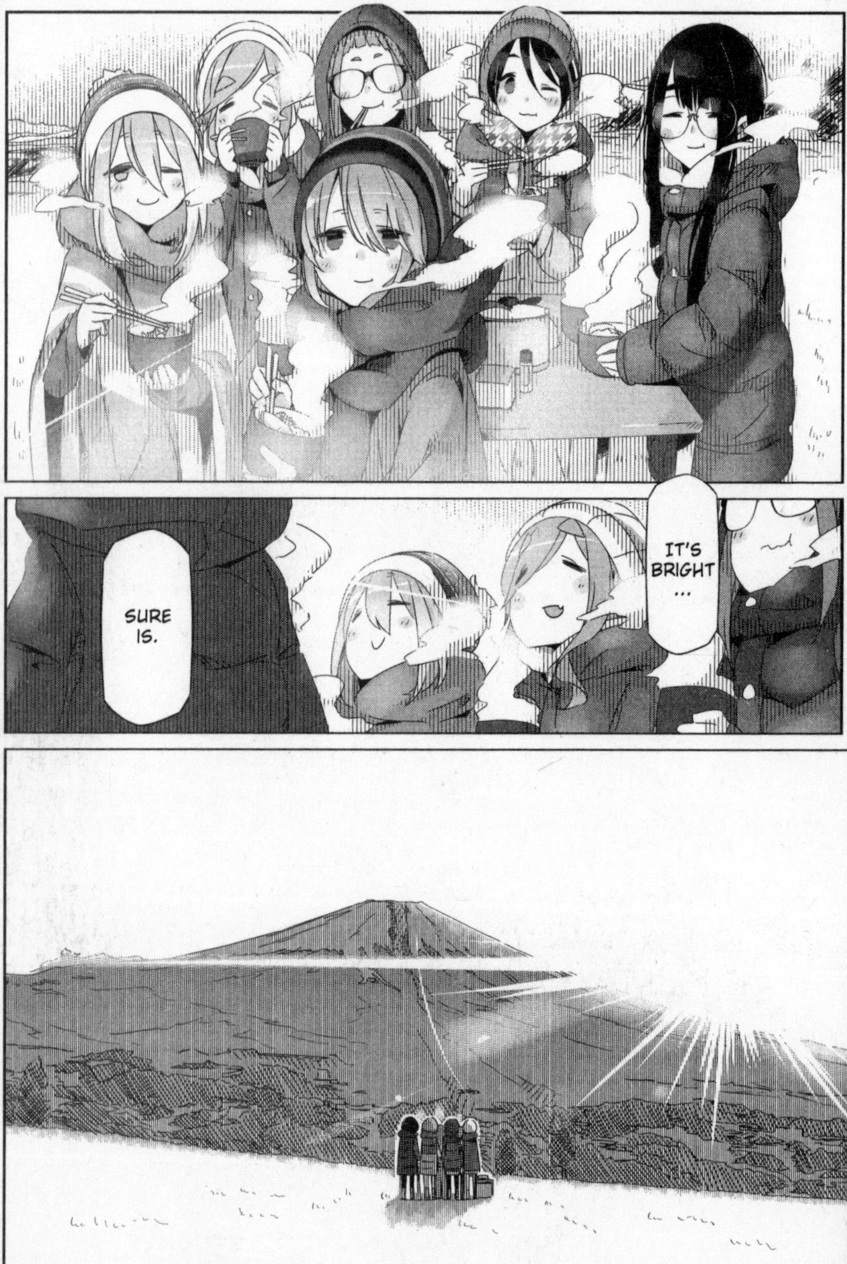
IT'S BRIGHT ...
SURE IS.

TRANSLATION NOTES

COMMON HONORIFICS

no honorific: Indicates familiarity or closeness; if used without permission or reason, addressing someone in this manner would constitute an insult.

-san: The Japanese equivalent of Mr./Mrs./Miss. If a situation calls for politeness, this is the fail-safe honorific.

-kun: Used most often when referring to boys, this indicates affection or familiarity. Occasionally used by older men among their peers, but it may also be used by anyone referring to a person of lower standing.

-chan: An affectionate honorific indicating familiarity used mostly in reference to girls; also used in reference to cute persons or animals of either gender.

-sensei: A respectful term for teachers, artists, or high-level professionals.

(o)nee: Japanese equivalent to "older sis."
(o)nii: Japanese equivalent to "older bro."

100 yen is approximately $1 USD.

Page 3
A-5-Grade Black *Wagyu* Sirloin: *Wagyu* (literally "Japanese cow") refers to domestically raised Japanese cattle. It's ranked according to quality, with A-5 being the highest grade achievable. Black (or Japanese black) is one of four breeds of Japanese cow.

Page 18
All bow-wow: In Japanese, Nadeshiko's last attempt has her say, "All *wanwan*?" Wanwan, in addition to sounding like "one-one" in English, is also the Japanese equivalent of "bark" or "bow-wow." It's also a cutesy way to refer to dogs in general.

Page 55
9.5: In Japan, milk products are labeled and marketed according to how much milk fat content they have. The milk carton here indicates that it is 9.5% milk fat.

Page 67
Christmas: Christmas in Japan is generally seen as more of a couples' holiday.

Page 90
Sukiyaki: A hot-pot-style dish where beef, vegetables, tofu, noodles, and other ingredients are simmered together in a special soup stock.

TRANSLATION NOTES (continued)

Page 99
New Year's cards: In Japan, it's tradition to write and receive postcards congratulating friends, relatives, wishing a Happy New Year. It originally began as a way to inform those you couldn't see often that you were doing okay.

Page 107
End-of-Year Squad Santa Rangers: The format of this joke caption, with its *End-of-Year Squad* subtitle, is a reference to how Japanese Super Sentai shows (the source material for the Power Rangers franchise) are commonly titled. For example, *Mighty Morphin' Power Rangers* is adapted from *Kyouryuu Sentai* ["Dinosaur Squad"] *Zyuranger*.

Page 109
"We're givin' it a new color!": In Japanese, Aoi uses the term *oiro naoshi* ("color revision"), which refers to the process of redyeing an outfit or costume. Traditionally, it was also used to mean when a newly married bride changed out of her ceremonial kimono to a different one.

Page 130
Shimarin Dango: *Dango* here refers both to a kind of Japanese spherical dumpling treat and the bun-shaped hairstyle named after it.

Page 143
Yamato stew: Known as *yamatoni* in Japanese, it's a dish made by boiling beef in ginger, sugar, and soy sauce. "Yamato" is a synonym for "Japan."

Page 149
Hardtack: Simple and firm crackers/biscuits with an extremely long shelf life that makes them ideal for emergency rations.

Page 152
Kuwabara, kuwabara: A phrase said to ward off bad fortune (the phrase itself refers to using a mulberry field to ward off lightning).

Page 163
The Go-Home Club: A tongue-in-cheek name given to the situation of students who elect not to join an extracurricular activity.

Page 167
Tako-san wieners: These are mini-sausages cut to look like octopus. As the word *tako* is Japanese for "octopus," Nadeshiko and Chiaki are arguing about whether the octopus or the wiener should be revered with an honorific like -san or even the more formal -sama (see above translation notes for more explanation on honorifics).

◁ SIDE STORIES BEGIN ON THE NEXT PAGE ◁

ROOM CAMP

AFTER-SCHOOL 13 MYSTERY OF THE TUNA CANS

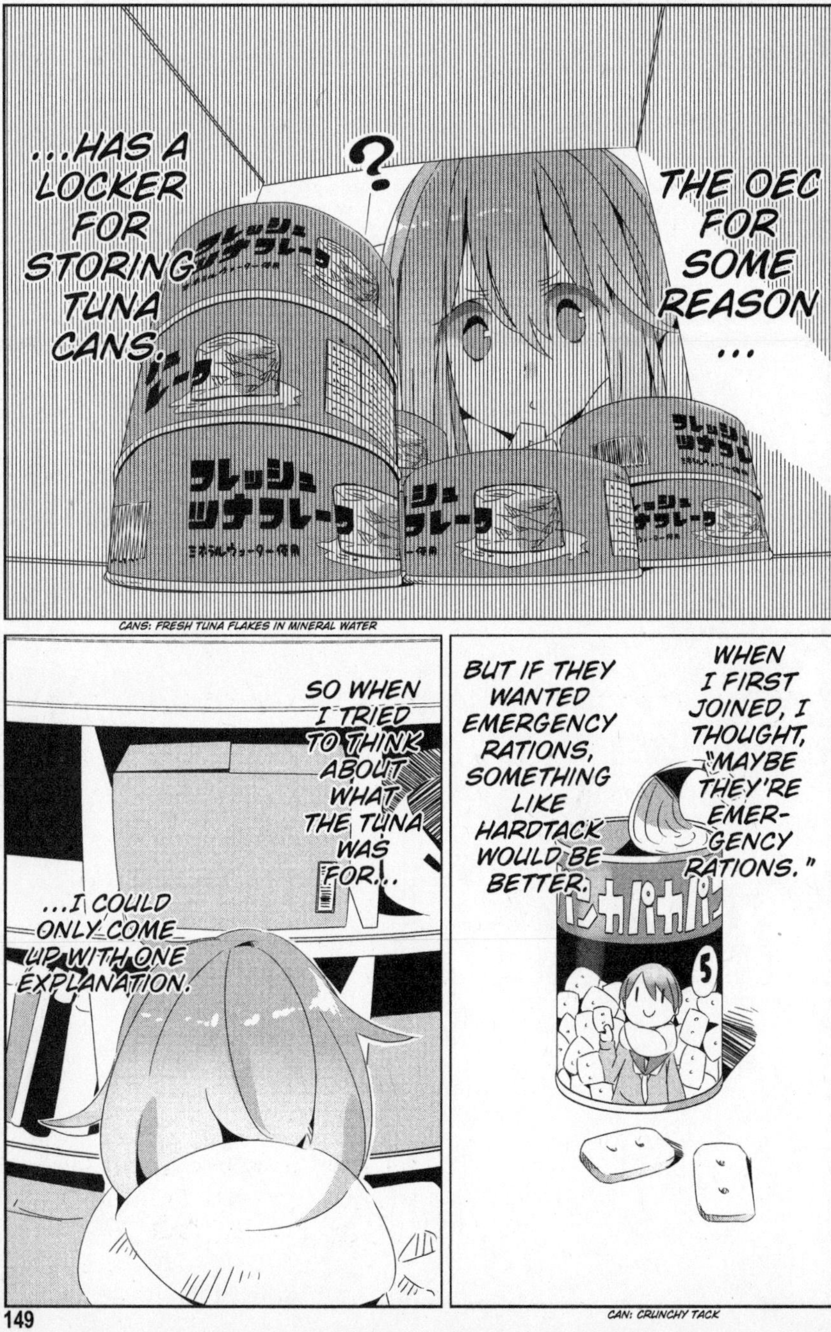
?
THE OEC FOR SOME REASON...
...HAS A LOCKER FOR STORING TUNA CANS.
WHEN I FIRST JOINED, I THOUGHT, "MAYBE THEY'RE EMER-GENCY RATIONS."
BUT IF THEY WANTED EMERGENCY RATIONS, SOMETHING LIKE HARDTACK WOULD BE BETTER.
5
SO WHEN I TRIED TO THINK ABOUT WHAT THE TUNA WAS FOR...
...I COULD ONLY COME UP WITH ONE EXPLANATION.

CANS: FRESH TUNA FLAKES IN MINERAL WATER

CAN: CRUNCHY TACK

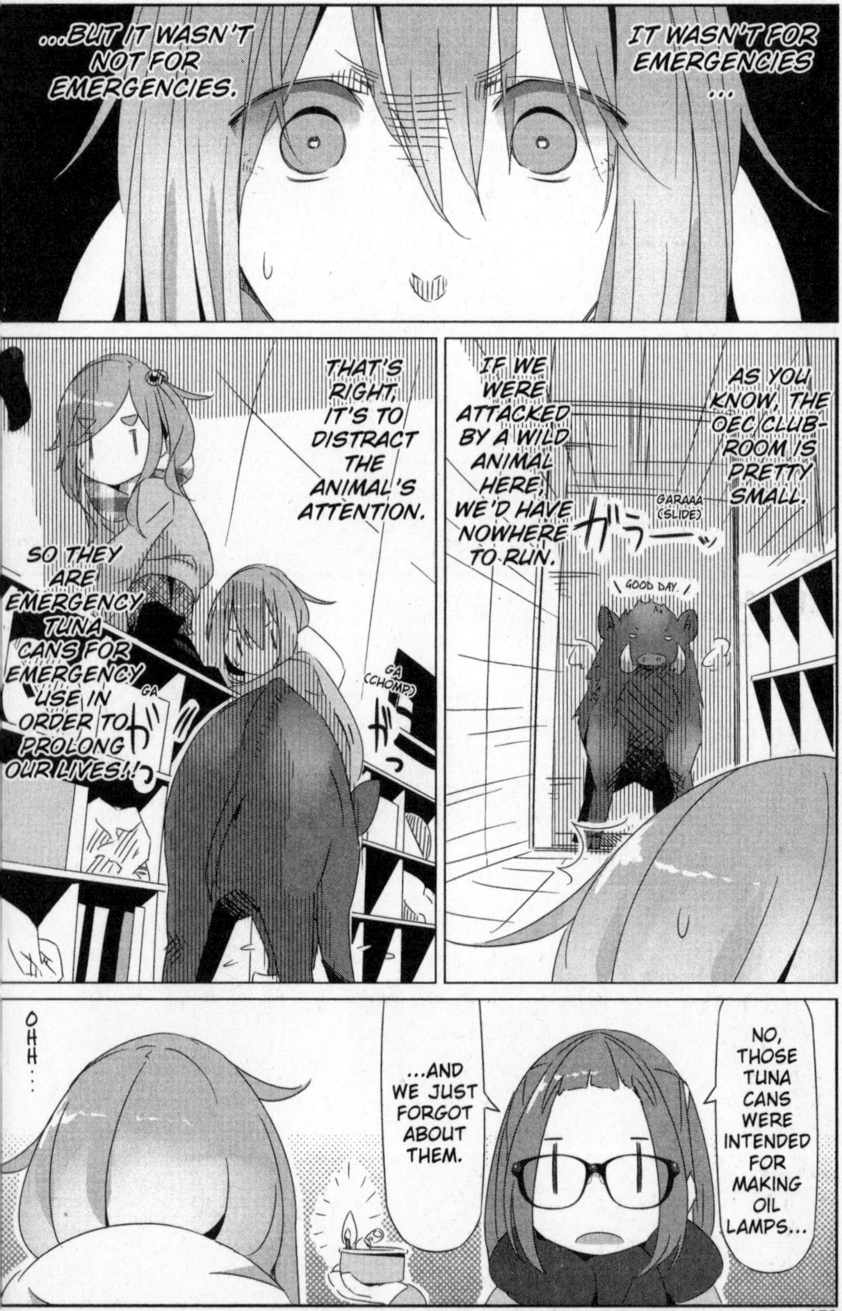
IT WASN'T FOR EMERGENCIES...
...BUT IT WASN'T NOT FOR EMERGENCIES.
AS YOU KNOW, THE OEC CLUB-ROOM IS PRETTY SMALL.
IF WE WERE ATTACKED BY A WILD ANIMAL HERE, WE'D HAVE NOWHERE TO RUN.
ガラーッ GARAAA (SLIDE)
GOOD DAY.
THAT'S RIGHT, IT'S TO DISTRACT THE ANIMAL'S ATTENTION.
GA (CHOMP)
SO THEY ARE EMERGENCY TUNA CANS FOR EMERGENCY USE IN ORDER TO PROLONG OUR LIVES!!
GA
NO, THOSE TUNA CANS WERE INTENDED FOR MAKING OIL LAMPS...
...AND WE JUST FORGOT ABOUT THEM.
OHH...

AFTER-SCHOOL 14 A REAL-LIFE SCARY STORY

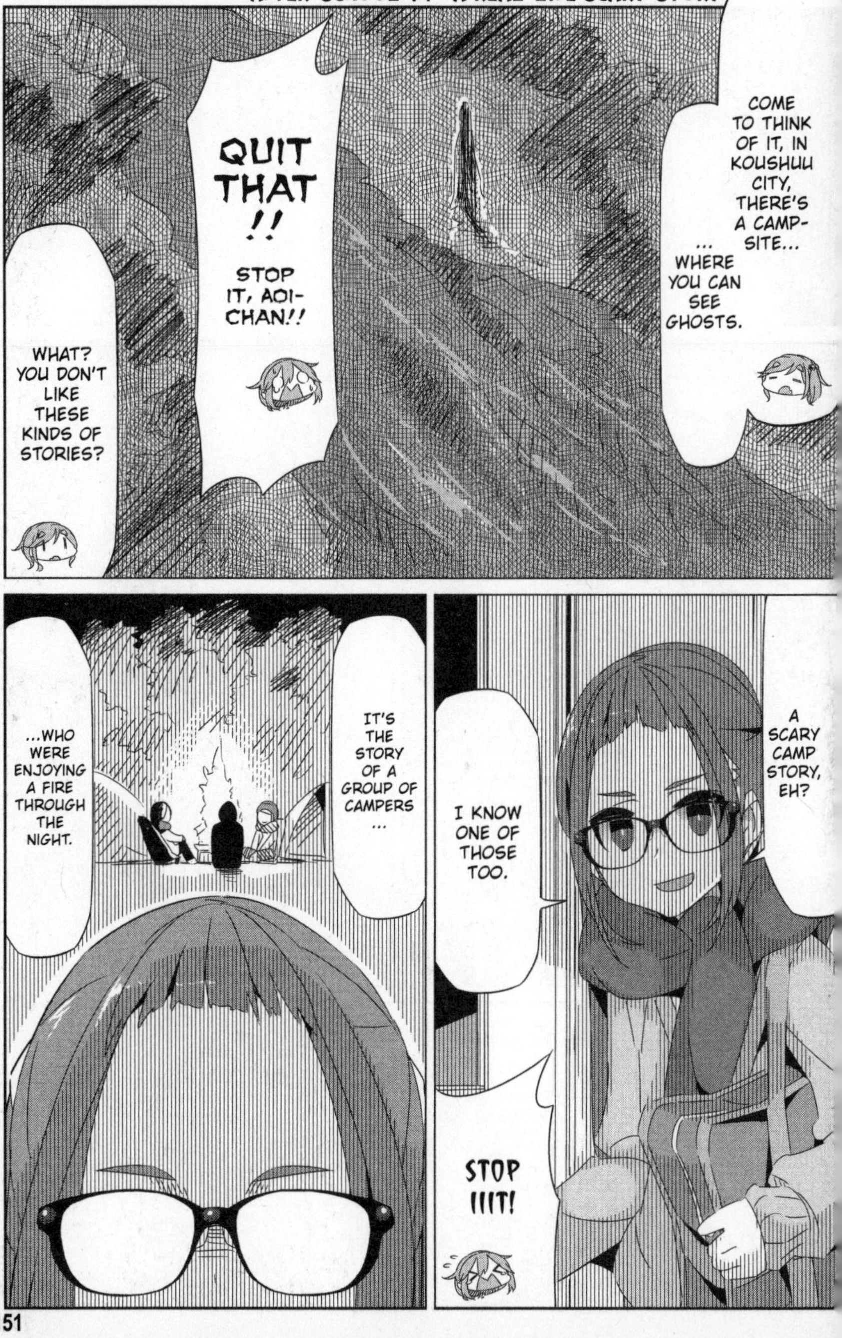
COME TO THINK OF IT, IN KOUSHUU CITY, THERE'S A CAMP-SITE...
...WHERE YOU CAN SEE GHOSTS.
QUIT THAT!!
STOP IT, AOI-CHAN!!
WHAT? YOU DON'T LIKE THESE KINDS OF STORIES?
A SCARY CAMP STORY, EH?
I KNOW ONE OF THOSE TOO.
STOP IIIT!
IT'S THE STORY OF A GROUP OF CAMPERS...
...WHO WERE ENJOYING A FIRE THROUGH THE NIGHT.

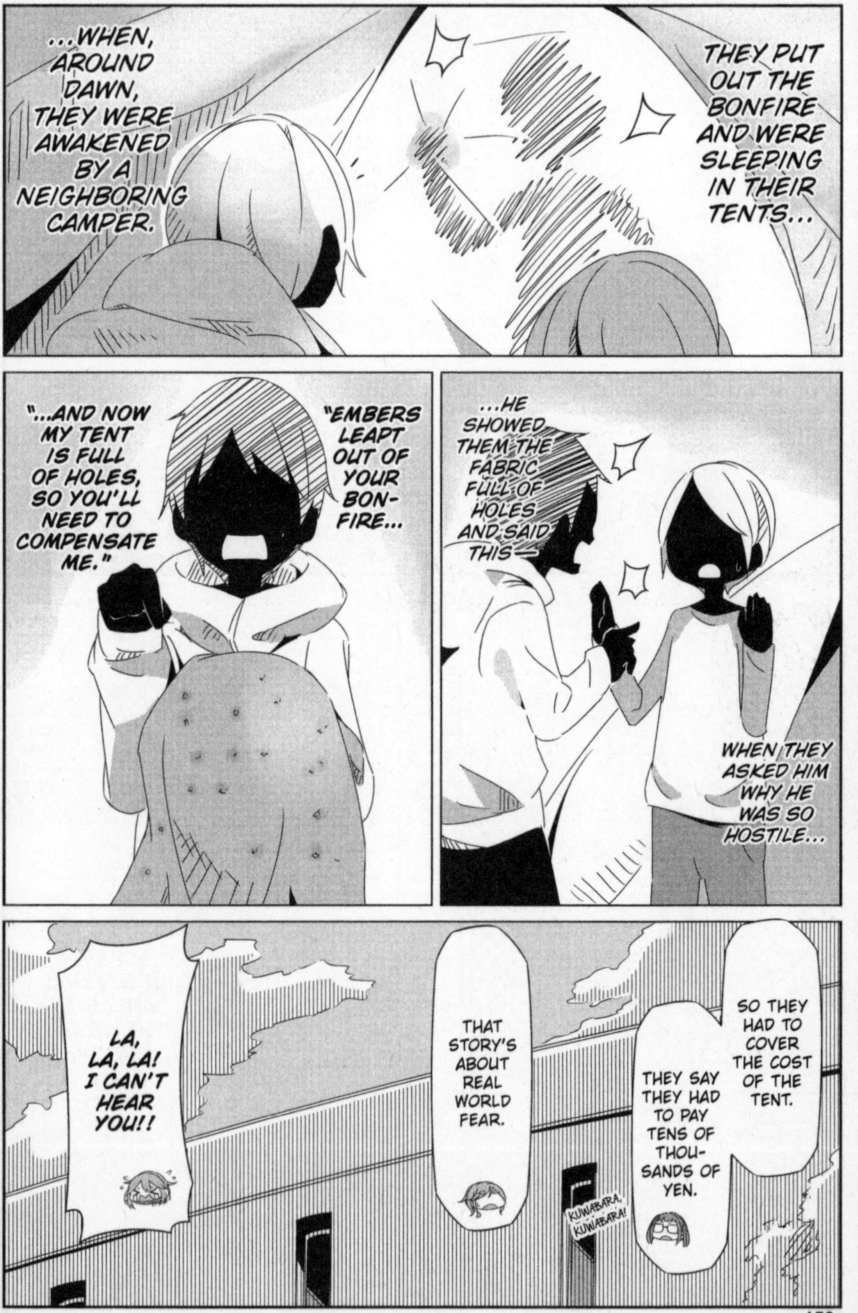
THEY PUT OUT THE BONFIRE AND WERE SLEEPING IN THEIR TENTS...
...WHEN, AROUND DAWN, THEY WERE AWAKENED BY A NEIGHBORING CAMPER.
WHEN THEY ASKED HIM WHY HE WAS SO HOSTILE...
...HE SHOWED THEM THE FABRIC FULL OF HOLES AND SAID THIS—
"EMBERS LEAPT OUT OF YOUR BON-FIRE...
"...AND NOW MY TENT IS FULL OF HOLES, SO YOU'LL NEED TO COMPENSATE ME."
SO THEY HAD TO COVER THE COST OF THE TENT.
THEY SAY THEY HAD TO PAY TENS OF THOU-SANDS OF YEN.
KUWABARA, KUWABARA!
THAT STORY'S ABOUT REAL WORLD FEAR.
LA, LA, LA! I CAN'T HEAR YOU!!

AFTER-SCHOOL 15 THE TRULY TERRIFYING CINEMA FESTIVAL

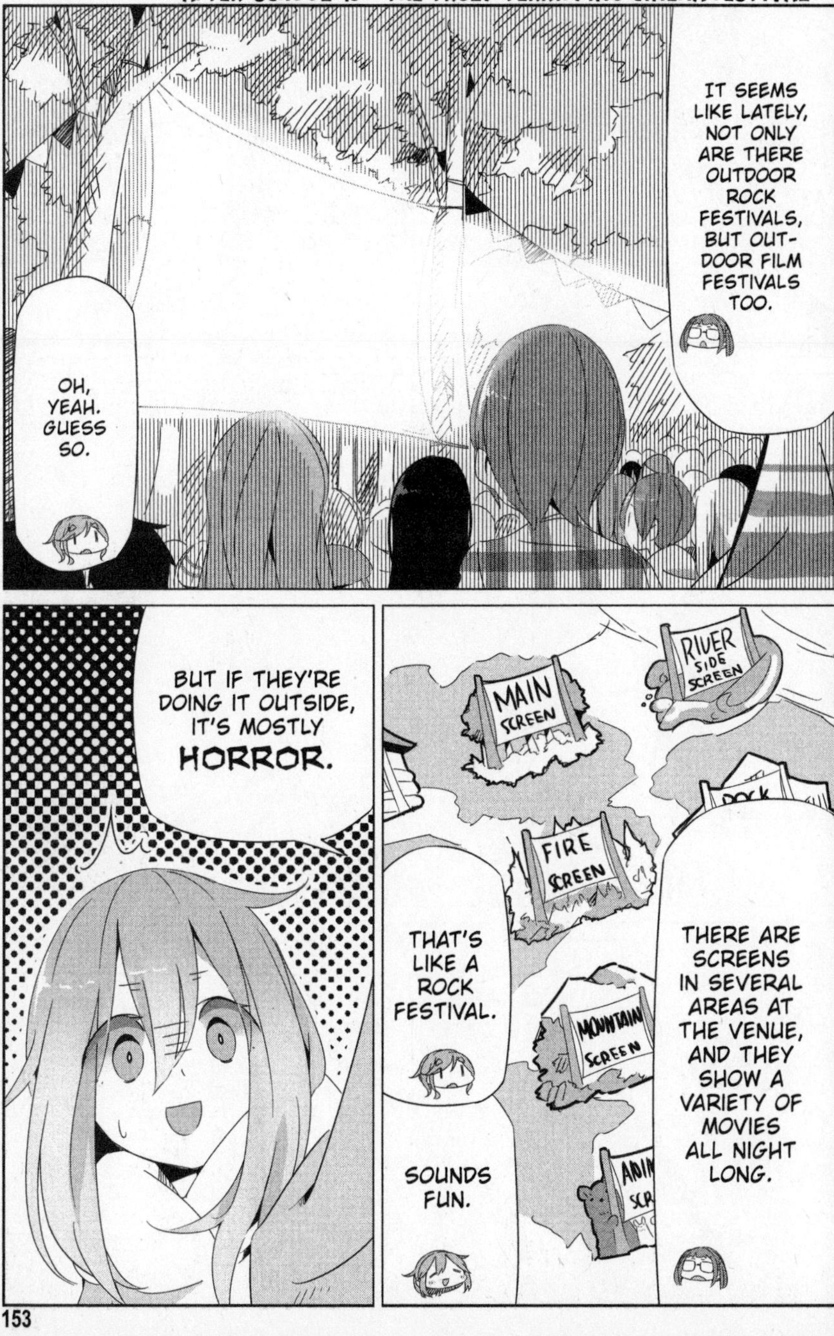
IT SEEMS LIKE LATELY, NOT ONLY ARE THERE OUTDOOR ROCK FESTIVALS, BUT OUT-DOOR FILM FESTIVALS TOO.
OH, YEAH. GUESS SO.
RIVER SIDE SCREEN
MAIN SCREEN
FIRE SCREEN
MOUNTAIN SCREEN
THERE ARE SCREENS IN SEVERAL AREAS AT THE VENUE, AND THEY SHOW A VARIETY OF MOVIES ALL NIGHT LONG.
THAT'S LIKE A ROCK FESTIVAL.
SOUNDS FUN.
BUT IF THEY'RE DOING IT OUTSIDE, IT'S MOSTLY **HORROR.**

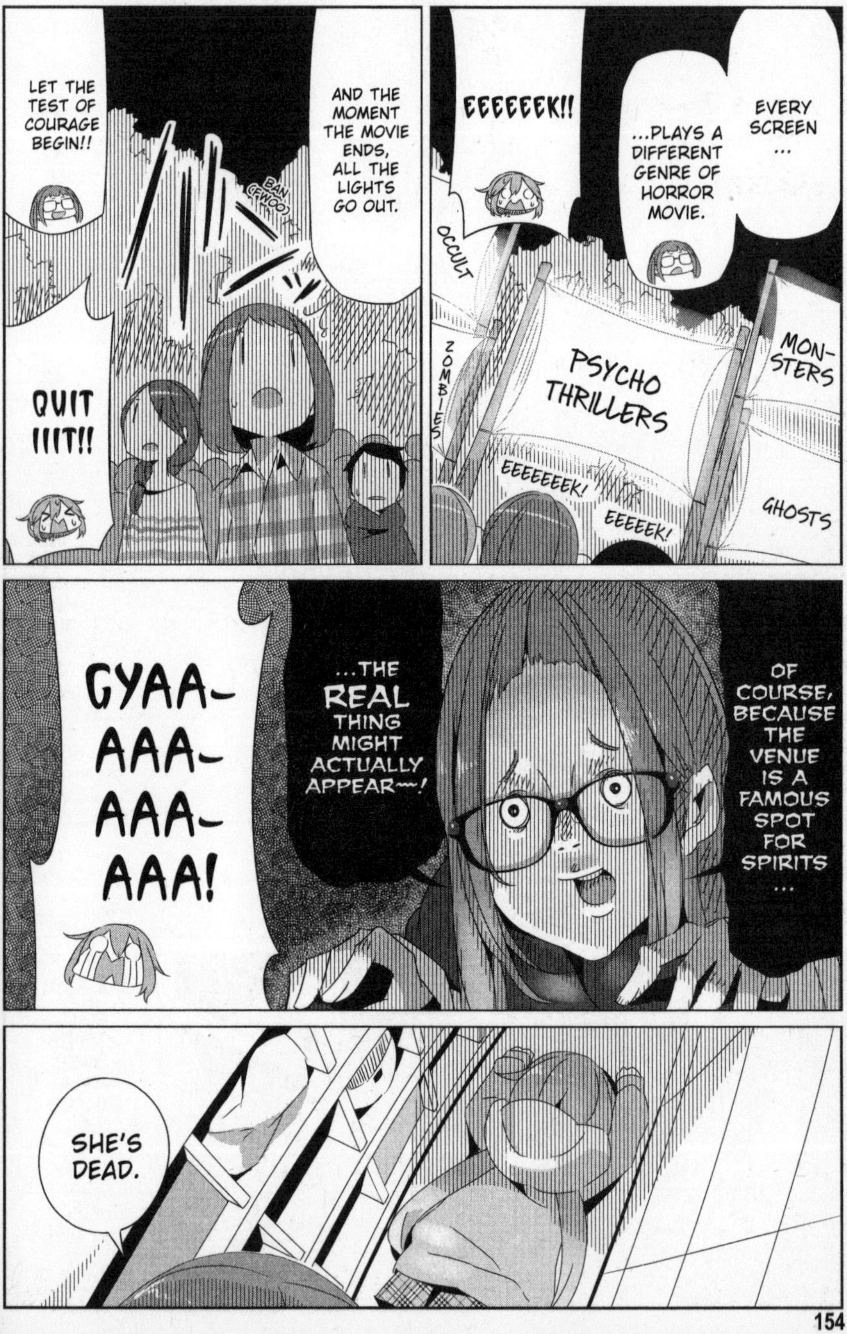
EVERY SCREEN...
...PLAYS A DIFFERENT GENRE OF HORROR MOVIE.
EEEEEEK!!
OCCULT
MON-STERS
PSYCHO THRILLERS
ZOMBIES
EEEEEEEK!
EEEEEK!
GHOSTS
AND THE MOMENT THE MOVIE ENDS, ALL THE LIGHTS GO OUT.
BAN (FWOO)
LET THE TEST OF COURAGE BEGIN!!
QUIT IIIT!!
OF COURSE, BECAUSE THE VENUE IS A FAMOUS SPOT FOR SPIRITS...
...THE REAL THING MIGHT ACTUALLY APPEAR~!
GYAA-AAA-AAA-AAA!
SHE'S DEAD.

AFTER-SCHOOL 16 CRAFTSMANSHIP

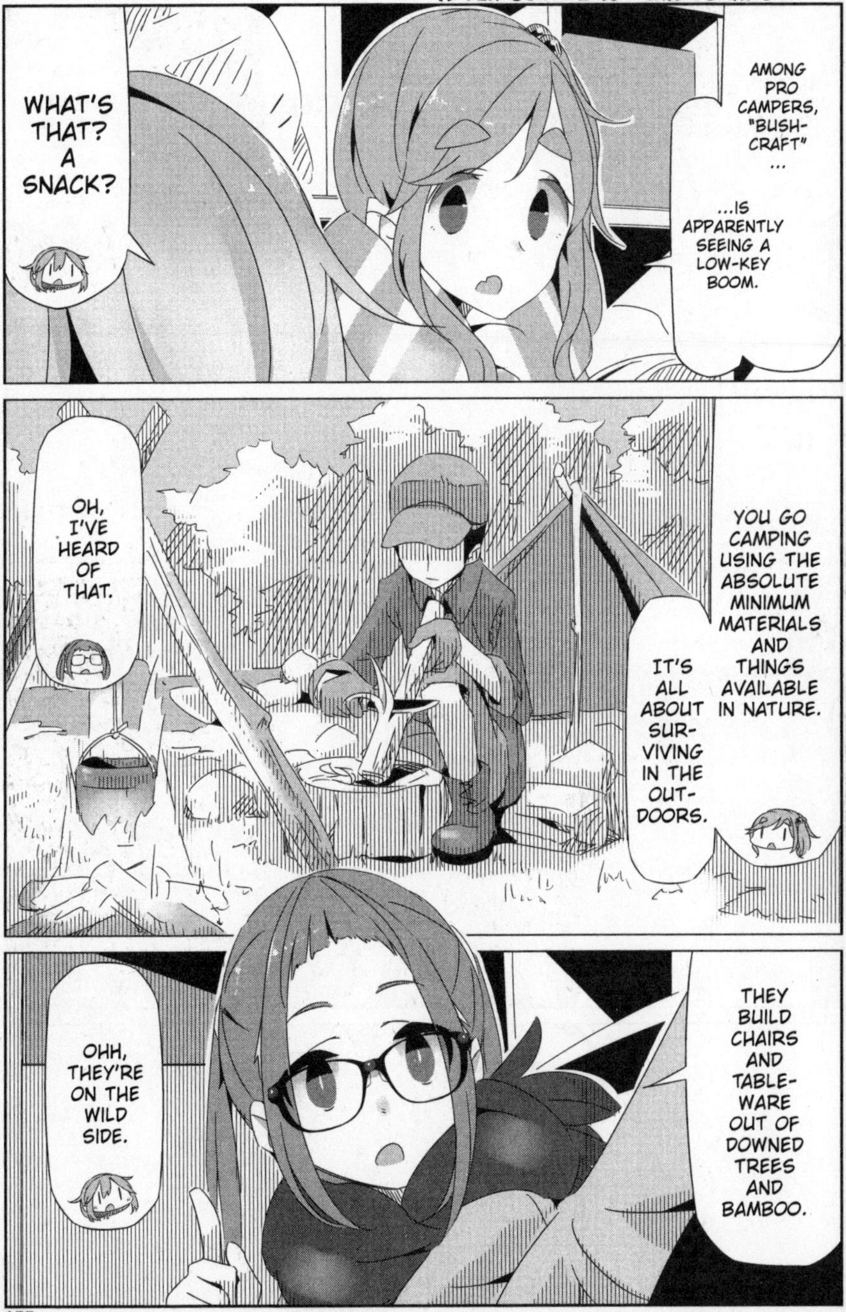
AMONG PRO CAMPERS, "BUSH-CRAFT" ...
...IS APPARENTLY SEEING A LOW-KEY BOOM.
WHAT'S THAT? A SNACK?
YOU GO CAMPING USING THE ABSOLUTE MINIMUM MATERIALS AND THINGS AVAILABLE IN NATURE.
IT'S ALL ABOUT SUR-VIVING IN THE OUT-DOORS.
OH, I'VE HEARD OF THAT.
THEY BUILD CHAIRS AND TABLE-WARE OUT OF DOWNED TREES AND BAMBOO.
OHH, THEY'RE ON THE WILD SIDE.

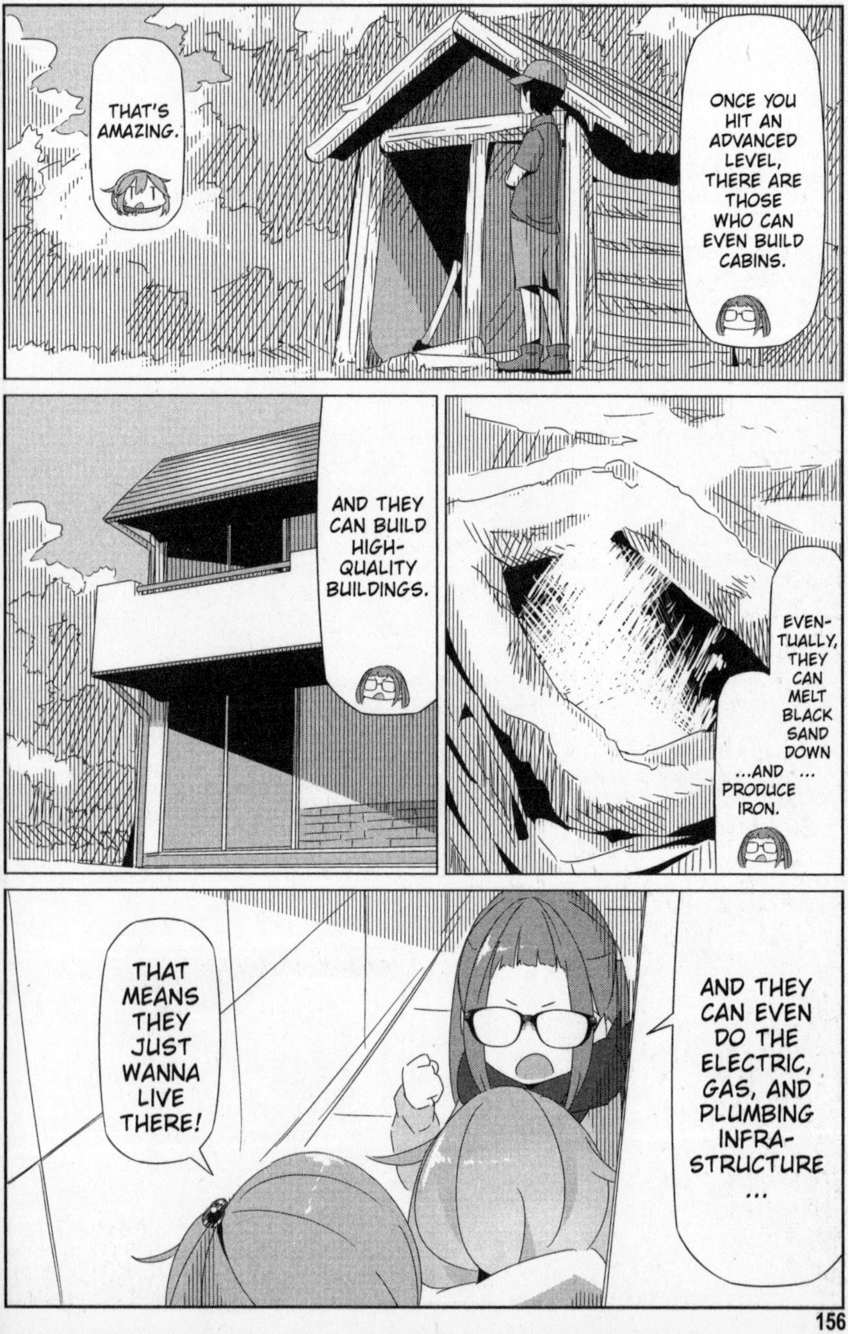
ONCE YOU HIT AN ADVANCED LEVEL, THERE ARE THOSE WHO CAN EVEN BUILD CABINS.
THAT'S AMAZING.
EVEN-TUALLY, THEY CAN MELT BLACK SAND DOWN ...AND ... PRODUCE IRON.
AND THEY CAN BUILD HIGH-QUALITY BUILDINGS.
AND THEY CAN EVEN DO THE ELECTRIC, GAS, AND PLUMBING INFRA-STRUCTURE ...
THAT MEANS THEY JUST WANNA LIVE THERE!

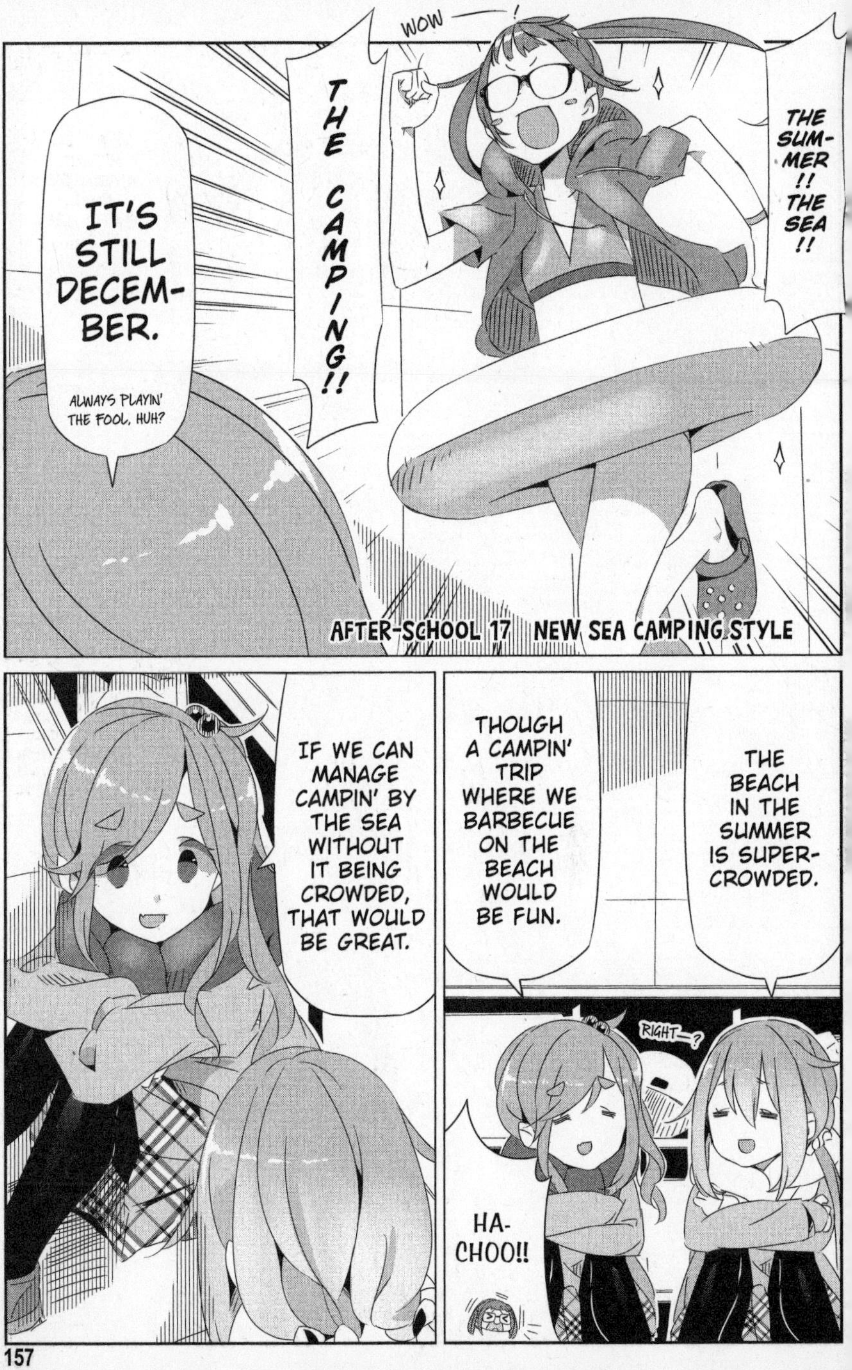
THE SUMMER!! THE SEA!!
WOW—!
THE CAMPING!!
IT'S STILL DECEMBER.
ALWAYS PLAYIN' THE FOOL, HUH?
AFTER-SCHOOL 17 NEW SEA CAMPING STYLE
THE BEACH IN THE SUMMER IS SUPER-CROWDED.
THOUGH A CAMPIN' TRIP WHERE WE BARBECUE ON THE BEACH WOULD BE FUN.
RIGHT—?
HA-CHOO!!
IF WE CAN MANAGE CAMPIN' BY THE SEA WITHOUT IT BEING CROWDED, THAT WOULD BE GREAT.

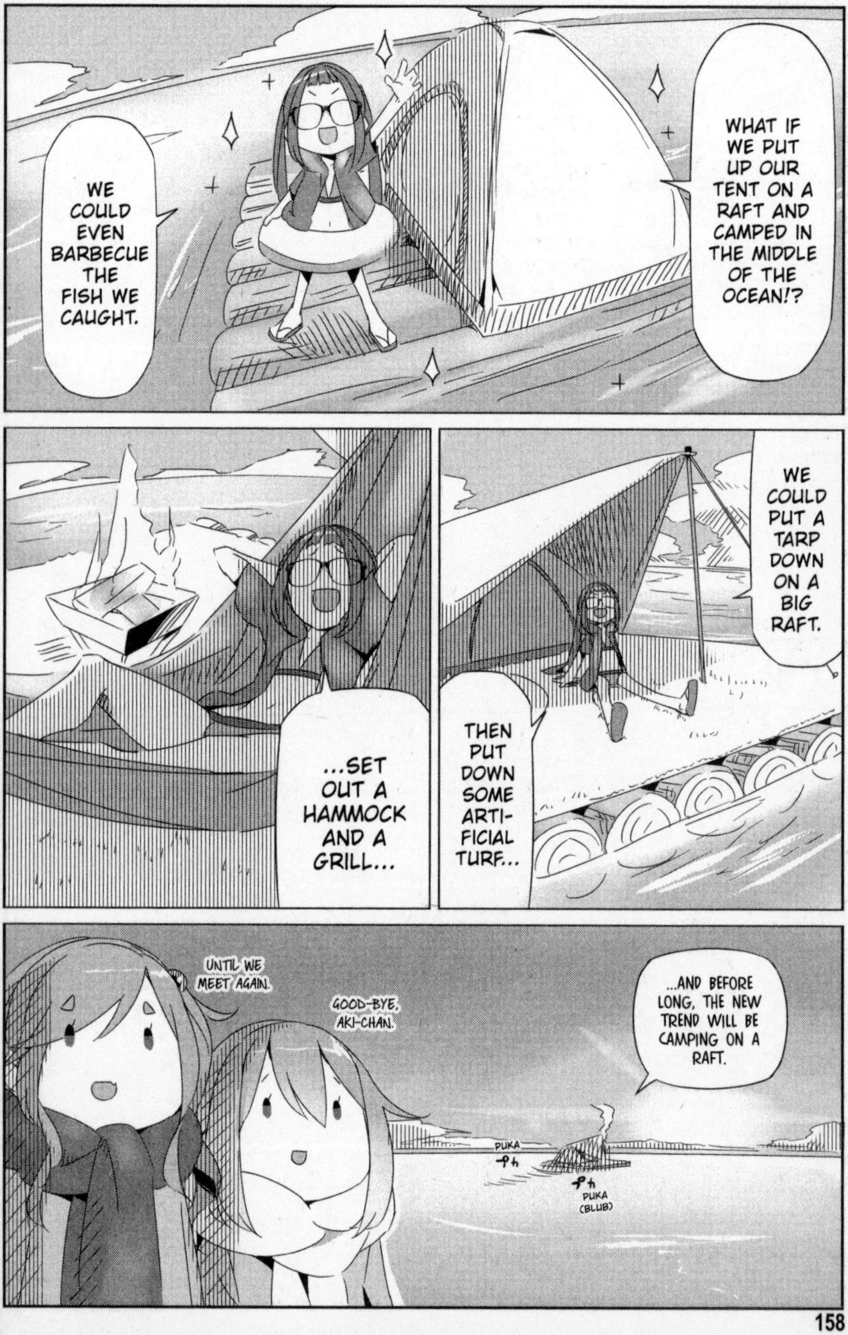
WHAT IF WE PUT UP OUR TENT ON A RAFT AND CAMPED IN THE MIDDLE OF THE OCEAN!?
WE COULD EVEN BARBECUE THE FISH WE CAUGHT.
WE COULD PUT A TARP DOWN ON A BIG RAFT.
THEN PUT DOWN SOME ARTI-FICIAL TURF...
...SET OUT A HAMMOCK AND A GRILL...
...AND BEFORE LONG, THE NEW TREND WILL BE CAMPING ON A RAFT.
PUKA
PUKA (BLUB)
GOOD-BYE, AKI-CHAN.
UNTIL WE MEET AGAIN.

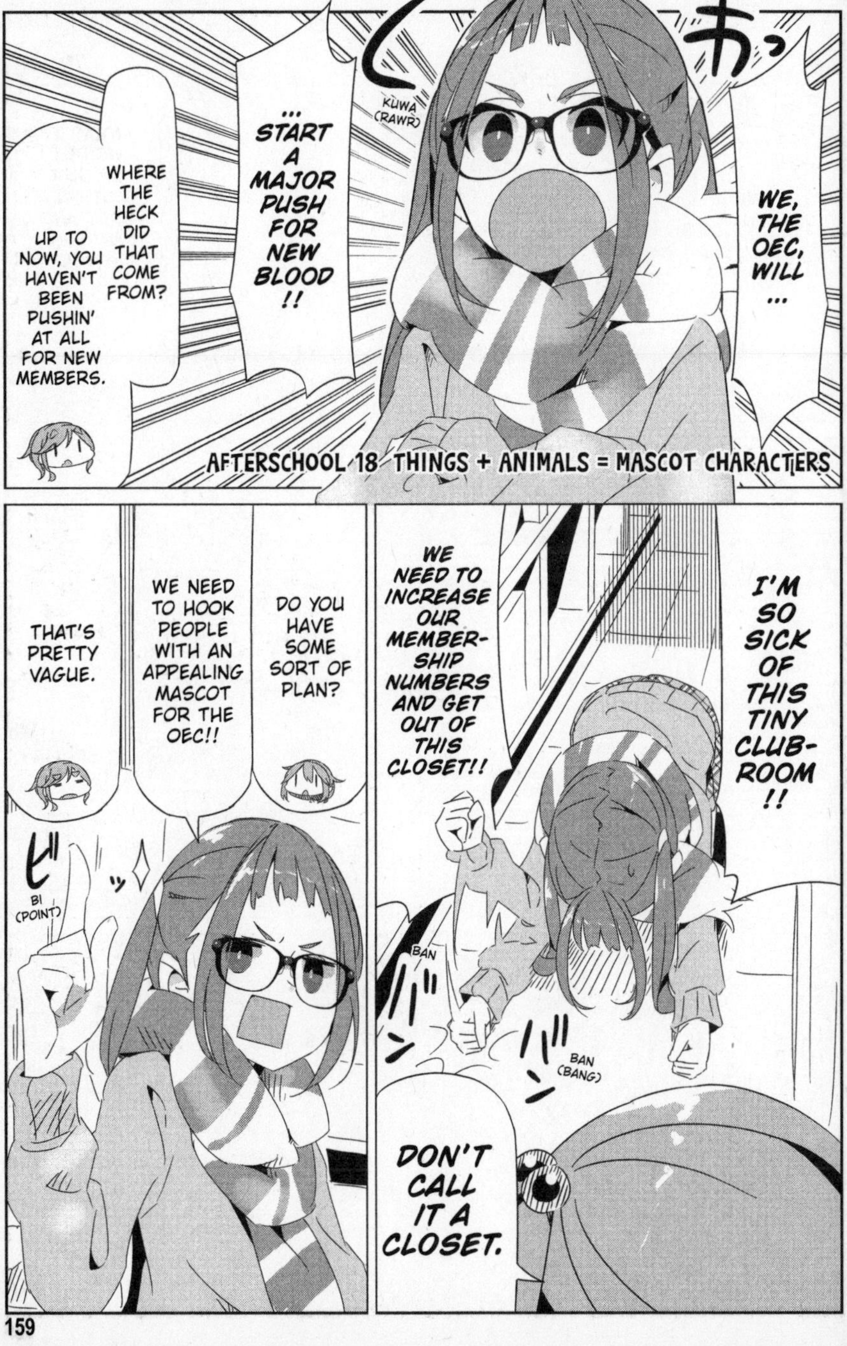
WE, THE OEC, WILL ...
KUWA (RAWR)
... START A MAJOR PUSH FOR NEW BLOOD!!
WHERE THE HECK DID THAT COME FROM?
UP TO NOW, YOU HAVEN'T BEEN PUSHIN' AT ALL FOR NEW MEMBERS.
AFTERSCHOOL 18 THINGS + ANIMALS = MASCOT CHARACTERS
I'M SO SICK OF THIS TINY CLUB-ROOM!!
WE NEED TO INCREASE OUR MEMBER-SHIP NUMBERS AND GET OUT OF THIS CLOSET!!
BAN
BAN (BANG)
DON'T CALL IT A CLOSET.
DO YOU HAVE SOME SORT OF PLAN?
WE NEED TO HOOK PEOPLE WITH AN APPEALING MASCOT FOR THE OEC!!
THAT'S PRETTY VAGUE.
BI (POINT)

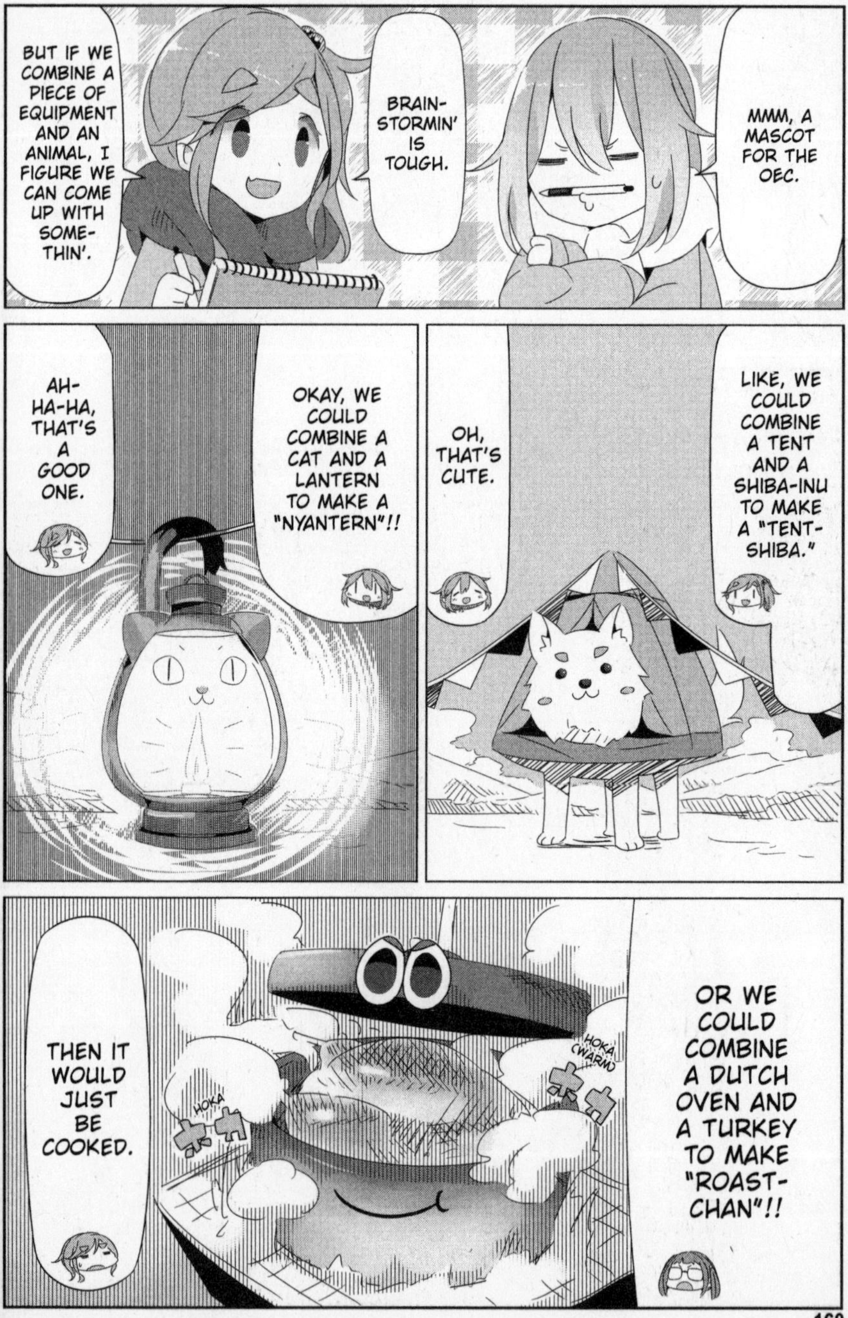
MMM, A MASCOT FOR THE OEC.
BRAIN-STORMIN' IS TOUGH.
BUT IF WE COMBINE A PIECE OF EQUIPMENT AND AN ANIMAL, I FIGURE WE CAN COME UP WITH SOME-THIN'.
LIKE, WE COULD COMBINE A TENT AND A SHIBA-INU TO MAKE A "TENT-SHIBA."
OH, THAT'S CUTE.
OKAY, WE COULD COMBINE A CAT AND A LANTERN TO MAKE A "NYANTERN"!!
AH-HA-HA, THAT'S A GOOD ONE.
OR WE COULD COMBINE A DUTCH OVEN AND A TURKEY TO MAKE "ROAST-CHAN"!!
HOKA (WARM)
HOKA
THEN IT WOULD JUST BE COOKED.

AFTER-SCHOOL 19 SAITOU-SAN IS RIGHT BEHIND YOU

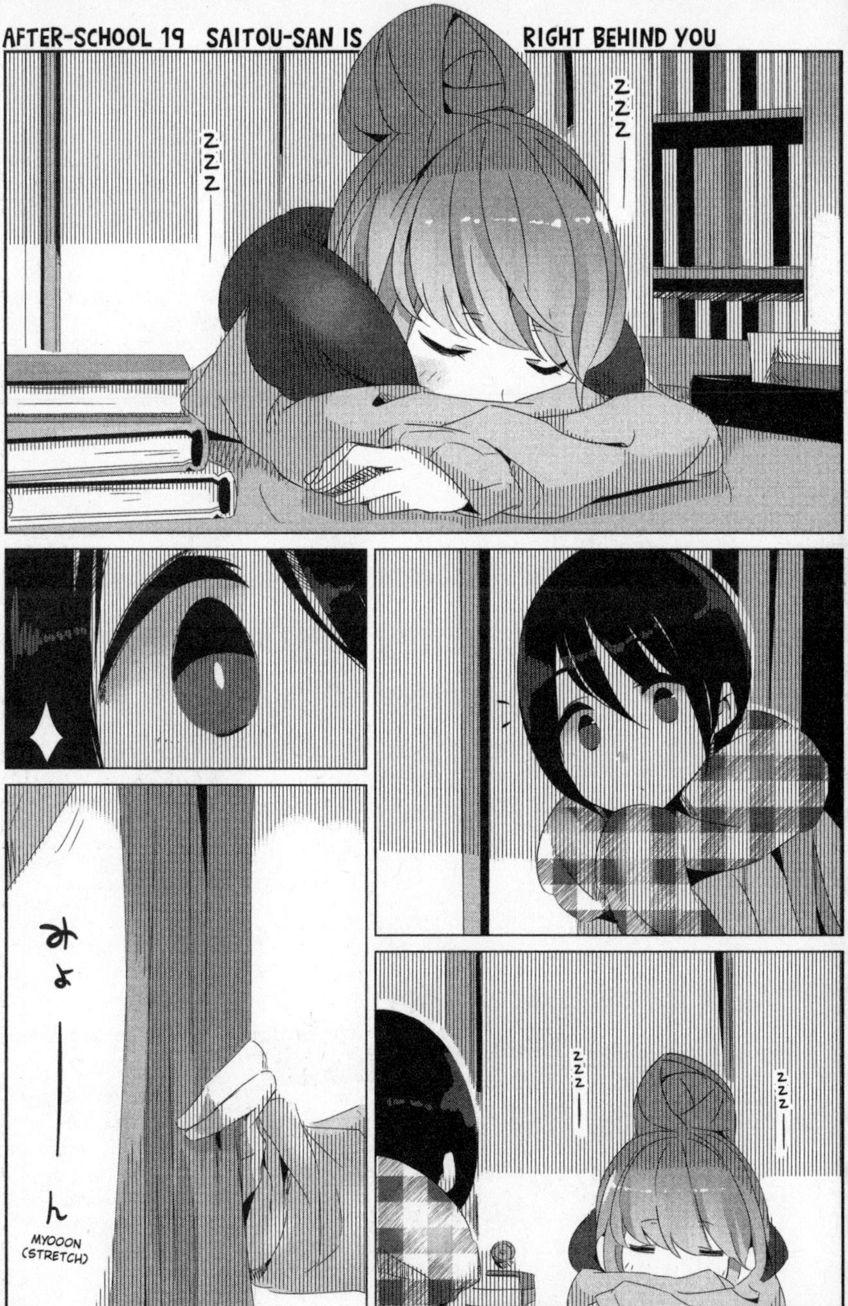

ZZZ—
ZZZ—
ZZZ—
ZZZ—
およーーーん
MYOOON (STRETCH)

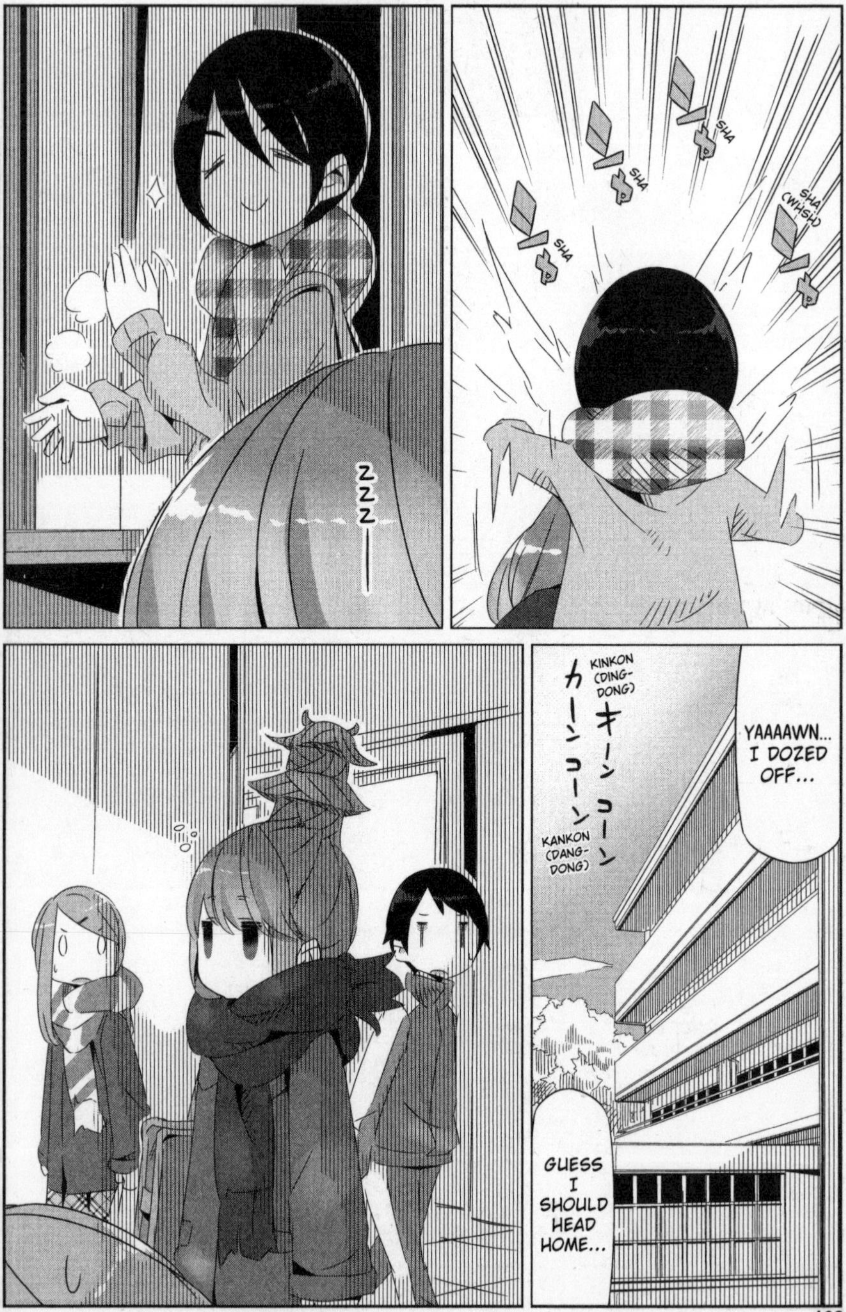
SHA
SHA (WHSH)
SHA
SHA
ZZZ—
KINKON (DING-DONG)
キーンコーン
カーンコーン
KANKON (DANG-DONG)
YAAAAWN... I DOZED OFF...
GUESS I SHOULD HEAD HOME...

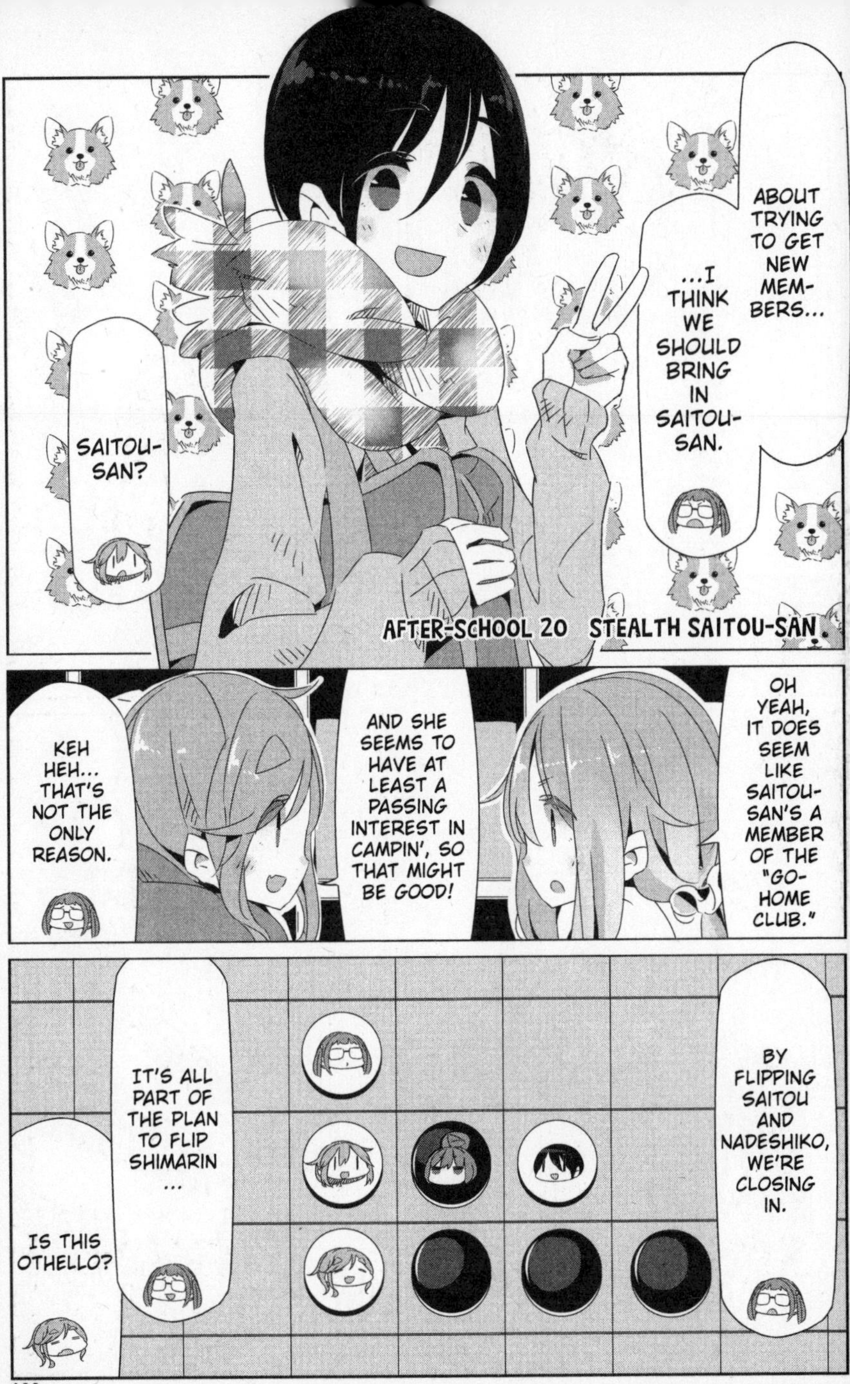
ABOUT TRYING TO GET NEW MEMBERS...
...I THINK WE SHOULD BRING IN SAITOU-SAN.
SAITOU-SAN?
AFTER-SCHOOL 20 STEALTH SAITOU-SAN
OH YEAH, IT DOES SEEM LIKE SAITOU-SAN'S A MEMBER OF THE "GO-HOME CLUB."
AND SHE SEEMS TO HAVE AT LEAST A PASSING INTEREST IN CAMPIN', SO THAT MIGHT BE GOOD!
KEH HEH... THAT'S NOT THE ONLY REASON.
BY FLIPPING SAITOU AND NADESHIKO, WE'RE CLOSING IN.
IT'S ALL PART OF THE PLAN TO FLIP SHIMARIN...
IS THIS OTHELLO?

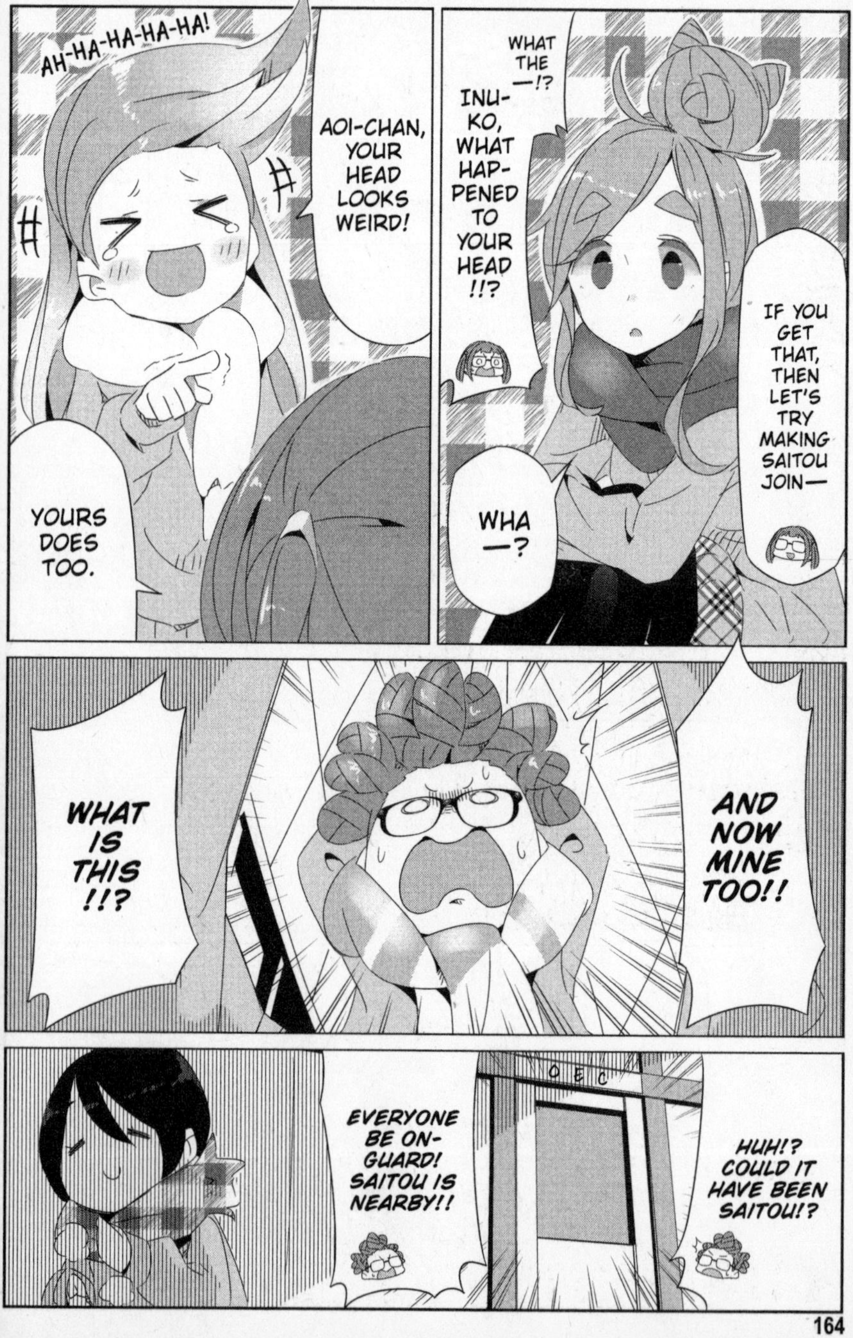
WHAT THE —!?
INUKO, WHAT HAPPENED TO YOUR HEAD!!?
IF YOU GET THAT, THEN LET'S TRY MAKING SAITOU JOIN—
WHA—?
AH-HA-HA-HA-HA!
AOI-CHAN, YOUR HEAD LOOKS WEIRD!
YOURS DOES TOO.
AND NOW MINE TOO!!
WHAT IS THIS!!?
O E C
HUH!? COULD IT HAVE BEEN SAITOU!?
EVERYONE BE ON-GUARD! SAITOU IS NEARBY!!

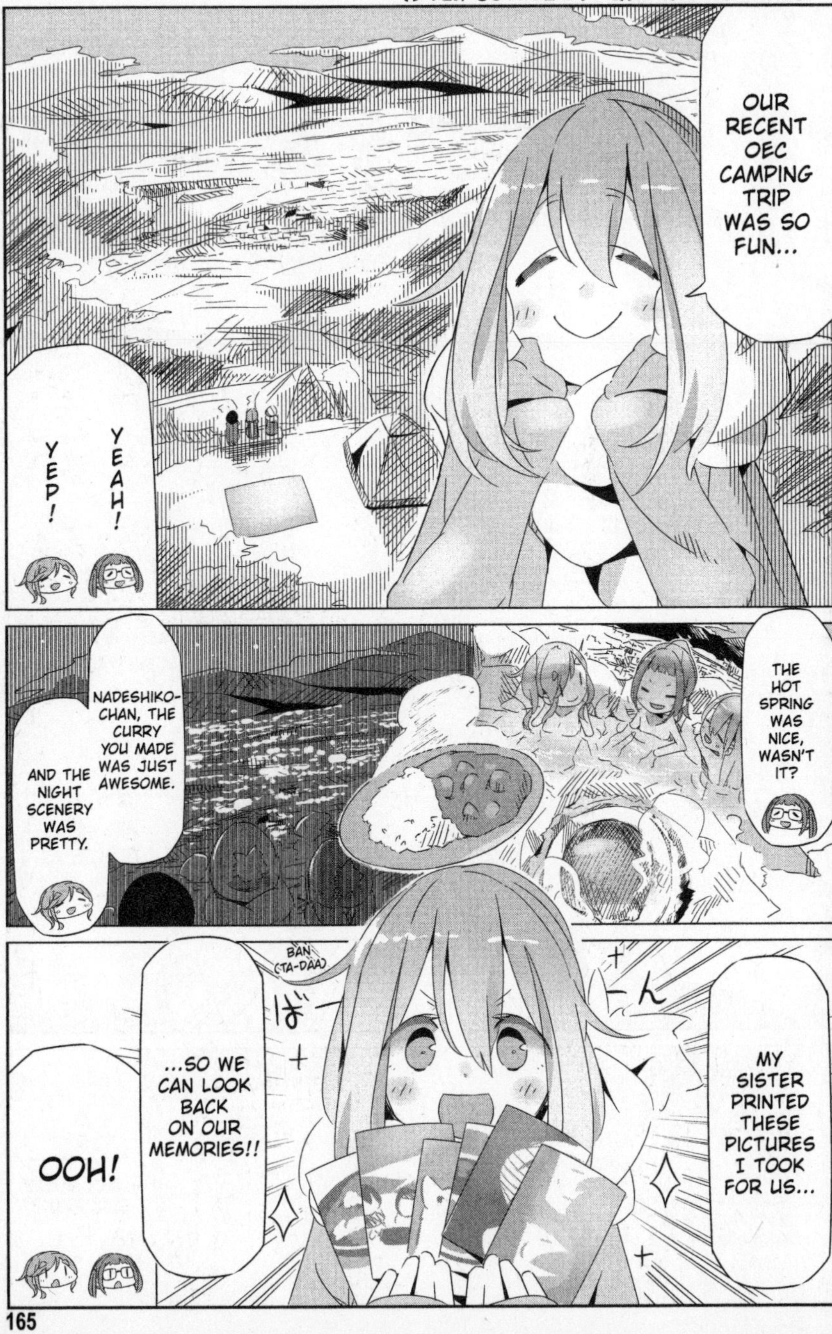
OUR RECENT OEC CAMPING TRIP WAS SO FUN...
YEAH!
YEP!
THE HOT SPRING WAS NICE, WASN'T IT?
NADESHIKO-CHAN, THE CURRY YOU MADE WAS JUST AWESOME.
AND THE NIGHT SCENERY WAS PRETTY.
MY SISTER PRINTED THESE PICTURES I TOOK FOR US...
ばーん
BAN (TA-DAA)
...SO WE CAN LOOK BACK ON OUR MEMORIES!!
OOH!

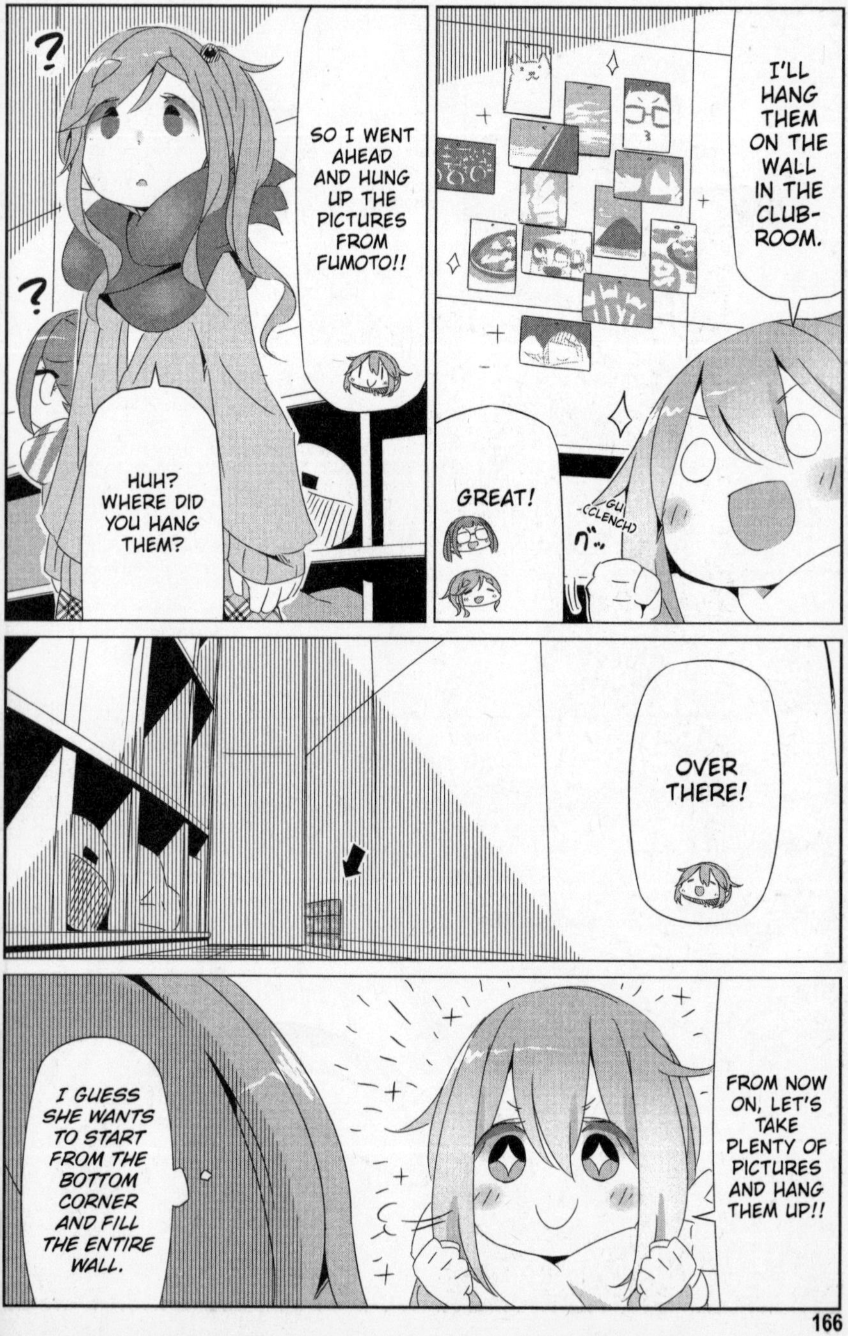

I'LL HANG THEM ON THE WALL IN THE CLUB-ROOM.
GREAT!
GU -(CLENCH)
グッ
SO I WENT AHEAD AND HUNG UP THE PICTURES FROM FUMOTO!!
HUH? WHERE DID YOU HANG THEM?
OVER THERE!
FROM NOW ON, LET'S TAKE PLENTY OF PICTURES AND HANG THEM UP!!
I GUESS SHE WANTS TO START FROM THE BOTTOM CORNER AND FILL THE ENTIRE WALL.

AFTER-SCHOOL 22 TAKO-SAN, WIENER-SAN

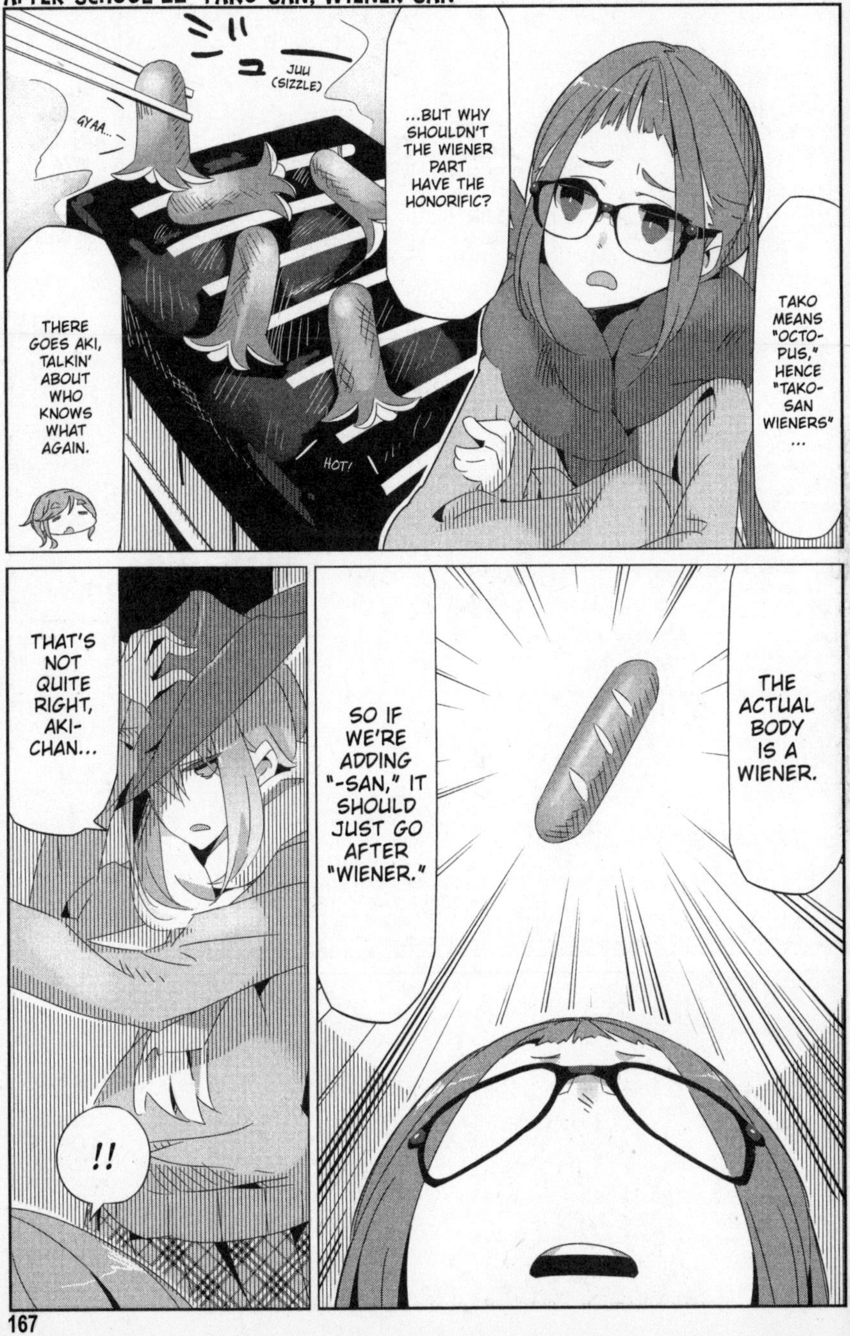
TAKO MEANS "OCTOPUS," HENCE "TAKO-SAN WIENERS"...
...BUT WHY SHOULDN'T THE WIENER PART HAVE THE HONORIFIC?
ジュー
JUU (SIZZLE)
GYAA...
HOT!
THERE GOES AKI, TALKIN' ABOUT WHO KNOWS WHAT AGAIN.
THE ACTUAL BODY IS A WIENER.
SO IF WE'RE ADDING "-SAN," IT SHOULD JUST GO AFTER "WIENER."
THAT'S NOT QUITE RIGHT, AKI-CHAN...
!!

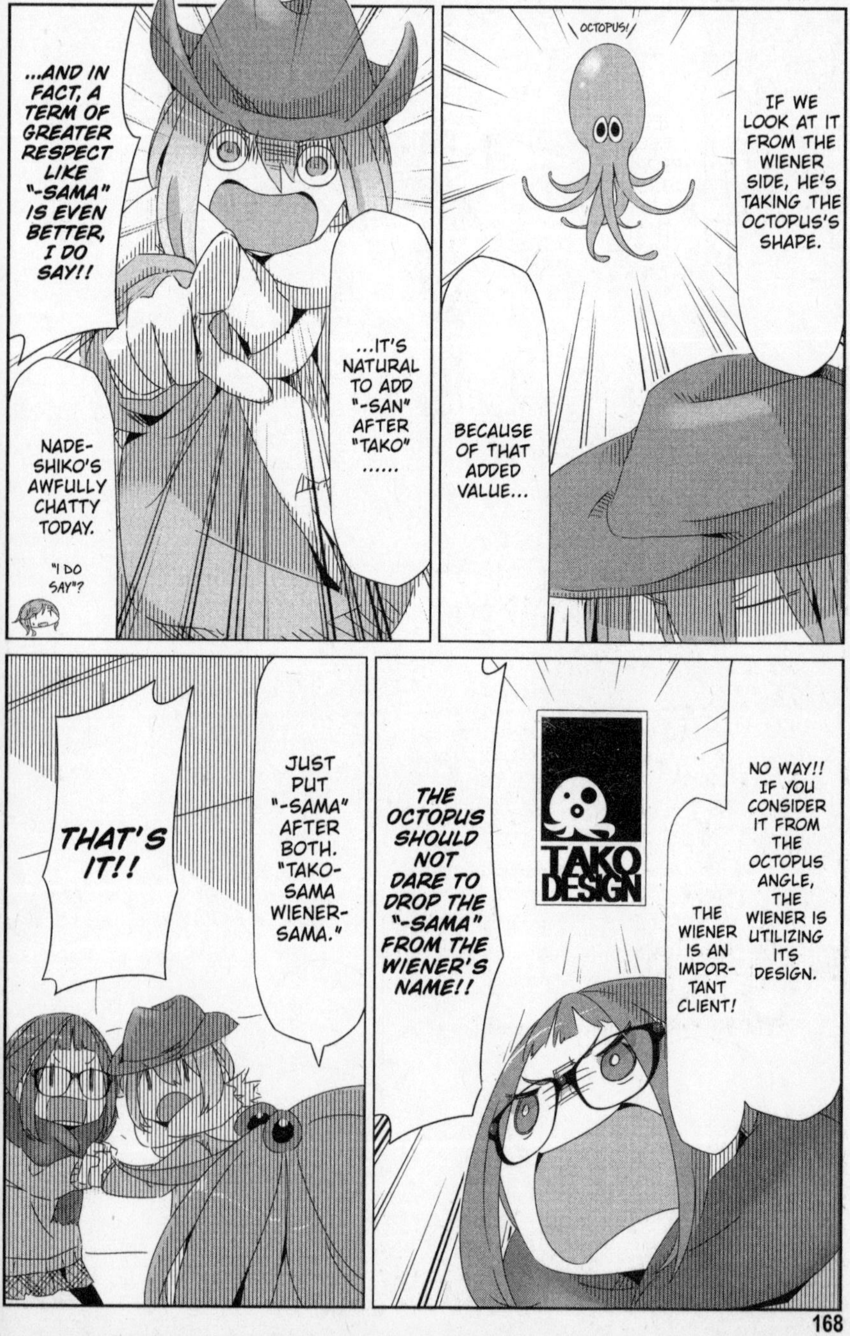
OCTOPUS!
IF WE LOOK AT IT FROM THE WIENER SIDE, HE'S TAKING THE OCTOPUS'S SHAPE.
BECAUSE OF THAT ADDED VALUE...
...IT'S NATURAL TO ADD "-SAN" AFTER "TAKO"......
...AND IN FACT, A TERM OF GREATER RESPECT LIKE "-SAMA" IS EVEN BETTER, I DO SAY!!
NADE-SHIKO'S AWFULLY CHATTY TODAY.
"I DO SAY"?
NO WAY!! IF YOU CONSIDER IT FROM THE OCTOPUS ANGLE, THE WIENER IS UTILIZING ITS DESIGN.
THE WIENER IS AN IMPOR-TANT CLIENT!
TAKO DESIGN
THE OCTOPUS SHOULD NOT DARE TO DROP THE "-SAMA" FROM THE WIENER'S NAME!!
JUST PUT "-SAMA" AFTER BOTH. "TAKO-SAMA WIENER-SAMA."
THAT'S IT!!

AFTER-SCHOOL 23 CAMPING BIKE

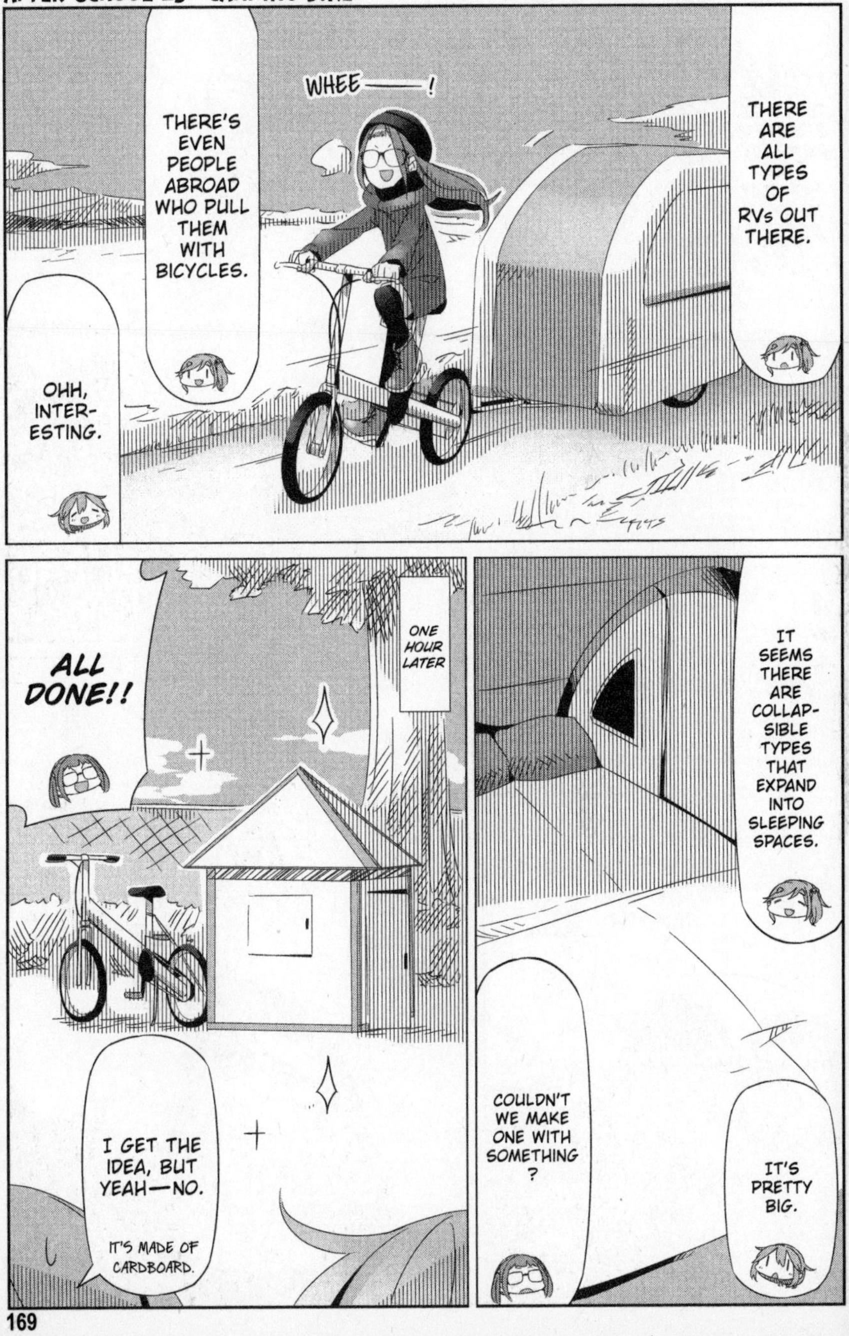
THERE ARE ALL TYPES OF RVs OUT THERE.
WHEE——!
THERE'S EVEN PEOPLE ABROAD WHO PULL THEM WITH BICYCLES.
OHH, INTER-ESTING.
IT SEEMS THERE ARE COLLAP-SIBLE TYPES THAT EXPAND INTO SLEEPING SPACES.
IT'S PRETTY BIG.
COULDN'T WE MAKE ONE WITH SOMETHING?
ONE HOUR LATER
ALL DONE!!
I GET THE IDEA, BUT YEAH—NO.
IT'S MADE OF CARDBOARD.

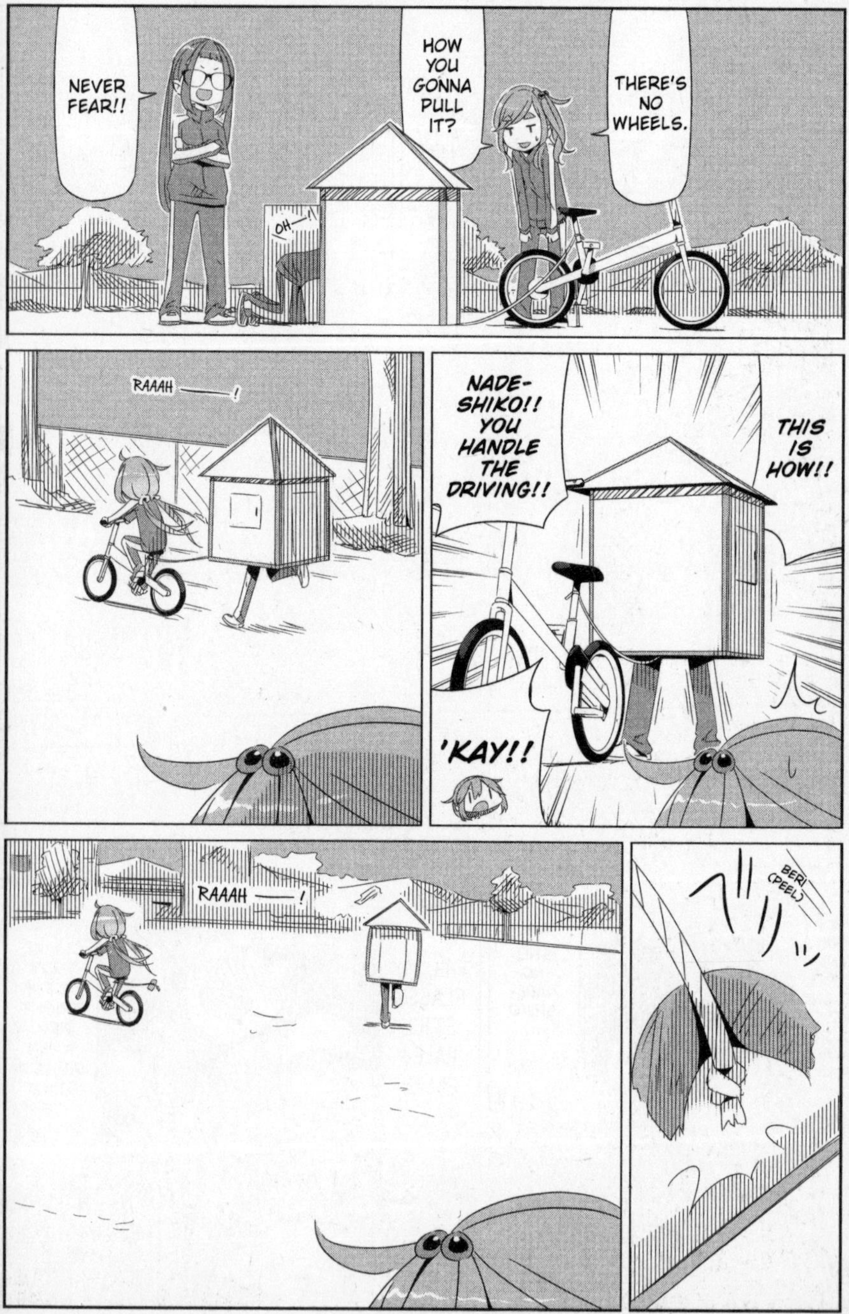
THERE'S NO WHEELS.
HOW YOU GONNA PULL IT?
NEVER FEAR!!
OH—!
THIS IS HOW!!
NADE-SHIKO!! YOU HANDLE THE DRIVING!!
'KAY!!
RAAAH—!
BERI (PEEL)
RAAAH—!

AFTER-SCHOOL 24 OEC, 10 YEARS LATER

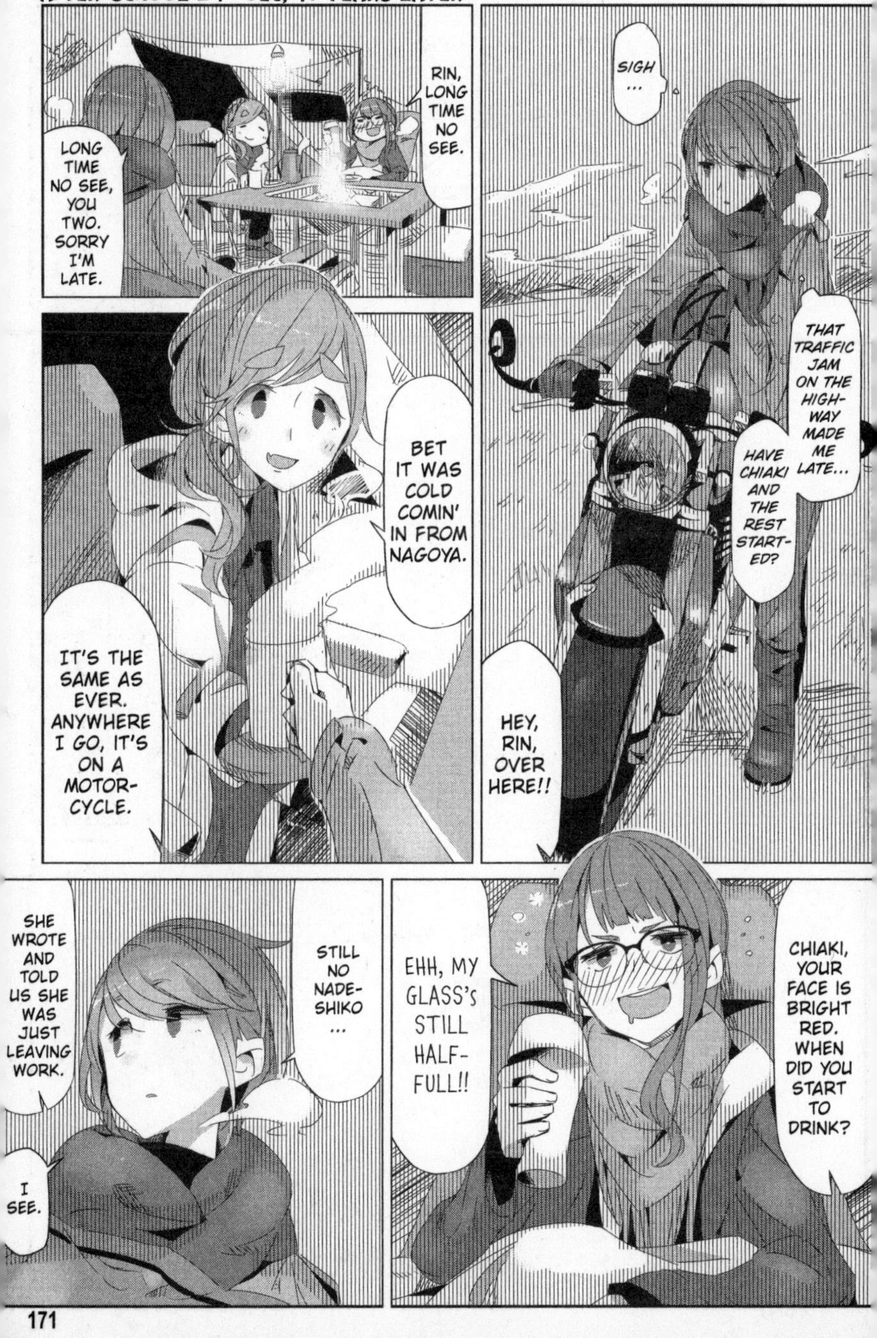
SIGH ...
THAT TRAFFIC JAM ON THE HIGH-WAY MADE ME LATE...
HAVE CHIAKI AND THE REST START-ED?
HEY, RIN, OVER HERE!!
RIN, LONG TIME NO SEE.
LONG TIME NO SEE, YOU TWO. SORRY I'M LATE.
BET IT WAS COLD COMIN' IN FROM NAGOYA.
IT'S THE SAME AS EVER. ANYWHERE I GO, IT'S ON A MOTOR-CYCLE.
CHIAKI, YOUR FACE IS BRIGHT RED. WHEN DID YOU START TO DRINK?
EHH, MY GLASS's STILL HALF-FULL!!
STILL NO NADE-SHIKO ...
SHE WROTE AND TOLD US SHE WAS JUST LEAVING WORK.
I SEE.

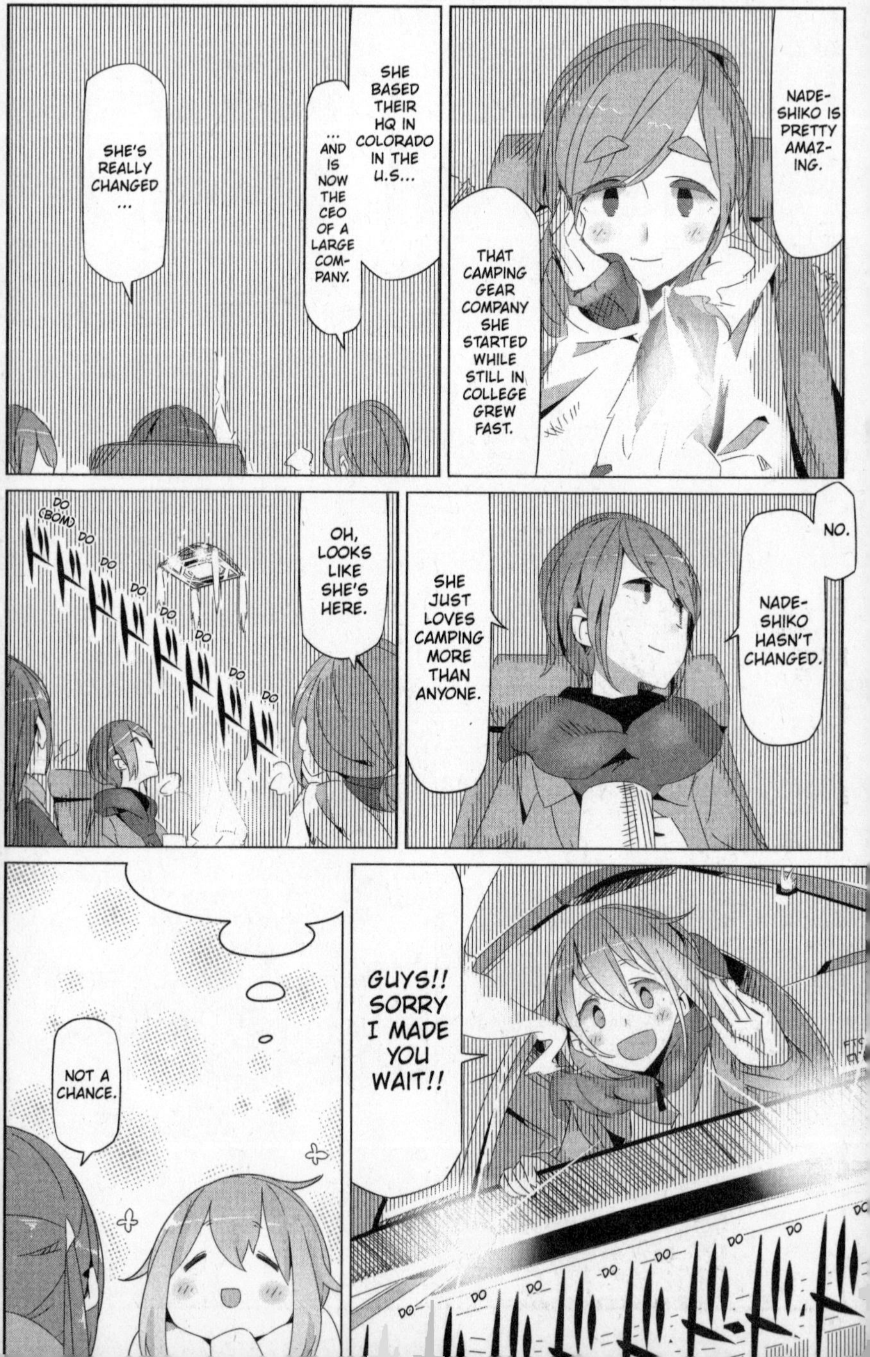
NADESHIKO IS PRETTY AMAZING.
THAT CAMPING GEAR COMPANY SHE STARTED WHILE STILL IN COLLEGE GREW FAST.
SHE BASED THEIR HQ IN COLORADO IN THE U.S...
...AND IS NOW THE CEO OF A LARGE COMPANY.
SHE'S REALLY CHANGED...
NO.
NADESHIKO HASN'T CHANGED.
SHE JUST LOVES CAMPING MORE THAN ANYONE.
OH, LOOKS LIKE SHE'S HERE.
DO (BOM) DO DO DO DO DO DO DO
GUYS!! SORRY I MADE YOU WAIT!!
DO DO DO DO DO DO DO DO DO
NOT A CHANCE.

AFTER-SCHOOL 25 OEC, 60 YEARS LATER

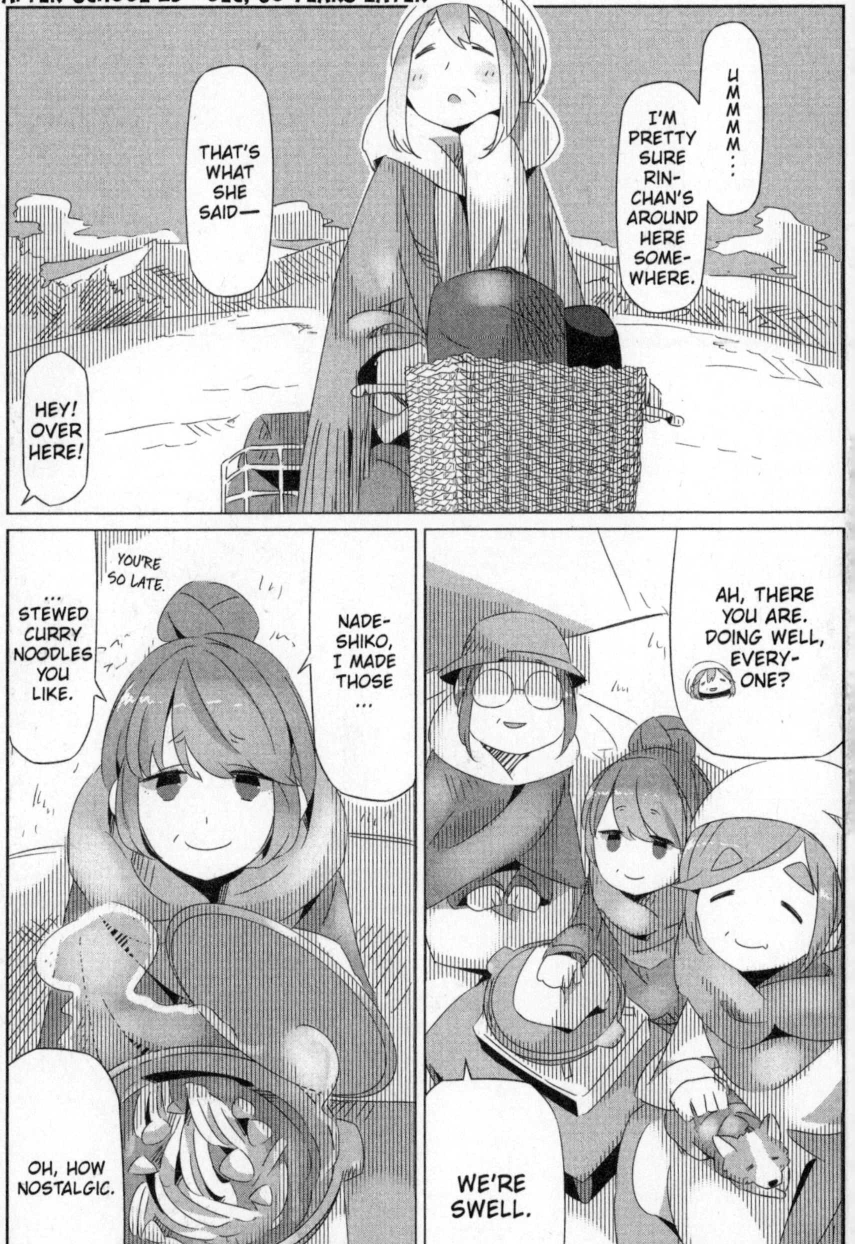
UMMMM...
I'M PRETTY SURE RIN-CHAN'S AROUND HERE SOME-WHERE.
THAT'S WHAT SHE SAID—
HEY! OVER HERE!
AH, THERE YOU ARE. DOING WELL, EVERY-ONE?
WE'RE SWELL.
NADE-SHIKO, I MADE THOSE ...
YOU'RE SO LATE.
... STEWED CURRY NOODLES YOU LIKE.
OH, HOW NOSTALGIC.

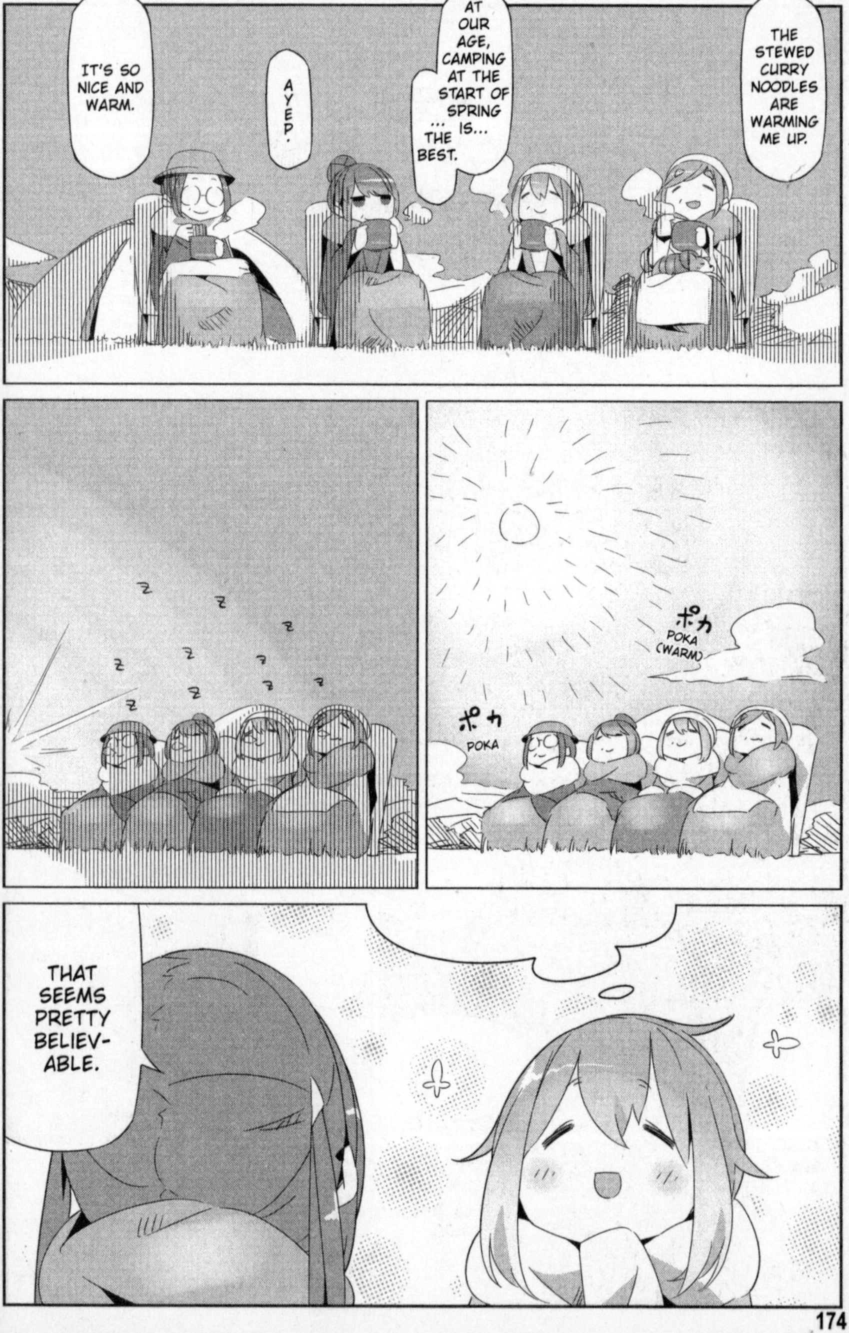
THE STEWED CURRY NOODLES ARE WARMING ME UP.
AT OUR AGE, CAMPING AT THE START OF SPRING IS... ...THE BEST.
AYEP.
IT'S SO NICE AND WARM.
ポカ POKA (WARM)
ポカ POKA
THAT SEEMS PRETTY BELIEV-ABLE.

AFTER-SCHOOL 26 NATIONAL CAMPING CHARACTERISTICS

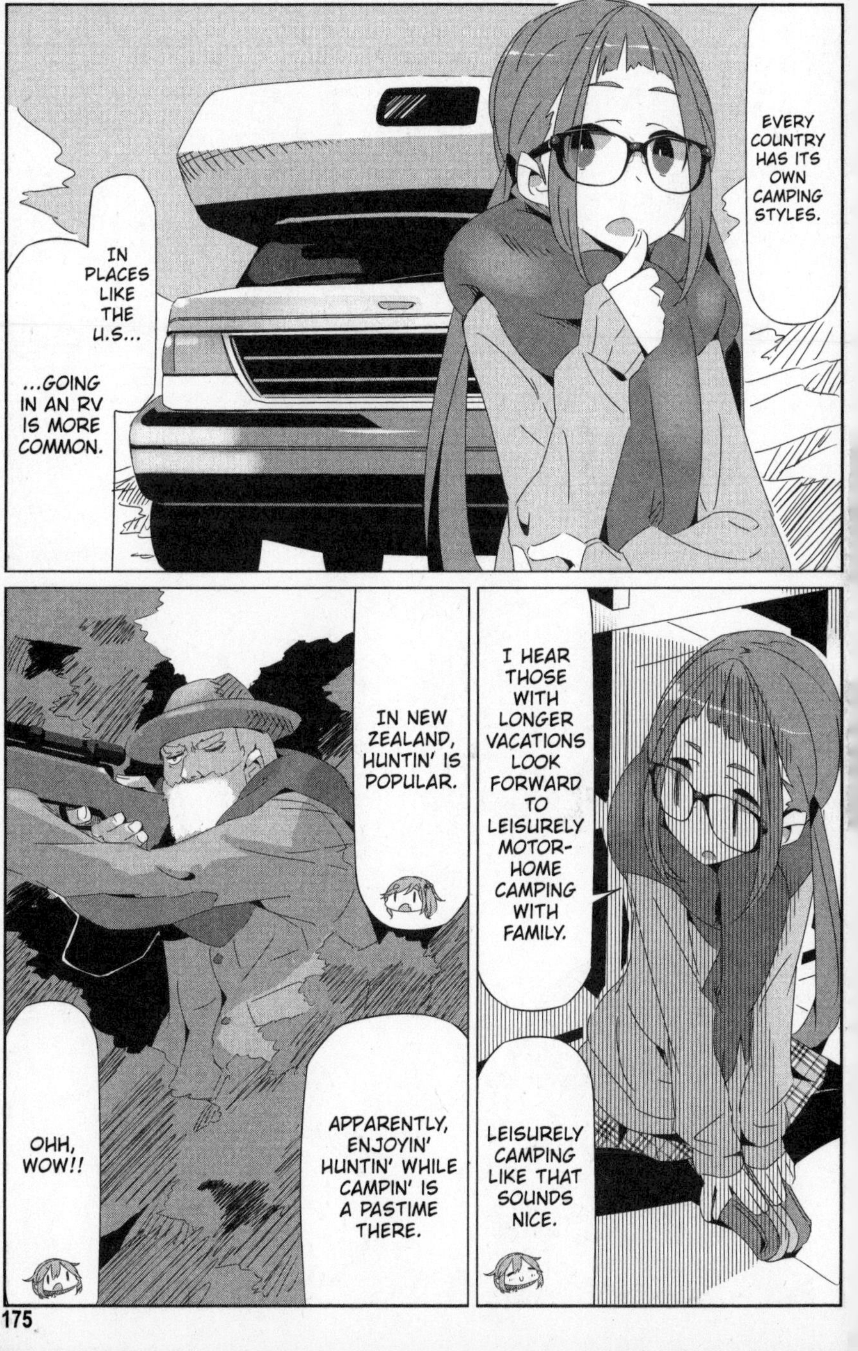
EVERY COUNTRY HAS ITS OWN CAMPING STYLES.
IN PLACES LIKE THE U.S...
...GOING IN AN RV IS MORE COMMON.
I HEAR THOSE WITH LONGER VACATIONS LOOK FORWARD TO LEISURELY MOTOR-HOME CAMPING WITH FAMILY.
LEISURELY CAMPING LIKE THAT SOUNDS NICE.
IN NEW ZEALAND, HUNTIN' IS POPULAR.
APPARENTLY, ENJOYIN' HUNTIN' WHILE CAMPIN' IS A PASTIME THERE.
OHH, WOW!!

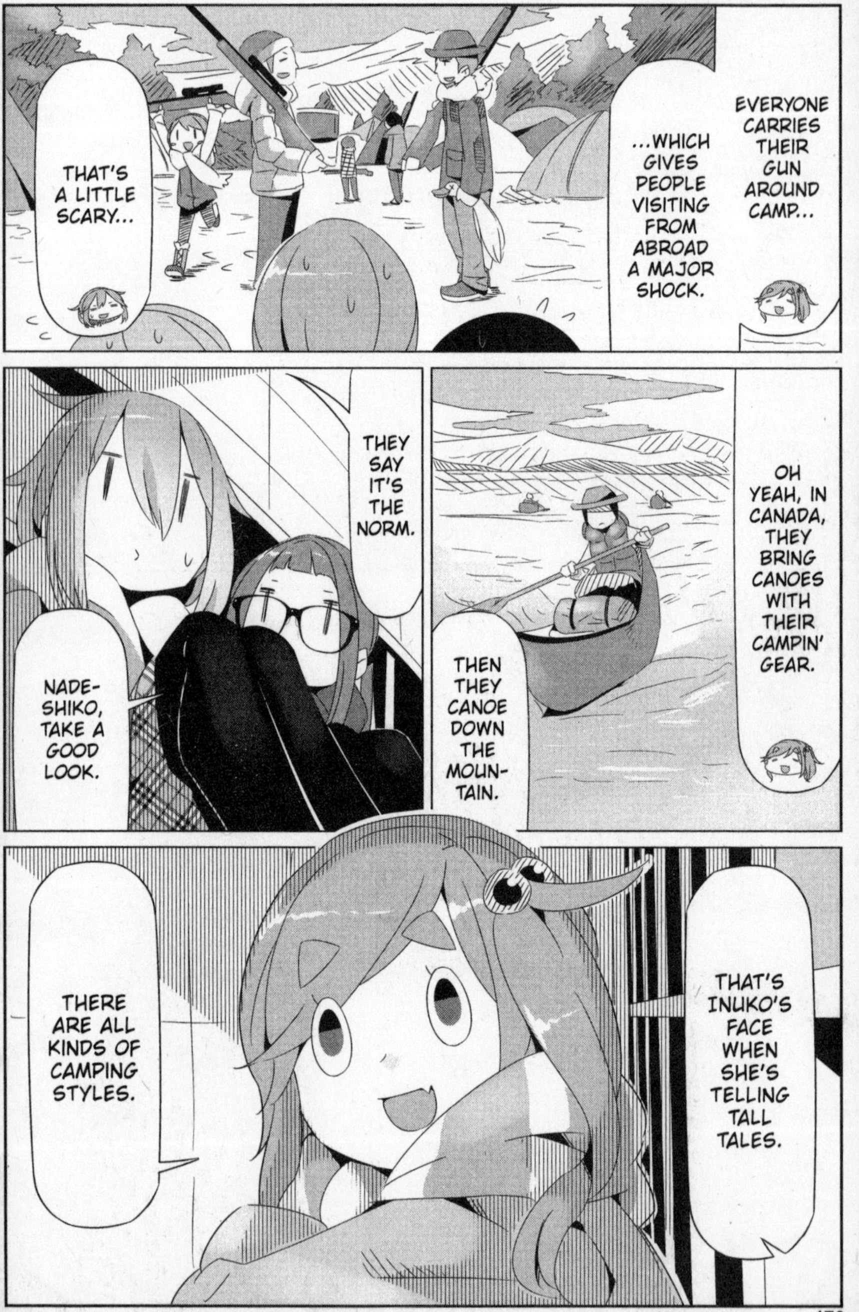
EVERYONE CARRIES THEIR GUN AROUND CAMP...
...WHICH GIVES PEOPLE VISITING FROM ABROAD A MAJOR SHOCK.
THAT'S A LITTLE SCARY...
OH YEAH, IN CANADA, THEY BRING CANOES WITH THEIR CAMPIN' GEAR.
THEN THEY CANOE DOWN THE MOUNTAIN.
THEY SAY IT'S THE NORM.
NADE-SHIKO, TAKE A GOOD LOOK.
THAT'S INUKO'S FACE WHEN SHE'S TELLING TALL TALES.
THERE ARE ALL KINDS OF CAMPING STYLES.

HOW WAS *LAID-BACK CAMP* VOLUME 4?

THIS VOLUME COLLECTED STORIES ABOUT PREPARING FOR CAMP,
CHRISTMAS CAMPING, AS WELL AS MORE ROOM CAMP.
WHEN I WAS STILL IN THE PLANNING STAGES, I USED GOOD MEAT
(A-5) TO MAKE BASIC SUKIYAKI, TOMATO SUKIYAKI, CHEESE
PASTA, AND BEEF YAMATO STEW. AS A BONUS, THE YAMATO STEW
REALLY BROUGHT OUT THE SAVORY FLAVOR OF THE BEEF. IT WAS
DELICIOUS.

THE NEXT VOLUME IS SET TO COLLECT STORIES FROM THE END OF
ONE YEAR AND THE BEGINNING OF ANOTHER, SO IT SEEMS WINTER
WILL GO ON FOR SOME TIME.

THIS HAS BEEN AFRO.

[FIRST PUBLICATION]
· *MANGA TIME KIRARA FORWARD* JANUARY-MAY 2017 ISSUES
· *KIRARA BASE* JUNE 28TH -JULY 12TH 2016, JULY 26TH-SEPTEMBER 27TH,
            OCTOBER 25TH ISSUES (UPDATED)
· ONE-SHOT (DRAWN FOR THIS BOOK)
THE MATERIALS IN THIS VOLUME WERE COLLECTED
FROM THE ABOVE SOURCES.

LAID ☕ BACK CAMP ④

Afro

Translation: **Amber Tamosaitis** ✳ Lettering: **D. Kim**

YURUCAMP Vol. 4
© 2017 afro. All rights reserved. First published in Japan in 2017 by HOUBUNSHA CO., LTD., Tokyo. English translation rights in United States, Canada, and United Kingdom arranged with HOUBUNSHA CO., LTD. through Tuttle-Mori Agency, Inc., Tokyo.

English translation © 2018 by Yen Press, LLC

Yen Press
1290 Avenue of the Americas
New York, NY 10104

Visit us at yenpress.com
facebook.com/yenpress
twitter.com/yenpress
yenpress.tumblr.com
instagram.com/yenpress

First Yen Press Edition: November 2018

Yen Press is an imprint of Yen Press, LLC.
The Yen Press name and logo are trademarks of Yen Press, LLC.

The publisher is not responsible for websites (or their content) that are not owned by the publisher.

Library of Congress Control Number: 2017959206

ISBNs: 978-1-9753-5480-0 (paperback)
       978-1-9753-5481-7 (ebook)

10 9 8 7 6 5 4 3 2 1

WOR

Printed in the United States of America